VEGAS
SUNRISE

Also by Fern Michaels . . .

VEGAS SUNRISE

Fern Michaels

Zebra Books
Kensington Publishing Corp.
http://www.zebrabooks.com

Kensington Publishing Corp.
850 Third Avenue
New York, NY 10022

All Kensington titles, imprints and distributed lines are available at special quantity discounts for bulk purchases for sales promotion, premiums, fund-raising, educational or institutional use.

Special book excerpts or customized printings can also be created to fit specific needs. For details, write or phone the office of the Kensington Special Sales Manager: Kensington Publishing Corp., 850 Third Avenue, New York, NY 10022. Attn. Special Sales Department. Phone: 1-800-221-2647.

First Kensington Hardcover Printing: October, 1997
First Zebra Paperback Printing: September, 1998
10 9 8 7 6

Printed in the United States of America

For two delightful sisters:
Anne Griffith and Carol Walderman

1

At three-thirty in the afternoon, the loudspeaker in the offices of Babylon crackled to life. The decibel level remained high; customers continued to gamble. "This is a reminder, ladies and gentlemen, that Babylon will close its doors promptly at 6:00 P.M. and will not reopen until one minute past midnight. This announcement will be repeated six times during the next three hours."

"Oh, Marcus, do you really think it's going to be a surprise?" Fanny asked her husband. "What I mean is, Bess and John are smart, don't you think they'll see through that little ruse we conjured up to get them out of the casino?"

"No, I do not. Bess knows you never ask her to do anything unless it's important. She thinks she's going to the chicken ranch to coax Ruby Thornton, your—what is she, Fanny, your half sister-in-law—to come to the casino? I think it's wonderful of you to want to include her in the family."

"She's part of this family even though Ash said she came in through the back door. She has Thornton blood, and that's good enough for me and the kids. The same goes for Ash's son. It's not right to deny either Ruby or Jeff Lassiter their rightful place. They're both wonderful people. I know it and so do my children.''

"I hope it works out, Fanny."

"Of course it will work out. Why wouldn't it? Don't rain on my parade, Marcus."

"As if I would ever do that. Did the boy really agree to come in here and take over for Bess and John? I find that . . . amazing."

"I had to do some fast talking. His mother helped convince him. He's worked in the casino summers and holidays while he was in college. He knows the business and what he doesn't know, he'll learn. We signed a three-year contract with him two days ago. It has to work, Marcus, because I had no other options. If Birch was here, it would be different. He isn't here, so I did what I had to do. It's settled, so let's not talk about it. What am I going to do if Bess and John balk at their retirement present? Just because I think a year-long trip around the world is wonderful doesn't mean she and John will think the same way. Her children packed her bags and brought them over earlier. The limo is coming for them at midnight to take them to the airport. Everything is set unless she balks." Fanny clenched and unclenched her hands as she paced around the office. "She won't, will she, Marcus?"

"Not a chance." Marcus's voice was airy, offhand. "She's going to love it. Stop fretting, Fanny. Let's check the dining room to see if your decorations are finished."

"Billie did it all. She even planned the menu, all of Bess and John's favorite foods. For five hundred people. She didn't even blink, Marcus. My daughter never ceases to amaze me. She said Bess and John weren't the only ones who were going to be surprised tonight. What do you think she meant by that?"

Marcus chuckled. "It's probably one of those inside Thornton family jokes. You love surprises. Guess you'll have to wait." He steered her into the dining hall, then watched as she darted across the room to embrace Billie.

"Oh, honey, it's beautiful. We have to take pictures." Fanny hugged her daughter.

"The ice sculpture goes in the middle of the main table," Billie explained. "There's a gizmo under the table that keeps it from melting. Sage hooked up the fountain. Chue brought the orchids earlier this afternoon. Aren't they gorgeous?"

"Only half as gorgeous as these tablecloths. Seed pearls sewn on linen, Billie?"

"I'm going to use them at our next trade show. I have a machine that does it. I wanted this to be really special. They're bringing the balloons at five o'clock. When Bess and John walk through the front door they'll drop. From there on, it's fun, fun, fun. Our own private night. Bess's family and friends, the Colemans, all our workers and their families. Josh Coleman is about to arrive from Virginia with his family. He called last night. We're going to have a full house. Think about it, Mom. Our blood family and our working family."

"It's like a dream. I just hope Bess and John love it all. Marcus and I are going upstairs. We'll be down at five-thirty. Call me when Aunt Billie and Thad get here."

"I don't miss this place at all," Fanny said as she unlocked the door to the penthouse. "It's a shame it sits here empty. I offered Jeffrey the use of it, but he said he prefers to live at home. I don't think his mother is well, and he likes to look after her. I respect that in a son. Ash was proud of the boy even though he wouldn't admit it. I think he's going to do very well."

"Does that mean you like our little house better than these sumptuous surroundings?"

"Marcus, I love our house. What I really love is seeing you cook in that state-of-the-art kitchen. It's cozy. I love cozy things. I guess I'm just a snuggler. It reminds me so much of our old house back in Sunrise. We have a front porch, a back porch, a garden for flowers and vegetables, a dog run, a gorgeous fireplace, a Jacuzzi. You to share it with. I couldn't ask for more. Retirement is so blissful. Being able to wake up and decide at a moment's notice to take a trip is ... what is it, Marcus?"

"It's wonderful. I have an idea, let's take a shower together."

"Mr. Reed, you do come up with delicious ideas from time to time."

"I do, don't I? Last one in has to wash the other one's back."

Sage Thornton stood at the end of the jetway, his stomach muscles churning. He wondered if he was going to get sick.

He would have known his twin anywhere even though he was seeing him in profile. And then Birch turned. Air hissed from between Sage's lips. He stared at his father's image. Somewhere during his life, he'd seen this exact same scene. Probably sometime during his teens when he picked up his father from the airport.

Even from this distance Birch looked lean and fit, with a bronze tint to his skin. A baseball cap that said Thornton Chickens was pushed back on his head. It was worn and frayed. A tee shirt with "Babylon" across the middle, equally worn and frayed, faded blue jeans, and scuffed hiking boots completed his outfit. A canvas carryall was slung over his shoulder. His eyes were bluer than sapphires against his tan. His teeth pearl white. At six-two, Birch could see over the heads of his fellow passengers. The moment he spotted Sage he dropped his bag and shouldered his way through the crowd of deplaning passengers.

They stood eyeball to eyeball as passengers milled about them. Sage's voice was choked when he said, "It's been a long time, Birch."

"Too long. The only thing I missed was you and Mom. C'mere, you big lug. Jesus, it's good to see you, Sage." His voice was just as choked as his brother's. "I knew you'd be the one to get married first and have a family. I want you to meet my wife."

Sage's jaw dropped. "You're married!"

"Yep, to the most wonderful girl in the world. We lived in a tent for three years so that should give you some kind of an idea of what she's like. She's simple and earthy like Mom. She's standing over there because she wanted to give us a few minutes alone. You're gonna love her." Birch motioned for his wife to join them.

She was tall like a showgirl, thin but well proportioned, with blond hair faded white from the sun. Her eyes were dove gray, almost translucent against her honeyed tan. An eerie feeling washed through Sage when he met Celia's gaze. Somewhere within him an alarm sounded. He backed off a step and held out his hand once the introductions were made. He saw the puzzled look on Birch's face. His brother had expected him to hug his wife and welcome her into the family. Later he was going to have to think about this scene.

Celia's voice was sweet, almost honeyed when she reached for Sage's hand. "I feel like I know you. Birch spoke about you every single day."

Sage forced a laugh. "I hope it was good."

"Only wonderful things. I'm looking forward to meeting your family. We hung the pictures of you and your family in our tent. We used safety pins. Those pictures were the first thing we saw in the morning and the last thing we saw at night."

"I'm flattered. You could have written more, Birch."

"You know me. I was never a letter writer. You aren't either. Who's kidding who?"

"Okay, I'll give you that one. Do you have a lot of luggage?"

Birch and Celia burst out laughing. They pointed to their duffel bags. "This is it. We lived very frugally. I'm going to have to borrow some clothes or else show up at the party in this attire. I'm assuming it's black tie.''

"You assumed right. Big doings. Mom and Billie have been planning this for weeks. Probably months. Is this just a visit or are you staying? You didn't say.''

"We're here to stay. When you wrote that Bess and John were retiring I knew it was time to come back and run the casino. That's why I'm here. It's time.''

Sage thought his stomach was going to lurch right out of his body.

"I figured we'd live in the penthouse if no one objected,'' Birch went on. "How do you like living at Sunrise, Mr. Family Man?''

"I love it. Iris and the kids don't even want to come to town anymore. She says we're hermits. Maybe we are.'' He could feel the translucent gray eyes boring into his back.

"We have to buy something to wear, Birch. I didn't realize how awful we looked until I saw all these people so dressed up. Living in a Third World country is not conducive to fashion.''

"It's not a problem, honey. We'll just go to one of the boutiques in the casino and get whatever we need.''

"Just like that!''

"Uh-huh.''

Sage concentrated on positioning the bags in the trunk of his car.

"God, I can't wait to take a shower. I'm going to stand under it until the water runs cold,'' Birch said.

"Sweetie, we have to shop. We don't want to embarrass your family.''

"No, Celia, we don't have to shop. We call downstairs and they send the stuff up. We pick and choose and they take the rest back. You can do that while I'm standing under that nice hot shower.''

Sage scrunched his big frame into the driver's seat. "Mom and Marcus are in the penthouse. I got you a room.''

"A *room?*" Celia said.

"Actually it's a suite," Sage said. He wondered why his voice sounded so defensive.

Birch's voice was cheerful when he said, "Guess you're going to have to wait a while to move into that fancy penthouse, honey."

"It doesn't look the same, Birch. Mom redid it when she moved in. She hated all those mirrors, chrome and glass. She smashed the place up one day. It kind of looks like Sunrise now. She's got a set of those red chairs."

"What does Sunrise look like?" Celia asked from the back-seat.

"Comfortable and worn. Green plants, bright colors. Home," Birch said.

"Oh," Celia said.

"You're gonna love it, honey."

"I'm sure I will."

"So, tell me about this party tonight. No, on second thought, tell me about the family. How's Mom?"

"Mom's great. She's happier now than she's ever been. She has a wonderful life with Marcus. They live on the outskirts of town in a small house. They garden, they travel, they take the kids for days at a time. She really is happy. She and Dad made peace the last few years. There at the end he turned out to be quite a guy."

"If you call pumping a bullet into your brother quite a guy, I guess so."

"You weren't here, Birch. It was wrong, but it was right, too, in a cockamamie way. It's over, and I don't want to talk about it."

"Sure. I want you to know, Sage, I tried to get a plane out but it was the rainy season and I couldn't. I was sick over it. Hell, we couldn't even get to a phone for ten days. I figured it was just better to stay where I was at that point. I did grieve, Sage."

"We all did." Jesus, what was wrong with him. Why was he acting so . . . so stupid? This was Birch. This was his twin. This was his best friend sitting next to him, and he was acting like he had a burr in his Jockeys. He struggled with his emotions. "Sunny's doing great. She's in a remission state right now, and she's living permanently at the center. She has a whole new life. There aren't any words to tell you how I admire our sister. She's good with the kids, too, considering her limitations."

"I don't think I could ever give up my children for adoption," Celia said from the backseat.

Loyalty ringing in his voice, Birch said, "If Sage was your brother, you could. I bet Iris is a wonderful mother to Sunny's kids. She's like Mom, isn't she?"

"Yeah. Yeah, she is. Mom gave her all her recipes. She taught her to sew and do all those mother things. She helped a lot with Dad at the end. Iris gets along with everyone. When the kids are older, she might want to go back to teaching at the university but then again, maybe she won't. Wait till you taste her strawberry-rhubarb pie. You can't tell the difference between hers and Mom's."

"Billie?"

"She's on top of the world. Three years in a row she was voted Woman of the Year by the textile industry. She managed to sell sixty-five million Bernie and Blossom dolls. They're still going strong. She's thinking of creating little brothers and sisters now. She's working on the prototypes. We'll test-market them in a few months."

"Guess that means the Thornton coffers are full, eh?"

Sage took that moment to look in the rearview mirror to check on an eighteen-wheeler behind him that wanted to pass. He felt his shoulders stiffen at the sight of Celia's glittering eyes.

A devil perched itself on Sage's shoulder. "You know Mom.

She siphons the money out as soon as it comes in. It goes right to the rehab centers."

"How is the casino doing? The last letter I had from Mom said it was bigger and better than ever. She even sent me a clipping from one of the newspapers. The article said Vegas expects to host 33,000,000 visitors this year. It went on to say each visitor is expected to gamble $154.00. That's some very heavy money."

"You never showed me that article, Birch," Celia said.

"I didn't think you'd be interested, honey. I threw it away."

Sage risked a second glance in the rearview mirror. The glittering eyes looked hard and cold to him. He knew in his gut Celia was trying to calculate the amount of money in her head. He could feel a nerve start to twitch under his eye.

Birch, oblivious to his wife's petulant face, continued to ask questions. "Can we stop and see Sunny?"

"She's at the casino, Birch. Mom brought her and her friend over early this morning. It was almost like old times except you were missing."

Celia leaned over the front seat. "In a wheelchair? Doesn't that create a problem?"

"No, honey. Dad was in a wheelchair. The whole casino is wheelchair accessible. My grandfather made sure of that so Dad wouldn't have any problems."

The devil on Sage's shoulder bounced back. "She has her dog with her. So does Harry."

"In the casino! That's so . . . unsanitary," Celia said.

"They're trained," Sage said tightly. He didn't like this girl leaning over the seat, didn't like her warm breath wafting into his right ear, didn't like the soap and water smell of her. He didn't like her, *period.* Talk about instant reactions.

"Will you relax, Celia. Mom is closing the casino tonight—so it will be just friends and family. The dogs are special. The dogs enable Sunny to get out and about more. I think it's great."

Celia flopped back against the seat cushion. Sage knew her eyes were glued to the back of Birch's head.

"Where are you from, Celia?"

"A small town in Alabama. Population twelve hundred or so."

"Are you going back for a visit?"

"No."

"Celia's family is gone. There's nothing to go home to. In a manner of speaking she's an orphan. Was an orphan. Now she has me and our family. Right, honey?"

"I know I'm going to love your family, Birch. We never talked about anything else but your family. Morning, noon, and night. I feel like I know every single one of you, even the children."

The devil on Sage's shoulder moved slightly. "Didn't you *ever* talk about your family, Celia?"

"There wasn't anything to talk about. Your family is so interesting."

And rich, Sage thought. "Do you want to go in the front door or up through the garage?"

"The garage. Neal would boot our asses right off the floor looking the way we look. What room are we in?"

"Dad's favorite room, 2711."

"What time should we be downstairs? Do you want me to hide and make a grand entrance? What's the drill here?"

"The party starts at six-thirty. Bess and John are coming in through the front door and everyone is going to yell, SUR-PRISE! Balloons will drop. Billie said you should weave your way around the crap tables and then we'll all yell SURPRISE again, at which point Mom will faint so be prepared to catch her. Nice meeting you, Celia. Oh, by the way, we all kicked in to get Bess and John a year's trip around the world. Tap that trust fund, big brother."

"A year's trip around the world. That probably cost more than I could earn in a lifetime. What trust fund? Do you have a trust fund, Birch? Shame on you for not telling me. It was nice meeting you, too, Sage.''

Sage leaned against the wall. "This is not good," he muttered. He sat on the trunk of his car, his thoughts chaotic as he smoked three cigarettes, one after the other. Maybe he was having an off day. Maybe he didn't see what he thought he saw in the new Mrs. Thornton's eyes. *Keep your thoughts to yourself. Don't look for trouble,* an inner voice warned.

Sage walked over to the elevator. He shivered and didn't know why.

"Here they come! Here they come! Get ready!" Fanny cried, excitement ringing in her voice.

The great doors opened. Bess and John Noble walked onto the casino floor to the shouts of "SURPRISE!" Colored balloons rained downward.

Fanny ran to her friends of forty years and swept them into her arms. "Don't cry, Bess, I don't have any tissues. We wanted to do this for you. It hardly seems enough for all you've done for our family." She couldn't hold the news back for one more instant. "We are giving you a trip around the world! A whole year, Bess, to do nothing but spend time with your husband. Please say you want it."

"I'm saying it for both of us," John said. "We were just talking about taking a trip last week. Nothing as grand as a trip around the world. We accept, don't we, Bess."

"Yes. But Fanny . . .''

"Shhh, it's our pleasure. All the kids chipped in. Your kids packed your bags. I know they packed all the wrong things so if you play the third machine from the left in aisle two you'll have enough money for a new wardrobe."

"Oh, Fanny . . . what a good, kind friend you are."

"Hey, I'm taking up too much time. The line behind me is getting longer and longer. Everyone wants to give you a kiss and a hug. Tonight you're Cinderella and your limo will be by the front door exactly at midnight. I'm going to miss you so. . . ."

"Mom, look over there by the crap tables," Sage whispered in her ear.

"Is that Birch? No! It is!"

Sage stepped aside as his brother swept his mother into his arms, twirling her around and around until she was dizzy. "Oh, Birch, it's so good to see you. You look so handsome. Actually you look just the way your father looked when he wore his tux. This is such a wonderful surprise!"

"Mom, this is Celia, my wife."

"You're married, and you didn't tell anyone!"

"Mom, she's special. I didn't think I'd ever meet anyone like her. She's so gorgeous she takes my breath away. We're here to stay. I'd like to start to work on Monday if that's okay with you."

Sage, his wife Iris next to him, watched as Birch drew Celia forward. He was in a perfect position to see his mother's raised eyebrows at the young woman's attire. He didn't think it was his imagination when he saw her shoulders tense.

Celia was wearing a strapless, backless black sequined sheath of a dress with a slit up the side. As she stepped forward, Fanny reached for her hands but didn't kiss or hug her. "I'm so pleased to meet you, Celia. Welcome to the family. How do you like Babylon?"

"It's . . . fantastic. I shopped all afternoon. Living in a tent and taking a shower under a waterfall is . . . this is just wonderful. I can't believe you *own* all of this."

"It is a bit startling at first. After a while, it's just a place of business."

Iris turned away to stare at the people surrounding Bess and John. "What would you do if I dressed like that, Sage? I feel like a Girl Scout leader compared to her. For someone who lived in a tent and showered under a waterfall she looks pretty good in those diamonds. I thought you said they only had raggedy stuff.''

''She went shopping,'' Sage hissed. ''Mom didn't hug her or kiss her the way she did you when she first met you.''

''She's taking a wait-and-see attitude. Birch was shock enough. Coupling that with a new bride who looks like she belongs in the chorus line should give you your answer. What do you think of her?''

Sage evaded the question. ''Birch is in love with her. It doesn't matter what anyone else thinks. She just got here. She's probably nervous, and by now she's aware that she isn't dressed right.''

''Oh, she's dressed right. Those shoes she's wearing cost $800. I saw them in the shop last week. What you're seeing is who that young woman is. She's a lot younger than Birch, too. She was pleasant enough, but I don't think I'm going to like her.''

Sage's sigh of relief was so loud, Iris shook his arm. ''You don't like her either, do you? You were waiting for me to say it first. We need to give her a chance. First impressions are not always what they seem. Let's agree, Sage, to stand back and be fair. Okay?''

''Sure, honey. You don't look like a Girl Scout leader to me. That's a nifty dress you're wearing, and you look great.''

''Aunt Billie made it for me. She made one for Sunny and Billie, too. Sunny's looking better than I've seen her look in a long time. I guess it's because she's happy.''

''Guess so. I'm going to check on the kids. Lexie's probably wading in one of the pools by now.''

''Marcus is watching them. They were picking flowers for Sunny in one of the hanging gardens.''

''I'll check it out. It's my turn to kiss Bess and John. I'll see you later by the banquet table.''

Sunny waved from across the room. Iris weaved her way toward her. She bent over to kiss her and Harry, whose chair was parked next to Sunny's, their dogs next to their respective chairs.

"There she is, one of my two favorite people in the whole world. Here comes the other one," Birch said, as Billie came up behind Sunny's chair. Iris watched as Birch kissed and hugged both his sisters before he introduced his new wife. She didn't know if she should laugh or cry at the expressions on Sunny's and Billie's faces. The expression of distaste on her sister-in-law's face was so fleeting she thought she imagined it until Sunny, in her own inimitable way, let her know she'd seen it, too.

"Harry and I were wondering if we dare head for the banquet table. We forgot our bibs." She looked pointedly at Celia when she said, "We drool and dribble our food at times. What would happen if you did that wearing such a fancy dress?" she asked Celia.

"I guess I'd have to get it cleaned." Celia looked pointedly at her husband, who was talking to Harry, Sunny's companion.

"The cleaners would ruin it," Billie said.

Celia made a little face. "I think I made the wrong choice when I picked out this dress. Birch has always said this was such a glittery, shimmering place, I thought it would be appropriate. I was wrong. I just itched to buy it. I lived in cutoff jeans and raggedy tee shirts for so long. I just didn't think. I hope I didn't offend anyone."

"Just my mother and me," Sunny said. Billie cleared her throat. Iris looked away.

"Did I miss something?" Birch asked.

"No. Sunny was just agreeing with me that I'm dressed all wrong. She said I probably offended your mother."

"See, I told you, but you wouldn't listen." Birch tweaked Celia's cheek before he walked over to Bess and John Noble.

"Are those diamonds real?" Sunny asked.

"The jeweler said they were. Birch insisted I get them. He said he wanted me to sparkle tonight."

Sunny's voice was prim when she said, "We're not a showy family. Actually, we're all rather modest. Mom always said less is more if you know what I mean."

"Yes. Thank you for pointing it out to me."

"My pleasure," Sunny said.

"Excuse me. Birch is motioning for me to join him."

"Sunny, that was uncalled for," Billie said.

"Damn straight it was. I saw the expression on her face when she looked at me and Harry. It was distaste. Ask Iris if you don't believe me." Iris nodded, her face miserable.

"She's in a new environment. We're all strangers to her. So she dressed wrong, so what. All of us at one time or another either overdressed or underdressed. Don't create a problem, Sunny, where none exists. She's Birch's wife," Billie said.

Harry, silent until now said, "I used to paint portraits. I was pretty good, too. The critics always said my eyes were the best. That's because they're the mirror of one's soul. That young woman has no soul. That's strictly my own opinion. Let's try the banquet table, Sunny. My hands are more steady than yours are today, so I'll hand you the food. We'll come back here to eat it out of the way, okay?"

"Sure. Will you guys watch our dogs?"

"Sure," Billie said.

"I admire Sunny so," Iris said, a catch in her voice.

Billie's voice was soft when she said, "Me too."

"Birch's timing was off. I think that's what this is all about. It would have been nice if he'd waited and made it a family thing where Celia could be the center of attention. However, I understand where he's coming from. Sage said he expects to start work on Monday. Did anyone tell him about Jeffrey? Sage said it wasn't his place to tell him. He also said Birch doesn't know how to play second banana. Does that mean there's going to be a problem, Billie?"

"Off the top of my head, I'd say yes. Let's not worry about

that tonight. We're here to have a good time, so let's have a good time.''

"Do I look dowdy and frumpy, Billie?''

"Absolutely not.''

"Then why do I feel that way?''

"Because your quiet, peaceful world has been invaded by a smashing blond bombshell. I feel a little dowdy myself. I thought I looked pretty good when I left the house.''

"So we're jealous is what you're saying.''

"No, that's not what I'm saying. We're who we are, and Celia is who she is.''

"Sage sees something we aren't seeing. He was so hyped about going to the airport to pick up Birch. He hasn't slept for three nights, that's how excited he was. He wanted to take the kids to the airport to show them off. He wanted his brother to see his kids. When he got back, it was . . . sad. I felt so bad I wanted to cry for him. He had these wonderful plans, these great expectations, and suddenly a new wife on the scene wiped all those plans away. He knows there's going to be some kind of blowup when Birch finds out Jeff signed on to run Babylon.''

"Everything will work itself out, Iris. Mom will step in and do what she always does, bring order and sense to everything.''

"Not this time, Billie. Birch has a wife now, and she's going to have a voice in everything he says and does.''

"There's Jeff now. He does look a lot like your dad. Ruby's really nice. I like her a lot. I'm glad your mom welcomed her into the family. She belongs. Right off she wanted to know what she could do. She pitched right in. She looks so damn normal compared to . . . Celia. I thought you were bringing your boyfriend tonight.''

"He had duty. Detectives are on call twenty-four hours a day. He might stop by later. It's not serious, Iris. We're good friends. I like him. He likes me. He doesn't just listen to me, Iris, he actually *hears* what I say. I like that in a man. I'm not about to get serious. I like being my own person, making my own decisions. It works for me the way being married and having kids works for you.''

"What do you think works for Celia Thornton?''

"The Thornton money.''

"I'm of the same opinion.''

"Sunny's dribbling. Let's go clean her up.''

"Billie, earlier Jake . . . what happened was Sunny was drinking a soda pop and she let the bottle slip. Jake . . . that little kid was so good about it. He wiped it up and said, 'Heck, Mom, I do that all the time.' Sunny's eyes filled up, and Jake wiped away her tears. He whispered to her for a long time. I guess he was giving her a pep talk because she started to laugh. He was grinning from ear to ear. He's really good with Harry, too. Ash made sure Jake understood his mother's limitations. He really understands, Billie. Do you think as he gets older that will stay with him? Every day I do my best to reinforce all that your dad taught him.''

"That boy idolized his grandfather. Trust me, his teachings will stay with Jake. I appreciate you telling me this, Iris.''

At ten minutes to midnight, Fanny asked for a drumroll. "Ladies and gentlemen, it's time for our guests of honor to make their way to the limo that is going to whisk them to the airport for the first leg of their journey. Let's all give them a big hand.''

Bess and John ran to the door. Tears rolled down Bess's cheeks as she waved to everyone, her eyes searching for Fanny in the crowd.

"Have a good trip, old friend. Take lots of pictures and send a card every week.''

"Fanny, this is the wrong time for me to be leaving. That girl spells trouble. I could feel it and I could smell it. My feeling has nothing to do with the outfit she's wearing either. John loved it. There's something about her that bothers me.''

"Bess, don't worry. I have your itinerary. I'll call if there's a problem. Hey, old buddy, this is me. The me who has a crisis in her life at least twice a month. Go and have a wonderful time. They're blowing the horn for you."

"Come on, Fanny, time to go upstairs. The doors are now open to the public. The party is over. You see, you worried for nothing. Your family is headed for the Harem Lounge for a nightcap. They asked us to join them," Marcus said.

Fanny nodded. "Marcus, how am I going to tell Birch he has to work under his half brother?"

"You just tell him, Fanny. Are you thinking of going back on your word?"

"I would never do that."

"Then there's no other way except to be up front and open about it. You said Birch and Sage both worked here together. Running this place is a full-time job for six people, never mind two. From what you said, this Birch is different from the Birch who went away a long time ago. He's older, wiser, more mature, and he has a wife now."

"I wonder if that's going to be a problem."

"Take a look," Marcus said. "I wonder what they're talking about."

Fanny looked into the lounge. Her children were seated at the bar. Celia was perched on one of the stools, a generous expanse of leg showing. To her right was Birch who was talking to Sage. To her left, Jeffrey Lassiter. Celia swiveled her stool until she was facing Jeffrey.

Celia's voice was playful, coy when she said, "And who might you be?"

Jeffrey Lassiter smiled. "Me? I'm the illegitimate son who's going to own this casino someday."

2

Sunny Thornton nudged the man in the wheelchair next to her. Her voice was a low hiss when she said, "You saw what I just saw, didn't you, Harry?"

The gangly redhead, whose face was a field of freckles, hissed in return, "And you were the one who said learning to sign and read lips was a mistake. Nevertheless, to answer your question, of course I saw what you saw."

"There is going to be trouble. Mom's back was to the wall when she asked my half brother to take on Bess and John's job. With Birch back there is going to be hell to pay. What should I do, Harry?"

"All he said was he was the illegitimate son, which is true, and that someday he was going to own the place. It's a stretch, but it is possible. If you start blabbing now, you might start something you aren't prepared to finish. When in doubt, do nothing."

"I don't like Celia. She's flirting with Jeff right under everyone's nose."

"You just met her, Sunny. Sometimes first impressions . . ."

"I saw the way she looked at you and me and our wheelchairs and the dogs. I'm an open-minded person. I could look beyond that, but I can't look beyond the revulsion I saw in her eyes. She didn't even try to hide it. I'm telling you, Harry, I see trouble, I feel trouble, and I smell trouble. If you expect me to keep my mouth shut, then we should go back to the center now."

"Then let's say our good-byes."

"Are you leaving so soon, Sunny?" Iris asked.

"Early to bed, early to rise. We aren't supposed to get excited," Sunny said.

Iris grinned. "Ohhh, I like the way that sounds."

Sunny's gaze swiveled to the bar. She shrugged. "Want to walk us to the van after we say our good-byes? One of the guys took the dogs out a few minutes ago."

"You bet. It's time for Sage and me to leave, too." Iris's voice trilled when she said, "I just love that brother of yours."

"Sage loves you just as much, Iris. He told me his world wasn't complete until you came into his life. It's so comforting to be loved." Again Sunny's gaze swept the length of the bar. She turned her chair with ease, increased the pressure on the hand control as she whipped down the room, ignoring Celia's outstretched leg.

"For God's sake!"

"How clumsy of me. Sorry," Sunny called over her shoulder as she brought the chair to a halt next to her mother.

"I saw that, Sunny."

"I swear, I'm getting worse and worse."

"Really," Fanny drawled. "Then how do you explain the wheelchair race you won two weeks ago at the center?"

"Pure dumb luck," Sunny drawled in return. "Harry and I are leaving now. We'll see you next week. Bye everyone!"

Birch wrapped his arms around his sister. He whispered in her ear, "So, big sister, what do you think of my new wife?

She's a knockout, isn't she? She's kind of reserved at first, but once you get to know her you're going to love her. She's really big on family.''

"I'm happy for you, Birch. Remember your promise to come out to the center to see me. What do you think of Harry?"

"A nice guy, Sunny."

"Yeah, he is. We look out for each other. He's doing better than me. He pushes me to my limit, and that's good. I'm glad you're back. I really missed you. We all missed you, especially Mom."

"Well I'm home now. You're going to get sick of looking at me. Iris is motioning to you, so you better get going."

Outside in the cool evening air, Iris looked up at the stars. "It's beautiful, isn't it? Do you want to talk about it, Sunny? I can come out to the center tomorrow if you want."

"What's wrong, Iris?"

"Nothing. I did see that little byplay in there." Iris dropped to her haunches and reached for Sunny's hands. "It's the strangest thing, Sunny, but suddenly I feel this fear. I don't think I ever experienced fear before. At least not like this. I shouldn't be telling you, and if Sage heard me, he'd say my imagination is working overtime. I'm afraid of her, Sunny. My God, I just met the woman, and I'm afraid of her."

"Come out to the center tomorrow afternoon. We'll talk on my turf. I'm a little braver there. If it's any consolation to you, I kind of feel the same way. It's like we've been . . . invaded. We do need to talk. Bring Billie if she wants to come. Three heads are better than two."

"Okay."

Iris watched until the van's taillights were dots of red on the winding road. She felt herself shivering until her husband's arms circled her shoulders.

"You okay, honey?"

"I'm fine."

"Why so quiet this evening? Everyone seems kind of pensive. This was supposed to be a happy night. Birch is back with his new wife, and he's happy. The family is together again except for Dad.''

"Do you think Birch changed? Being his twin, you would be more aware than the rest of us.''

"He's happy. That's the only change I see in him. I would imagine there will be fireworks when Mom tells him Jeff is going to run the casino. I think he'll accept it. It was his choice to stay away. Life goes on. Mom will never go back on her word.''

"What do you think of Celia?''

"Didn't we have this discussion a little while ago? It's a loaded question if I ever heard one. She seems pleasant. Birch is crazy in love with her. Sunny detested her on sight. They got off to a bad start, but I think Birch can make it right. No one wants to be on the receiving end of Sunny's wrath. It doesn't matter that she's disabled—her brain is as sharp as ever, and that mouth of hers is still the same. She listens to Harry, though. Strange, isn't it?''

"They're so good for one another. I can't tell you how much I admire Sunny.''

"We all do, Iris. If we're lucky, maybe they'll find a cure for multiple sclerosis in our lifetime.''

"Sage, Birch must have told Celia about Sunny and Harry. Yet . . . I saw the way she looked at Sunny. It wasn't distaste. It was revulsion. Sunny saw it, too. I'm not sure about Harry, though.''

"Iris, that's a terrible thing to say. Sunny . . .''

"I know what I saw, Sage. It's not my imagination. It's too nice a night to argue about something that . . . I was going to say that doesn't concerns us, but it does concern us. Celia is now part of the family. You need to know, Sage, that I will step in if it looks to me like Sunny is getting the short end of the stick. I won't tolerate it. Neither will your mother.''

"Jesus. It sounds like the three of you drew battle lines, and this is only the first shot. Is it possible you misinterpreted the whole thing?''

''Wrong. Count us as four. Billie saw it, too; she was steaming. I'm afraid, Sage, and I don't know why.''

''Fearless Iris. I don't believe what I'm hearing,'' Sage said, trying to make a joke of the whole thing. When his wife's expression didn't change, he felt his own first stirrings of fear. No, second stirrings of fear. The first ones were at the airport and on the ride home. Dependable, down-to-earth, common-sense Iris never got rattled, never showed fear. She looked problems in the face, studied them, resolved them. He kissed her lightly on the cheek, praying his own fears would dissipate.

Iris snuggled into her husband's embrace. ''I love you so much, Sage. There aren't any words in my vocabulary to tell you how much.''

Sage felt his heart start to pound. His wife was professing her love and yet the words had an ominous ring to them. Fear jumped into his throat. He felt the urge to roar like a lion, giving notice he was protecting his own. He almost snarled when Birch came up behind him. His voice was less than cordial when he said, ''What's happening?''

''Nothing. I came out to get some air. I guess I really did miss this place. I like Marcus Reed. Mom seems really happy. Now, tell me, how do you like Celia?''

Sage's heart continued to thump and grind in his chest. Birch looked like his answer was something he waited for all his life.

''Trust you to pick a real looker. We just met and didn't have a chance to get acquainted. By the way, where is she?''

''Playing twenty-one. This is all so new to her. She's like a kid at Christmastime. It'll wear off in a week or so. I figured I'd let her indulge herself. Iris, you'll take her under your wing, won't you?''

''Well . . . ah . . . sure. I don't have much free time with the kids and all. You know me, I cook and bake and take the kids on outings. Do you think she'll like being around kids?''

"Are you kidding? She loves kids. She can't cook or bake or do that homemaker stuff. I was hoping you could teach her, Iris."

"For you, Birch, anything. Give me some notice, and I'm all yours."

Sage slapped his brother on the back. "Time for us old married people to hit the road. We get up with the kids at the crack of dawn. We're usually in bed by ten, so it's past our bedtime. We'll say good night. If we don't see Celia, explain for us."

"I'll do that. Good night."

"I'm glad you're back, Birch."

"Me too."

"What can I do to make that frown disappear, Mrs. Reed?" Marcus asked.

"Until six o'clock my world was almost perfect. Then, in one instant, it changed. Right now I should be the happiest woman alive. All my chicks are in the nest, my wonderful husband is at my side, my two best friends are finally going to get the vacation they deserve. Billie and Thad are here, and so are Josh Coleman and his family. I haven't seen any of them all evening. I'm a terrible host. What's wrong with me, Marcus?"

"Your son brought a wife home. A wife you didn't get to approve or disapprove of."

"I'm sure she's a lovely girl . . . woman. This wasn't exactly the ideal time to introduce her. We all gave her short shrift as my father would say. Tomorrow we'll arrange dinner or something so she can be the center of attention. If not tomorrow, then maybe this weekend at Sunrise. Josh said his family was staying on through the weekend. I really want to get to know all of them."

"Honey, when are you going to tell Birch about Jeff?"

"In the morning. I invited him for breakfast. He said Celia likes to sleep late. What do you think of her, Marcus?"

"In my day we would have called her a dish. She's a beautiful young woman. It's obvious to anyone who looks at Birch that he's completely in love."

"But what do you *think* of her?"

"I think I want to know why you didn't do that Fanny thing with your arms and your lips. I don't think I ever saw you act so formal. Even with the Colemans whom you just met. Everyone kissed and hugged."

"I meant to and wanted to. Then I looked in her eyes. I knew I didn't want to hug or kiss her. I reacted to my feelings. Did Birch notice?"

"If he did, I don't think it bothered him. Men are usually oblivious to things like that. How would Ash have reacted?"

"Oh, Marcus, I was just thinking the same thing. Isn't it wonderful that you and I can talk about the children's father without either one of us getting upset. To answer your question, Ash would have sized her up in a heartbeat. He had such a way with women. In minutes he would have known her strengths and weaknesses. He'd go on from there, well armed. He could outthink and outguess just about everyone except me. He admitted that to me once. I'm sorry to say Ash wouldn't have liked Celia one little bit."

"You look tired, Fanny. Let's say our good nights and head upstairs. Tomorrow is another day."

"This is wrong, Marcus. We've all formed opinions on the run where that young woman is concerned. I'm sure she's wonderful if Birch chose her for his wife. This . . . can be overwhelming at first. There was the long plane ride, choosing clothes quickly, the apprehension of meeting our family, all these people. Tomorrow I'm sure we'll meet the *real* Celia.

"It's wall-to-wall people," Fanny said a moment later. "Unless we page everyone, we're out of luck. Let's just head upstairs to bed."

"My thoughts exactly."

Celia Thornton watched her mother-in-law make her way to the private elevator that would take her to the penthouse. The penthouse that Birch promised would be hers.

The champagne flute in her hand started to shake. She set it down next to one of the slot machines as her gaze swept around the entire floor. She tuned out the world as she listened to the bells and whistles, the voices, the sounds of money dropping into metal trays. This was certainly very different from Ardmore, Alabama, population 1096. She shivered when she thought of her last day in the small town.

"I've been looking all over for you, honey."

"I've never seen anything like this, Birch. Money smells, did you know that?"

Birch laughed. "Tomorrow or the day after, I'll take you into the counting room. We had to buy a hydraulic lift to move the money from place to place. Money is heavy and, yes, money smells. Amazingly, people get sick from handling money. Are you ready to call it a night?"

"Yes. How do you get used to this?"

"After a while it becomes just a place. The noise, the smoke, the late hours, it gets to you eventually. My father loved it. They called him The Emperor of Las Vegas. It was in his blood."

"Will they call you The Emperor if you take over?"

"I doubt it. Tell me, what did you think of the family. Aren't they great?"

"Absolutely. I know I made the wrong impression. I should have listened to you about this dress. Do you think they sell sackcloth in the boutiques?"

"My sisters and mother aren't glitzy people. Aunt Bess and Aunt Billie are plain people, too. We even eat plain stuff. My father was the glitzy one because he had a very high profile. He tried to mold Mom into what he wanted her to be, but it didn't work. In the end he wanted her just the way she was.

My mother is probably the most wonderful woman in the world with my sisters close runners-up. You'll fit right in. Didn't you just love Iris? I was jealous when Sage started going with her. Mom, Sunny, and Billie loved her on sight. I think she's perfect.''

Celia's head bobbed up and down. "Are you saying you want me to be like your sisters, Iris, and your *mother?*''

"Hell, yes. When something's perfect, don't mess with it. You're going to fit right in, honey. Iris will take you under her wing and show you the ropes. Wait till you see Sunrise. We're all going to go up there this weekend. I just made a snap decision here, but I know Sage and Iris will agree to a weekend get-together.''

"I see. What if I don't fit in, Birch?''

"Why wouldn't you?'' His voice was so puzzled that Celia grimaced.

"I'm not a nester, Birch. I've always been a free spirit. You told me that was one of the reasons you fell in love with me. I don't like rules and regulations. I like new things, new places, new interesting people. Costa Rica was fine for me because of you. I was somebody else there. I had to conform. That was part of the deal when I signed on. I didn't make a deal with you, Birch, to cook and sew and do all those housewifely things. Maybe later. For now I want to experience this wonderful place. I don't want a schedule, and I don't want someone making decisions for me. Is this going to be a problem for us?''

"I think the question is, what will you do? Do you plan to get a job?''

"A job!'' She made the word sound obscene. "Will we need another income? We never discussed this. If you need me to work, I will. I thought . . . hoped, I could stay home for a while. I guess everyone in your family works, huh?''

"Yes. Iris worked for a bit while she was pregnant. She tutored for several months after Lexie came along. The kids and Sunrise are a full-time job now. Billie loves working. Sunny would, too, if she could. She has great ideas and shares them in the middle of the night when she can't sleep.''

There was a nip to Celia's voice when she said, "How cozy."

"Obviously we need to talk, Celia. We can do it upstairs or tomorrow. I don't like things to fester. It might be good to do it after I have breakfast with my mother."

"Does that mean I'm not invited?" The nip took on an edge of frost.

"It's not a question of inviting. We have business to discuss. You like to sleep late. Breakfast is at seven."

"Does that mean I'm not part of this business? In Costa Rica you never made a decision without talking to me about it. We were a team. We worked together, and we shared together. Why is this different?"

"You know what I mean. You aren't going to be working here, so what's the big deal?"

"The big deal is I thought we talked about everything. You know all there is to know about me. Now, suddenly, I'm finding out all these things you never bothered to share with me. I'm beginning to think you were deliberately hiding things. Is there anything else you haven't shared with me?"

"I resent your tone and your implication, Celia. Those things weren't important to me over there."

"How could a trust fund not be important? How could all this wealth and prestige not be important?"

"To me it isn't important. I've seen firsthand what money does to people. I'm just as plain and ordinary as the rest of my family. You said you felt the same way."

"I had no choice but to feel that way. I wasn't born with a silver spoon in my mouth the way you were. I like the idea that you and I will never have to scrounge for money. I don't think that makes me any less a person. Security is important to everyone."

"This is a family business. I don't make solitary decisions. I don't think Mom would mind if you tagged along."

"Tagged along." The frost in Celia's voice could have chilled milk.

"Poor choice of words. I'm tired, Celia. Mom won't mind if you sit in on the meeting."

"I beg to differ, Birch. Your mother doesn't like me. I saw it in her eyes. Maybe it was the dress, maybe it's something else. Maybe she doesn't like me because you married me without her approval. Some mothers are like that."

"My mother isn't like that. You're imagining things. My mother is the fairest, most impartial person walking this earth. She waits till she has all the facts before she makes a move. Everyone loves her, and she loves everyone in return. This town owes a lot to her. I take umbrage, Celia, at what you just said. I saw her welcome you."

"You make her sound like a saint," Celia sniffed.

"If you knew the half of what my mother has had to endure, you'd swear she *was* a saint. We're bickering, and if we don't watch it, we're going to have a fight. I don't like fighting, and I don't like confrontations. I had enough of that to last me a lifetime. I'm going upstairs. If you want to stay down here, then stay."

"If that's the way you feel about it, I will."

Birch stalked across the casino floor. He didn't look back.

Celia headed for the Harem Lounge. She settled herself on the same stool she'd vacated earlier. "Scotch on the rocks. I'm Celia Thornton. I'll run a tab."

"I'm buying. Put it on my tab," Jeff Lassiter said smoothly as he slid onto the stool next to Celia.

The sole occupant of Room 2711 paced the floor, his eyes going to the small travel clock perched on the nightstand. The minutes and hours ticked by slowly. Twice, Birch ordered double shots of scotch from Room Service. The third time he ordered, he asked for a bottle. At 3:45 he slipped between the sheets of the huge double bed. He thought he was drunk. If he were *really* drunk, he wouldn't be able to see the bright, red numerals on the travel clock. More minutes ticked by.

The numbers on the clock read 5:25 when he heard Celia's card key slide into the lock. He rolled over, his head in the crook of his arm. His position allowed him to observe his wife as she stumbled into the bathroom and undressed. What in the goddamn hell was she doing all this time? Well there was only one way to find out.

"Birch! I thought you were sleeping. I tried to be quiet."

"You're drunk, Celia," Birch snarled.

"I am not. I did have a few drinks, though."

"How many is a few? All I have to do is pick up the phone and call every bar in the casino. They'll tell me right down to the number of ice cubes in your drinks. I'd rather hear it from you."

"What's gotten into you, Birch? So I had a few too many. So what. I enjoyed myself by talking to people, nibbling on pretzels, watching the entertainment in the lounge. I didn't object when you said you wanted to go to bed. You were tired, and I wasn't. That's the bottom line. You have to get up in the morning as you pointed out. I don't since I wasn't invited to share breakfast with you and your mother the saint."

Celia took the slap high on her cheekbone, reeling backward to clutch at the shower curtain. The second slap caught her full on the mouth, splitting her lip. "Don't ever, by word or look, talk about my mother like that again."

"You hit me! You struck me!" Celia howled as she staggered to the mirror. The horror of what she was seeing made her shriek at the top of her lungs. Birch slapped her again.

"Shut up or Security will be knocking on the door. You stepped over the line, Celia. The women in my family do not hang out in the bars. The women in my family are ladies. I don't want you to forget that. I'll get you some ice."

"I don't want your goddamn ice. I just want you to get the

hell away from me. How dare you strike me! How dare you! Another thing, Birch, don't ever tell me what to do again. I won't tolerate it. We aren't in a Third World country now where women have to endure abuse like this. Do it again, and I'll personally fry your ass. I don't want *you* to forget *that*."

"You sound like some floozie in a backroom bar. I won't tolerate that kind of talk from my wife. My God, Celia, what's happening to us? We never had a cross word between us the whole time we were in Costa Rica. I'm beginning to wonder what kind of life you led before I met you."

Celia's shoulders tensed at her husband's words. Her voice was a hushed whisper when she said, "It's the liquor. You know I can't drink. Look. I'm sorry. I behaved like . . . unlike myself. Let's start over. I'm apologizing, Birch."

Birch's eyes were wary, his shoulders stiff when Celia stepped close to lay her head against his chest. "Just hold me the way you used to. Let's put this behind us and forget today ever happened. I have an idea. I'm going to take a shower since I reek of cigarette smoke. Order us some coffee from Room Service, and we'll sit and talk until it's time for you to get ready for the meeting with your mother."

Birch strode to the French doors that led to the balcony. He stared out at the city of lights, a city that never slept. His city now. His and Celia's. Suddenly he wanted to cry the way he had when he was a small boy. He looked at his watch. Sage said he got up with the chickens. He walked back inside, called Room Service, then dialed his brother's number. "Did I wake you, Sage?"

"No. Is something wrong, Birch? You sound funny."

"I just hit my wife. Not once but three times. I needed to tell someone."

"Uh-huh. I guess my question should be, why?"

"She was out all night drinking. She said things, I said things, she took shots at Mom and I blew up. Would you ever hit Iris?"

"No."

"What would she do if you did?"

"If I had to take a guess I'd say she'd kick my ass all the way to Arizona, then she'd take the kids and beat feet. Dad never laid a hand on Mom, Birch. Grandpa Philip never touched Grandma Sallie. Maybe you need to talk to someone."

"I am. I'm talking to you. You're better than any high-priced shrink. You know me. Can you get away for lunch, Sage?"

"Sure. Name the place."

"The Fox and Hound at twelve-thirty."

Birch opened the door for the waiter, tipped him, then poured coffee into two cups just as Celia emerged from the bathroom, her golden blond head wrapped in a white towel, her body wearing a second towel sarong-style. Her left eye was swollen shut and her lips were puffy and bruised. Birch blinked.

"I don't think I can drink the coffee, Birch. Maybe if I had a straw. I wanted it more for you than me anyway. When you go downstairs would you send up some papers and magazines. I don't think I'll be going out for some time. Makeup won't cover what you did. I want your promise, Birch, that you will never do this again. If you do, I'll leave. The only reason I'm staying now is that I was wrong to do what I did. However, that doesn't give you the right to use me as a punching bag."

"I'm sorry. Now, what do you want to talk about?"

"Us. Here, this place. Your family and what they expect from us, me in particular. I want us to share everything like before. I don't want us to have secrets from one another. I don't want things between us to change just because we're living in a new place. We'll deal with the rest of the stuff as it comes up. Were you jealous, Birch?"

Birch sipped at his coffee. It didn't feel right. Something was missing. Sadness welled in him. He tried putting his arm around Celia's shoulders. In the past he always felt good when she snuggled against him. For some reason he felt empty now. Things were moving too fast for him here in Sin City. In that one split second he knew that he'd made the biggest mistake of his life by coming back to Las Vegas. His eyes burned unbearably. "We'll talk later, Celia. I have to shower and dress."

"You're still angry, aren't you?"

"Disappointed would be a better word. You have my word that I'll never hit you again."

Celia's voice was that of a little girl when she said, "Okay, Birch."

His back to her, Birch didn't see the ice-cold calculation in Celia's eyes. He was also unaware of the way her hands balled into tight fists of anger as she pummeled the sofa cushions.

"Where do you think you're going, Mrs. Reed?" Marcus asked, his voice tinged with sleep.

"I was going to order us some coffee. You don't have to get up, Marcus."

"It doesn't work that way, Fanny. You get up, I get up. Let's just lie here and talk."

Fanny snuggled closer. "I love waking up knowing you're next to me, and I can touch you if I want to. I'm so glad you found me that night, Marcus. My whole world had just been knocked right out from under me. And then, suddenly, there you were. I knew right at that moment something good was going to happen for us."

"I knew, too. It happened. Look at us now."

"Are you sorry you retired, Marcus?"

"Are you kidding!"

"You led such an exciting life flying to the Orient, Europe, South America on a moment's notice. You met wonderful, exciting people who controlled huge corporations, even small countries. This must be so tame compared to that time in your life. I worry, Marcus, that you will start to miss the excitement."

Marcus leaned up on one elbow. "Fanny, look at me and

listen to me. It was a job. I hated the hotels, the thick, rich food, never knowing from one day to the next where I'd be. My body never seemed to catch up with the different time zones. I lived in fear that I would get sick in some damn foreign country and die because I couldn't speak their language and they couldn't speak mine. I should have quit or retired a long time ago. I would have but there was nothing on my horizon but work. I settled. Until I met you. The only thing I can say for all those years was it paid well and helped me to help make my sister's life more comfortable. She was all I had. When she died, I worked harder because it was all that was left for me to do.

"Then I met you and your family, and I knew what I'd been missing all those years. I wanted to belong to someone. The sweetest words I ever heard were when you told me to drive carefully because you cared what happened to me. You gave me the key to that little house in the cottonwoods. I was so bone tired that day. I knew then that I loved you."

"I knew I loved you then, too. Just think, Marcus, if I hadn't been in the Harem Lounge that night, if my feet hadn't been hurting, we might never have met. We wouldn't be lying here right now."

"Don't think that, and don't say it," Marcus said.

"I like it that we're going to grow old together. We need a purpose, though. We should both start to think about doing something meaningful, something we can do together. It's important to give back, to contribute."

"I agree. When the people across the street engaged my services it was impossible to get them to understand that little adage. They were so locked into the old ways they refused to open their eyes. They were eaten with jealousy over you and couldn't understand how you, a mere woman, could be so successful. In some ways it was quite comical. That was one of the reasons I made up my mind to meet you. I heard just last week that your colleagues across the street donated three million dollars to add an extension on to the main library. It was done anonymously. You're responsible for their generosity. They all look out for you and your family. You are aware of that, aren't you?''

"Yes. I know in my heart you had something to do with that.''

"They listened. This town, these people, they take care of their own, Fanny. They watched Sallie for years. She never asked for anything. She was fair, and she gave back. Then you came along and did the same thing. It doesn't matter that you're on one side of the fence and they're on the other.''

"It sounds so nice when you explain it like that. They helped me, Marcus, more than once. I hope they know they can count on me.''

"Trust me, they know that.''

"Marcus, I would trust you with my life. I know my kids feel the same way about you.''

Marcus leaned back into his pillow. "Until I met you, Fanny, my life was like a page in a notebook with a few scribbles on each page. After I met you there were more words on the pages and then, when I had the good sense to marry you, the pages became full and made sense. I think I have a whole book now.''

"Do you think we should get it published?'' Fanny teased.

"No. However, I do think we should make meaningful entries from time to time. Like now. I'd like it very much, Mrs. Reed, if you'd make love to me.''

"Would you now, Mr. Reed?''

"Oh, yes, Mrs. Reed, I would.''

"If I make love to you, will you make love to me?''

"Absolutely.''

"Then I think we should get on it right away so we don't waste any more time.''

A long time later, Fanny stirred. "Shhh, Marcus, there is no reason for you to get up. I have just enough time to shower and meet Birch. Later, let's go on a picnic.''

"Hmmmnn."

"You look like a satisfied man. I like that, Mr. Reed."

Marcus rolled over and opened one eye. "Wait till you see what I can do on a picnic."

Fanny giggled. "Promises, promises. I'm going to hold you to that promise, Mr. Reed." Marcus's light snores followed her into the bathroom. "Thank you, God, for blessing me with this wonderful man."

Birch took a moment to watch his mother at a table set far back in a corner. She must have chosen it for privacy. She was pretty, as pretty as he remembered. He felt sad when he noticed the fine wrinkles on her face and the gray in her hair. His mother was getting old. Had he expected her to be forever young? Yes, yes, yes. She noticed him then and smiled, her gentle loving smile he had thought about thousands of times over the years. Suddenly his world was bright, warm, and wonderful. He smiled in return as he strode toward the table.

"You look wonderful, Mom."

"I was going to say the same thing to you. You look so much like your father it's downright spooky. It's not a bad thing," Fanny added hastily.

"You look happy, Mom. I don't think I ever saw your eyes sparkle until now."

"I am deliriously happy. My family is doing well. Sunny has exceeded mine and the doctor's expectations. Jake, Polly, and Lexie are super little kids. Jake is so good with his mother. Sometimes I want to cry at the way he loves her. Your dad did a wonderful job with him. He talks about Ash all the time. Sage and Billie run Sunny's Togs and Rainbow Babies like the pros they are. We're on the Big Board now. The Colemans are doing well. I guess I should say the Kingsleys. Billie really doesn't like the fishbowl life in Washington, though. I'm meeting later today with the other branch of the family. Last night you barely got to say hello. Marcus is a wonderful man. I want you to get to know him. He makes my life complete. Someday, I don't know when, we'll talk about your uncle Simon. Please don't be bitter where your father is concerned. He did what he felt he had to do. That doesn't make it right. It was his choice. In the end, when it counted, he came through for all of us. That's what we have to remember. We made our peace, Birch.''

"I guess I have a lot of catching up to do. One minute I feel like I've never been away, and the next minute I'm sorry I came back. Life was simple back then. I hope you don't feel like I let you down.''

"I never thought that, Birch, even for a minute. You did what you had to do. Life is too short for recriminations. I wish you had let me know you were coming back. Because I didn't know what to do when Bess and John announced their retirement, I offered the job to Jeff Lassiter. He has a three-year contract. He knows the business since he worked at the casino summers and holidays when he was in college. You'll be working under him, Birch. When Jeff's contract is up, we'll discuss our options. I can't and won't go back on my word. Your salary will be $100,000 plus the penthouse. Do you have a problem with any of this?''

Hell yes he did, but he wasn't going to admit it. "Since it's a done deal, I guess not. How are we going to, you know, divvy up the workload?''

"Jeff's waiting for your input. I don't think he'll step on your toes, and I don't expect you to step on his. I want you to work in harmony. The others like him. He's got a good head on his shoulders. I'm sorry, honey, if this isn't what you expected.''

Birch forced a lightness into his voice he didn't feel. "You know me, Mom, go with the flow. I can handle it.''

"If things go awry, or they aren't working, I expect you to come to me. We'll work it out. I want your promise, Birch.''

"Okay, Mom.''

"I scheduled a meeting for you and Jeff for two o'clock in the office. This place is now yours, Birch."

Mine, but my half brother is calling the shots. How the hell was he going to tell Celia he was second banana?

"So, what else is on your agenda today, Birch?" Fanny asked when she finished her coffee.

"Actually, Mom, I'm going out to the center to see Sunny. Celia will probably sleep the day away. I'll be back in time for the meeting. I missed you, Mom."

"And I missed you. Give Sunny a hug for me."

"Will do."

Birch stared at the rehab center where Sunny now lived. As pretty and picturesque as it was, it was still an institution. He felt a lump form in his throat. Why Sunny? Of them all, Sunny had always been the most vibrant, the most daring, the most courageous. As a youngster and then as a teen and young woman she'd been fearless. Her athletic prowess was beyond measure. She'd bragged last night about winning a wheelchair race here on the grounds. The lump in his throat seemed to be getting bigger as he roll-called memories of Sunny besting him and Sage in every sport—their father, too. How had it come to this for his sister?

Eyes burning, Birch climbed from the car. He loved Sunny almost as much as he loved Sage and Billie, maybe more. Sunny was special. She was always in his face telling him like it was, sparing nothing. He should have been here for her. Caught up in his own misery, he'd left her to flounder.

Birch's sneakers slapped at the flagstones as he loped his way to the reception area inside the center. He waited patiently until the young doctor finished working on a chart. He held out his hand, a smile on his face when he introduced himself and asked to see Sunny.

"Sorry. Visiting hours are Sundays only unless arrangements are made earlier."

"Are you saying I can't see my sister?"

The doctor nodded, his pen poised in midair.

Birch's mind raced. What would his father have done? Would he have used charm or bluster? Charm on a woman doctor, brash bluster and intimidation on a male doctor. Well, hell, if it was good enough for the old man, it was good enough for him.

"Then I guess you better start filling out your résumé because I'm going to cut off your funding in about three minutes flat. Do you care to rethink that negative nod?"

"Why don't I get Dr. Samuels for you?"

"That's not necessary. Point me in the direction of my sister."

The pen in the doctor's hand trembled as he pointed to a colorful, flower-bordered path outside the reception area.

"Write this down, Doctor. I will come here as often as I please and when I please. I won't interfere with any of Sunny's schedules. Write that down, too."

The dog saw Birch before Sunny did. He was a whirlwind of motion, circling Birch's feet, his tail between his legs. Birch froze in his tracks.

"Birch! What are you doing here? Did you sneak in? Oh, I'm so glad to see you. We hardly got to say hello last night. Come here, give me a big hug? Easy, Fred, he's okay."

The shepherd's tail swished back and forth as he escorted Birch to Sunny's chair.

"Good boy, Fred. What brings you out here today, Birch?"

"I wanted to see you. I didn't want to wait till Sunday. What the hell kind of place is this that limits visits? I thought friends and family helped situations like yours. I didn't sneak in, I bulldozed my way in with a threat."

"The rules are why this place works, Birch. You didn't know that, so it's okay this time. I have free time in the morning at eleven and again at four. A half hour each time. When you want to come out, use that time. I'm surprised they didn't boot your ass out of here. What did you say?''

"I said I'd cut off their funding in three minutes."

Sunny frowned. "Birch, I don't trade on the Thornton name here. Sometimes I want to, but I don't. I'm just like everyone else. That's another reason it works. Harry wouldn't be able to stay here otherwise. I had a real hard time with the rules at first. There were days I would have killed to see Jake and Polly. I got over that real quick because I had no other options. Now, I'm the welcoming committee for new patients. I pep-talk them, the whole nine yards. When there's a problem they call me. Enough, already, why are you here? What's wrong? Don't tell me nothing because I can see it in your face."

"I hit Celia. Three times. She really pissed me off. It's no excuse, and I promised I'd never do it again. She stayed downstairs till five-thirty this morning, and she was drunk when she came up. I think, Sunny, I might have made a mistake in coming back here."

"Oh, Birch, no, it wasn't a mistake to come back. It was a hell of a mistake, though, to hit your wife. Listen to me. I started hitting Jake, and Dad let me have it. I was out of control. Tyler had just left, I was getting worse, Dad was sick, Mom and I weren't speaking. I couldn't handle it. I took it out on Jake. That little boy didn't deserve what I did to him. No one in this family will tolerate that kind of battering. You come and talk to me. I want your promise."

Birch nodded. "You really got a handle on all of this?" Birch asked, waving his arms about. "Are you and Harry an item?"

"Yes and yes. If your next question is, do we have sex the answer is yes. It isn't easy but we manage. His family tossed him out. They didn't want the responsibility of caring for him. He's a dear, sweet man. We watch out for each other. We have teams here. The dogs look out for both of us. I see your eyes filling up. Don't be sad for me. I've come to terms with my life. It's what it is. Fortunately for me I have a wonderful family. We're Harry's family now, too. Remember how we used to talk about family where Dad was concerned? He just didn't get it till the end, and then it was too late.''

"I want you and Celia to be friends, Sunny."

"Birch, I don't think that's going to happen. For starters, I don't think I like your wife. I know that hurts your feelings, and I'm sorry about that. You see, we learn here that we have to say things just the way they are. We don't sugarcoat anything. Everything has to be out in the open. We can't hide behind doors, words, or people. Celia looked at Harry and me with revulsion. We're both used to that, but we shouldn't see it from our families. Sure, I smear myself sometimes if my hand goes someplace else instead of my mouth. I spill and dribble and drop things. Sometimes I want to cry. Sometimes I do cry. Fred licks my tears or Harry wipes them away. I'd kill to be able to hold a chicken leg or pop a lid from a yogurt cup. The big word here is tolerance. They have signs posted everywhere. I've learned to live by that word. Please don't say anything to Celia. It will just make things worse. Some people can't handle other people's handicaps.''

"Sunny, I'm so sorry. I want to do something for you. I'm sorry I wasn't here for you. For whatever consolation it is to you, I did think of you every single day I was away. I wondered what you were doing, what kind of mess you got yourself into with that mouth of yours. I used to talk about you so much Celia would tell me to shut up.''

"You did write five whole letters, so I forgive you. Now it's my turn. Are you okay with Jeff? He's all right, Birch, but . . . there's something off-key about him. I have to be honest and say no one agrees with me. It's just a feeling. Mom's back was to the wall. She really didn't have a choice, Birch. She's done her best to do things the way Dad would have wanted her to, and his first rule was that only family should be involved.

When you own your own business you don't let strangers or outsiders run it for you.''

"My first thought was, how is Celia going to take it?" Birch said. "I was a little upset, but it was okay. A hundred grand a year and the penthouse isn't shabby.''

"Will Celia think it's shabby?''

"My gut says yes. The day before yesterday I would have said no. Sunny, I feel like a net is getting ready to drop on me. It came out of nowhere. Maybe I don't belong in society.''

"I wish I could help you, but it's all I can do to help myself. I'll try to like her for your sake. If it doesn't work, it won't be because I didn't try. Remember the rules now.''

"You want me to apologize to that doctor, don't you?''

"Only if you want to. What are you going to do now?''

"Go look for a car. I'm going to need some wheels.''

"Want mine?''

"Your Volvo? Do you still have it? You really have the old gray ghost?''

Sunny smiled at the excitement in her brother's voice. "I sure do, and it's in mint condition. It's candy apple red now. Dad had it overhauled, repainted, new upholstery, the works. Feel free to use it. God, how I loved that car.'' She fumbled in the side pocket of a canvas bag attached to her chair. "Here's the key. Swear you won't drive it over forty miles an hour. Sometimes when I have trouble falling asleep I think about all the good times, running to the car, running here or there. I'm always running, and then I slide into the car. Oh God, Birch, I'm never going to be able to do that again. Never, ever.'' Her high-pitched keening wail sent shivers up Birch's spine.

His heart breaking for his sister, Birch lifted her out of the wheelchair and into his arms. He walked with her, around the old tree and then back and forth, his tears mingling with Sunny's as he crooned to her. Until that moment he wasn't aware of how thin and bony she was under her layered clothes.

"Okay, I'm done bawling now. You can put me back in the

chair. Jeez, I haven't done that in a long time. Did I mess up your shirt?''

"Nah. Are you serious about the Volvo? Sage and I were so jealous when Mom let you get that car. At night when you were sleeping we'd go out and sit in it.''

"I know.''

"You knew and you didn't beat on us.''

"You're my brothers. Take Jake out in it sometimes, okay?''

"Sure.''

"What's Celia going to say when she sees you driving around in a fifteen-year-old Volvo?''

Birch shrugged. "She wants a Cadillac.''

"Dad always called them pimpmobiles. Thanks for coming by, Birch.''

"I'll be here every week, maybe twice. I'll go pick up your car and drive out to Mom's house. I can't wait to see it.''

"Did Mom tell you about Daisy's pups? She had four. Sage took one, and Bess took one. Mom kept two. She calls the girl Growl Tiger and the boy is Fosdick. Mom and Marcus just love them. All three of them sleep on the bed with them. Jake baby-sits the dogs when they travel. He really keeps them spruced up. Oh, oh, here comes my therapist. Don't go yet, I want you to meet her. Her real name is Libertine. Don't laugh. We call her Libby.''

Birch turned, hands jammed into his khaki trousers. She looked golden in the early-morning sun, her reddish hair a nimbus of curls around her head. Her eyes were cornflower blue and crinkled at the corners. Her smile was so warm it wrapped itself around him. Her handshake was bone-crushing.

"You must be Birch. Sunny described you perfectly. I think I'd know you anywhere. I'm Libby Maxwell. I lost ten dollars two weeks ago at Babylon.''

"Oh. Well . . . ah, are you going to try and win it back?''

"Probably not. I work too hard for my money. It was nice meeting you. Sunny has to go to therapy now.''

"C'mere and give me a big smooch," Sunny said, holding out her arms to Birch.

Birch leaned over. Sunny whispered in his ear, "I had it all planned. Libby was supposed to be your destiny. She already knows you're hers. I've been showing her pictures. You blew my big plan by getting married. Now Harry and I are going to have to find someone else for her."

Birch's body felt red-hot when he turned to say good-bye. On the way home he had the urge to turn back and tell Sunny to hold off on finding a replacement for her therapist. Libby Maxwell's crinkly smile stayed with him all the way back to town.

His destiny?

3

Birch let himself into Room 2711. He stood still for a moment listening to the silence before he tiptoed into the bedroom. Celia was still sleeping. He stared down at her for a long time, his heart racing. What in the goddamn hell was he doing here?

He kicked off his shoes and shucked his clothes. He pulled on worn, faded jeans, a sweatshirt and sneakers. He searched for his baseball cap, the last thing his father had given him. His index finger traced the raised threads that spelled out Thornton Chickens. He settled it firmly onto his head.

The key to Sunny's Volvo in hand, Birch made his way to the underground garage. His eyes filled as he stared at Sunny's pride and joy. He unlocked the door, settled himself, marveling at the new-car smell of the vehicle. His smile stretched from ear to ear when he turned the key in the ignition. The car purred like a contented lioness. His hand caressed the mahogany knob on the gearshift as he slid it into reverse. Sunny had always boasted she could shift on the fly. Both he and Sage had been eaten alive with jealousy when Sunny made it look so easy.

Neither he nor Sage had been able to work the clutch until they got older.

It was all so long ago.

Fifteen minutes later, Birch was on his way up the mountain; his destination, Sunrise.

Iris Thornton's jaw dropped when she saw Sunny's red Volvo screech to a stop in the cobbled courtyard. Her jaw dropped farther when she saw her brother-in-law climb from the car. She watched as he turned to get his bearings before he took off running like the demons from hell were on his heels. The phone was in her hand before she even realized she'd picked it up.

"Sage, Birch is here. He drove up in Sunny's Volvo and then he . . . he started to run. He ran down the mountain. At least I think he did. Maybe you should come home, Sage." She listened for a long time as her husband spoke. "You give me too much credit, honey. Okay, I'll call you when he leaves. Everything's fine. I probably shouldn't have called you, but Birch was the last person I expected to see today. Bye."

Iris checked the huge pot of stew simmering on the stove. She took a quick peek at the two loaves of bread and the peach cobbler browning in the oven before she put a fresh pot of coffee on to perk. Birch, like Fanny, drank coffee all day long. She eyed the two rockers next to the fireplace. She threw on two logs. Sparks spiraled every which way. She likened the shooting sparks to Birch's emotions and wondered how she knew her brother-in-law's emotions were spiraling in all directions. She listened to the sounds of the percolator. Rosie, Daisy's pup and the runt of the litter, raised her head from her nest on the red-checkered cushion on the rocker. When the last plop-plop sound ricocheted around the kitchen she jumped down.

Iris waited, her eye on the kitchen clock. When the timer

went off, she removed the bread and cobbler from the oven, sniffing appreciatively. She slid a cookie sheet full of cloves and orange peels onto the top oven shelf and turned off the oven. The whole house would smell wonderful in ten minutes. A trick Fanny had taught her.

Her housework done, Iris busied herself by cutting vegetables for a dinner salad. She set butter on the counter to soften because Sage hated hard butter on fresh bread. Soon Chue would be bringing the kids home from school with his own grandchildren. Usually they stopped to play for a half hour or so, then walked the rest of the way home. *What is Birch doing here? What's wrong?* Whatever it was, it was going to affect her and Sage.

Rosie's head jerked upward. A second later she ran to the door, barking and growling, the hair on the back of her neck on end. Iris's sigh could be heard in the next room. She set out cream and sugar and two large mugs.

"Just in time for coffee, Birch. It's fresh."

"I feel like I just came in from school. It's almost time for the kids to come home, isn't it?"

"Yes, but today is Chue's day. We take turns alternating the after-school snacks. They love the mountain, Birch."

"Sage and I loved it, too. Celia won't like it up here. It's too quiet and peaceful. I don't know if I could live here either."

"Sage loves it."

"He always loved it here. We used to lie in bed at night and talk about what we'd do when we were old and married. He always said he was going to build a house next to Mom's. We assumed back then that she'd live here forever. I've found out that nothing is forever, Iris. I thought coming back here was the wise thing to do. Now, I think I made a mistake. I think I ran twenty miles up and down and around the mountain trying to get a fix on things."

"Did it work?"

"Hell, I don't know. I think I've lived in the bush too long, and I don't think I thought this through. I'm sure Sage told you about what I did. I didn't think I was capable of violence, but I am, and it bothers me. Who knows what I'll do the next time someone ticks me off?"

"By someone, do you mean Celia?"

"Celia, Jeff Lassiter. That's sitting, but not well. I'm pretty sure I can handle working with him. The burning question is, is working with Jeff really what I want to do? A hundred grand a year isn't all that much."

"Many people work for far less and raise families. You'll have no rent or mortgage, your food is free, no utilities, your car maintenance and gas are charged to the business. The only cost to you is clothing you get at a thirty percent discount and your taxes. You also have the option of taking a check every month from the trust fund. If you and Celia can't manage to live on that, then something is seriously wrong. You have no children, Birch. Am I missing something here?"

"Christ, Iris, I don't know. I have this ominous feeling that something is going to happen. On top of that I have this fear that I'm going to turn out like Dad. I'm tied in knots. When I was in Costa Rica, I never had a moment's worry. I know this is going to sound corny as hell, but my soul was at peace over there."

"Go back, Birch. If that's how you felt, then get that feeling back before it's lost to you. Take your trust fund and do some good with it. Talk to Celia, explain how you feel. I'm sure she'll understand. I'd follow Sage to the ends of the earth, so would the kids. I think you need a new baseball cap. I'm pretty handy with a needle. I could redo the lettering on your cap if you want."

Birch shook his head. "This is the last thing Dad gave me. Actually, he threw it at me. Celia hates it. She says it's dirty and cruddy. As much as I regret what happened, it made me stop and think. God, this kitchen smells good."

"I'm making stew. It's your mother's recipe, the one with

the horseradish in it. The bread is fresh, the butter soft. The cobbler is still warm, and I finished cutting the salad greens right before you came in. Want some?''

''All of Sage's favorites. I hope he knows how lucky he is.''

''I remind him every day. Are you saying you don't want any of my home cooking?''

''I'll take a rain check. I need to get back. Sunny gave me her car. Actually, she lent it to me. I felt like king of the hill when I drove up this mountain.''

Iris smiled. ''Sage has had his eye on that car for years. He's the one who polishes it. He doesn't have a key, so he couldn't even sit in the seat. Sunny wouldn't give him the key. You should feel honored. I understand. You and Sunny were very close, more so than Sage and Sunny.''

''I don't know why that was. Sage is closer to Billie than me. I guess it's just the way it worked out.''

''I think it's because you and Sunny are so much alike. The only difference is she's a girl and you're a guy. Sage is serious and so is Billie. They work very well together.''

''Sunny's wasting away. If anything goes wrong, it's gonna kill me.''

''Nothing is going to go wrong. Sunny isn't wasting away. The truth is they put some meat on her bones. You should have seen her before she became a permanent resident at the center. Being thin has nothing to do with things. Harry is thin, too; so are most of the other patients. Some of them are elderly, which proves my point. Sunny is contented, Birch. That's the most important thing. More coffee?''

''No thanks. I need to get back. I shouldn't have left Celia.''

''But you did.''

''Yeah. Me first. Just like Dad.''

''There are worse things in life, Birch. The last few years you would have been proud of him. He came through for all of us. Your mom and dad became best friends. Ash liked and approved of Marcus.''

"And he killed his brother."

"We don't talk about that, Birch. Your uncle Simon stalked your mother, he beat your father to a bloody pulp, and he burned Sunrise to the ground. He also enlisted Jeff Lassiter's help to take some big bucks out of all the casinos. In the end it was the consensus that Simon would have ended up killing your mother. We can't change the past, Birch. It happened, and it's history now."

"My brother is one hell of a lucky guy. I'll see you Sunday. Can we do anything?"

"Show up. Be careful going down the mountain in that sporty car."

"Sunny says I can't drive it more than forty miles an hour. She was serious, too."

"You agreed to that?" Iris asked in awe.

"Damn straight," Birch said, using his sister's favorite expression. "I would have agreed to ten miles. Thanks for the coffee."

"My pleasure."

"Kiss the kids."

"Sure."

"Iris . . ."

"What?"

"Would you think I was crazy if I went to work for Thornton Chickens?"

"I'd say that would be one of your smarter moves. Ruby's great. You'll like her. She admits she doesn't know much about the chicken business."

Birch nodded as he climbed behind the wheel. He leaned out the window. "I love you guys. You know that, don't you?"

"We know that, Birch."

* * *

"Celia, I'm back."

"I'm right here, Birch. I pulled the drapes because the light hurts my eye. Where were you?"

"Here and there. We can move into the penthouse now if you want to pack up your stuff. Mom and Marcus left after breakfast. Are you up to it? We'll talk when we settle in. Again, I'm sorry, Celia."

"I know you are, Birch. There is nothing to pack. I threw out all my stuff because it was so ragged and worn. I see you kept yours."

He noticed the ice bag on the end table. He tried not to look at what he'd done to his wife. "You go on up and I'll bring our stuff. I can make it in one trip." He handed over the card key his mother had given him earlier.

"I can't wait to see it," Celia gushed. "I bet it's beautiful."

Birch's voice was short and clipped when he said, "I think I'd go with the word comfort opposed to beautiful. Looking out at the city is pleasant at night."

"And your mother controls all of this. I can't even begin to imagine what a powerful feeling that must be. I'll see you upstairs."

"Yeah," Birch muttered.

Celia, dressed in one of the casino's terry-cloth robes and slippers, took the private elevator to the penthouse. She sucked in her breath and squeezed her eyes shut when she slid the card key into the lock. She just knew this new home of hers was going to be gorgeous beyond belief. She wailed her displeasure the moment her gaze fell on the two red chairs. The braided rugs didn't bear a second glance. The oak tables and potted plants made her retch. The kitchen with its old claw-foot table and plaid cushioned chairs made her want to cry. She ran to the bedrooms, her eyes full of anger. Who in their right mind slept on flannel sheets? She clenched her fists so she wouldn't rip them off the beds. "I hate it, I hate it, I hate it!"

"What do you think, honey? Can you see yourself living here?"

"Well—"

"It looked different when my father lived here. It was cold and impersonal, slick and shiny. The stuff's in storage if you don't like my mother's decorating taste."

"It isn't that I don't like it, Birch. I don't think I could be comfortable with this stuff. It's too hot-looking. The furniture is heavy and cumbersome. The pictures I've seen in magazines of different penthouses were light and airy-looking. They used mirrors to make the place bigger. I like glass and chrome, and I'm partial to black and white. It's so clean and stark-looking. If you don't mind, I would like to switch up. Guys usually don't care about stuff like decorating. Do you care?"

"Let's make some coffee and talk, Celia."

"Why don't we order Room Service?"

"Because it gets charged to the family. That's one of the things we need to talk about. There is every staple imaginable in the kitchen. I'll make the coffee."

"I didn't know you were such a skinflint, Birch. How much could they charge?" she muttered.

"Fifteen bucks plus a tip."

"For a pot of coffee?"

"For two cups."

Celia sat down.

Birch returned from the kitchen to sit down on the low, comfortable red-and-brown sofa next to his wife. He put his arm around Celia's shoulder. "What would you say, honey, if I asked you to go back to Costa Rica with me? I'm here two days, and it seems like things are closing in on me."

Celia bolted upright. "It's just anxiety. You know, like opening night jitters, that kind of thing. You've been away a long time. Things will calm down. You'll relax in a few days. I don't want to go back. It was fine while we were there, but we've moved on now. We talked about this. It was your idea to come back. You said you were ready. I'm not going back, Birch.''

"Look what I did to you. I don't want to turn out like my father. That's always been the biggest fear in my life. If we stay here, things are going to happen. I know it as surely as I'm sitting here. This is a totally different kind of life. It sucks you in, and you aren't even aware of it happening until it's too late. I don't think I want to spend the rest of my life in a casino. Mom told me she gave my half brother Jeff a contract to run the casino. I would be working with him for a salary of $100,000 a year.''

"A hundred thousand dollars! You said it was worth $250,000. Is that what she's paying your brother?'' Birch cringed at the greed in his wife's voice.

"My half brother. I don't know. My mother made the decision, and she never goes back on her word. It's my own fault. I should have told her I was returning. So much for big surprises.''

"At least you have your trust fund. Do they give bonuses?''

"I wish you'd forget that trust fund. No, they don't give out bonuses. Since we got back, all you talk about is money. In Costa Rica the word wasn't in our vocabulary.''

"That's because we didn't have any and, even if we had, there was nowhere to spend it. You're right though, I do talk about money, and I think about it, too. I'm tired of living like a ragpicker. I want nice things, good food, and a house to live in. I also want a car. Of my own. Does a car come with this job?''

"No. Sunny gave me her treasured Volvo. The one I used to tell you about. It's like a bright red bonbon. I can pick up a station wagon for you in a few days.''

"Watch my swollen lips, Birch. I do not want some stodgy station wagon. I want a bright colored, low-slung sports car.''

Birch removed his arm from his wife's shoulders. "Tell me,

if you had married someone else, how would you get those things?''

"I didn't marry someone else, Birch, I married you. I had no idea you were such a scrooge where money is concerned. How much money is in that trust fund?''

"I have no idea. It's just there. No one uses it. None of us draw from it. If I ever have children, it will go to them. That's how it's set up. If I don't have children, it will go to Sunny's kids.''

"You need to change that. You have a wife now. We could have children one of these days. Things like that need to be taken care of. You must have some idea of how much money is in the fund.''

"Look at me, Celia. Yes, it's mine, but there are strings and restrictions. It was set up by my grandmother and my mother. I cannot undo it. It's airtight. It goes down the line to the family heirs. *You* cannot inherit from it. Ever.''

"Are you saying I don't count for anything in this marriage?''

"No, I'm not saying that at all. I'm explaining it to you the best way I can. I can't help it if you don't like it.'' Birch watched his wife's shocked face when he said, "There is around five million in the trust. That was years ago. I don't know what it's worth today.'' He felt sick to his stomach at the greedy, calculating look he saw reflected in Celia's eyes. He got up and moved to one of the red chairs that gave him a frontal view of his wife. "Children are not in my game plan, Celia. I'm not father material like Sage is. My sister Billie is the first one to tell you she isn't mother material. Don't ask me why that is. We agreed, Celia, that children wouldn't be part of our lives. I haven't changed my mind.''

"When are you going to decide about the job? We need to talk about this or doesn't my opinion count?''

"Of course it counts. Iris said something this afternoon about following Sage to the ends of the earth. I found myself wondering if you'd do the same thing. You seem to be changing in front of my eyes, or is it my ears."

"Changing! What about you, Birch? In my worst nightmares I never thought you'd strike me. Let's be fair here. You certainly have been busy today, haven't you?" This last was said so snidely, Birch felt the control he'd kept on his anger begin to slip.

Birch stretched his neck to relieve the tension in his shoulders. "I don't want to stay here and work with Jeff. Yeah, it bothers me. For some reason I don't think my father would have approved of this. I suppose I could do it. Since I have choices, I'd like to opt for something else. I'm going to go out to the ranch tomorrow and talk to Dad's half sister Ruby. Dad worked the ranch for many years. Between him and my grandfather they put Thornton Chickens on the map."

"Are you telling me you'd give up working here at the casino to clean up chicken shit? That, I think, doesn't even bear discussing."

"If I go to the ranch, we have to give up the penthouse. I prefer a house myself with a garden. A small house."

"A little house! Birch, I don't like the sound of any of this. Two days ago our lives were settled. Now, things have switched up, and nothing is like you said it would be. What about me?"

"Get a job. Keep busy. Do volunteer work at Thornton Medical Center. When did you become so selfish?"

"The minute I stepped back onto American soil. I want to know when you became so stingy?"

"I was always frugal. Mom taught us all to save. We were taught to spend some and to save some. Sage and I used to save ten cents every week from our allowances. Sunny saved twenty cents. She always had to go one better than us. Billie saved her entire allowance. Once she lent me five hundred dollars when my clunker broke down. Billie and Sunny always had the most money in the bank."

"All that money, and Sunny can't enjoy it. It doesn't seem

fair. Money should be enjoyed. That's my philosophy. So, what are you going to do, Birch?''

''I'm going out to the ranch tomorrow. We're going to Sunrise on Sunday. I'll decide before then.''

''And if I don't agree?''

''I would hope that you loved me enough to want what is going to make me happiest. Celia, working here wouldn't give us any time alone. When I thought it was just going to be me running the casino, I planned on doing days and training someone for nights. Jeff gets the plum spot, and I'd have to do nights. I'd be sleeping all day. I saw what it did to my father. I had a plan all worked out in my head. It's not feasible now. I think I'll make some dinner unless you want to do it.''

''It's hard for me to chew. I'll just have some soup or a scrambled egg.'' Her voice was so pitiful-sounding, Birch felt his stomach muscles bunch into a knot.

In the kitchen Birch jammed his hands into his pockets to stop them from trembling. He wished he could cry the way he had when he was little. He longed for Sage to clap him on the back and tell him things would be better. Right now, this very minute, Sage was probably sitting down to the wonderful dinner Iris had made. The kids would be chattering, Iris would be talking to Sage, and there would be flowers from Chue's greenhouse on the table. ''Son of a bitch!'' The expletive hissed from between his clenched teeth.

He recognized his anger and disappointment as he banged pots and pans in his search for the frying pan. His dream of a happy marriage was crumbling right before his eyes. He thought about his father then because he always thought about Ash Thornton when things didn't go right. It always comes down to money, just like he said. His thoughts took him into the future and words like prenuptial agreements, settlements buzzed around inside his brain. He'd been crazy in love with Celia three days ago and today he didn't even like her. He didn't discount his own violent behavior. He could make up for that by making sure it never happened again. What he couldn't alter or change was the monetary situation. He couldn't take the greed out of Celia's eyes, couldn't take away the revulsion Sunny said she saw in those same eyes.

Birch looked around the homey kitchen. His mother had done her best to make the penthouse comfortable so she could live here and work at a job she'd hated. She'd put her life on hold to do what his father wanted. Marriage was one sacrifice after another. Even when she'd divorced his father, she hadn't given up on him. In his gut he knew Celia would never be the woman his mother was.

"Dinner's ready," he called.

Celia picked at the scrambled eggs on her plate. Birch stared at her across the table. Aside from a little puffiness on her bottom lip and a darkening patch under her eye she seemed okay. She was milking it, and they both knew it.

Birch wolfed his food. "You can clean up. I'm going to go out to the ranch. I don't feel like waiting till tomorrow. Don't wait up for me."

"You're leaving me alone! Are we going to get a maid?"

"Yes and no. You didn't seem to mind leaving me alone last night while you partied downstairs. If you want a maid, you're going to have to get a job to pay for it. This apartment isn't so big that you can't handle a few housekeeping chores. My mother raised me to be neat, so you won't have to pick up after me. We have two bathrooms. You take care of yours and I'll take care of mine."

"I'm not a housekeeper, Birch. I'm not even a good cook."

"I guess you're going to learn. Mom and Iris will help you."

"Stop jamming your family down my throat. When my face is healed, I want to do some shopping. Do we have credit cards?"

Birch's stomach rumbled. "They're invalid since they haven't been used in years. I'll look into it when I have time."

"Do we have any cash money? What am I supposed to do if I need toothpaste?"

"We'll hash this out tomorrow. I have decisions I need to make right now, and this shitty stuff that's consuming you isn't a priority with me."

"Maybe I should pack up my underwear and leave. This isn't working for me."

"Suit yourself. While you're packing that underwear, you might want to ask yourself what it is that isn't working for you. Guess what, it may not be working for me either. You don't seem the least bit interested in how I feel and what is going to work for me. I'm the one who has to bust his ass for that toothpaste and that credit card you want. Women work today. In a few short hours you've focused on the Thornton money to the exclusion of all else. That bothers me. Were you always like this and was I too blind to see it?"

Celia started to cry. "This is new and . . . so thrilling. Why can't you let me enjoy it for a little while? I love you. You love me. What we have is good. I'm not going to hold the violence against you. I can forgive you because I love you. If I can be forgiving, why can't you bend a little? Both of us could use some fun. The truth is, Birch, I'm starved for the good life. You always had it. I didn't. If you want me to get a job, I will. I'll still need money to outfit myself. I'll need a car to get to work. I'd like to stay here and live in this penthouse. If you let me, I can make it a showplace. I hate it that you're even thinking of working at that chicken place. You'll come home smelling like chickens. Chickens smell nasty. Chicken feathers will be on your clothes, stuck to your shoes."

Birch turned around. "I don't think you have any idea of the size of Thornton Chickens. It's a megabucks industry. My grandfather and my father worked their asses off to make it the company it is today."

"So what! Your father's half sister owns it. You'd just be the hired help. What do we get out of it beside your salary if you work there? Free chickens? What exactly does megabucks mean in chicken lingo?''

Birch snorted. ''Try rolling a billion-dollar-a-year industry off those puffy lips of yours, sweetheart.'' The door slammed behind him. In the hallway he leaned against the wall to stop his internal shivering. Who was that person in there?

Celia tossed the silverware and dishes into the sink, the fry pan on top. Toast crumbs on the table were brushed onto the floor. She dusted her hands. Her job was done.

A *billion*-dollar-a-year industry could hardly be called chicken feed. Celia smiled all the way into the bedroom, where she climbed into bed, pulled up the covers, and switched on the television set. She leaned back in her nest of pillows and immediately began to spend money in her thoughts.

So much money. So little time.

When her mental closets were full of designer clothes and furs, her jewelry box overflowing and her new sports car garaged, Celia picked up the phone and placed a person-to-person call to Huntsville, Alabama. ''Solly, this is Celia Connors. Celia Thornton now. You know the Thorntons of Las Vegas. I'm one of them now. Can you believe it? Have I got a story to tell you. Listen up, Solly.''

Birch picked his way up the winding path that led to the ranch's main house. The low-wattage lighting hidden in the shrubbery twinkled as he walked along. It was quiet here. Somewhere off to the left he could hear night birds chittering in the trees. He liked the comforting sound they made. For one brief moment he felt like he was back in Costa Rica.

Long ago, when he was in his early teens, his father had brought him and Sage to the ranch to see the way things were done. All he remembered now was what a monster operation it was, and profitable. Now, at night, it looked different. He wondered if the chickens were asleep. For the first time in days he felt genuine amusement. He jumped to the side when he felt something brush against his ankle. He looked down to see a large yellow cat. He dropped to his haunches. "You're a big guy, aren't you?" The cat allowed his head to be stroked. He purred contentedly. On his feet again, the cat followed him to the front door, where he rang the bell.

Ruby Thornton opened the door. "Birch! Come in, come in. Is anything wrong? Did something happen? I'm babbling here. Please, come in. Can I get you a drink or some coffee?"

"Coffee would be good. Nothing's wrong. Listen, what should I call you?"

"Ruby's fine. Do you like kitchens?"

"My favorite room in a house. We used to live in our kitchen at Sunrise. So, how do you like living way out here?"

"I hate it. I hate the chicken business even more. I'd like to unload the whole thing."

"I'm looking for a job."

"But ... I thought ... what about Babylon? You want to work here at the ranch? Tell me what you want. This is so strange. I was upstairs cursing this business, this town, my life, the whole ball of wax. I was a hair away from throwing my clothes in my suitcase. Then you ring my doorbell. Is this divine providence or what? Talk to me, Birch."

It was almost midnight when Birch wound down his hours-long-monologue. They had replenished the coffeepot twice. "I'll never sleep now," Birch said ruefully.

"Mr. Thornton, sir, you are this lady's answer to her prayers. If you think you can handle this business, it's yours to run. Cough up some bucks and you're my partner. The books say you can take a half million out a year in salary. My father and your grandfather started a wonderful pension plan and initiated a bonus system that will keep you comfortable for the rest of your life. The house goes with the job. I don't want your answer tonight, Birch. I want you to talk this over with your mother. Fanny's been wonderful to me. She made me feel a part of your family. Ash ... didn't want me anywhere near any of you. I'm like my mother was in many ways. I came on to your dad like gangbusters. I wanted to know my brothers. He didn't want to know me at all. I never did get to meet Simon. End of story."

"What will you do?"

"Travel the world, write a book. Find a man who will love me unconditionally. Don't send me any reports. Stick them in a paper bag under the sink. If I ever come back, I'll know where to look."

The awe on Birch's face was total. "You're serious, aren't you?"

Tears welled in Ruby's éyes. "Your mother made my life bearable. When Ash got sick, really sick there at the end, she called me. We sat in the kitchen at Sunrise and talked for hours and hours. She put her arm around me and let me cry. She never had a mother, so she knew how I felt. I had a mother, but I didn't have the family. Your grandmother was a whore and so was my mother. I had a hard time with that for a while. All your family's riches, all my mother and father's riches came from two frightened whores. It's amazing when you stop to think about it. Now, I want you to tell me how you're going to present this plan to your wife."

"You're gambling on me, Ruby. I know nothing about chickens. I'm going to flub up. That's a given. As to Celia, well, I guess I'll just tell her. Whatever happens, happens. Who's your attorney?"

"Forget that legal stuff. We're family. A handshake will do it. That's how my father did things, and your father did them the same way. That's good enough for me. Give me your answer Sunday when we all go to Sunrise. If you agree, I'm out of here come Monday morning. Deal?"

Birch's hand shot out. Ruby pumped it vigorously. "This calls for a toast. Let's switch to lemonade. The cat goes with the deal. Will you take care of her? Her name is Cleo. She's a real love. Smart, too.''

"Okay.''

"I'm going to miss Sunny. Your sister is a real piece of work. I admire her so, and yet I cry for her. Will you keep me up-to-date on her? I know she can't respond, but I'll write to her anyway. I can't believe she gave you her car. By the way, there is a Ford Mustang in the garage. It's in good shape, and I just had it serviced a few weeks ago. Your wife can use it if she wants. It will save you some bucks.''

Birch nodded his thanks. "Do you know anything about free-range chickens?''

"No. Should I?''

"That's what the health-food industry wants. I'd like to give it to them. Profits could double. I read about free-range chickens on the flight from Costa Rica.''

"Go for it.''

Birch nodded. "It's late. I should go home. Would you mind showing me the house?''

"Go ahead. The upstairs is lighted. Take your time. Mom had it done over before she died. The bathrooms are all new and so is this kitchen. The floors are solid oak. The cross ventilation is great. There are four central air-conditioning units. The fireplaces are great in the winter. There is enough wood in the shed to last you all winter. We have about twenty generators in one of the barns. Make sure they're always in working condition. That was one of the things Dad always drilled into the workers. Listen to me. I sound like you've already agreed to take on the business. I hope you do, Birch. I can go away knowing Pop's legacy is in good hands.''

It was after two when Birch said good-bye. He whistled when he strode down the dimly lighted path. He knew what his answer was going to be on Sunday. He couldn't wait to tell Sage.

It occurred to Birch as he drove up the mountain that it

should be Celia he wanted to share things with, not his twin brother. Here he was, driving to Sunrise in the middle of the night. Sage would understand. He'd wait till five o'clock, when Sage said he got up, to ring the doorbell.

Instead of waiting for a light to go on inside the house, Birch climbed from the car and headed to the private cemetery behind the house. He sat on the low brick wall Chue had built years ago. He thought about the past, the present, and what the future was going to hold for him.

Inside the house, Rosie ran up the steps to the second floor and, with a mighty leap, landed on Sage's stomach. She growled and tugged at his pajama top.

"Okay, okay, I'm coming," Sage said groggily. "How come you can't do your business at ten o'clock? All right, all right."

He saw the car when he opened the kitchen door. What the hell was Birch doing here at four in the morning? More to the point, where the hell was he? "Go fetch him, Rosie." The little dog raced off. A sheepish-looking Birch followed Rosie to the kitchen.

"You were in the neighborhood and thought you'd stop and visit, huh?"

"Nah. I didn't feel like going home. I don't have a home. I think I'm what you might call a displaced person. I was out at the chicken ranch all night talking to Ruby. We worked out a deal. I'm going to take over the ranch."

"Birch, what in the hell do you know about the chicken business?"

"Not a damn thing. Don't you see, Sage, that's the beauty of the whole thing. I didn't know a damn thing about building a village either, but I did it. I can do this, too. Ruby thinks I can do it. I like her. I'm going into the free-range chicken business and in a year I can double profits."

"Uh-huh."

"I can do it, Sage."

"What exactly are free-range chickens?"

"Ask the health-food industry. Free-range chickens are what organic vegetables are to the produce industry. I think I came up here to have you pat me on the back and say, good idea, Birch. Celia isn't going to like the idea. The house and a cat named Cleo go with the deal. Good bonuses, pension plan, and a half million in salary."

Sage whistled. "Not shabby."

"It's not the money. It's the challenge of the job. I want what I do to count for something. I want that adrenaline rush when I know I pulled it off. The casino isn't going to do it for me. Too many bad memories there. I would have given it my best shot, though."

"Mom's going to take it personally."

"She'll understand when I explain things to her. You got any of that stew left over?"

"I'll fix it," Iris said from the doorway. "Promise me you won't make visiting at this time of night a habit."

"Honey, Birch is going to take over Thornton Chickens. He's going to raise free-range chickens."

"No kidding. Put us down for a crate a month. They are so delicious! The Thornton coffers are going to bust wide open. What a super idea, Birch."

"You know about free-range chickens?" Sage said.

"Of course. I'm a cook. They're hard to come by, and they're very expensive. I want mine free."

"You got it," Birch beamed.

Sage slapped his brother on the back. "Leave it up to you, you son of a gun. Go for it, big brother."

"It's almost like old times, eh, Sage."

"Yeah. Yeah it is. All we need is Sunny and one of her fried-egg sandwiches."

"Ruby said I should cut you all in on the free-range end."

"This family is something, isn't it, Birch?"

"Yep."

4

Fanny Thornton Reed stood in the driveway waiting for Marcus to lock the doors and close the garage. "Do you know what I love best about our house, Marcus?"

"That I came with the deal?"

"That too. This house doesn't remind me of anyone or anything. We built it, and the only memories are ours. There were days when I hated Sunrise, days when I hated the cottage in the cottonwoods. Before you, Marcus, I hated a lot of things. I love you so much. This," she said, waving her arms about, "is as good as it gets. You garden and work in your shop in the garage, I cook and sew. We have the dogs to keep us company. We can pick up and go away on a moment's notice. My family is together now that Birch is back. We are definitely blessed."

"I love you, Fanny. I think I waited all my life for you. Remember our pact, we don't dwell on the past."

"After today, we won't. We need to make a decision where Simon's estate is concerned. I can't believe he never changed his will and everything was left to me. I shiver every time I think about it. It's been hanging over my head since the will went through probate. I just want it to be over and done with.''

"It's a mind-boggling amount of money, Fanny. You need to make the right decisions.''

Fanny's voice was weary. "I know, Marcus. I wanted to turn it all over to Mr. Hasegawa's estate, but they wouldn't take it. Do you believe that? He was so generous with his help in building the other rehab centers. No one wants Simon's money. Even the kids don't want it.'' Fanny stared at the diamond-shaped windows on the second floor of her house. Her heart hammered in her chest when she turned and ran to the car, gasping for breath. "I swear, Marcus, I thought I saw Sallie at the window.''

Marcus put his arm around his wife's shoulders. "It was a trick of light, honey. I know you have feelings where she's concerned but ghosts, spirits, whatever, even if I did believe in them . . . they haunt old places, not brand-new ones. Lay her to rest, Fanny.''

"I know, I know, and I feel foolish when things like this happen. It's Simon. Even his memory can do this to me. I've been thinking, Marcus. The truth is I've been doing nothing but thinking where Simon's monies are concerned. Do you remember me telling you about the property Ash had me buy in Atlantic City?'' Marcus nodded. "What do you think about building a casino there? Sunny was in on Babylon from the ground floor, and she finished up with my brothers. It might be good for her to get involved from the ground up. Sunny has always been an idea person. It wouldn't have to be on the same scale as Babylon. My brothers are still in business. We could give them some kind of percentage annually. They've been saying they're going to retire for years now. This could put their business over the top so their sons will never have to worry about money.''

"It sounds good to me. Do you think the others will go along with it?"

"It's either that or divide the money up among them. I can't see us *giving* the money away. When the casino is finished we could transfer Jeff to Atlantic City and have Birch take over Babylon or vice versa."

"For some reason, Fanny, I don't think that's going to fly. You might want to rethink that idea. Jeff might not take kindly to that kind of shift. As it is, I see trouble ahead where Birch and Jeff are concerned."

Fanny's voice was anxious when she said, "Do you think I made a mistake, Marcus?"

"Yes and no. Your back was to the wall. Birch should have informed you of his plans to return. You might want to give some thought to six months on and six months off, that kind of thing."

"I don't understand what you mean, Marcus."

"Jeff at the helm for six months and then Birch takes a crack at it. You'll see who's doing the best job and go on from there. Look, I'm the first to admit I know nothing about the gambling business, but we're talking people here. If Jeff does a lousy job, and I don't think he will, what are you going to do, boot his tail out the door? This way you'll have a better handle on things. Put it to a vote with the kids."

"Things were settled. This is the kind of thing I object to. I don't want to be involved in the business anymore."

Marcus's voice was gentle and sad. "Fanny, you can never walk away from your family," he said. "They need you and depend on you. You're their port in a storm, and a storm is coming. You need to batten down your hatches and steer everyone to clear, safe waters. These are little interludes, small passages in time that are troublesome. *We* can do this together. Enough business. Did you bring the potato salad?"

"It's in the backseat. I brought it out earlier. Did you put the racing cars you built for Jake and Chue's kids in the trunk?"

"Did it last night."

"The doll cradles for Lexie and Polly?"

"They're in there, too."

"Then let's get this show on the road." The gurgle in Fanny's voice brought a smile to Marcus's face. It stayed with him all the way to Sunrise.

"How much do you want to bet Iris has the front porch decorated for Halloween?"

"I'm not betting on that, Fanny. That young woman could make a holiday out of every day of the week. She's going to have pumpkins, haystacks, scarecrows, spiderwebs, and whatever else goes with the deal. She's going to have pumpkin pies and she'll decorate them like pumpkins. I bet she decorates the plates and napkins, too. The big question is, what do we think the centerpiece will be?"

"That's a biggie all right. I say Billie made something exquisite and came up early to set it up. A fifty-cent bet, Mr. Reed."

"You're on. Iris and Billie get along so well. Iris is so *craftsy*. She told me the kids are making all their own Christmas presents this year. I think it's wonderful. She's also thrifty, to Sage's delight. Mine, too. She's like Billie in that respect. When you can create something out of nothing, you've earned my respect."

"What do you think Celia's strong point is?"

"I have no idea. Maybe we'll get to know her today. Do you think she'll fit in?"

Marcus reached out his hand to Fanny. "You're worried about that, aren't you?"

"I suppose so."

"Are the Colemans coming?"

"They said they were. Billie and Thad left last night. Thad said he had a lot of paperwork to catch up on. He has to clear his desk so they can go on that cruise with us in November. I'm really looking forward to it. Then before you know it, the holidays will be here. We'll be so busy we won't have time to catch our breath.''

Fifteen minutes later, Marcus said, ''Looks like we're the last to arrive. You were right, Fanny, look at the porch!''

''My goodness, it's a whole scene complete with a tombstone.''

Marcus chuckled as he opened the trunk of his car. He was surrounded immediately by whooping children, their voices carrying down and around the mountain. ''This is man stuff, Fanny. You take your potato stuff in the house and us guys are going to *play*.''

Fanny laughed as she hugged the children. She knew if she looked out the window in five minutes she'd see her husband sliding down the mountain while the children watched.

''Mom's here!'' Sunny shouted.

''Hi, honey. Harry, it's good to see you.'' Fanny tweaked Fred's and Gus's whiskers as she made her way around the kitchen.

''Are we in the way with our chairs and dogs?'' Sunny asked.

''Absolutely not. I'm so used to skittering around kids and my own dog, I'm an expert,'' Iris said from the far end of the kitchen. ''Sage is handling the bar. What will you have to drink, Fanny?''

''I think I'll have an ice-cold beer,'' Fanny said smartly. ''I'll swig from the bottle the way my husband taught me.''

''She's one of us now,'' Sage boomed as he handed his mother a beer. ''Where's Marcus?''

''He made some racing cars for the kids, and they're trying them out on the hill.''

Sage and Birch were like tornadoes as they collided at the door.

''We'll never get them in now,'' Iris moaned. ''Sage is going to get that contraption he built with Birch when they were kids and show off.''

Sunny started to laugh and then choked. The dogs were on

their feet in an instant. Harry held up his hand. "She's okay."
Both dogs lowered themselves to the floor.

"Sorry about that. Sage and Birch made this racing car out
of milk crates. They used the wheels from Billie's baby buggy
and the steering wheel came from Chue. That baby could really
fly. We used to take turns riding it down the hill to Chue's
house," Sunny said, her eyes watering.

"I didn't know Myrtle was still in the garage. I forget, who
painted the name on the side?"

"I did," Billie said.

"Where are your uncle Josh and his family?"

"They walked down to Chue's earlier. Uncle Josh is going
to have a horse sent here for the kids. Jake can't wait. He's in
the cowboy stage right now. I think it will be good for the
kids, and we certainly have the room. They were absolutely
mesmerized with the greenhouses."

Fanny sat down across from Celia. "What do you think of
Sunrise?"

"It's very beautiful. It must be heavenly in the spring and
summer. I love mountains. Alabama is so flat."

Today Celia was dressed in a plum-colored wool dress that
was so plain it shrieked money. A single strand of pearls hung
from her neck. She fiddled with them.

"Do you like the penthouse?" Fanny probed.

"It's lovely. Birch said I could toss . . . remove the furnishings and do it over. He said his father's things were in storage.
I think I'll look at them tomorrow or the next day."

"Oh." Everyone in the kitchen suddenly looked somewhere
else.

"Did I say something wrong?"

"No, of course not. Is Ruby here, Iris?"

"She went out to the cemetery. She brought some flowers
for her father's grave."

"I think I'll go out and talk to her. You young people can
chat. Is there anything you want me to do?"

"It's under control, Fanny."

"I love it when you say things like that." Fanny laughed. She pecked Iris on the cheek.

Outside in the crisp October air, Fanny drew a deep breath. Ruby was walking toward her. They embraced.

"I love autumn."

"Me too. Want to go for a walk?" Fanny asked.

"I'd love to go for a walk. You don't like her much, do you?" Ruby said.

"I'm sure she has some wonderful qualities."

"Don't count on it," the outspoken Ruby replied.

"I have to count on it for Birch's sake."

Ruby jammed her hands into the pockets of her hunter green coat. "Birch came to see me the other night. I want you to hear me out, Fanny, okay?"

"Sure." Fanny listened, her heart fluttering in her chest. "Will you hear me out, Ruby?"

"Shoot."

Fanny recounted the conversation she'd had with Marcus on the ride up the mountain. "Can you hang on for six months, Ruby? If Birch really wants to work the ranch, I'll go along with him. Your offer was more than generous."

"I'm taking this family thing real seriously. I'm so grateful to you, Fanny, for allowing me to become part of your family. I love all of you."

"Ash talked about you a lot at the end. He knew I wouldn't let it lie and he was okay with it. You belong. That's the fact."

"Jeff?"

"I have mixed feelings where he's concerned. I had to try. I'd like him to be part of the family. The kids don't seem to have a problem with him. Birch might, but he's always been fair. When he acts on impulse, Sage reels him in. All we can do now is take a wait-and-see attitude. About that six months?"

"I can hold on. God, I hate chickens. My father used to name them."

"I know. At the time I thought it was cute."

"There is nothing cute about a chicken, Fanny."

Both women burst out laughing.

"Let's go inside and see what's happening," Fanny said.

"You are such a brave soul." Ruby grinned.

"Marcus says I'm the quintessential optimist when I'm not being a quintessential pessimist. Go figure."

"Here come the guys," Ruby said, her hand on the kitchen doorknob.

It happened so fast, Fanny found it impossible to describe later. Ruby held the door, Sage brushed past her just as Celia got up from the table to take her glass to the sink when Fred, Sunny's dog, rose, his eyes and ears alert to the sudden noise and commotion. Harry took that moment to wheel his chair out of the way, his dog Gus colliding with Birch, who then fell over Sunny's chair which then fell backward, knocking Celia to the floor. Everyone rushed to help everyone else as the kids barreled through the door, Marcus bringing up the rear. He took in the situation at a glance and bellowed at the top of his lungs, "FREEZE!"

All movement ceased but the babble of voices continued. "Jesus, Sunny, are you okay?" Birch said as he scooped his sister into his arms, Fred pawing his pant leg and Jake yanking at his other leg.

"I'm okay. It's okay, Fred. Down, boy. Jake, it was just a little spill. It's okay. See if Harry is okay."

"I'm okay, Sunny," Harry called from the other side of the kitchen. His dog let out one shrill bark. "Gus is okay, too."

"I don't suppose anyone cares if I have a concussion," Celia snapped as she struggled to her feet.

Sage, his hand outstretched to help Celia to her feet, froze when he heard his brother say, "You fell on your ass, how could you have a concussion?"

As before, everyone started talking at once. Fanny made her way to Marcus's side, where she reached for his hand. Her eyes tear-filled, she watched her son Birch cuddle his sister, smoothing back her hair and crooning soft words that were indistinguishable.

"Dammit, the heel broke on my shoe!" Celia seethed. "They cost $400. I suppose you're going to blame me for wasting your money when I throw them out."

"I can fix it for you, Celia," Harry offered. "I know how to do that. My hands are still good."

"I don't want *you* touching my shoes," Celia screeched, as all eyes swiveled toward her.

Birch settled Sunny in her wheelchair. Iris and Billie rushed to her.

"That does it!" Birch strode across the room and grabbed his wife's arm and dragged her to the door. He turned, and shouted over his shoulder. "I'm taking her home. I'll be back. Wait for me."

"Holy hell!" Sage said when Sunny's Volvo streaked out of the courtyard.

"Is he driving faster than forty miles an hour?" Sunny grumbled.

"Heck, Mom, he was crawling," Jake said. "Are you sure you're okay?"

"Honey, I'm fine. Birch caught me. Take the kids upstairs and play a game or something. The grown-ups need to talk."

Fanny sat down next to Ruby. "I don't know what to say."

"We could ignore it and pretend it never happened," Billie said.

"We can talk it to death," Iris said.

"It won't change anything," Sunny said.

"Why don't we just get on with the day? How about a beer, Harry?" Sage asked.

"That sounds good." He motioned for Sunny to wheel her chair next to him. "You can swig from mine. I'll hold the bottle."

"Mom, do you think I should go after Birch?" Sage asked.

"No, honey. He said he'd be back."

"Why don't you guys adjourn to the living room and us girls will get on with our food preparations? The Colemans and Chue and his family will be back soon. We're running a little behind."

"You sit right here with your husband, Fanny. You did your share for years. I'll step in for you," Ruby said. "I'm no cook, though," she confessed.

The women hooted when Ruby donned an apron. Marcus left to join the others in the living room.

"This is not good," Fanny said. "We have some business to discuss today. Celia and Birch need to be here."

"Why?" Sunny demanded. "I can see Birch being here, but why does Celia have to be here? I promised Birch I'd try to like her. I don't even want to be in the same room with her. What does he see in her?"

"Love's blind. I'm an authority on the subject," Fanny said.

"I don't think I like her much myself. What she said to Harry was unforgivable. Where does she come off acting like that?" Iris demanded.

"Harry's okay with it," Sunny said. "We're used to stuff like that."

"Oh, honey, don't speak for Harry. I saw his face. Her words hurt him unbearably. No one ever gets used to things like that. We all love Harry, and he knows it. I wish there was a way to shelter you two, but there isn't."

"Mom, trust me, it's okay. Harry and I will talk about it tonight. Tomorrow we'll talk to a counselor, and this will just be an unpleasant memory. Maybe we shouldn't go out as much as we do. Maybe we should stay where we belong. It was such a freak thing," Sunny dithered.

They jumped on her as one. "No more talk like that. This is your home, too. It will always be your home. You have a right to be wherever you want to be, and you belong wherever you want to be. That's the end of it," Ruby said, summing things up.

Fanny smiled, but the smile didn't reach her eyes. "You wanted to belong to a family, Ruby. This is what it's like. We go from one crisis to the next with hardly a break between. I do hope Birch can mend things."

"Some things aren't worth mending, Mom," Billie said.

"It sounds to me like you've all made up your mind not to like Birch's wife. That doesn't seem fair. Maybe we need to try harder."

"There's nothing to like. Look into her eyes sometime. Nothing comes back. They're empty. I had her number from the git-go," Sunny muttered.

"Where's Sage going?" Billie asked, as her brother whizzed past the kitchen window.

"He's going to run down the mountain and wait at the base for his brother." Iris's voice was so low the others had to strain to hear the words. "He's hurting for Birch, and he knows Birch needs him right now. Twins are like that, you know, tuned to one another."

"While we're waiting for those two hunks to come back why don't I show you my table decoration. I want you all to know I have one for Thanksgiving and one for Christmas too. On the drawing board that is. I left them in the trunk. I'll just be a minute."

The bad moments were set aside as they waited for Billie to return.

Sage ran in place at the base of the mountain, marking time as he waited for the first sign of the red Volvo. His heart flip-flopped inside his chest when his brother brought the Volvo to a stop at the side of the road. Sage climbed in. "I cleaned out my ears this morning when I took a shower. Talk, Birch."

"It's all wrong, Sage. I feel like somebody put a hex on me, and the worst is yet to come. I think it started when Dad died, and I couldn't make it back. Then I had to deal with the fact that he killed Uncle Simon. On top of that I feel like I let Sunny down. Mom's got me on probation whether she admits it or not. I'm definitely not the favored son. I'm not sure I ever got over the mountain crash. I still have nightmares about it. Someone I thought I loved died in that crash. Dad bamboozled me, and I fell for it. Do I have some kind of invisible mark on my forehead? Now Celia. How do you go from all-out love to revulsion in a matter of days? How, Sage? Where did I fuck up? Christ Almighty, you'd think I'd have my shit in one sock at my age. Everything is wrong. I haven't even touched on Jeff Lassiter yet.''

"You want to cut and run, don't you?"

"Hell yes. I don't want to deal with this shit."

"If you don't deal with it, who will, Birch? You can't keep running away. You need to stare it in the face, get a handle on it, and go from there. We aren't kids anymore. You don't pick up your marbles and go home because something doesn't go your way. I'm not an advocate of divorce, but if it's your only option, do it. Talking solves a lot of things, Birch. Iris and I fight. We say what we have to say. We never go to bed angry with one another. You can't always be right, Birch.''

"It's the money, Sage. She believes she should have carte blanche. I'm beginning to wonder if I talked in my sleep, and she married me for my money.''

"What did Celia say on the way home?''

"Nothing. We didn't say one word to each other. I dropped her off in the garage, turned around, and headed back. Getting together today was my idea and we screwed up. I'm sorry, Sage.''

"It's no big deal. Iris is up for anything that gets the family together. It's good for Sunny and Harry to get out and be among family. The guy is a real sweetheart. The kids love him. He can tell stories better than Mom used to. More important, Sunny loves him. Birch, I gotta tell you, it kills me that Sunny is . . . you know. Sometimes I goddamn cry when I think about it. She's so damn good about it.''

Birch clapped his brother on the back. ''Yeah, I know.''

''What are you going to do, Birch?''

Birch reminded him of his visit to Ruby's. ''I'm considering it. It kind of depends on Mom today. I have this fear of disappointing her.''

''What are you going to say about Celia?''

''Nothing. It is what it is. Everyone saw it. What's to talk about? We've moved on now. I'll deal with Celia and my marriage in my own way.''

''I'm here for you, Birch.''

''I know that, Sage. I knew you'd be here at the base of the mountain. How long were you waiting?''

''Fifteen minutes or so.''

''Ha. I would have made it right on schedule but I promised Sunny not to drive this heirloom over forty miles an hour. Want to drive it halfway up the mountain?''

''Do birds want to fly? Get out so I can move over! Jeez, finally I get to drive the gray ghost. Do you know how often I dreamed about this? It's a secret, right?''

''Damn right it's a secret.''

Sage smacked his hands gleefully as he shifted gears. ''Jesus, this is great. I'd kill for this car.''

''Going forty miles an hour has its drawbacks.''

''Who cares,'' Sage chortled as he downshifted.

Halfway up the mountain Sage said, ''Birch, why do you think Sunny had this car done over? She knows she can never drive it. Dad took care of it for her. She picked out the leather and the paint, though.''

''A dream. Hope. Maybe someday by some miracle she might be able to drive it. If not, maybe Jake will want his mother's car someday.''

''You realize both of us could go out tomorrow and buy a

Porsche, a Corvette, or a Lamborghini and not even blink. Instead, we're both lusting after a fifteen-year-old car that will never belong to us.''

''That's why. It can never be ours. It's all tied up with Sunny. Pull over. We're almost to Chue's house.''

Birch climbed into the driver's seat and continued up the mountain. He pocketed the keys. ''Not a word to Sunny. Swear, Sage.''

''My lips are zipped. I won't even tell Iris.''

''It's about time. We've been waiting. Dinner's almost ready,'' Iris chastised.

''You drove my car, didn't you, Sage?'' Sunny accused.

''Where'd you get an idea like that?''

''Because you *look* like you drove it. Tell the truth.''

''I never lied to you, Sunny,'' Sage said.

''I know you drove it. I forgive you this once.''

''You do. That's great, Sunny. I'll never touch it again, I swear.''

''Ha! Gotcha. I knew it. I knew it!''

''You didn't know?''

''Sure I knew, but how could I prove it?'' Her voice turned wistful when she said, ''So how did it drive?''

''Better than ever.''

Sunny turned to hide the tears puddling in her eyes. ''I hear a car. Quick, Sage, see if it's Libby? Iris said it was okay to invite her. Don't tell her what happened. She gets like a tiger when someone beats on us. Billie, warn Harry.''

Birch felt his heart thud inside his chest. Someone should have told him the therapist was coming to Sunrise. He backed up a step and asked himself why. He moved then, quicker than he'd ever moved in his life, to lope up the steps to the second floor, where the children were squabbling good-naturedly. He wasn't ready to deal with what Sunny perceived as his destiny. He should call Celia to be sure she was okay. He wouldn't apologize, though.

He stood in the doorway for a moment observing the children. They were all best friends, Chue's grandchildren and his nieces and nephews. It was blond, blue-eyed Jake and dark-haired, dark-eyed Sami who were in charge. Both were the same age. He had to wonder if Sami was Jake's destiny. His heart was thudding again. He walked to the room at the end of the hall. He closed the door. It was quiet and peaceful here though he could hear the muted voices of the children. A deep sigh escaped his lips as he picked up the phone to call the penthouse. He let the phone ring twenty times before he hung up. Why didn't the answering machine come on? He picked up the receiver and dialed again, paying careful attention to the numbers he dialed. The phone rang twenty more times. His gut started to churn.

Birch dropped his head into his hands. He wanted to bawl his head off and put his fist through the wall all at the same time. He was so engrossed in his own misery he didn't hear the door open or close. He did hear the heavy footsteps cross the oak floor, though.

"What's wrong, son?" Josh Coleman asked gently.

"Everything. My life seems to be spiraling out of control. I should be trying to get a handle on it, but I just keep making things worse."

"Let's talk about it. I'm an old man, and I've lived through more misery than you can ever begin to imagine. I'm just going to sit here, and you let it rip, boy. Ain't nothing I haven't seen or heard, so don't be shy."

Birch looked at the old man's eyes that were the color of worn denim. He thought he saw a twinkle. The hand on his shoulder felt so warm and comforting he leaned into the pressure his great-uncle's hand created. "Just let it rip, boy."

He did.

"Life wouldn't be worth a tinker's damn if there weren't some upsets along the way. Hell, boy, you got the world by the tail. In my day we called it a tiger's tail. You swing that bastard and move right with it. You got Coleman blood in you, boy. That makes you one of a kind. We ain't never been misfits, cowards, or followers. We're leaders. You got a mouth, a brain, and you got fists. Fists don't work nowadays. That leaves your mouth and your brain. Your ma saw to it that you got a fine education. Don't you be disappointing her now. Women don't always make the right decision where their young'uns are concerned. You git in your half brother's face and tell him the way it is. You're full blood. He came in through the back door. That counts for a poke. That little filly you married—Well, hell, boy, you tell her like it is, too. You're the boss. It sounds to me like you let her get out of line. Reel her in. A few pretty words ain't going to hurt. Maybe a few posies from time to time. Marriage needs to be worked at. You gotta give her some pocket money that's all hers. You don't ask any questions when she spends it either. If she pisses it away, it ain't no never mind to you. You following me, boy?''

''Yes, sir.''

''You feeling any better since we had this little talk? You ain't said if you love your wife or not.''

Birch stared into the denim eyes. ''I thought I did.''

''It was a yes or no question, son.''

''It isn't that simple, Uncle Josh. Words can never be taken back once they're spoken. I can't undo the physical part of it. I wanted to beat the living hell out of Celia this afternoon. It was almost as though she was taunting me to do it.''

''She probably was. You do it again, boy, and you'll find yourself in court. Sometimes you have to cut your losses and move on. Happened to me a time or two. You don't look back either. You might have to pay out some of those Thornton dollars if you ain't careful. You best think about that. What you need is a plan. Your ma wants you downstairs. The eats are ready to go on the table. It pays to mind your ma no matter how old you are. I'm going to ponder the matter for you. When I come up with a solution, I'll let you know. You come from good stock, so don't screw things up along the way." His uncle's slap on the back almost propelled Birch across the room.

Dinner over, Jeff, Ruby, Josh Coleman and his son Colin prepared to leave. Their good-byes took half an hour before the parade started down the mountain.

"Time for family business," Fanny said as she motioned for everyone to sit at the kitchen table. Marcus, Libby, and Harry adjourned to the living room where the children were watching a horror video.

"We're together again," Fanny said in a choked voice. "Some decisions need to be made. Your uncle Simon's will has gone through probate. His holdings passed on to me. I didn't know . . . I thought he'd changed his will, but he didn't. It's a sizable fortune. I could pass it on and divide it among the four of you. I could also use the money to build more rehab centers. I tried to pay back the Hasegawa estate, but they refused the offer. Before your father died he . . . he had an idea. He sent me to Atlantic City to buy up some property. My thinking is this. We could build a casino there and either Birch or Jeff could operate it. It wouldn't be as grand as Babylon. My brothers could build it for a fraction of the cost of Babylon. We would, of course, give them a percentage. Sunny was in on the building from the ground up. I thought it might be a challenge for her to start on this. Providing you're up to it, honey."

"Really, Mom? You'd trust me with something like that?"

"Sunny, I'd trust you with my life. Of course. You'll be in charge."

"But, Mom, that's New Jersey. This is Nevada."

"Did you forget about the center we built in Cape May? You could stay there while the building is going up. You could take Libby if she's willing to relocate for a while. I was hoping, Birch, that you would want to be part of it. I realize you have to discuss it with Celia. Ruby did tell me about her offer to you. I asked her if she could wait six months to see if . . . if you might change your mind.''

"What about Harry?"

"He goes where you go, Sunny, if he's willing," Fanny said. "Let's take a vote."

"Wait. Wait," Sunny said. "I need to talk to Harry and Libby first."

"I guess we know what the vote is going to be," Sage grinned. "Mom, this is the best thing in the world for Sunny. I think it's going to hang on you, Birch. How does it stack up against free-range chickens?"

"You got my vote. When do you want to get this under way, Mom?"

"Brad and Daniel are standing by the phone. Either you or Sunny should call them. Marcus and I are leaving it all in your capable hands."

"Did you vote?" Sunny demanded from the doorway.

"Didn't you tell us to wait for you?" Sage shouted. "Well, we're waiting."

"Harry and Libby said yes."

"Okay, let's vote. A show of hands will do nicely." Four hands shot upward.

"Then it's a done deal. Marcus, we're ready to leave now."

"I can do this, can't I, Mom? You aren't just handing me pity crumbs, are you?"

Fanny cupped her daughter's face in her hands. "Your dad said you could handle it. That's good enough for me. I would never pity you, honey. All I have for you is admiration. Your brothers and sister feel the same way. Don't ever think thoughts like that again. Marcus!"

"Marcus wants to see if the three-headed monster gobbles up Arizona," Harry said.

"I saw that movie with Jake. Tell him a helicopter chops off all three heads. Time to go, Marcus!"

"It was nice seeing you again, Mrs. Reed. Thank you for

the opportunity to go with Sunny and Harry. I'll watch over them.''

"I know you will, Libby.''

"I enjoyed seeing you again, Birch.''

Birch reached for Libby's outstretched hand. He held it a moment longer than necessary. He felt like a schoolboy as he grappled for suitable words. He wanted to say things like, you're prettier than the first spring flower or you're more beautiful than the first sunny day in summer. Instead he said, "Thanks for coming to Sunrise. I guess we'll be seeing more of each other as the days go on. Sunny was always a hands-on person.''

"That's good. I am, too. Hands-on, I mean.''

"Yeah, me too. That's the only way to go. Being right there, seeing, observing, reacting.''

Libby nodded as she withdrew her hand.

Birch turned as Sage offered up a sly wink. Birch felt warm all over. The warmth stayed with him all the way down the mountain.

The penthouse was dark and empty when Birch entered. He turned on the lights, checked the answering machine that was turned off. He looked around for a note and found none. He made a pot of coffee before he called Ruby. He explained the situation. "I hate putting you on hold, Ruby. I want to do this for Sunny. I hope you understand. I'll see you in six months. If you get bored, come to Atlantic City. Thanks for understanding.''

Birch carried his coffee into the living room. He kicked off his shoes, turned on the television set, and was asleep five minutes later. He didn't wake until eight o'clock the following morning. He showered, shaved, dressed, and was making coffee when Celia entered the kitchen.

"You made enough noise for six people,'' she said, frowning. "Where are you going so early in the morning?''

"I have some things to do. I'm going to make this short and quick. I decided I don't want to live here in this penthouse and work at Babylon. Ruby offered me a job at the ranch that paid a half million a year with generous fringe benefits and bonuses. I turned her down last night. Instead of dividing Uncle Simon's estate among us, the family has decided to build a casino in Atlantic City. Sunny and I will be overseeing it and my uncles, Mom's brothers Daniel and Brad, will be building it. The pay is zip. That's as in zero, nada, nothing. I'm going out now to buy some work clothes, do some banking, then I'll be leaving later today to get things set up for Sunny, Harry, and their therapist. I'll be driving in Sunny's car. It's going to be a long trip since I can't drive the car more than forty miles an hour. I personally don't care if you go with me or not. Give me your answer when I get back. When I leave, the penthouse gets closed up tight.''

''Wait just a minute. You already made this decision?''

''After yesterday's incident you have no voice in anything I do. I will never forgive your behavior yesterday, nor will my family. I think you showed all of us who you really are. It was my misfortune to have married you.''

Celia stared at her husband as she tried to comprehend what he was saying. ''You gave up a $100,000 job with free rent and a job offer that pays $500,000 plus bonuses, to work for free building a casino in another state!''

''Yep. Your dishes are still in the sink from the other night. I suggest you clean up the kitchen because I'm not going to do it.''

''Where does all your decision making leave me?''

Birch stared at his wife. Makeup was smeared all over her face in streaks. She must have fallen into bed without removing it. Where was the warm, caring, fresh-faced girl he'd married? Was it all an illusion? Who was this hard-as-nails-looking person staring at him with such righteous indignation?

''I plan to leave around four this afternoon. I'll drive through the night. If you decide to join me, be ready. If you elect to stay, I'll give you enough money to tide you over until you can get a job. The decision is yours. If you decide to join me, know this, we'll be living in an apartment that's economical. You'll have to get a job. I'll finance a car for you. We'll discuss our future and do whatever's best for both of us. I suppose your next question is, what is my share of Uncle Simon's estate? I don't know because it wasn't left to me, it was left to my mother. Neither my brother nor my sisters wanted to take it. Your greed is showing again, Celia.''

"How . . . how can your sister, who is in a wheelchair, help you build a casino? You people boggle my mind. What kind of family do you belong to?''

"Sunny has a brain. Before her illness she was absolutely tops in everything she undertook. She can run circles around me. She helped my father build this casino and she's the one who managed to bring it in on schedule after my father fucked it all up. You, Celia, crapped on the wrong person. Do you have any idea how you hurt Harry yesterday? As to my family, they're aces in my book. What that means is you could look the world over and not find a better family.''

"By telling him I didn't want him fixing my shoe? That hurt his feelings?'' There was such perplexity on his wife's face, Birch sighed deeply.

"Forget it. I'm leaving now.''

Celia poured herself a cup of coffee, her hand trembling so badly she could barely lift the cup to her lips. It was scalding hot. She barely noticed. What was she supposed to do now? Did she want to stay here in Vegas, work a nine-to-five job and live in a one-bedroom apartment? She'd had that in Alabama. If she hadn't split when she had, she'd probably still be living there.

Should she stay here or should she leave with Birch? If she stayed, it would be the same as it was in Alabama. Maybe there was a way to make peace with Birch, weave a little magic, make nice to the cripples and possibly, just possibly, the pot at the end of the rainbow really could be hers.

Celia cleaned the kitchen in minutes, was in and out of the shower in less than ten minutes. She had to strike while the iron was hot and do some shopping. Once she bought everything she needed from the boutiques downstairs and removed the tags, Birch wouldn't be able to make her return the things. The moment her shopping was finished she would head for the first lawyer listed in the phone book to find out what her marital rights were in case of a divorce.

Driving cross-country at forty miles an hour with her husband wasn't going to be a picnic. The alternative left her panic-stricken.

5

Celia eyed the digital clock next to the wide-screen television set. Her hands were sweating. She wiped them on her new stone-washed Wrangler jeans. She felt herself wincing at the reflection she saw on the blackened TV screen. She looked exactly the way she'd looked that first day when she rode into the village Birch was building in Costa Rica. Her face was scrubbed clean, her hair pulled back in a ponytail, her drugstore sunglasses perched on the end of her nose. Her navy blue Kmart sneakers with their pristine shoelaces glared up at her. She'd tried scuffing them, even wetting them in the bathtub to take away their new look. She hadn't been successful.

A large khaki duffel and a small canvas bag stood next to the front door. They were holding two other bags for her downstairs behind the registration counter. A tidy pile of receipts and a bottle of mineral water sat on the table next to her chair. The *real* stuff, the designer outfits, pricey shoes, jewelry, and receipts were in the bags downstairs. She'd zipped through the boutiques running up a $25,000 bill in less than two hours. She'd gone crazy when one naive salesclerk told her the bills would go to the corporate offices and be paid by the family accountant. What that told her was that Birch would probably never see the bills. At some point in time he might *hear* about them. She was not going to worry about something that might never come to pass. She had to look out for number one.

She'd had a busy day, shopping, talking to an attorney, lining up an apartment she had no intention of living in, filling out job applications at the Board of Education and arranging a supper date with Jeff Lassiter.

Celia did one last run-through of the speech she'd worked up for Birch's benefit. She felt confident Birch would listen. All she had to do now was wait. Her gaze locked on the digital clock.

The numerals flashed to 3:35 when Birch returned. "Hi, honey," Celia called. "Birch, can we talk for just a minute? Can I get you a soda pop?"

Birch nodded, his eyes wary as he took in his wife's appearance. He felt something tug at his heart.

"Honey, let me talk, okay? I need to apologize to you. Whatever this thing is between us is my fault. I'm so sorry. All I did today was think. I came up with this. I'm going to stay behind. For now. We both need some space, and we both need to do some thinking. I'm going to get an apartment in town. I found a small efficiency for $300 a month, but I didn't have any cash to put down. It's on hold. It's late into the school term to get a job, but I can sub. I can get a job waitressing if the sub jobs are few and far between. I can lease a car with nothing down to help me at first. I will need to borrow about fifteen hundred dollars. I'll pay you back monthly. Not much because I won't be making much. It'll be something, though. We'll take it a month at a time. We'll decide if we want to stay married as time progresses. My punishment will be staying here without you. I think I can handle it. I'd like to know, though, if I can't, will I be welcome in Atlantic City? I don't know what else to do. I'll apologize to Sunny and her friend and to your family. I think I went temporarily insane there for a little while and have this awful sick feeling in the pit of my stomach. I love you, Birch. I never loved anyone the way I love you. You need to know that. Oh, I spent $180 downstairs for a few things. Here are the receipts. I tried to be frugal. Say something, Birch.''

Birch stared at the young woman he thought he'd loved with all his heart. He remembered the day she rode into the makeshift village on a donkey, remembered the weary smile on her face. The first words out of her mouth had been, ''What do you want me to do, Mr. Thornton?'' He'd replied, ''Start calling me Birch. Mr. Thornton is my father.''

Celia saw the indecision in her husband's face. She stepped closer. ''I want us to start over. I want you to do what you feel you have to do, and I don't want you to worry about me. I want you to think about me, though. I can make this right, I know I can. Please, Birch.''

Birch didn't trust himself to speak. He nodded. She stepped closer and then closer still. He found himself wrapping his arms about her. The hard look in his eyes softened as his arms tightened around her slim form. She felt so good, so right in his arms. ''We'll try it your way, Celia.'' His voice was a low murmur.

''Oh, Birch, I'm so happy to hear you say that. You won't be sorry. Before you know it, it's going to be like old times.'' Celia's voice dropped to a hushed whisper, ''I haven't forgotten one day of our time together. I made up this mental list in my head, and all day I kept referring to it. What we had was good, and it was special. I don't want us ever to lose those feelings. Just meet me halfway.''

She kissed him and he forgot all his good intentions. ''Are you sure this is the way you want it?'' he whispered against her cheek.

"It's just time, Birch. We're young. We have all the time in the world. Depending on how you look at it, it could be an eternity or the time could go by in a flash. It will be what we make it. I'm going to try so hard, honey, to be the person you want me to be. Let's make a date for New Year's Eve. Either I'll go to Atlantic City, or, if you can free up the time, you can come here. It will give each of us something to hold on to. Will you agree to that, Birch?"

Birch nodded. His tongue felt thick in his mouth. "I have to go, Celia. I changed my mind about driving Sunny's car and scheduled a flight for 5:20."

"I'd like to go to the airport with you if you don't mind."

"I'd like that, Celia. I have a taxi waiting. Just let me get my gear." The moment Birch was out of sight, Celia's clenched fist shot in the air.

On the ride to the airport, they held hands, Celia's head on her husband's shoulder.

"Do you want me to go inside with you, honey?"

"No point, Celia. I'm just going to make it. Jesus, I almost forgot, here is some money and a credit card. I'll leave word at the desk when I have a phone and an address. You leave yours with the desk, too. I'll call."

"I guess I better get an answering machine. If I'm going to work two jobs, I might miss your call. Good luck, Birch. I miss you already, and you haven't gone yet. I'll count the days till New Year's Eve. This is too much money, Birch."

"It's okay, Celia. An emergency might come up. You might not get any subbing jobs right away. If anything goes awry, talk to my mother or Jeff. Listen, I'm sorry about everything."

"I know. I'm sorry, too. I love you, Birch," Celia said.

"I love you, too." It was a lie. He knew it was a lie, and yet the words escaped his lips.

"Everything's going to be okay. Every marriage has a few bumps. I know we can weather this because we love each other. Whatever came before this moment is history. Have a safe trip.

I'm going to write Sunny and her friend a letter. Tell her that for me, okay?''

"Her friend's name is Harry."

"Yes, Harry. Have a safe trip, honey."

Birch waved as he loped off, his bags slamming against his legs.

Celia smiled all the way back to the casino.

Jeff Lassiter sat back in the special chair that had once belonged to his father. He propped his feet on the corner of the desk the way he'd seen his father do when his legs were working. A perfect smoke ring spiraled upward to settle over his head like a halo.

One brother down, one brother and two sisters to go.

As a numismatist, he couldn't want or ask for a better job. It had come to him, literally falling in his lap. Babylon was the best place in the world to apply his profession. He wondered if anyone, including the Thornton family, knew exactly what a numismatist was or what one actually did. He'd graduated second in his class, which put him a notch above his half brother. Studying money and monetary objects was what had led Simon Thornton to him several years ago with his grand plan to wipe out Babylon. If his father and mother hadn't clapped an iron hand on him that night along with the threat of the Internal Revenue Service, he could have been the new emperor of Las Vegas. He'd been younger then, frightened at what he knew he was capable of doing. That fear was gone now, and so was his father and his brother Simon. His mother was older and in frail health. She didn't care what he did these days as long as her meals were on time and her game shows weren't interrupted.

What he needed to do now was set up a network of loyal employees and get rid of all the deadwood that might be tempted to carry tales. For weeks now, off the clock, he'd been watching, observing, taking notes. He knew the smart money on the street was already down. The odds were ten to two that he'd step into his father's shoes. He had his own bet down across the street. With Birch out of the way there was no way he could fail. With Birch's wife on the periphery, the odds were even more in his favor.

Jeff wondered what Birch's decision to go to Atlantic City would do to the odds that were so heavily in his favor. He stubbed out his cigarette. Birch Thornton didn't interest him in the least. He had more important things to occupy his mind.

Within minutes, Lassiter was engrossed in his charts and lists to the exclusion of all else. In his mind, his office was now called the War Room. In thirty minutes he would be hosting a meeting of electrical and mechanical engineers, systems and software designers, graphic artists, and mathematicians. Their combined object: the development of a killer game inside a perfect slot machine.

He wanted a device that would be fast yet simple. He wanted to seduce the player with a modicum of risk, yet let the player think he was in control. He wanted near addiction but needed to stay within the bounds of legality. He wanted the player to smile as the machine gobbled up his money. Could it be done? With the right team players and the proper incentives, and he knew a thing or two about incentives, it absolutely could be done. Before long they'd be calling his device Lassiter's Holy Grail.

Jeff wondered if he was ahead of the pack by hooking his ideas to the MTV generation. So far he thought he was. With 70 percent of the twenty-three billion gambling take coming from the slots, it was imperative he come up with the ultimate gambling machine. To his mind it was a make-or-break situation. Flipping the dial on the television set one evening he'd watched MTV until he was dizzy with ideas. He knew when he turned off the set it was going to take more than three cherries to hook the joystick generation of MTV viewers since they got bored so easily. He needed exactly the right combination of game and gizmo with plenty of bells and whistles. He had to come up with a killer category that was better than video poker.

His first order of business after today's meeting was to introduce twenty-five new slot machines and take away another twenty-five. Bess and John Noble had followed through, waiting a whole year for the new game to go from concept to design to focus-group evaluation to regulatory approval to casino testing and finally onto the floor. Cost per machine, a cool two hundred grand. His baby now that the Nobles were on a round-the-world trip. In three months' time, possibly sooner, customers would call the new slot Lassiter's Machine. They would forget Bess and John Noble. Out of sight, out of mind.

The buzzer on Jeff's desk alerted him that his guests were in the conference room. He looked at his watch. He had three hours until it was time to meet Celia Thornton for dinner.

"This was such a pleasant surprise, Adam. It isn't often you take time off from chasing criminals to take me to lunch. In a casino no less. I don't think my family would understand me lunching at a competitor's casino, though," Billie Thornton said.

"The food's good. My jacket safely hides my hardware. I'd like us to see more of each other, Billie. How about dinner this evening?"

"Can't. I took a long lunch break to be with you. We've been here two hours and I need another half hour to get back to the office. How about Friday?"

"Sure. By the way, where were you yesterday? I called around lunchtime and no one knew where you were."

Billie's voice was testy when she said, "Are you checking up on me, Adam?"

"No. I wanted to take you to lunch yesterday. I'd take you

every day if you'd let me. I thought I saw you on the Strip but by the time I found a parking place you were gone."

"It must have been someone who looked like me. Gotta go. I'm parked in the underground garage, so I have to go back inside. We're on for Friday then?"

"I'll count the hours."

Billie stared at the man she'd been seeing off and on for almost two years. He was more than pleasant. Handsome, too, lean, and hard-muscled. He topped the growth chart at six-three. Wearing high heels, she still got a stiff neck looking up at him. She leaned closer for him to kiss her lightly. His shoulder holster pressed against her chest. "I hate guns," she murmured.

"I do, too," Adam said. "If I don't wear it, who's going to catch the bad guys?"

"Some other detective. No, huh. It's a jungle out there, so be careful."

"Now, where have I heard that before?"

Billie laughed. "Probably the same television show I heard it on. Bye, Adam."

Inside the casino, Billie looked around to get her bearings before she headed for the rest room. When she walked onto the casino floor fifteen minutes later, her own mother wouldn't have recognized her. She headed straight for the twenty-one table. She played steadily until four-thirty, losing $26,000. She returned to the rest room and dressed in her original attire to return to the office. She'd work till eight or nine. After that she'd go home, change, and head for another casino.

On the way back to the office, her forehead beading with sweat, she mouthed the words, "I do not have a gambling problem. I positively do not have a gambling problem."

Yet.

Entering the office, Billie worked a smile onto her face. "For someone who has always brown-bagged her lunch, I'm having trouble with these four- and five-hour lunches, Billie," Sage said. "You have at least twenty-five calls, and you missed the meeting with one of our key distributors. Maybe it's time for you and Adam to get married. What the hell do you talk about for five hours?''

"Things. I'll still be here tonight when you're getting ready for bed. What is the big problem, Sage?''

"When you're running a business, you need to be on the premises and keep regular working hours. You have a better rapport with these people than I do. When they call they want you, not me. I've been making up stories for months now.''

Billie felt her heart start to flutter at the look in her brother's eyes. "Maybe you should start to mind your own business. This is how I see it, this company owes me years and I mean years, of overtime and vacation time. If you don't like the way I do things, there's the door. I'm sick and tired of you minding my business. Do I interfere with you and Iris? No, I do not. Do you know why I don't interfere? Because your business is your business and not mine.''

"My personal life has nothing to do with my business life. We're talking business here, Billie. Another thing, how does a cop get to take five-hour lunches? What the hell kind of police force do we have in this town that would permit something like that?''

Billie knew her voice sounded lame when she said, "Adam was . . . is a workaholic like me. He's got as much vacation and overtime accumulated as I do. Detectives have more leeway than beat cops. He's got his beeper, pager, and cell phone with him all the time. Not that it's any of your business, Sage.''

Sage tried another tack. "I have this feeling, Billie, that something's wrong. I just want to help. I'm your brother for God's sake.''

"Do I look like I need your help?''

"Yeah, you do.''

"Well, you're wrong. I'm here now, so you can go home to your wife. When I leave here this evening, things will be caught up-to-date. I will even work on tomorrow's schedule so you don't get your Jockeys in a wad if I decide to go out to lunch.''

"Iris is pregnant, Billie.''

"That's nice. You really should go home, Sage. Everything is fine.''

"That's nice. That's all you have to say?''

"What's going on here, Sage? Why do I have the feeling it isn't just me? Or is it me because you can't attack Birch and Sunny because they're gone. You need to be nice to Iris, so that leaves me. It's okay; I can take it since it's deserved. Is it Jeff Lassiter? Is it all of the above?''

Sage sat down and fired up a cigarette. "I don't know what it is. I'm happy Iris is pregnant. We want a boy. I'm glad Sunny went with Birch, and I'm glad she feels she can handle her end of things. I'm not real pleased with Birch, but I understand him not wanting to work with Jeff. Yeah, I like the guy. But then I liked Uncle Simon and look how he turned out. I resent Mom giving Lassiter a three-year contract. Celia stayed behind. Did you know that? Birch called this morning and asked me to look out for her. How the hell do you look out for a barracuda?''

"No, I didn't know Celia stayed behind.''

"I have this feeling that something bad is going to happen. Something that's going to affect all of us. I worry about Sunny. I'm concerned that Birch and Celia are having a problem. Iris has the morning pukes really bad. I'm not sleeping well. I'm piss-assed scared about Lassiter. I keep thinking about that stunt he pulled with Uncle Simon a couple of years ago. The guy's a numismatist for God's sake. He can do whatever he wants with the casino numbers. I tried talking to Mom about it, but she didn't want to hear anything I had to say. Marcus listened, though. Then you, our rock, suddenly get fed up and start taking five-hour lunches. I'm sorry I snapped at you, Billie.''

"How about if I cut them back to a measly two? Can you handle that? Is there anything I can do? I can call Celia, take her to lunch or dinner. I can poke around at the casino to see if I can get any feedback where Jeff is concerned. If you think you can handle things here, I can go to Atlantic City on the weekends to check on Sunny. I really think Birch can take care of himself and Sunny, too. Harry's there, too, don't forget that. Our lives are changing, Sage. Mom isn't standing behind us anymore. I guess it's time for all of us to either sink or swim on our own.'' She paused, took a deep breath. ''What could he do, Sage?''

''By 'he' I guess you mean Jeff.'' Billie nodded. ''Dad had every fail-safe method known to man installed. That doesn't mean Jeff will keep them in place. He could do a lot of things. He's got three years to do whatever he wants. Mom gave him carte blanche. It was a mistake. If it were up to me, I'd go over there right now and boot his tail out of there and take over myself. Of course that would mean leaving you in the lurch, so to speak.''

''Are you overreacting? Forget I even said that. Of all of us you've always been the most methodical, the most cautious. Why don't we talk to Mom again, the four of us? We could get Sunny and Birch on an extension. By rights, she should have talked with us before she decided to hire Jeff. Better yet, maybe we should talk to Marcus.''

''Let's think about this for a few days.''

''That sounds good. I really am happy for you and Iris, Sage. What are you going to do if she has twins? You're a twin. You look a little green, Sage.''

''I wasn't going to tell you, but it is twins. The doctor said he heard two heartbeats. I guess that's why I'm not sleeping.''

''Oh, Sage, it's wonderful. Sunrise is going to jam again. Kid voices carrying down the mountain. It's going to be just like it was when we were growing up. Do you have any idea how lucky you are? Did you tell Mom?''

''Not yet. We will, though. I think Iris and I are still in shock.''

"A nice kind of shock, though. Go home, Sage. I'll be here if any problems crop up. Say hi to Iris and hug the kids."

"Billie . . ."

"Go already. It's okay."

Sage hugged her. "See you tomorrow. I'm going to stop by the casino to get Celia's phone number and address. I'll give her a call. Mom might want to invite her out to the house or something."

"Or something," Billie said as she shoved him out the door.

Billie locked the office door. She was shaking when she sat down behind her desk. She hadn't counted on Sage being so astute and outspoken. She pulled the adding machine closer. From her locked desk drawer she withdrew a small yellow notebook and began to feed the numbers to the machine in front of her. The tally at the end of the strip of paper turned her face white. She leaned back in the deep comfortable desk chair, drawing her knees close to her chest, and cried as if her heart would break.

"Nice seeing you again, Mr. Thornton," the desk clerk said.

Sage smiled. "How's your family, Myra?"

"We're all good. And yours?"

"Couldn't be better. Do you have Celia Thornton's phone and address? I promised my brother I'd pick it up."

"I have it already, Mr. Thornton. If you're looking for Mrs. Thornton, she's here in the casino. I saw her a little while ago when I took a message out to the floor for one of the customers. She was heading toward the office."

"Thanks, Myra."

Sage pocketed the envelope. Should he go to the office or shouldn't he? What the hell, he was here. A little family nicety might help Birch. He looked at his watch—twenty minutes past five.

It was ten minutes to six when Sage finally made his way

across the floor, stopping to shake hands with pit bosses and money changers. He stood outside the door of the office, remembering the day he'd walked out of the casino for the last time. He'd never forget the awful look on Birch's face that day. Time and life didn't stand still for anyone. He was about to knock on the door when he heard low, intimate laughter from inside. He jammed his hands in his pockets. Leave? Stay? What did that laughter mean? They, and exactly who was the they? As if he didn't know. Jeff and Celia must be standing right next to the door. He was about to leave when he heard his half brother say, "There is a room here that no one ever uses. My father kept it for himself. Out of respect for him they never assigned the room. It's at the end of the hall on the seventh floor. There is no master key, so you can stay there and no one will be the wiser. Room 719. You'll be on your own as far as housekeeping goes. Actually, it's a suite. My father, in case you haven't heard, was a lady's man."

Sage swallowed, his tongue thick and dry in his mouth. What the hell was going on here? Room 719? How did Lassiter know about Room 719? To his knowledge only Birch, Sunny, and he knew. He wasn't sure, but he didn't think his mother knew. No master key, my ass. There was a master key to everything. Sunny had turned her key ring over to him the day she moved to Sunrise. His father had given his set to his mother the day Fanny had taken over the management of Babylon.

Sage walked back to the registration desk. "Myra, do we ever rent out Room 719?"

"No, Mr. Thornton. That was one of your father's strictest orders. To my knowledge, they have never rented it. It's never been used, even when we're at a hundred percent capacity. There's no key here. I don't think I've ever seen a key to that room. If I'm not mistaken, it has a special lock of some sort. Your mother or Mrs. Noble might know."

"It's not important. Thanks, Myra."

Sage walked over to one of the house phones. He identified

himself before he asked the hotel operator to place a long-distance call, person to person, to the rehab center in Cape May for Sunny Thornton Ford. A wave of dizziness swept over him when he heard his sister's voice.

"Sunny, it's me, Sage. Listen, I want to tell you something, and I want to ask you something. This is just between us, okay? Did you have a key to Room 719? Did Mom have one? You're sure? Did she know what it was for? Think, Sunny. Hell yes it's important; otherwise, I wouldn't be calling. Listen up."

Sage held the phone away from his ear at Sunny's furious squawking. "You actually took Dad's card key and put it in the back pocket of Dad's spare wheelchair that's in the garage. You taped it there. Good girl, Sunny. I don't know what I'm going to do. Not a word. Of course I'll let you know. I know you hate her. I'm not sure I like her myself. For Birch's sake I'm going to try very hard to like her. Are you feeling okay, kiddo? Good. How's Harry? All right. Don't overdo it. If you need me, call. I'll let you know when I know what's going on. To use your favorite phrase, damn straight something is going on. Bye, Sunny. Hey, don't mention this call to Birch, okay."

Sage turned when he felt a light tap on his shoulder. "Neal, how's it going?"

The floor manager wore a tight expression when he said, "I was going to ask you the same question."

"I'm fine, and I don't miss this place at all. You now, it's in your blood the way it was in my father's blood. Is everything okay?"

"I don't know, Sage. All kinds of rumors are flying around here. We're all walking on our toes. The word's out a major shakeup is coming. The word is we 'old-timers' are going to be the first to go."

"Where did you hear something like that?"

Neal shot Sage a disgusted look. "Right here on the floor."

"It's not going to happen. You have my word. Birch, my sisters and I own this place, not Jeff Lassiter. You have my number, Neal. If it looks like it's going to happen, call me. This place would fall apart without all you, quote, old-timers. When someone new comes on the scene, rumors like this always start. It's that new broom sweeps clean thing. When I tell you your job is safe, it's safe. Tell the others.''

''That's a load off my shoulders, Sage. This probably is none of my business, but for what it's worth, I'd put a harness on that young woman.''

''What young woman?''

''The one wearing the tight green dress who's headed for the registration desk. Your brother's wife. In just a few short days she's made a name for herself here at the casino. In my opinion, and I know you didn't ask for it, but I'll give it to you anyway, she's too damn friendly with Lassiter. It's out in the open for everyone to see. Listen, Sage, I have to ask you something. Is it going to be us against them? By them I mean all the new people who have been going back and forth to the offices and conference room.''

''I don't know, Neal. I'll check it out.''

''Nice seeing you again, Sage. Say hello to Birch for me. I only got to see him for a few minutes before he left. He did ask if me and the guys would consider going to AC when the casino is up and running to sort of train and keep an eye on things until everyone gets their feet wet. We all said yes. All of us are loyal to your family, Sage.''

''I know that, Neal.''

Sage snagged a beer from a passing server, his eyes on his sister-in-law. He watched as Myra talked, then pointed in his direction. Sage stared boldly at his brother's wife, using the beer bottle as a salute. He thought she looked nervous. Maybe jittery. Nervous and jittery. Maybe arrogant and cocky. She was coming toward him. Some of the more rambunctious customers whistled and leered at her. She waved nonchalantly at them, acknowledging their approval.

''Sage, what brings you here to the casino?''

"I was just going to ask you the same question." The score was one to one if you were counting. He was counting.

"Do you have time for a drink?"

"Got one." Sage held his beer bottle aloft. The score was two to two if you were counting. He was counting.

"Want to gamble?"

"Been there, done that." The score was three three if you were counting. He was still counting.

"The desk clerk said you were looking for me. She said she directed you to the office."

Sage swigged from the beer bottle. "Yes, she did." Sage swore he could see straight through the translucent eyes to the back of Celia's skull. "It sounded like you and Jeff were . . . ah . . . busy so I left." The score was four three in his favor.

"Busy? Sage, that's too funny for words. I just stopped by to pick up some paper for my résumé. Jeff told me the funniest joke."

Sage eyed the form-fitting green dress. No pockets and what Iris would call an itt-bitty purse hanging from her shoulder that could only hold lipstick and a hankie. "So, where's the paper?" The score was five–three if you were counting. He was counting.

The translucent eyes glittered. "That almost sounds like you don't believe me, Sage."

Sage set his beer bottle next to a slot machine. He smiled. "Seeing is believing. I don't see any paper. Nice seeing you, Celia." Sage felt like he'd been dipped in ice water as he made his way to the elevator that would take him to the underground garage.

On his drive up the mountain Sage used his mobile phone to call Sunny a second time. He felt better the moment he blurted out the details of his meeting with Celia. "What's your assessment, Sunny?"

"She sounds like she's up to no good. You need to stay on top of it. Are you going to tell Iris?"

"No. Sunny, Iris is pregnant with twins. She's into her fifth month."

"No shit!" the outspoken Sunny gurgled. "That's wonderful, Sage. It is, isn't it?"

"Yeah, it is. It was a shock at first."

"Will Jake and Polly be too much for her, Sage?"

"Of course not. We're getting a mother's helper, and one of Chue's relatives is going to help when the babies come. I think Jake is more excited than all of us put together. Our family is growing, Sunny. This other crap is taking the edge off our happiness."

"Harry said he thinks Celia's a slut. Harry's always right. He also said you should hire a private dick to look into her past. I agree. It's a shitty thing to do, but it's better to know what you're up against going in. If you don't do it, later you might wish you had. For Birch's sake."

"Think about what old Birch will do if he ever finds out."

"Who's going to tell him? Certainly not me or Harry. That leaves you, Sage. If you keep your lip zipped, no one will ever find out. Are you gonna do it?"

"I'll think about it. I don't like being in this position. Maybe we should just mind our own business."

"Do you want sleepless nights for the rest of your life?"

"No."

"That's your answer. I gotta go, Sage, the dinner bell is ringing. Call me."

"Yeah. Don't eat too much."

"Are you kidding? I lose more than I get in my mouth. I eat all day long. Slow and easy, Sage. Résumé my ass."

Sage laughed. He loved it when Sunny reverted to what he called the old irrepressible Sunny.

Iris watched her husband through the kitchen window. A frown built between her eyebrows when she saw him go into the garage. Sage was rarely late, always calling ahead if he thought he'd be delayed. Today he was almost two hours late, and he wasn't barreling into the house shouting, "I'm starved, what's for dinner?" Instead he was in the garage.

"Okay, kids, Daddy's home. Time for homework, Jake. Polly, help Lexie get her pajamas on. One television program and one bowl of popcorn. Daddy's late so that means he's probably tired. Low voices and big kisses. Scat."

"Honey, you look absolutely frazzled. Is everything okay? Your dinner's warming in the oven. Banana cream pie for dessert."

"Sounds great, honey. How are you feeling?"

"Today was pretty good. I think my morning sickness is easing up a little. I was starting to get worried, Sage. Jake kept going out to the road every ten minutes."

"I'm sorry. I stopped at the casino to get Celia's address and phone number from the desk clerk. You know how it is. I stopped to talk to Neal and some of the guys. I'm sorry I didn't call. Time got away from me. I did kind of have a run in with Billie today."

"Billie! I find that hard to believe. Is anything wrong?"

Sage threw his hands in the air. "Would you call five-hour lunches something to get concerned about?"

"Occasionally or all the time?"

"For some time now. It started being two, then three, four, and today it was five. She looks very tired, as though she isn't sleeping. She stays late to make up the time. I feel terrible for the way I came down on her. She reminded me the company owes her years of vacation and overtime. She's absolutely right about that. She spoiled me by always being there. She's always been a workaholic. I guess she's spreading her wings a little. I just don't get a detective having so much time off in the middle of the day. She had that one covered, too. She said he has as much time coming to him as she does. The whole thing just didn't ring true to me."

"Adam works nights a lot. Maybe they .. ah ... you know ... afternoon trysts."

"Trysts?"

"Assignations."

"Assignations?"

"Sex, Sage, in a hotel."

"Billie?"

"Yes, Billie. She isn't a nun, honey."

"In the middle of the day? I just never thought ..."

"You need to mind your own business, Sage."

"Somebody has to look out for her. Sometime, hell, most of the time, she acts like she's in another world."

"Creative people are like that. Artists are dreamy, writers are flaky, designers are spacey. Do you get it?"

"Yes. Thanks for sharing that. Supper was great as usual. I'm going to take a shower. I promised the kids we'd play Monopoly. We won't be able to finish tonight, so is it okay to leave the board set up in the dining room? You don't want me to do anything, do you?"

"Yes, no, go."

Later, when her family gathered in the dining room, Iris made her way upstairs to turn down the beds. She laid out clean clothes for the morning, hung up Sage's wet towels, and turned down her own bed. She picked up Sage's suit, checking the pockets before she placed it on the pile of clothing to be taken to the dry cleaners in town.

Iris knew what she had in her hand even before she looked at it; a Babylon room key. In her husband's pocket. A husband who was two hours late coming home. In a trancelike state, she slipped the card key back into the pocket before she replaced Sage's suit where she'd picked it up. She sat down on the edge of the bed, her hand going to her stomach to feel the protrusion that would one day be twins.

From her position on the bed she could see her reflection in the bureau mirror. When she woke this morning, she'd felt good, robust, healthy. The mirror told her she was heavier, fuller, rounder. She squeezed her eyes shut and saw Celia Thornton behind her closed eyelids. Shapely, sexy, gorgeous Celia.

Iris's gaze swiveled to her husband's jacket. The card was a special card. She'd been able to tell that by the feel of it. Once, a long time ago, Sage had told her about a special room his father kept at Babylon. A card key that fit into a special lock. A tamper-proof card, according to Sage. A one-of-a-kind lock and card key. Logic said Fanny would be the owner of the card now that Ash had passed away. Why would she give such a key to Sage? Fanny would have changed the locks and opened the room for rent, knowing what she knew. Fanny would never keep the room as a shrine to Ash. Never in a million years.

Iris reached for the phone, pressed the buttons that would give her the switchboard at Babylon. Her voice was tremulous and full of tears when she said, "Room 719."

"One moment, please."

In Room 719 Celia Thornton twirled about the sitting room. Yes, this would do very nicely as a nest. Yes, indeed. The phone rang. Thinking it was Jeff Lassiter wanting to know how she liked the suite, she picked up the receiver and purred, "You sweet thing, this is just fabulous." She reared back when she heard the phone click in her ear.

Miles away, on top of the mountain, Iris slammed the phone into the cradle and rushed to the bathroom, where she lost her dinner. She'd know that throaty purr anywhere. Her world shattered around her as she stumbled back to her room. Not bothering to change into her nightgown, Iris slipped between the sheets where she cowered, her knees drawn up to her chest.

6

Sage woke slowly, instantly aware of two things: his wife was at the far side of their king-size bed, and she was feigning sleep. In all the time they'd been married, neither one of them had slept on "his" or "her" side of the bed. They always woke pressed against one another. He squinted at the clock. There was still five minutes before the alarm went off. His gut told him it wasn't going to be a good day. He reached out, pressed the alarm button.

Beneath the spray of the shower his mind raced. He tried to recall what kind of day he'd scheduled at the office. If he wanted to, he could take a few hours off. The question was, what would he do with the few hours if he did take them off? He needed to get his ducks into the water and line them up. For starters, he could try to get a handle on Celia Thornton in order to report back to Sunny. He could apologize again to Billie and see if he could figure out what was bothering her. A visit to his mother and Marcus wouldn't be out of the ordinary. A brief meeting with Jeff Lassiter was definitely on his agenda. Maybe he needed to take the whole day off.

He made a mental note to call the airlines to see if he could make a trip to Atlantic City and return the same day. Not necessarily today, but at some point when his silent investigation provided hard, conclusive facts.

Sage stepped from the shower to poke his head out of the bathroom door. Iris was still buried under a mound of covers. Normally he could smell bacon and coffee when he stepped from the shower. Iris never missed making breakfast. The kids were stirring. Cold cereal this morning. He shaved, nicking himself twice. He cursed under his breath. A headache started to hammer at the base of his skull. He popped three aspirin and knew he'd regret it. Aspirin on an empty stomach wasn't good where he was concerned. He dressed, sticking his tie in his pocket. His gut started to churn as it fought with the aspirin and Iris's still form in the bed.

"Honey, are you okay? Is there anything I can do?"

"Get the kids off. I went downstairs earlier and made some oatmeal. Warm it up and cut a banana for each of them. Their lunches are packed. I made coffee."

"Okay. I hope you feel better later. I'll call you." He leaned over to kiss her, but Iris rolled over. "I'll see you later, honey." Uncertain now, Sage gathered up his suit to add it to the pile of dry cleaning. He remembered the card key in the pocket. He slipped it into his shirt pocket. He hung up his wet towel and dried the sink. His footsteps were quiet when he left the room.

Iris sat up in bed. Did he take it? Didn't he take it? She swung her legs over the side of the bed, glad that Sage had turned the heat up, something she always did since she got up first. She knew in her heart the card key would be gone, and it was. Whimpering, she climbed back into bed, hugging her knees, tears streaming down her cheeks.

The moment she heard Sage's car start up in the courtyard,

Iris put on her robe and went downstairs. She eyed the coffeepot. Would coffee stay down? She poured a cup and drank it in two gulps. When her stomach didn't rebel, she poured a second cup. The illogical side of her personality argued with her logical side. She should have talked to Sage, asked him to explain the card key. She had no right, even in her thoughts, to accuse Sage of infidelity with his brother's wife. Sunny would say she was going off half-cocked. She wondered if she dared to call Sunny or Billie to ask for their advice. The Thorntons stuck together like glue on flypaper when one of their own was threatened. Fanny? Never. Marcus? No. The only people left were Ruby and Jeff Lassiter. She negated Jeff almost immediately. Men stuck together. For all she knew, Jeff might be covering for Sage. Ruby was worldly, and Ruby liked her as much as she liked Ruby.

It occurred to Iris as she poured a third cup of coffee that she had her husband tried and convicted without any proof. Suspicions weren't enough to convict someone when that someone was your husband.

At the end of an hour's time, Iris had herself convinced she'd acted rashly and that sweet, wonderful Sage would never do what she suspected him of doing. The feeling stayed with her while she showered and dressed. The feeling left her when she gathered up her husband's pile of cleaning to carry downstairs.

Iris looked at the sink full of dishes, at the messy breakfast table without seeing it. She called Chue's house and asked him to watch the children after school. "I might be late, Chue. I'll call you if I'm going to miss dinner. Thanks."

By eleven o'clock, the cleaning had been dropped off and she'd bought her sundries at the drugstore that now belonged to Bess Noble's son. She stopped at a small variety store to buy coloring books and new crayons for all the young children. For Chue's older grandchildren and Jake she bought a pile of comic books. With nothing but time on her hands, Iris walked down the street to Babylon. She could say hello to Neal, spend ten dollars in the slots, go to lunch, and head home. Or, she could stop by the office and offer to take Sage to lunch. After she *grilled* him. On the other hand, maybe she should go to the office first in case her husband had a meeting or a business lunch with a supplier or a distributor.

Iris retraced her steps and headed for the office. She opened the door and was about to offer a cheery greeting when she saw Billie's startled expression that to her mind looked guilty. She pretended not to see her sister-in-law shove a yellow notebook into one of the desk drawers and then lock it. She also pretended not to see the annoyed look on Billie's face. "I thought I'd stop by and take Sage to lunch. Am I too late?"

"Actually, Iris, Sage didn't come in this morning. He called me at home and said he had some things to take care of. It looks like a slow day for both of us."

"Is he coming back?"

Billie shook her head. "He didn't say, so I assume he has his end under control and that he won't be back. Want some coffee?"

"I had my quota for the day. How about you, Billie, want to have lunch? My treat."

"Iris, I can't. Adam asked me yesterday. Would you like to join us?"

"Absolutely not! I'll shop. Can I get you anything?"

"No, but thanks for offering. Iris, Sage told me yesterday that you're expecting twins. I think it's wonderful. Congratulations. If there is anything I can do, just let me know. When are you going to tell Mom? She's going to be so excited. Have you thought about godparents? Put my name down."

"I'm asking Sunny and Harry, and I thought you and Birch might want the honor?"

"What about Celia?"

Iris's face closed up. "No, not Celia."

"Okay, I'm your girl."

Iris sensed that Billie wanted her to leave. "Billie, is everything okay? You seem, I don't know, jittery, for want of a better word.''

"Yeah, I am. It's that time of the month. Too much coffee, not enough sleep.''

"If you're free Sunday, come for dinner. I should be leaving. I think I'll take a ride out to the desert to see Fanny and Marcus. Bye, Billie.''

"Bye Iris. If Sage comes in, I'll tell him you stopped by.''

Outside in the crisp October air, Iris drew a deep breath. On a whim, she walked back to Babylon, where she took the elevator to the underground garage where Sage kept his reserved parking space since parking spots all over town were at a premium. When she saw the vacant slot, her eyes filled. Was Sage in the casino or had he parked his car somewhere else? He could have walked anywhere in town if he wanted to, which meant he could be anywhere. He also had spare keys to all the casino's shuttle vans. She sat down on the back bumper of Sunny's Volvo, parked in the space next to Sage's. Tears rolled down her cheeks. What was she doing here? She should go back to the mountain where she belonged. That's exactly what she would do when she'd had lunch and checked out Room 719.

"Sage! Marcus, Sage is here!" Fanny called out to her husband. "I can't remember the last time you just stopped by, honey," she said, hugging her son.

"Mom, I didn't just stop by. In a way I did. I came by to tell you something and to ask you something. The good news is Iris is expecting twins."

Fanny's hand flew to her mouth. "Twins!"

"Twins!" Marcus echoed his wife's startled comment.

"Yep. They're due on Valentine's Day."

"Valentine's Day," the Reeds said in unison.

"Yep."

"How's Iris?"

"She had a lot of morning sickness, but it's getting better now. She slept in this morning for the first time ever."

"I hope you're being considerate of her, sweetie."

"Mom, Iris and the kids are my reason for living. How could you even think I might not be considerate of her."

"Your father . . ."

"I'm not Dad, Mom. I remember what it was like. Trust me when I tell you I will never be like him."

Fanny nodded. "What was the other thing you wanted to talk about?"

"Jeff Lassiter."

"What about him, Sage?"

"I stopped by the casino last night to get Celia's phone number and address at Birch's request. By the way, here it is in case you want to call her." He handed his mother a slip of paper. "I spoke to Neal and some of the other employees while I was there. Are you aware that a rumor is going around concerning layoffs? Out with the old and in with the new. Did you give Jeff that authority?"

"It all went with the job. You didn't want it, Sage. Birch wasn't here. Bess and John wanted to retire. My back was to the wall. I explained that to all of you."

"So you just gave him carte blanche?" The indignation and outrage on Sage's face were palpable. Marcus moved closer to his wife, his hand on her shoulder.

"Yes."

"Does that mean you're going to go along with laying off Neal, Todd, Steve, and all the others? They have families, Mom, kids in college, mortgages, ailing parents. There's a lot of new faces roaming around over there. You can't let him do that. It's not going to be good for morale. They're all loyal to this family."

"Sallie ran the Silver Dollar into the ground with that kind of thinking. We all cut our teeth on that story. Business is business. I'm sure a nice, healthy severance package will go with the layoff.''

"Aren't you forgetting what all those guys did for you when you took over from Dad? Mom, you owe them. Babylon would have gone down the drain if it wasn't for their dedication and loyalty to this family. Mom, I never heard you talk like this. You were always the most family-oriented person I knew. Marcus, what do you have to say?'' Sage all but snarled.

"It's not my business, Sage. I promised all of you and your mother when we got married that I wouldn't interfere in your family business. I have to stand by my decision.''

"That's it then! You won't talk to Jeff?''

"Until he does something wrong, no, I won't interfere,'' Fanny said.

"Then I guess I have to go the other route and talk to my siblings. Your vote only counts, Mom, when things are tied. Would it bother you at all if I told you your golden boy is pussyfooting around with your new daughter-in-law? Here's one for the books. I think Jeff has Celia stashed in Room 719, Dad's little private whorehouse.''

Fanny's face drained of all color.

"The apple doesn't fall far from the tree, Mom. You backed the wrong horse.'' His face murderous, Sage stormed from the room. Marcus marched after him.

"Sage, wait.''

"Don't talk to me, Marcus. You had your chance back there, and you blew it. She's wrong, and we both know it. This is the goddamnedest fucked-up family I ever came across. I wish to hell I'd never been born into it.''

"You don't mean that, Sage. Take a deep breath, son, and calm down.''

"I'm not your son, so don't try pulling that shit on me. There's going to be a war here, so you better get the hell out of the line of fire. Mom taught us about honesty and loyalty from the time we were old enough to walk and talk. Obviously she no longer practices what she preached all those years. To say I'm disillusioned with my mother would be putting it mildly. I think I can speak for my brother and sisters on this.''

Marcus gasped. ''Are you threatening your own mother? Sage, I don't believe I'm hearing this from you.''

''I'm threatening her *decision* because it is a bad decision. If she stands behind it, then yes, I'm threatening her. Both of you, stay away from Sunrise, too. Don't call us. We'll call you.''

''Sage . . .''

''Get the hell out of my way, or I'll run you over.''

Sage drove for a mile before he realized he'd taken a wrong turn. He pulled to the side of the road until his breathing returned to normal. He eyed the mobile phone. He fumbled through his wallet until he found the number Birch had given him for the building site in Atlantic City. He placed his call, his breath exploding in a loud sigh when he heard his brother's booming voice. Sage explained his encounter with Fanny and Marcus.

''Jesus, I'm glad Sunny and I are out of there. You got my vote. Sunny's here if you want to talk to her.''

''Yeah, put her on.''

Sage explained again.

''That sucks, Sage. Of course you have my vote. I say we fire the son of a bitch!''

''He has a contract, Sunny. I'm sure it's airtight. We can outvote Mom, though. I'm sure Billie will go along with us. It will get down and dirty, Sunny.''

''You know what, Sage, I'm spoiling for a good fight. Say what you will about Dad. He kept Jeff at a distance for a reason. He probably knew this would happen somewhere along the way. Dad was, among other things, shrewd and wise in the ways of trickery and deceit. Whatever you decide to do, it's okay with Birch and me. We can be home in four hours if you need us. Say hello to Neal and the guys for me. Neal always took my side when Dad thought I wasn't doing something to his liking. Do you have any *other* news?"

"By tonight I might. I'll call you. Don't call me at the house. I don't want to get Iris involved in any of this. She's not feeling too good. She gets paranoid when she thinks there are family problems. As it is, she's acting weird."

"Wait. The longer the pregnancy goes, the weirder she's going to get. It isn't easy being pregnant. Try being a little more understanding. Take her some flowers."

"With sixteen greenhouses on the premises!"

"They're free. *Buy* them. Present them. Sometimes you're so stupid it's hard to believe you're my brother. Harry and I are going to get married."

"Huh?"

"You heard me. On New Year's Day. We want you and Birch both to be our best man, men, in this instance. Say something." Sunny's voice was anxious when she said, "You like Harry, don't you?"

"Like a brother, Sunny. Congratulations. When are you going to tell Jake and Polly? Man, this will give Iris something to do beside thinking about twins. Can I tell her?"

"Sure you can tell her. I'll call the kids this weekend. We want to get married at Sunrise at sunrise. You know, the start of the day, a new year, that kind of thing. I'm doing real good now, and so is Harry. We'll finally get to live in the same cottage."

"That's great, Sunny. What about Mom?"

"Whatever will be will be, Sage."

"Okay, I'll talk to you later. Say hi to Harry for me."

"Will do. We want a really smashing present. I was thinking along the lines of a fifty-six-inch television set. A Mitsubishi."

"I'll tell Iris. Bye, Sunny."

"Sage, wait, don't hang up. I think you're going to need a lawyer. Hire Clementine Fox before Mom or Jeff gets to her.

She's the best. Give some thought to all of us buying out Jeff's contract.''

"Okay. I'll call Clementine today."

Sage's next call was to Billie at the office. He went through his spiel for the third time. "What's your vote?"

"The same as you guys. Sunny's right. Talk to Clem before you do anything. Who drew up Lassiter's contract? Do you know?"

"His own attorney. Mom didn't even use a lawyer. She read it, said it was simple, cut-and-dried, and she signed it."

"Nothing is cut-and-dried. Forget simple. The lawyer hasn't been born who knows what simple means. Cover our asses, Sage. By the way, Iris stopped in to take you to lunch. I didn't think she looked well."

"She wasn't feeling well this morning. She was still in bed when I left. I'm sorry I missed her. Do you need me for anything?"

"It's quiet today. I was just getting ready to go to lunch. Is that okay with you, big brother?"

"Take as long as you like, Billie."

"Let me know what happens. Was Mom mad?"

"Stubborn. I blew up at Marcus. I hate it when people are tight-minded. Doesn't Mom care?"

"She paid her dues. I guess she figures she did the best she could at the time. We need to allow for that. She's very fond of Neal and the guys. When she took over from Dad, she relied on all of them. If it wasn't for those guys, Babylon would have gone down the tubes. Maybe you should have reminded her of that little fact."

"I did, Billie, but it didn't make a difference."

"Do what you have to do. You have my vote. Mom's vote only counts if it's a tiebreaker."

"Sunny's getting married on New Year's Day. She wants to do it when the sun is coming up at Sunrise."

"God, that's great. I'll call her tonight. I can make her gown and veil if she wants me to. Thanks for telling me. See you tomorrow.''

Next stop, Babylon.

Iris opted for the buffet at the Country Kitchen dining room, nestled at the far end of the casino, that was frequented mostly by the staff. Sage had said he always ate here. Until today she'd watched her weight, eating only vegetables, fruits, and chicken. Her weight gain, even though she was five months pregnant and carrying twins, was minimal. As she walked down the line with her oval-shaped plate, she eyed everything before making her final decision. When she sat down at the table, she had a slab of ribs, two deep-fried chicken legs, two scoops of mashed potatoes with gravy, one small spear of broccoli, and a half loaf of garlic bread spread with thick butter. She ate everything except the broccoli. She went back for cherry pie and soft ice cream, washing it down with a bottle of lemon-lime soda.

Once in a great while she smoked but hadn't smoked at all since her pregnancy began. She fired up a stale cigarette from the bottom of her purse. She coughed and sputtered but kept on smoking. She smoked two more cigarettes before she got up from the table. Waiting in line at the cashier's counter, she popped three Rolaids for the heartburn she knew would overtake her once she started moving.

Iris walked slowly, her eyes canvassing the casino floor. When she didn't see anyone she recognized, she looked around for a courtesy phone. She stopped once to change a ten-dollar bill for silver dollars. She fed them one at a time, yanking the handle violently nine times, at which point a siren over her head went off and a whistle blasted her eardrums. She stared at the blood red triple sevens in front of her. People were staring at her, hooting and hollering. She wished the floor would open and swallow her.

Out of the corner of her eye she saw Neal approaching her, a broad smile on his face. "You tapped the big one, Iris," he said, putting his arm around her shoulder. "Twenty-five big ones!"

"You mean I won twenty-five hundred dollars!"

"Twenty-five *thousand* dollars! How do you want the check made out?"

Run and hide money. Now, where did that thought come from?

"My name," she said smartly. Neal spoke softly into the walkie-talkie in his hand.

"Attagirl." Neal laughed. "You aren't going to believe this, Iris, but your new sister-in-law fed this machine for close to two hours a little while ago. I think she pumped three hundred bucks into it. Smile. Here comes our new boss with your check."

So Celia was in the casino a little while ago. Probably, Iris thought, *while I was stuffing my face in the Country Kitchen.* She smiled for Jeff Lassiter, who handed over the check, a strange look on his face. "Dumb luck," she muttered. On the ride home, she'd think about the strange smile she'd seen on Lassiter's face.

"If you're looking for Sage, I saw him about fifteen minutes ago. Do you want me to look for him?"

"Nope. I'm going to take my money and run. To the bank." *Fifteen minutes versus Celia a little while ago.*

Smiling at her well-wishers, Iris made her way to the courtesy phone. "Room 719," she said in a harsh voice.

"That room has not been assigned, ma'am. Are you sure you have the right number?"

"I'm sure. This is Iris Thornton. Ring the room, please."

"Yes, ma'am," the flustered voice said.

The phone in Room 719 was picked up on the fourth ring. Iris listened to her husband's husky, cautious hello. When she heard him say hello a second time, she hung up the phone.

Sick to her soul, Iris made her way to the underground garage. She cried all the way up the mountain.

In Room 719 Sage replaced the phone in the cradle. A signal? The call had been made from the casino floor. He didn't need to be a rocket scientist to recognize the bells and whistles of the slot machines. Lassiter checking on Celia? What was he thinking this very minute?

Sage knew he should leave, but he wanted to see if there were any traces of Celia's presence. When he reported in to Sunny later, he wanted to make sure he was telling the truth. He checked the bedroom closet, bug-eyed at the costly garments, the price tags still attached. Six pairs of glittery, spike-heeled shoes were on the floor. The dresser drawers showed him his sister-in-law had fine taste in lingerie. The stuff looked like cobwebs to him. The bathroom was chock full of cosmetics and crystal perfume bottles. He removed the glass stopper on one of the bottles and sniffed. He swiped at his nose and then sneezed three times in succession. He recognized the scent as one his mother wore. Four hundred fifty dollars a half ounce. Possibly more in today's market. Once when they were kids they had pooled their money to buy their mother the half ounce bottle. He'd used up almost a whole year's allowance, as had his brother and sisters.

Sage placed the perfume bottle exactly where he found it. He felt the towel. It was wet. Supersleuth Sage Thornton. He grimaced at his reflection in the mirror. He looked around the sitting room, his eyes searching for a sign that he'd been in the apartment. It was probably a mistake to answer the phone. He couldn't worry about that now. He left the room, checking the door to make sure it was locked. The elevator door started to swish shut just as the elevator on the right opened. Sage stepped next to the panel catching only a glimpse of his half brother Jeff Lassiter. "Supersleuth Sage Thornton makes a clean getaway," he muttered.

Sage looked at his watch. Fifteen minutes to get to Clementine Fox's office to keep the appointment he'd made earlier. His visit to the seventh floor was a can of worms. The appointment with Vegas's hot-shot attorney would be opening a *bucket* full of worms. Sage shrugged, remembering his father's famous words, "You play the hand you're dealt."

Fanny sat at the kitchen table with her hands folded, her eyes full of tears. Marcus set a cup of steaming coffee in front of her. He emptied the dishwasher, cleaned the now empty coffeepot. He eyed his wife out of the corner of his eye as he picked up the small rug under the sink. He carried it outside to shake out the crumbs. He let the dogs in and out. Fanny hadn't moved. The tears were still glistening in her eyes. Her coffee was untouched. "No matter what I do, it's never right. I can never make my children happy. Why do they expect so much from me? Sage was so ... *bullish*. Was I wrong, Marcus?"

"In my opinion you were wrong."

"You're on *their* side?"

"I'm not on anyone's side. I said I wouldn't interfere with your family, and I meant it. You asked my opinion, and I gave it to you. You always said Sage was the level-headed one, that he was the one who thought things through. You said Birch acted on impulse."

"That's true. Sage was almost *violent*. Ash used to act that way when things didn't go his way. I don't for one minute believe what he said about Celia and Jeff. Do you believe it, Marcus?"

"Are you asking my opinion, Fanny?"

"Yes."

"I believed everything Sage said. He has no reason to lie.

Ask yourself why Celia stayed behind. Don't you find it a little strange considering what went on at Sunrise?''

"I don't think Sage has forgiven Birch for going off to Costa Rica. I think that has something to do with things."

"I don't believe that either. Again, it's my opinion. Why do you suppose Ash kept that young man out of the way? He did it for a reason. He didn't want him to be a part of your family. There had to be a reason for that, too. From everything you told me, Ash went out of his way to make sure what is happening now never happened. I can respect that in a man. You took matters into your own hands, and this is the result. There were options available to you, Fanny. You chose not to exercise them. I never asked why. Neal is more than capable of running the casino. I also think he had every right to expect the job. Bess and John both told me he was the logical choice."

"Everyone's right, and I'm wrong."

"Fanny, it's all right to make a mistake, to make the wrong decision as long as you make it right in the end. I think you're being stubborn now. Do you want your family divided . . . *again?*''

"No, of course not."

"You, Fanny, divided your family this morning. You aligned yourself with your husband's son this morning to the exclusion of your own children. Sage told me this was the goddamnedest, fucked-up family he ever saw and wished he'd never been born into it. Then he told me there was going to be a war and to get out of the line of fire. After that he threatened to run over me if I didn't get out of his way. He'll freeze you out, Fanny, just the way Sunny did. Birch and Billie will side with their siblings."

"Then I didn't do my job right when I raised them." Her voice was harsh and tortured sounding.

"On the contrary. You did your job so well your children believe, and rightly so, that they have every right to expect their mother to back up those teachings. You're going against everything you taught them. The question is why? Personally speaking, Fanny, I don't blame them. I think, this is only my opinion again, your children feel like you betrayed them. If Ash wanted Jeffrey Lassiter in the family, he would have jammed the boy down all your throats. You know it as well as I do.''

''Are you turning on me, too, Marcus?''

''Good heavens no. Drink your coffee, Fanny. I'm going to try to fix the television antenna. I think the wind knocked it loose last night.''

''You should call a repairman.''

''I could. I like tinkering. When I tinker, I don't have to think. I'll probably think about Iris and Sage having twins and what it will be like. I wonder if they'll let *me* see them.''

Fanny's head jerked upward. ''That's tantamount to blackmail on their part. I won't stand for something like that.''

''Then it will be your loss, Fanny. You're going to have to turn the television on, so I'll know if I'm doing the right thing when I'm on the roof. When you get a good picture, call up to me.''

Fanny marched into the living room, her body stiffer than the board under her mattress. She turned on the set. It crackled with white wavy lines. As she watched the screen, she thought about everything her husband had said. Marcus always made such perfect sense. In essence she was throwing away her family by siding with Jeff Lassiter. If she gave in to Sage and the others, she would be going back on her word. In her entire life she'd never reneged, never broken a promise. As early as five years of age her father and brothers had drilled into her head that a person was only as good as their word. She'd seen and felt the repercussions when Ash went back on *his* word.

''Anything yet, Fanny?'' Marcus bellowed from the roof.

''It's still the same. Try jiggling it.''

''Any better?''

''No. Turn it the other way or let me call a repairman.''

"A piece broke off. Okay, I'm coming down. Call a repairman."

Fanny turned off the television and closed the front door. She walked back to the kitchen to call for a repair. Her call completed, she sat down to finish her now cold coffee, her mind whirling in every direction. She snapped out of her reverie when she saw the television antenna fall outside the kitchen window. Had Marcus thrown it off the roof? She raced to the door calling her husband's name. She looked around, her eyes wild, for some sign of him.

"Fanny . . ." The voice was faint, muffled.

Fanny ran to the front of the house. Her heart in her throat, her eyes searched the roof, then the ground. "My God, Marcus, don't move. Don't even twitch. I'll call an ambulance." She was back in minutes, dropping to the ground. She wanted desperately to cradle her husband's head in her arms, but she knew better. It was all a bad dream. This whole day was a bad dream. It was one of those horrible nightmares one had from time to time. *Oh God, Oh God.* "I'm here, Marcus. The ambulance is on the way." Fanny's voice was hysterical when she said, "Don't try to talk and don't move. Please, Marcus. I hear the siren. If they allow it, I'll go with you in the ambulance."

"Move out of the way, ma'am."

"Yes, yes, out of the way. He fell from the roof. He hasn't moved. I told him to lie still. Can you help him? Please, you have to tell me, is he going to be all right?"

"I don't know. We'll do everything we can."

"Take him to the Thornton Medical Center. I'm Fanny Thornton. Do you want me to call ahead for you?"

Fanny raced into the house. She was incoherent when she started to babble into the phone. "Get every doctor in the hospital to stand by. They'll be bringing him in soon. Be ready. Yes, yes, I'll be with them. Yes, yes, I'll tell them."

Fanny's voice was filled with fear when she said, "Is it safe to move him? They're waiting at the center for you to call. Is he unconscious? That isn't good, is it? Did he talk? What can you tell me? I need to know. Can I ride with him in the ambulance?''

"We'd prefer that you follow us. Are you capable of driving? Perhaps you should call someone to fetch you. Okay, on three, lift.''

Fanny ran into the house for her car keys and purse. The ambulance, siren blasting, was a half mile down the road as she backed out of the driveway, her tires squealing on the asphalt. She floored the gas pedal. *Please, God, don't let him die. Please, God. Don't take him away from me. I need him. Please, God, hear my prayers.*

Fanny sat alone in the waiting room. She was numb with shock as she drank cup after cup of bad coffee. She wished she could cry and wanted to cry. She needed to cry, but her eyes were dry, tired, and full of grit. She wished for John Noble's comforting presence, but he'd retired from the medical profession. Su Li was in China. She had no idea who the new doctors were who manned Sallie Thornton's medical center. The best of the best according to a newspaper article she'd read. She should have kept up with the workings of the center instead of letting trustees oversee everything. Something else she'd fouled up. Par for the course.

A nurse wearing crepe-soled shoes walked up to her. "Mrs. Thornton, I'm sorry, Mrs. Reed, can I get you anything? Do you want me to call anyone for you?''

"No. I'm fine. It's been so long. Somebody must know something by now. Can't you find out anything? Don't they give updates? John Noble always did when he was in charge of this center. When did things change around here? I'm going to have to look into this. I want to know what's going on, and I want to know now. It's been seven hours. Seven hours is an eternity when you're sitting out here.''

"I'll see what I can find out, Mrs. Thorn . . . Mrs. Reed."

Fanny started to pace, her eyes on the carpet. Such a strange color for a hospital. Hours ago she'd worn a path down and around the small sitting area. She reversed her steps, hoping to erase her footprints. She was completing her ninth lap when she felt a presence behind her. She turned. She blanched at the pale green garb, at the sight of the surgical mask hanging askew around the doctor's neck.

"Mrs. Reed?"

"Yes."

"I'm Dr. Oliver. I operated on your husband. He's in recovery right now. A round-the-clock nurse is with him. There is good news and bad news. The good news is your husband survived the surgery. He no longer has a spleen. We had to remove his left kidney. His right leg is broken in three places. He's got three broken ribs and two that are fractured. He's suffered a severe concussion. It's too early to make a prognosis. You can see him for a moment or so through the glass. He's still out of it. He's in good health, so we're hopeful. The next seventy-two hours will tell us more. My advice would be to go home and come back in the morning. Everything that can be done has been done. Now we wait. I know that doesn't sound encouraging, but it's all I can offer right now. Are you alone, Mrs. Reed?"

"Yes. Why?"

"Are you capable of driving home?"

"Yes. I'd like to see my husband."

"Come with me."

Fanny stared through the glass at the still form lying in the stark white bed. The array of tubes and monitors made her light-headed. She leaned her forehead against the cool glass as her body started to shake. He'd been so upset with her over the children, and now this. She never should have allowed him to go up on the roof. She should have insisted he call a repairman. It was all her fault. Everything was her fault. Like Sallie, she couldn't do anything right. No matter what she did, no matter how hard she tried, everything came back to slap her in the face. Sallie all over again.

Fanny wept for the past, what she was now facing, and the unknown future. Dr. Oliver gently led her back to the waiting room. "I can have one of the orderlies drive you home, Mrs. Reed. You look very tired."

"I'm fine, Dr. Oliver. I'll be back in the morning. Thank you. Thank everyone for me."

"It's our job, Mrs. Reed. Try to get some rest. We'll talk again tomorrow."

Fanny left the hospital, her shoulders slumped, her feet dragging. She sat in the parking lot smoking for a long time before she started the car's engine.

She felt like a thief in the night when she climbed from the car in her own driveway. She stared at the antenna on the ground, at the towel and blanket in the driveway. How had they gotten there? The sensor lights sprang to life as Fanny crossed the driveway. How quiet and still it was. The dogs must sense something wrong, she thought. She knew the animals were fine. Earlier in the day she'd put down dry dog food and fresh water. The doggie door Marcus had installed allowed the dogs to go in and out at will. Thanks again to the privacy fence Marcus had put up a week after they moved into the house. There was nothing for her to do inside except cuddle with the dogs.

Fanny sat down on the railroad ties that bordered the driveway and dropped her head into her hands. What would she do if Marcus died? Unable to come up with an answer, she ran across the yard to the fallen antenna. She kicked it, slammed it, yanked at it and finally, using all the strength she could muster, heaved it sideways into the fence. It splintered into sections, hanging drunkenly on protruding nails along the fence line.

She walked back to the railroad ties and sat down. A harvest moon glared down at her. She'd always loved harvest moons. Tonight it seemed ominous, a malevolent evil eye.

She was truly alone. Decency said she should notify her children of Marcus's accident. Because her children were decent human beings, they would say the right things even though they had no real interest in Marcus. They might even stop by the hospital or send flowers. They'd schedule their visits when she wasn't there and go on with their lives that no longer included her. Because of her stubbornness. Ash always said one of the things he liked most about her was her ability to stand tall and not back down.

Fanny started to blubber. "I miss you, Ash. Those last months with you were some of the happiest months of my life. You finally came to understand me, and I truly got to know who you were. I love Marcus, but not the way I loved you. I wish you were here so I could talk to you. I need to know about Jeff. I need to talk about the kids. That's funny. They aren't kids anymore. It's so hard down here, Ash. I don't know what to do. All night long I kept asking myself what you'd do."

Fanny pounded the railroad ties with her clenched fists. Pain ricocheted up her arms. Grimacing with pain, she finally got up and made her way to the kitchen door. The dogs circled her feet, each vying for her attention. She played with them for a few minutes and dispensed dog biscuits before she went upstairs to shower.

Dressed in her ratty old robe, Fanny settled herself in the kitchen, the scotch bottle and a glass in front of her, the dogs at her feet. She drank steadily until she knew she would be able to sleep. She staggered to the living room, the dogs trailing her. The animals sat at attention until they were certain their mistress was asleep. Their heads on their paws, their eyes and ears alert, they remained sentinels all night long.

7

Birch Thornton grappled with the phone stapled to a telephone pole at the construction site. Receiver in one hand, five rolls of blueprints in the other, he barked a greeting, "Thornton here."

"Birch, it's Sage. Listen up. Marcus Reed fell off the roof and is in critical condition. It was in yesterday's paper, but I didn't see it until last night. Mom didn't call Billie or me. I assume she didn't call you or Sunny either. It happened five days ago. I thought I'd stop by the hospital today and send some flowers. Billie isn't interested in going. Iris is waffling. I don't really want to go, but I feel like I should since my last words to Marcus were less than kind. Mom will probably boot my ass out on the street. However, it's the right thing to do. My ass has been skinned before. I don't know if you want to call Mom or not. Sunny . . . Sunny might want to. Like you, she went up against Mom once before. Your choice."

"I talked to Celia last night, and she didn't say anything.

When was it in the paper? I can hardly hear you. Bad connection or else it's all the noise.''

"Yesterday. Right on the front page. Maybe Celia didn't get the paper. How's she doing?"

"She subs one day a week and waitresses two days during lunchtime at the Golden Nugget. She says she likes it. I thought you were going to take her to dinner or lunch."

"Birch, I've called her six or seven times and left a message. She doesn't return my calls. I hope you aren't expecting me to stick my nose into your wife's business. Things are getting wild around here. Lassiter won't give me the time of day. I need you and Sunny to send Clementine Fox your power of attorney. I met with her the other day, and she's getting a handle on everything. She said the buzz on the street is he's going to step into Dad's shoes big time. And, get this, he's trying to develop something the street is calling the Holy Grail. The asshole probably started the rumor himself, just the way Dad used to do when he wanted word to get out about something he did. Clem is looking into that, too. I think Sunny had the right idea when she said the four of us should pool our money and buy out Lassiter's contract. Neal can run the place. What do you think?"

"Sage, whatever you think is right is okay with me. Sunny's right here, and she's nodding agreement. What about Billie?"

"She's in."

"That makes it unanimous. Send the flowers from all of us. I wouldn't go to the hospital though. If Mom wanted you, she would have called. You said it was going to be a war. I take that to mean the lines are drawn. We're stepping outside the family now if it works and Neal is in. I'm okay with it, though."

"Dad would have done it," Sage replied.

"Yeah, this is exactly what he would have done. Do it!"

"Okay. Lassiter doesn't have to take the offer, you know."

"Then make his fucking life miserable. You have the power now to shut down the casino in the time it takes him to blink.

Once his foothold is secure, he's in the catbird seat. Shut it down, and he's out of a job. Play hardball like Dad did. Eyeball to eyeball and make him blink first. Our old man was a whiz at that. Can you handle it?''

Sage gritted his teeth. "Yeah, I can handle it."

."How's Iris?"

"Moody. Withdrawn. It seems like she just goes through the motions. She goes to bed at eight o'clock and stays in bed in the morning. She goes to see Ruby pretty often. They like each other."

"That's good, isn't it?"

"Hell, do I know?"

"Listen, Uncle Daniel is calling me. I'll put Sunny on. Do what you have to do, Sage. Sunny and I are behind you."

"How's it going, Sage?" Sunny asked.

"It's going. Listen, Sunny, Celia isn't subbing. I called every damn school in the district. She registered, but that's all. The woman I spoke to said they called her twice and left a message, but she didn't get back to them. She isn't waitressing at the Golden Nugget either the way Birch said she was. I checked that one out yesterday, and no one's even heard of her. When I said her name was Celia Thornton they laughed in my face. In my opinion the apartment she took is just for Birch's benefit. I know she's holed up in Room 719. I thought I'd stay in town tonight and hang around. Lurk or skulk are probably better words. Try to get those power of attorney forms to me by tonight or early tomorrow morning. Send someone to the airport and put them on the next flight. Clem wants to pay a visit to Jeff tomorrow. I'm going to talk to him myself this afternoon. Meanwhile I have some dummies I can doctor up to throw in his face if need be."

"Don't say anything about Celia," Sunny warned. "Call me tonight. I don't care what time it is. You know me, I always sleep with one eye open. Try not to get caught. Are you okay with the Mom thing?"

"No, Sunny, I'm not okay with it. I hate it. I don't think this family is ever going to know peace."

"Maybe someday. Have you spoken to Neal in the past few days?"

"We're meeting for coffee in a little while."

"Say hi for me."

"Will do. Take care, Sunny."

Sage looked up from his desk. "Where to, little sister?"

"Meeting on the other side of town with my button supplier. Want to come along? No, huh? I had flowers sent to the hospital and put all our names on the card. I also called the hospital and Marcus is holding his own. When are you going to talk to Jeff?"

"After my meeting with Neal. Where's your power of attorney?"

"Under your elbow. See you later."

Sage spent another hour clearing off his desk. He returned phone calls, separated his mail into two piles, "must deal with" and "delays." As he shifted papers, he called Iris. "Listen, honey, I'm going to stay in town tonight. I'll probably take a room at Babylon or if they're full up I'll crash at Billie's. I'll see you tomorrow evening. You okay, honey?"

"I'm fine, Sage."

"You sound funny. Not funny ha-ha, funny as in something's wrong."

"What could possibly be wrong?"

"That's my question. Since you don't have an answer, I'm going to head out of here. I'm meeting Neal for coffee, then I'm going to surprise Jeff Lassiter. At some point I have to meet up with Celia since I promised Birch. Billie sent flowers to the hospital. She said Marcus is holding his own. Have a good day, honey."

Sage slipped into his jacket and was out of the office in seconds. He did double time going down the street and around the corner to Babylon, entering by the front door. He weaved his way through the narrow aisles filled with a visiting contingent from Boise, Idaho, coming to a stop at the Country Kitchen, where Neal was waiting for him. They shook hands and headed for a table in the back where it was quiet.

"What is going down around here, Neal?"

"The pink slips are going out next week. Supposedly they have already hired new people to replace all twelve of us. We can't confirm it, though. Some kind of secret meetings are going on in the executive dining room all day and all night. Lassiter refers to his office now as the War Room. The ax is getting ready to fall, buddy."

Sage smiled grimly. "Not likely, Neal. I'll have my brother's and sisters' powers of attorney by tomorrow morning. We override Mom when it comes to a vote. None of you are out. If Lassiter paid out any sign-on money, he's going to have to eat it. If possible, we're going to try to buy out his contract and put you in charge. If he doesn't go for the buyout, you're still in charge. He'll just be a figurehead going through the motions to save face. The job should have been yours to begin with. Mom made a mistake. We engaged the services of the Silver Fox."

Neal whistled.

"I'm going to talk with Jeff after we have our coffee. What else is going on?"

"Sage, I hate telling you this crap, but that sister-in-law of yours is on the payroll right here in the casino. Bitsy Drake in Payroll called me at home early this morning to tell me. In this business you have to have spies everywhere, you know that." His tone was defensive-sounding. Sage shrugged.

"Celia? What does she do?"

"No job description. Her salary is $800 a week. That's gross, not net. Hortense, the maid on seven, said she's using Room

719. She asked the head of Housekeeping if she had a key to clean the room. Delphine went to Lassiter, who assured her Hortense was seeing things and no one is in 719. Hortense is now on the unemployment line and Delphine already got her pink slip. Friday's her last day. Sage, those women have been here since Babylon opened. Your father loved both of them. Hell, Delphine knitted him a sweater one Christmas. He left each of them $5000 in his will; you know that, so it should tell you something.''

"We'll just see about that. Tell them both their jobs are secure for as long as they want them. Make sure you get Hortense back here today, even if you have to go to her house to get her. She stays on seven, too. She could probably tell us both stories about that room that would curl our hair. She never, ever breathed a word to anyone. She was definitely loyal to Dad. I guess my next question as much as I don't want to ask it is, does Lassiter hang out in that room, too?''

"The indications are that he does. What the hell is going on, Sage?''

"I don't know. That's the truth. My skin is starting to crawl, though. How about doing a little detective work for me this morning. Check all the stores in the casino and see if Celia has been charging stuff to the family account. If you can, get a copy of the receipts.''

"Sure, no problem. Listen, Sage, there is one other thing. I've been agonizing over this for months now. I've wanted to call you or your mother, but I didn't. It isn't my business, and yet it is my business. Someone came to me the other day. It isn't important who that person is. What is important is the story he told me, complete with pictures. Here, take a look,'' Neal said, withdrawing an envelope from his breast pocket.

"Why do I have the feeling I'm not going to like what I see? Your bald head is glistening with perspiration. That's making me even more nervous.''

Sage rifled through the pictures. "She looks like Billie.''

"It is Billie, Sage. She's wearing different-colored wigs."

"Where the hell did you get these?"

"I told you, a friend. She's gambling. Big time. On the other side of the street."

"Billie! I don't believe that."

"Then why do you look like you believe it? Every day and half the night. We're talking some very big bucks, Sage. She's hooked. That was your old man's biggest fear."

"What was?"

"That one of you kids would get hooked. He made me swear on his life, and I'm not joking, that if I ever got wind of one of you hitting the tables, I would let him know. I'm letting you know, and I'm off the hook."

"I feel sick," Sage said.

"How do you think I felt? The only thing that could make me feel worse would be if it were Sunny. If it were Sunny, I would have dragged her out and demanded an explanation. Your sister Billie and I never had the rapport Sunny and I had. It's always the one you least expect who throws you the curve. If I can do anything, let me know. Good luck with Lassiter."

Sage shoved his coffee cup to the middle of the table. Neal hadn't touched his coffee at all. Billie gambling? Sweet, gentle, workaholic Billie. How had this happened? Why hadn't he seen the signs? He was with her every day, how could he not know something like this was going on? He wondered *exactly* what big bucks meant where Billie was concerned. It certainly explained the four- and five-hour lunches and the dark circles under his sister's eyes in the morning. It probably explained the locked drawer in her desk, too. "Son of a bitch!" he muttered.

Sage stopped at the first phone he came to. He placed five calls, issuing orders in a soft voice before he stomped his way out to the casino floor and then down the corridor that led to Jeff Lassiter's office.

"Sorry, sir, no one goes beyond this point except Mr. Lassiter."

"Get out of my way, you pipsqueak," Sage said as he shouldered the nattily dressed guard aside.

Sage didn't bother knocking. He opened the door, closing it behind him. "It's time to talk, Jeff."

Jeff swiveled his chair around until he was facing Sage. "How did you get in here?"

Sage looked down at his feet. "I walked." He waved the copies of his siblings' powers of attorney under Jeff's nose. "What this means to you is this, you can't fire anyone unless we all agree. We don't agree. If you hired anyone without our approval to replace any old employees and paid sign-on bonuses, you eat those. Neal and the others stay. So does Delphine. Hortense is on her way as we speak. Don't ever do anything like this again. My sisters, my brother, and I are prepared to buy out your contract. Seven hundred and fifty thousand dollars, cash on the line."

Lassiter laughed, a fiendish sound to Sage's ears. "The contract is airtight. Five million, and I might *think* about it." It was Sage's turn to laugh.

"I rather thought that would be your answer. Know this, though, you're going to have a thousand pairs of eyes on you. Every person in this casino is loyal to our family. I want you to remember that. The books are open to every member of this family. A team of forensic accountants will be here starting tomorrow. I don't know what your game is, but whatever it is, it's not going to be at the expense of my sisters and brother. It's obvious to me you have a gripe where the Thornton family is concerned. That gripe might even be justified. I can't undo something my father did, nor can my sisters or brother. My mother made a mistake when she hired you. Legally, we can undo that mistake. However, a deal is a deal. If you plan to earn your livelihood in the gaming business, it is not our intention to thwart those endeavors. My father provided for you and your mother very handsomely. I'm sorry if it wasn't to your liking. As I said, we can't undo his arrangements. All we can do is try to honor, to the best of our ability, the plans he set in motion. So, you collect your pay, you keep your sign-on bonus, and the rest of the casino will be run by Neal. It's a take it or leave it offer.''

Jeff's voice was shaky when he said, ''My contract calls for total control of this casino. Your mother signed it.''

''My mother is only in control when a tiebreaking decision occurs. We outvoted her. Birch, Sunny, Billie, and I are in control. We could force you out of here if we wanted to. My offer stands to buy out your contract. Room 719 goes on the occupancy list at noon today. Hortense is on the way. She'll see to it. If there is anything in that room that doesn't belong there, it's going in the trash.''

Jeff leaned back in his father's old chair. He made a steeple of his fingers just the way Ash Thornton had always done when a problem surfaced. It was uncanny how much he looked like their father, Sage thought, much more so than he or Birch. Sage wasn't sure, but he thought Jeff had the same single-minded determination his father had.

''This is about Celia Thornton, isn't it?''

''No. It's about our employees. We don't like it when strangers mess with other people's lives and destroy their livelihood. If you hadn't done that, we would have taken a backseat and watched your operation. We wouldn't have interfered. Now that you brought up my sister-in-law's name, perhaps we should discuss Celia's role here and what she does to warrant an $800 a week job. That's some very heavy money. No one seems to know where she is or what she does. Would you care to offer an explanation?''

''She came to me and said she needed a job. She said your brother left her with what she called a pittance. She called him a miserly scrooge. I thought your family would want me to help. I did. The two part-time jobs she has, according to her, aren't enough to cover her rent and car rental. Perhaps I was too generous. I find it strange that you object to employee wage problems but aren't the least sympathetic to a family problem.''

''Birch and Celia's affairs are no concern of yours or mine for that matter. You stepped over the line where Celia is concerned, which leads me to believe you have an ulterior motive. What exactly does she do to earn such a princely salary of $800 a week?''

''I hired her as a goodwill house ambassador. As a home economics teacher she wasn't qualified for much else. As I said, I thought I was helping your family.''

''A goodwill house ambassador? You need to define that title, Lassiter.''

''She dresses up. She walks around, smiles, makes nice, that sort of thing.''

''We have at least two hundred goodwill ambassadors who do the same thing for minimum wage, plus tips, plus a bonus at the end of the week. My family has always called them waitresses. It's a damn hard job, that's why we give the girls bonuses at the end of the week. That way we don't have a turnover. It was one of my father's rules. You took away those bonuses, didn't you, you son of a bitch? That's how you were going to pay Celia. It looks to me like you're going to have one hell of a busy day calling all those people back to work and firing their replacements.''

''No.''

''No? Oh, yes.''

''I think we need to call your mother.''

''That's entirely up to you, Lassiter. You look kind of boxed in right now. What's your game anyway?''

The steeple wavered slightly. ''No game. I'm trying to do my best. There is a lot of unnecessary money being spent here. Cutbacks occur all the time. My intentions were and are still honorable. My plan was to save this casino a million dollars a year on wages and bonuses and another two million on over-head.''

"Of which you get a percentage according to your contract."

"I have people working on a game within a game for the slots. That game can triple your revenues the first year. It won't happen overnight, though."

"Using our money, our time, and when it's ready to fly you shop it around to the highest bidder, right?"

Lassiter blinked.

I scored with that one, and I just pulled it out of my head, Sage thought. "Is that why they call these offices the War Room? I understand the executive dining room is off-limits. Where the hell do you get off doing something like that? It's being cleared out as we speak. You are, of course, free to develop anything you want on your own time with your own private payroll. If it happens, Babylon will bid on your game like every other casino. Did I forget anything?"

Lassiter smiled. "Off the top of my head, I'd say no. I'm staying."

"That's your right, according to your contract. As an employee of this casino I'd like it now if you'd accompany me to the seventh floor."

"I'll pass," Lassiter said.

Sage walked around Lassiter's desk. He bent down and yanked the telephone wire out of the wall. "My father used to do that on a regular basis. Actually, my mother did it a few times, too. Sometimes my father was so wise it boggles the mind. Other times he was downright stupid. Will you take care of Celia's pink slip or should I handle it?"

"I'll take care of it."

"Then I guess our business is finished. For now."

"For now. You know the way out."

"War Room, my ass," Sage muttered as he closed the door behind him.

A grim look on his face, Sage rang for the elevator and

punched the number seven. Delphine, the cherub-faced head of Housekeeping, Hortense, and a two-man maintenance crew, along with a locksmith, were waiting. Sage hugged the women, shaking hands with the men before he fit his key into the lock. "I want the room cleaned and aired. It goes on the occupancy list at noon. I want a regulation lock installed. Buck, service the AC. It probably needs Freon. *Everything* in that room goes in the trash. I'll be downstairs in Neal's office if you need me."

Celia Thornton's shrieks and curses followed him to the elevator. How in the hell was he going to explain this to Birch?

"Sunny, would you and Harry like to go out to dinner to an honest-to-God restaurant? I don't think I can eat another burger or bag of french fries. I'm sick of soda. There are a couple of good seafood restaurants on the boardwalk. Your chairs won't be a problem."

"I'm kind of tired. What about Uncle Daniel and Uncle Brad?"

"They turned me down, too."

"Uncle Brad said they're staying on for a half hour or so. They ate lunch late, too. Uncle Daniel said they'd grab something on the way back to the apartment. Why don't you invite Libby? I bet she'd love to go. It's just dinner, Birch. There is nothing wrong with going to dinner. You like her. She's good company, and she knows you're married. You know you're married, too, so what's the big deal?"

"Do you think she'd go? I don't know, Sunny, it might not be a good idea. People start to talk."

"What people? Dinner is dinner. You have a drink, you eat, you go home. Big night in Atlantic City. You could of course take in one of the casinos. Make a night of it. You've been working sixteen hours a day. You deserve a break. Go on, call her. You can always call Celia and tell her your plans if that's what's bothering you."

"Okay, I'll do it."

"Do it now before she makes other plans."

Sunny winked at Harry, who grinned as Birch walked over to the construction phone. "It's just dinner, Harry," Sunny sniffed.

"She said yes."

"Everybody has to eat. The food at the center is good, but it's nice to go out to a restaurant once in a while. Libby's partial to good white wine. I bet you don't have a thing to wear." There was a giggle in Sunny's voice that did not go unnoticed by Birch.

"Can you get back to the center okay?"

"Of course. Uncle Brad is driving us. It's amazing how fast this whole thing has taken hold. One day this was just a wide-open space, and now we're up and running. Four full crews make all the difference in the world. Harry and I won't be here till noon tomorrow. Have a nice dinner, Birch."

Birch leaned over to kiss his sister's cheek. "Have a good night, Sunny. I'm going to call Mom and the medical center before I leave. If I hear anything you should know, I'll give you a call."

"Birch, I've called every day. Marcus is the same. There hasn't been any change."

Birch nodded. "I'm going to call anyway."

It was seven o'clock when Birch escorted Libby through the creaky doors of the Crab Shanty. "It has a seafaring smell to it, doesn't it?" Birch grinned.

"Do you suppose being on the ocean has anything to do with it? Maybe it's all these fishnets and anchors. Or maybe it's the pirate getups the help wears."

"Probably all of the above. I heard this is the best place on the boardwalk. I've always been partial to red-checkered tablecloths and peanut shells on the floor." Birch held a chair for Libby at a table that was nestled in a far corner next to a blazing fireplace.

"This is pleasant. I love a fire. A friend of mine told me that makes me a nester. I like to curl up with a book or just sit and stare into the fire. I've always been a homebody. How about you, Birch?"

"I like a fire myself. Believe it or not, Sage and I were Boy Scouts. Mom used to send us out for firewood that Chue cut. We'd haggle over the logs, betting which one would burn the longest. We do come from a gambling family after all. My mother had these wonderful big, old red chairs. Two people could sit on one. They were in her studio. We'd all huddle and drink hot chocolate. It's a very pleasant memory. How about you?"

"Growing up those things were in a wish book. I grew up in an orphanage. I was out and on my own at seventeen. I worked my way through college with student loans I'm still paying off. Another year and I'm free and clear. By then my car will finally surrender to some junkyard and I'll be in debt again." Libby's voice was wistful when she said, "What's it like to live in a real family? Sunny told me what it was like from her perspective. I'd like to hear what it was like for you." She looked up at the waitress. "I'll have a bottle of Budweiser."

"Make that two. Sunny said you liked good wine."

"Sometimes."

Birch stared at his dinner companion. She wasn't beautiful, but she was attractive in a wholesome way. Sunny had said she wore glasses from time to time. He wondered if they were wire-rimmed or shell-framed. It would be a shame to hide her eyes, which were the same color as the bluebells Chue raised in the greenhouse. He said so. She smiled. He thought he'd never seen a nicer smile. It crinkled around her mouth and up to the corners of her eyes. She made a self-conscious face and laughed, a sweet sound of mirth.

"So what do you think?"

"About what?"

"You were studying me as though you were committing me to memory. Tell me what you see. You also didn't answer my question about what it was like to grow up with a real family."

"It was pretty wonderful. We lived on an incredible mountain. Mom's the greatest. Dad left a lot to be desired during that time. We hung out together. I guess that's why we're still so close. When my grandmother was alive she'd tell us stories about what it was like back in the old days when Vegas was just a dust ball. It was the best of all times. No worries, no one was jealous of anyone else. I think Sage and I spent our entire youth trying to figure a way to best Sunny. I would have been happy to beat her at marbles. That's pretty much it. I'm a people person. I used to watch the customers at the casino sixteen hours a day. Sometimes I'd make up these little scenarios, but I never knew if I was on the money or not. I'd say you're a what-you-see-is-what-you-get kind of person. You know your business. You like what you do. You're probably grossly underpaid and yet you can't see yourself doing anything but what you're doing. That makes you a dedicated person who has ideals and principles."

"Sunny talks too much."

Birch leaned across the table. "Sunny didn't tell me anything where you're concerned. She said she liked you and that you were a good therapist. That's all. I would have figured it out on my own because you have to be damn good to work at any of our centers. Your turn."

Libby leaned into the table, the yellow glow from the candles highlighting her hair, bringing out its rich copper color. A small parade of freckles marched across the bridge of her nose. "I see an unhappy man. I read an article once by some psychologist who said a person's eyes are the mirrors of his soul. I think I believe that. You don't smile much, do you? Tell me something. What would it take to make you happy?"

Birch sipped at his beer. "Right now I can't answer that.

Not too long ago I thought I knew the answer. Man, was I wrong. I need to fall back and more or less regroup. I guess you could say I'm in my search mode. What would it take to make you happy?''

''I'm quite happy now. I know there is more out there. When it's my turn, it will happen. Having a husband who loves me and whom I love, kids, pets, a small house with a real fireplace. I'd like to see my husband mow the lawn and grumble when the dog pees on the carpet. I don't want a husband who someday might break my heart. My game plan calls for one marriage, one husband. My biological clock is ticking, and I can hear it. If it doesn't happen, I'll adopt a child and find a way to buy my own little house. My life won't depend on a man, but I would like to have one included in my life. Don't get the idea I'm one of those women's libbers because I'm not.''

''My next question was going to be, why haven't you married?''

''I got close a couple of times. When it was down to the wire, I realized they didn't want the same things I did. At one point I bought a wedding gown on time payments. It's still in the box. I paid it off, too.''

Birch laughed. ''Look at it this way, if someone sweeps you off your feet, you're prepared. How about another beer?''

''Okay. I'm going to have the all-you-can-eat crab legs with a loaded baked potato, blue cheese on my salad, garlic bread with a side order of shrimp.''

''I'll have the same thing.''

Libby shivered inside her heavy sweater. ''I like your sweater with all those reindeer prancing about,'' Birch said ''It's unusual.''

''That's because I made it. I ski when I can. Do you ski?''

''Oh yeah. Maybe we can find a place and do it some Sunday. I haven't skied for a long time. Sage does it every winter. Iris skis, too. They're teaching the kids. They do everything together as a family. I like that.''

"I love Iris. She's so *normal*. I don't think I know anyone, and I know a lot of people, who could have stepped in and adopted kids and loved them like they're her own. You have a very nice family. At first Sunny used to break my heart when she'd talk about her family. She's okay with it now, though. Working for your uncles is the best thing you could have done for her. Harry too. He loves your sister so much. It's so good to watch the two of them as they help each other make up for their shortcomings. All we're doing is talking about me. Tell me about you. Come on now, share, what would it take to make you really happy?"

"Okay, but this is off the top of my head. To feel at peace. To wake up next to someone I knew would be waiting for me at the end of the day."

"Like someone who would make you stay in bed when you have a cold, someone who would bring you chicken soup and who would keep the kids quiet and the dog off the bed?"

"Yeah, yeah. Exactly." Birch felt like she'd just given him the answer to life's problems. "How did you know?"

"Sunny told me. She said you just didn't know it yet. She loves you very much. You shouldn't be so tormented where Sunny is concerned. She picks up on it."

"I feel like I let her down. I should have been here for her, but it was at a time in my life where I was having trouble helping myself. I regret it now. God, it's great having her here. Sunny could always run circles, physically and mentally, around Sage and me. Things are so limited for her now. Is she truly contented?"

"Look at me, Birch. We are on a first-name basis, right?" Birch nodded and grinned. "Sunny is happy. Sunny is contented. She deals with everything right up front. Now, if things change somewhere along the way, I don't know what she'll do. I tend to think she'll deal with it then in her own forthright way. Every day I try subtly to reinforce that in some way.

Someday I might leave, and Sunny would have to deal with that loss.''

''You wouldn't do that, would you?''

''I might. It isn't the best-paying job in the world. I'm also on call, so I can't moonlight. I don't want to get burned out. My white knight might appear. Sunny and I have discussed all of this. She's okay with it; so is Harry. Would you look at the size of those platters? Do you think we can eat all of this?''

Birch stared first at Libby and then at the seafood platters. She might leave. At some point in time. For a single second he thought his heart stopped beating.

''What's wrong?''

''This is weird. I started to miss you.''

Crab leg in one hand, crab cracker in the other, Libby stared into Birch's eyes. She didn't mean to say the words. They just tumbled out. ''Then I won't go.'' She looked away to cover her confusion. ''I did say that, didn't I?''

''Uh-huh. I feel a lot better now.''

''I feel kind of foolish,'' Libby said.

''Is something happening here?'' Birch asked softly.

''I'm not sure,'' Libby said.

''We should probably eat this mountain of food in front of us.''

Libby nodded.

''Who named you Libertine?''

''Sunny. It's a joke. My name is Liberty. I named myself when I was seven years old. Someone just . . . dumped me off in a basket at the front door. Liberty seemed appropriate at the time.'' She cracked one of the crab legs. Juice spurted across the table and onto Birch's face. ''Oh, God, I'm sorry.'' A second later she was on her feet, leaning across the table, wiping Birch's face with her napkin.

Birch's heart thundered in his chest. He could smell the sweet soap and water scent of her, smelled the ocean in her hair and the fish on her fingers. He wondered if Libby could hear his heart beating. He reached for her hand. "It's okay. Really, it's okay." Flustered, Libby sat down and stared at her plate.

"You're married," Libby said bluntly.

"Yes," Birch responded just as bluntly.

"These crab legs are probably the best I've ever eaten," Libby said.

"I'd say so," Birch said.

"Neither one of us has tasted them yet," Libby said.

"I know. I'm assuming they're good."

"Oh," Libby said.

"Would you like to walk on the beach? It's cold but we're both dressed for it."

Libby had her jacket on before Birch finished speaking.

Birch laid some bills on the table. He followed Libby from the restaurant.

Halfway down the beach Birch said, "Sunny told me you were my destiny. Are you?" His voice was so hoarse and gruff-sounding, Libby shivered as his words were carried away on the wind.

"You're married."

"I know. You didn't answer my question."

"Yes. And we can do nothing about it."

"I know," Birch said. He reached for her hand. She clasped it tightly in her own.

"It's getting late. We should be getting back."

"Is that what you want?"

"No, but it's what we're going to do. Until you can tell me your middle name is Liberty, the way mine is, it's the way it has to be. Liberty means free, did you know that? I don't think I could live here year-round. I miss Nevada and the desert."

They were back on safe ground. "You adjust. I didn't think I would ever get used to living in a Third World country, but I did. Race you to the pier!

"You beat me!" Birch growled, startled at Libby's athletic ability.

Panting, Libby said, "Sunny said you were a fast starter and played out quickly. She said the secret to beating you was to take it slow and steady. The sand was a hindrance, and you're wearing those cloppy work boots. I'll give you another chance to beat me someday."

Someday.

"Oh, Ruby, I'm so glad you came. I need to talk to you," Iris said as she fell into Ruby's outstretched arms.

"Iris, nothing is so bad that it can't be fixed. Honey, all you have are suspicions. You need to talk to Sage. Why are you being so stubborn?"

"Ruby, Sage came home last night smelling of perfume. It's the same kind my mother-in-law uses. Sage hasn't seen his mother. Why would my husband smell like perfume? Give me one reason. Just one, Ruby. He's not coming home tonight. He called earlier. Do you know what I did an hour ago, Ruby? I called Celia. Just to chat. She was very pleasant on the phone. My blood ran cold. I managed to work my way around to perfume and what do you know, she said she bought a bottle of the same stuff. I can't pronounce it, and neither could she. She knew exactly what I was talking about, though. She even described the damn bottle."

"What if you're wrong, Iris?"

Iris burst into tears. "That's why I can't say anything to Sage until I'm one hundred percent certain. He knows something's wrong. I'm having a hard time pretending. I'm blaming everything on this pregnancy. I'm buying emotional time, Ruby, because I don't know what else to do. If I'm wrong, I don't want Sage ever to know I doubted him."

"Oh, honey, honesty is always best. I've seen a lot of bums in my day, but your husband isn't one. All you have to do is look at that sweet guy to know he'd never do anything like that.''

"Sage is his father's son. I can't discount that either. There is such a pile of incriminating evidence. The perfume was the clincher. He isn't coming home tonight. It isn't as though he works at a job that would keep him in overtime, much less double overtime. Be honest, Ruby, this whole thing is suspect. If there was a problem, Sage would have confided in me. He always likes two minds that come to the same conclusion.''

"You could go to town. Or, we, as in you and me, could go to town and do some spying on our own. Two sets of eyes are better than one. It has to be your decision, Iris.''

Iris started to whimper. "What if . . . what if we . . . find out something that's conclusive? If that happens, I have to make a decision. I could never stay with a man who cheated on me. Where am I going to go with the kids? I can't get a job now because I'm pregnant. I want to be with my babies when they're born. I could never go off and leave them with a sitter. I'm between a rock and a hard place.''

"So what you're saying is you want to stay here and be miserable and believe the worst rather than deal with it?''

"It sounds terrible when you say it like that, Ruby.''

"How else can I say it, Iris? Why don't we talk to Fanny?''

"Fanny has more on her plate than she can handle right now. Something's going on with Jeff Lassiter. I heard Sage on the phone with Birch. Whatever *that* is, it involves Fanny. I don't need to add to her problems.''

"Then why don't I go to town and do some spying on my own. I'll do anything not to deal with those chickens. If I leave now, I can be in town by ten-thirty. Things just start to heat up around that time.''

"If you find out anything, will you tell me the truth?''

"Of course I'll tell you the truth.''

"Even if it's bad?''

"Even if it's bad. I'm going to stop by the medical center.

Things always seem really bad at night when you're waiting for word the way Fanny is. Do you happen to know if anyone called Billie Kingsley or Bess?''

''I don't know. I think Fanny would have called them. Those three women are like the Three Musketeers. When one is in pain or trouble, they appear. It's the way it is. I want you to know, Ruby, I would have gone down, but Sage forbade it. I'm sorry to say I listened to him. Some days I think I don't have a mind of my own anymore. Will you tell that to Fanny for me?''

''I'll tell her, Iris. Now, tell me exactly what you want me to do?''

''I want you to find out who's in Room 719. Check out Jeff Lassiter. Try to find out where Sage is. He said he might stay with Billie or take a room at Babylon. This is Celia's address and phone number. Check her out, too. Find out about that perfume. If you're going to see Fanny, ask her for the name of it. She only uses one kind, and she knows the French pronunciation. I'll wait up for your call. I appreciate this, Ruby.''

''I know you do, honey. Don't be surprised if I come up dry.''

''I have a feeling, Ruby, in the deepest part of my gut, that you're going to need a heavy-duty raincoat.''

Ruby wrapped Iris in her arms. ''My mother, who might have been many things to many people, was the wisest and best mother in the world. She always told me no matter how dark the tunnel was, there was always a light at the end. If you weren't pregnant, you'd be viewing this whole situation differently. I want you to go to bed, and I want you to sleep. Those dark circles under your eyes are not becoming. I'm going to go back to the ranch to change my clothes after I stop to see Fanny. I prefer to look a little flashy opposed to this schoolmarm look I'm sporting. I'll call you first thing in the morning.''

"Thanks for coming to the mountain, Ruby. Thanks for everything."

In the car with the engine running, Ruby stretched her neck to look into the rearview mirror. "Ruby, you are a fool for getting involved in other people's lives. It sure beats watching the chickens roost," she answered herself.

8

Fanny leaned her head back on the chair rest. She made a mental note to write a letter to the board of trustees asking for new comfortable chairs in the waiting room. On second thought, instead of asking, she'd *demand* they order new chairs. She wondered what the theory was behind the chair she was sitting in. Did the purchasing agent deliberately set out to order these miserable chairs in the hopes people would go home instead of staying here for all hours? Or, was he taken advantage of because of the Thornton name? She looked around at the shabby furnishings. The center hadn't looked like this when John Noble was in charge. The two sofas were worn, the armrests frayed the way the edges of the cushions were. The artificial rubber plants were dusty, the artificial Spanish moss trailed limply down the sides of the lopsided wicker baskets. Nothing in the room matched the pictures on the walls whose frames were a mix of metal and wood. The pictures were ordinary splashes of dull, annoying color. The carpet, whose color defied description, had worn paths that crisscrossed. Probably because families paced their way around the room the way she'd been doing for the past five days. Or was it six days? Maybe it was seven. Just this afternoon she'd counted the wet towels in her bathroom at home. Was it six or seven? She couldn't remember.

They wanted her to go home. They kept offering to drive her home. *They.* The staff nurses, the doctors that were taking care of Marcus. As if she cared what *they* thought. She poured coffee from a thermos she'd brought from home. *They* didn't like that either. They offered her coffee every fifteen minutes. Coffee that looked like colored brown water and tasted like colored brown water.

Maybe she should go home and mow the grass. Fanny's brow furrowed. Did Chue mow the grass yesterday before he came down to visit Marcus? He'd said he was taking the dogs to Sunrise since she spent so much time at the center. He'd brought her rice cakes. Did she eat them? Did she eat at all yesterday? She couldn't remember.

Pull the plug. Nobody was saying the words aloud, but it was what they wanted her to do. Pull the plug. Couldn't they come up with a better way of phrasing such a horrible thing? You pulled the plugs on lamps, refrigerators, and televisions when there was an electrical storm. Couldn't they say disconnect, turn off the current? No, they whispered among themselves as they covertly looked at her from their two-way windows, mouthing the hateful words. *They* weren't God. Nobody had the right to take her husband's life. Nobody.

Fanny emptied the thermos. She panicked until she remembered she had another thermos in her knitting bag. She closed her eyes, wishing for the miracle of sleep, but it eluded her. Maybe she would never sleep again. Maybe she'd stay in this uncomfortable chair for the rest of her life. She looked around at the empty waiting room. For days now, she'd been the only occupant. She wondered if it was because of the worn, ugly furnishings. Was it possible Marcus was the only ill person in the whole center?

So alone. Was it supposed to be like this? First Ash, then Simon, and now Marcus. Was she meant to live out her days alone? God must think so since He took two husbands from her and was currently working on her third. What kind of God did things like that? Maybe she was only supposed to have one husband. Maybe God thought she was a loose woman. Maybe God didn't want her to have three husbands. Maybe a lot of things. *Please, God, let me sleep. Let me wake to find this is all a bad dream. Please.*

Fanny heard whispering behind her hair. God talking to her? She drank the last of the coffee. She didn't think she had the strength to fumble for the second thermos or to open it. "Stop whispering. If You have something to say to me, say it."

"Fanny, it's Billie. Bess and John are here with me. Fanny, why didn't you call us? How long have you been here?"

"I don't know. Six towels. It seems like a long time. I wish you hadn't come. How did you find out?"

"Thad's staff reads all the newspapers. He saw the article on Marcus. I called Bess on the ship to shore phone. Come on, we're taking you home. John's here now. He's going to meet us back at the house. My God, Fanny, you must have lost twenty pounds. When was the last time you ate or slept? Where are the kids?"

Fanny shrugged. "They deserted me."

"I don't believe that," Bess said.

"I wouldn't do what they wanted, so they deserted me. It's no big deal. They've done it before. They sent flowers. Do you believe that? Even an idiot knows you can't have flowers in ICU. They smelled sickening, like death. I told the nurses to throw them out. Chue came. Good old Chue. I can always count on Chue. You can never count on your children. All they do is break your heart. Sallie was right. Sallie was always right.''

Billie stopped in mid-stride. "No, Fanny, Sallie was not always right. More often than not she was wrong. Bess, take her other arm. She can barely stand up."

"How have you been getting back and forth, Fanny?" Bess asked.

"I drove. Sometimes off the road. I got here, didn't I? It doesn't matter. Don't you understand, nothing matters? I give up and want everyone to know I give up. Tell everyone for me. Tell my shitty kids, tell Ash's son and his sister. Tell the whole damn world. Fanny Logan Thornton Thornton Reed finally gives up!"

"Oh, no, that's too easy," Billie said.

"Billie's right, that's too easy," Bess said. "Easy, Billie, I have a good grip on her."

"Where are you taking me? I don't want to go. I want to die in that ugly chair. Don't you get it? I—don't—care."

"Get in the car, Fanny," Bess said.

Too weak to argue, Fanny fell across the backseat. Billie started the engine.

"Are you going to talk about me now the way the nurses do?"

"Yes," Bess snarled. "How did you let yourself get like this?"

"It was easy. When you don't care anymore, everything gets easy. They think it's easy to pull a plug. You have to be tough to do that. You have to have guts to do that. I'm not tough, and I don't have any guts because I don't care. What time is it? What day is it?"

"If you don't care about anything, why do you want to know?" Bess asked from the front seat.

"Just for the record. I don't want you here. Go back on your cruise ship and send Billie back to Washington. Go home."

"We don't care what you want," Billie called over her shoulder. "We're here, and we're staying. Get that through your head."

"I want to be by myself. I have to think about everything and don't want you here pep-talking me. I told you, I give up. When you give up there is nothing to talk about."

"So think. No one is stopping you from thinking," Bess said. "Only quitters give up. You're no quitter, Fanny. You worked damn hard to get to this point in time, and Billie and I aren't about to let you give up. Think as much as you want as long as you come up with the right answers."

Fanny struggled to sit up. "I can't do anything right. How do you expect me to come up with right answers to anything?"

"We're here to help you. We're friends, Fanny. Did you forget that? The answers are there. You simply have to explore all of your options. It's a weeding-out process. You've done it all your life, so you can do it again."

"That's a laugh," Fanny snorted. "I don't want to go in there, I hate this house. I sit in the garage with the door open. When I called for the ambulance, I told them my name was Fanny Thornton. Why did I do that? It means something. Stop looking at me like that. I know I look terrible, and I don't care."

"Why do you hate your new house? You and Marcus built it together. Saying you were Fanny Thornton doesn't mean diddly-squat. You've been a Thornton most of your life. It was a slip of the tongue. Somewhere in your mind you probably thought the ambulance would get here sooner if you used the family name. You were in shock, Fanny. You're still in shock," Bess said.

"Those are just words. You're trying to humor me. Go away."

"Why?" Bess asked again.

"Because something will happen to you if you stay. Something happens to everyone who . . . everyone dies. You have husbands who love you. I'm not supposed to have a husband.''

Billie shook Fanny's shoulders. ''Who told you something like that?''

''Me. Nobody has to tell me anything. Something's wrong with me. Just go away and leave me alone. I didn't invite you here.''

''Listen to me, Fanny. I want you to sit on this kitchen chair and not move. I'm going to make you something to eat, and you're going to eat every bite of it. Bess and I are here, and we're staying as long as you need us. After you eat you're going to bed to sleep the clock around. Bess and I won't let anything happen while you're sleeping. When you wake up, we'll talk.''

An hour later, Billie looked at Bess across the kitchen table. ''This isn't good, Bess. In all the years I've known Fanny, I've never known her to be anything but strong and positive. The first thing we need to do is call the kids to find out what went wrong. I think we'll have a better handle on the situation once we talk to them. You call, Bess, and I'll make some fresh coffee.''

''That's it, Billie,'' Bess said, hanging up the phone. ''Sunny has retired for the night and no calls are put through after nine o'clock. Birch is out for the evening. Iris said Sage stayed in town. Billie's answering machine comes on, so that must mean she's out for the evening, too. All Iris knows is there is a problem with Jeff Lassiter and the casino. Now what?''

''Now you open the door since someone is knocking.''

''Ruby!''

''Am I intruding? I stopped by the medical center, but they said Fanny left with two women. I was hoping it was you two. How is she?''

''She's feeling down. She hasn't slept or eaten. What's been going on, do you know?''

''I only know what Iris told me. It doesn't concern Fanny,

so I don't think I should betray her confidences. It's a personal thing between her and Sage. They're having twins, you know. Everyone gets emotional over something like that.''

"Twins!'' Billie and Bess exclaimed as one.

"Yes, twins. Is there anything I can do?''

"No. There's nothing for us to do either. We're waiting for John to come back from the center.''

"Try calling the casino to have Sage paged or ask for Neal and have him locate Sage. Iris said he might take a room or stay with Billie this evening. I'm going to stop at the casino on my way home. If I see Sage, I'll tell him to call. I called the center every day for an update on Marcus's condition. I asked to speak to Fanny, but the nurses said she wouldn't take the calls. The children should be here. I wish I understood this family a little better. Call me if you need me.''

"We will. Thanks for stopping by, Ruby. I'll tell Fanny you were here when she wakes up.''

"Now what?'' Bess asked.

"We wait. Gin rummy?''

"Sure.''

Jeff Lassiter opened the door to his office. He reached out and yanked Celia Thornton into the room.

"Do you mind telling me what the hell is going on here? Those housekeepers made me move out of the room. I'm lucky I got my stuff out. Now what am I supposed to do?''

"That's only part of it. You're off the payroll, thanks to your brother-in-law Sage.''

"I don't understand. What does Sage have to do with this? You told me you were in total control.''

"He knew about Room 719. The others knew about it, too. It seems they've banded together to get me out of here. They offered to buy out my contract, but I stood firm. At the moment, I'm a figurehead. It's ugly, and it's going to get uglier because they've consulted an attorney. I'm not worried about that, though. I heard just a little while ago that all those fancy things you bought are now public knowledge. Sage has the receipts. I would imagine he's going to present them to your husband. He knows you moved into 719. I don't know how he found out, Celia. I suppose he has spies the way I have spies, the way Neal Tortolow has spies. No one trusts anyone in this business. I think he thinks something is going on between the two of us.''

''He can think whatever he wants. I know how to take care of Sage Thornton. You disappointed me, Jeff. I believed you when you said you were going to own this place someday. Now you tell me you're a mere figurehead. This is not going according to plan.''

''You can't blame me for this. It's a temporary setback, nothing more. Fanny didn't tell me her children held the controlling interest in this casino. It's fine. I have three years to take over this place. It's a wise man who bides his time and strikes when the time is right. It simply means I switch to Plan B.''

''Where does that leave me?''

''Exactly where you were before. You work at your jobs and stay in your apartment. You can win enough at the tables with my system to keep you in the style you wish to accustom yourself to. Just don't get greedy. Your brother-in-law is in the casino. I think it's safe to say he's spying. Let's give him something to spy on. Hit the twenty-one tables. You know what to do. My advice would be to pay off those bills. I have this feeling your brother-in-law isn't buying into that sweet, innocent act you put on when you first got here. At some point he's going to share that knowledge with his brother and sisters. He may already have done that for all we know. Everyone knows what a close-knit little group they are. Sage sees you as the opportunist that you are.''

"Tell me again why I put my eggs in your basket instead of my husband's, Jeff," Celia snarled.

"You aligned yourself with me because you know I have the capability to take this casino for every dime in its coffers. I also have the capability of making all the other casino owners sit up and beg. It might take me every bit of the three years on my contract, but it will happen. Your take is 10 percent as we agreed. If things change, that percentage can go up or down. Your future will be secure, and you'll never have to worry about money. Did I miss anything? Oh, yes, Celia, what are you going to do about your husband? Your part of the deal was you'd be on the inside and able to feed me information. You got greedy, and now we're in this fix."

"I don't agree. I can wrap Birch around my fingers, and there are ways to get information without being on the inside. Being a Thornton has its advantages. I'm not sure I want to give that up."

"What will you do if Birch wants to give *you* up?"

"It won't happen. If it does, then I get down and ugly. He's the one who slapped me around. It was pure dumb luck that I remembered the Polaroid camera Birch brought back in his duffel bag. All I had to do was stand in front of the mirror and snap. The bruises showed up magnificently. Spouse abuse works wonders in divorce cases. Especially when there is proof. Tap into that fancy-dancy computer of yours and tell me which room Sage booked for the night." Jeff's eyebrows shot up to his hairline. He tapped at the keys.

"He's in Room 1611. You are a little devil, aren't you?"

"A key would be nice, Jeff. A girl's gotta do what a girl's gotta do. I found out the hard way if you don't look out for number one, no one else will." Celia pocketed the master key Jeff handed her. "I'll probably be calling you later, so be available. We discussed this a few days ago. You know what you have to do. I'll see you later."

*   *   *

Sage was dodging a group of tourists exiting the hanging gardens when he heard the high-pitched babble of excited voices coming from the twenty-one tables. He worked his way across the floor in time to see Celia rake in a pile of chips. She scooped them up into a large cardboard bucket. She tossed one of the chips to the dealer before she turned to leave the table, her winnings clasped tightly against her chest.

"Lucky night?" Sage said. His voice was cool, matter-of-fact, his eyes openly suspicious as he eyed the bucket of hundred- and thousand-dollar chips.

"You wouldn't believe how lucky. Here, these are for you to pay off the things I charged. We're square now. I suppose you plan to tell Birch."

"What makes you say that?"

"My womanly intuition. How about buying me a drink? There are some extra chips in the bucket that will cover the bar tab. It's almost time to head home. Gambling is very stressful. A drink will help me unwind. I have a subbing job tomorrow. You just wouldn't believe the trouble I've had. I bought this answering machine and hooked it up wrong. I'm not the least bit mechanically minded. I guess I lost more messages than I got. Jeff was good enough to put me up here at the hotel when my apartment got overrun with roaches. They used some kind of killer spray that wasn't good for humans to breathe. You know, the fumes. Anyway, I'm back in the apartment, my machine is working, and I'm working. My job here fell through. You'd think being a Thornton would help my résumé. Did you have anything to do with that, Sage?" Celia asked playfully as she wagged a finger under Sage's nose.

Sage laughed as he headed for the Harem Lourge, the bucket of chips clasped securely in his hands.

"Gin and tonic," Celia said to the bartender.

"Beer," Sage said. He set the container of chips on the bar.

Celia crossed her legs as she swiveled the barstool till it was facing Sage. "What are you doing in town tonight? Birch said you hated this place."

"Business."

"At this time of night! Oh, I get it, monkey business, right?"

"Wrong. It's late now, so there's no point in heading up the mountain. It's one of the nicer perks about this place. Birch asked me to take you to lunch or dinner."

"Are you asking me to go to lunch or dinner or are you telling me that's what Birch wants you to do?"

"Would you like to have lunch, Celia?" His voice was so prim and polite, Celia smiled.

"I would, Sage, if I thought you genuinely wanted to have lunch with me. Taking me to lunch because someone asked you to doesn't make for an enjoyable luncheon. Besides, I work the lunch hour at the Golden Nugget. I was never big on lunch to begin with. I suppose I should thank you for asking, though. What is it about me that you don't like, Sage?"

"Where did you get the idea that I don't like you?"

Celia smiled. "From you. It's okay. I have a whole list of people I don't like. You aren't on my list, Sage. Thanks for the drink." Celia slipped off the barstool. Before Sage knew what was happening, she kissed him soundly on the mouth. "No hard feelings, Sage," she cooed as she playfully tweaked his nose. "I'll see *you* later." She raised her voice to make sure the bartender heard her and also noticed her little byplay.

Ruby stood in the doorway to the bar. Her jaw dropped. She turned around just as Celia exited the bar. What did, I'll see *you* later mean?

"Celia! What a surprise! It's so nice to see you. How's Birch? I was just going to treat myself to a nightcap before heading back to the ranch. Would you care to join me?"

"I don't think so, Ruby, but thanks for asking. I have a teaching job tomorrow, so I have to get up early. Perhaps another time."

"We could make it a cola. When I was your age, I could stay up till the wee hours and still go to work. Stamina is such a wonderful thing. I insist, Celia," Ruby said, leading Celia to a sofa in the hotel area across from the registration desk. "Maybe we should have coffee. How was your night?"

"Actually, Ruby, it was quite wonderful. I won a lot of money at twenty-one, but I had to give it to Sage to pay off some things I charged. I pretty much went berserk when I went shopping. Birch frowns on things like that. I'm just lucky I won. Birch is such a . . . tightwad."

"I would have thought he was generous. The others are. How is he? Does he like Atlantic City? I'm still hoping he'll give the ranch serious consideration."

"He said he's into it. He likes building things. He took some great pictures of the village he built in Costa Rica. We could have dinner one night this week, and I'll show them to you. They're Polaroids, though." Celia's voice turned wistful when she said, "I miss him. I wouldn't count on him as far as the ranch is concerned. Personally, I thought it was a very generous offer."

"If you miss Birch, why don't you join him? I don't understand you young people today. If I was married to someone like Birch, I'd be all over him twenty-four hours a day."

"We have some things to work out, Ruby. I made some mistakes when we first arrived, and now I have to find a way to make them right. Birch wanted . . . expected certain things and . . . I got caught up in the glitz and glamour. Things didn't work out the way either of us expected. Birch got violent and used his fists. I couldn't go out for a few days. Don't get the idea I was blameless because I wasn't. I'm even willing to take the blame for my part in the whole thing. A little distance between us for a while will help things. We'll work it out because we love each other. How are you doing, Ruby?''

Ruby pretended shock for Celia's benefit. ''Very few changes occur in my life on a daily basis. For the most part I lead a very orderly existence. I'm still looking for someone to take over the ranch. Have you been to the medical center to see Marcus?'' Ruby said in one long rush.

''No. I've been thinking about it, though. I sent a card to Fanny, one of those cheerful, keep your chin up things. I made so many stupid mistakes in the beginning I didn't want to make another one by invading her privacy. I did call earlier. I wanted to be able to tell Birch something tonight when I called.''

''Tell him Billie, Bess, and John arrived a few hours ago.''

''Thanks for telling me that. I know Birch will be relieved. Something's going on with all of them and their mother. Birch didn't elaborate, and, as I said, I learned my lesson earlier, so I don't question him. Now, let's firm up a dinner date for the end of the week. I've really got to go home, Ruby. Six o'clock rolls around quickly. It was so nice running into you. Be careful driving home.''

''How about Friday evening? Sevenish at Peridot. Peridot is Fanny's favorite restaurant. Actually, I think it's everyone's favorite restaurant.''

''I'll look forward to it. Take care, Ruby.''

''Give my regards to Birch.''

''I'll do that.''

Ruby watched Celia weave her way across the casino floor. She wondered why she wasn't exiting by the hotel door if she was really leaving the casino. She stood, her eyes following the electric blue beaded gown that was brighter than the neon overhead. She decided to follow Celia. She didn't know how she knew, but she knew Celia Thornton wasn't going back to her apartment. The night was too young to retire the sparkly blue dress. She was proved right minutes later when Celia left the casino by one of the side doors. She risked a glance at her watch; 10:55. Somewhere along the way, Celia had picked up a matching shawl. She watched as Celia threw it over her shoulder with a carelessness of long practice. Ruby's eyes narrowed. "Just what do we have here?" she murmured aloud.

Following Celia to the casino across the street was easy, the glittering dress showing her the way. Ruby watched as Celia flirted outrageously with the customers. At one point she playfully swatted a slot player when he reached out to pat her rear end. She stopped just long enough to take a sip from a glass he held out. This young lady had definitely been "around the block," Ruby thought.

Ruby stayed on the fringe as Celia fought her way to the twenty-one tables, where she patiently waited for a seat. When a seat opened, Celia sat down and to Ruby's inexperienced eye, proceeded to act like an experienced gambler. Ninety minutes later, Celia carried her chips to the cashier's window, $17,000 richer for the experience.

"I'm not cut out for this detective business," Ruby muttered to herself as Celia bought herself a drink at the bar. She chatted and flirted with the bartender as well as the men at the bar for thirty minutes. *It's like she's on a time schedule*, Ruby thought as Celia kept glancing at her watch.

Ruby looked at her own watch and was dismayed to see that it was five minutes past two. She wished she were home in bed.

Again she followed the sparkly dress out of the casino and back to Babylon. Ruby made sure she stayed far enough away to observe the young Mrs. Thornton, but not close enough to be seen and recognized. At twenty minutes past two, Jeff Lassiter strolled nonchalantly into the Harem Lounge. He exited almost immediately, followed by Celia a few minutes later. Ruby stayed on her trail until she felt a light tap to her shoulder. Panic-stricken, she whirled around.

"Are you having some kind of problem, ma'am? I've been watching you all night. Why don't we go somewhere that's quiet so we can talk?"

He looked like a nice young man but Ruby was having none of it. She shook off his hand, her eyes searching for the shimmering blue dress that was headed for the elevators. "Listen, I'm undercover," she hissed, "and you're interfering with my job. My name is Ruby Thornton. Run it by your boss, what's his name, Neal? He'll vouch for me. Now, scat, before I make a scene." The elevator door closed just as Ruby reached it. There was nothing for her to do but watch the lighted arrows at the top of the elevator. The elevator stopped at the sixteenth floor. Were there other people in the elevator? She had no way of knowing. When the elevator door opened, she emitted a sigh of relief. Good. Now all she had to do was find out what room Sage was in?

"Ma'am?"

"I thought I told you to stop bothering me. You made me lose . . . Never mind. What do you want now?"

"I want you to come with me."

"That's not likely to happen, young man. I don't like pushy people. I'm not doing anything wrong."

"You look like you're stalking someone."

"Your eyes are deceiving you, young man. I do not stalk. Men do that to unsuspecting women. You're trying to put me on the defensive. You're stalking me! The things we Thorntons have to put up with. I want you to leave me alone."

"I work here."

"Well, guess what, my family owns this casino. Are we having a standoff here?"

"It would appear so," the young man said, his voice edgy.

"Is there a problem, Anthony?" Neal Tortolow, head of Security and floor manager, asked, coming up behind his Security guard.

"Yes, there is a problem," Ruby said. "You know me, don't you?"

"Of course, Miss Thornton. What's the problem?"

"I'm conducting family business here this evening. Your man here just crimped my style. The person I was observing got away from me. This is not something the family would want to . . . you know, get out. Do you mind if I leave now?"

"Can I help? Do you care to be more explicit?"

Ruby sighed. "Without mentioning names will it help if I say it's about the young you-know-who and the other young you-know-who, both newcomers to this establishment?"

Neal's brow furrowed. "Oh." He nodded and waved her on.

"Anthony, this is one of those things you learn to deal with as you gain more experience. You were diligent and I commend that in my employees. Miss Thornton is family. Take a break and wind down."

Neal kept his eyes on the bank of elevators. What the hell was going on and *where* was it going on? The old lady was undercover on a matter that concerned two people known as "you-know-who." At two-thirty in the morning, it was par for the course.

Neal scribbled a note to himself and stuck it in his breast pocket. The elevator stopped on sixteen—Anthony said customer in blue dress took elevator to sixteen prior to his discussion with Ruby Thornton.

Celia stepped from the elevator on the sixteenth floor. She scanned the arrows on the walls to see which corridor she should follow to 1611. She sucked in her breath. Was this a mistake? Would it backfire? She desperately needed an ace in the hole. But, would what she was about to do give her that ace? It was a gamble. Solly, her old buddy from BBT, which meant Before Birch Thornton, always said you fuck them before they fuck you. Then you divide and conquer at which point the pie is all yours. What she was about to do would drive a wedge between Sage and his wife, another wedge between Birch and Sage which, in turn, would bring mother Fanny into the foray and drive a third wedge between her and her son Sage. Internal family matters would take precedence over business matters and pave the way for Jeff Lassiter to carry out his plans. Jeff would send, anonymously, the little sister's photographs to one and all along with the astronomical sums of money she'd lost gambling. All the internal strife would cause extreme stress to big sister Sunny, who would collapse under said stress. Yes, what she was doing would definitely be an ace in the hole. For 10 percent of the Babylon empire she'd sell her soul to the devil.

Celia took another moment to savor the situation she was in. She'd planned this little caper from the day she found out who Birch Thornton was, back in Costa Rica. She'd been clever, too, having the others on the team ask the sticky questions so Birch wouldn't think she was interested in his money. She'd written letters to everyone she could think of, to verify the Thornton wealth, saying she was a foreign student doing a paper on the gambling business in Las Vegas. The whole process had taken a full year. Her reward at the end of the year was marriage to Birch Thornton.

Playing the role of the girl next door, a.k.a. Miss Simpleton, had worked wonders. She knew everything there was to know about the Thorntons. Birch loved talking about his family, loved sharing confidences and secrets. She'd soaked it all up like a giant sponge. Sage slept like the dead, according to Birch. According to Birch, waking Sage was impossible, once he was asleep. Once, Birch had gone on to say, he, Sunny, and Billie had tied Sage's legs and hands and carried him outside and left him in the bushes. He didn't wake until eight the following morning, when he bellowed like a bull to be cut loose.

Time to get on with it. Card key in hand, Celia followed the arrow just as the elevator started upward. She slid the card key into the slot, waited a second for the small green dot to appear before she opened the door and slipped into the dark room. The elevator stopped. She heard the door open. She'd made it without a moment to spare.

Celia waited for her eyes to adjust to the darkness. She removed her shoes and tiptoed over to the bed. Sage lay sprawled across the bed, the flowered spread in a heap at the bottom. He wore only his Jockeys. She took a moment to admire his leanness, his hard flat belly. She wondered if he was half as good as his brother in bed. Birch was wild, but she was wilder. She'd shown him things he'd only dreamed of until he became a sex addict. She knew how to hold him in line, though. When he did something she didn't like she withdrew her favors until he made things right. That was in Costa Rica. Those tricks didn't work here in Vegas. Other tricks were required here in this fast-track paradise of neon light. That was okay—she knew every trick in the book and then some.

Celia reached behind her to pull at the zipper of her dress. It made a slithering sound when it fell to the floor. The lacy underwire bra and string bikini made no sound as they fell on top of the sparkly dress. She moved closer to the bed, trying to figure out the best camera angles. All she needed were four shots. One with Sage's head between her breasts, one with her on top of him, up high and one low. The last one would be the clincher. She wouldn't have to disturb him at all for that shot. She could flip him over on his back, strip off his underwear, and get the other three shots in a matter of seconds. Her adrenaline kicked in when she picked up the phone to dial Jeff's extension. "Now," she whispered.

She was perched on the side of the bed when Lassiter let himself into the room. Celia turned on all the lights, her eyes never leaving Sage's body. He didn't stir. "Let's make this quick."

"Jesus H Christ," was all Lassiter could say repeatedly as he snapped the pictures with his Polaroid. "Let me take a couple of extras just in case. I have to tell you, Celia, this is one obscene shot. Good, but obscene. I really didn't think it was possible to get a full shot of your face, his face, your breasts and his dick all in one shot. We need a couple of these."

"Shut up and be done with it already."

Five minutes later, Celia was completely dressed. She turned off all the lights. She waited until Jeff left, then waited five more minutes before she opened the door. She looked to the left and right before she stepped into the hall to head for the elevator.

"A very productive night's work," she murmured on the ride down to the lobby.

Ruby Thornton peered between the leaves of a palm tree. A quickie? Obviously. She watched as Celia left the building by the hotel entrance. For all her efforts the only thing she knew for certain was that Celia Thornton had gone to Room 1611. She'd followed the young woman's perfume trail that ended at the room registered to Sage Thornton. The only thing she didn't understand was why Jeff Lassiter took the elevator to the sixteenth floor shortly after Celia. She almost choked when the word "threesome" ricocheted inside her head.

"I need a drink," she muttered.

"Is anything wrong, Miss Thornton? You look like something's bothering you," Neal said.

"Nothing's wrong. I'm leaving now."

"It's a long ride out to the ranch. Would you like me to get someone to drive you? It is close to three-thirty. I worry about women out alone at this time of night."

"Perhaps an escort to my car. Thank you for the offer. I'll keep my doors locked."

Neal watched Ruby leave. He knew something had gone on

in the casino. Something he wasn't privy to. It irked him that he had no proof, no one to blame. If Ash Thornton were here, he'd have the answer within minutes. He sighed. As much as he wanted to be like Ash Thornton, he wasn't ever going to reach that status. All he could do was keep his eyes and ears open and deal with the real problems that surfaced every five minutes. He had to deal in facts and what his eyes saw and what he could prove if it came to a court of law.

Celia let herself into the small one-bedroom apartment. It was a rathole pure and simple. She looked around at the Goodwill furniture, the threadbare carpets, the crusty lampshades on rusty lamps. The only thing that could be said about the apartment was it came furnished. There was no way she was sleeping here. She would never put an ounce of food in the filthy refrigerator. She wouldn't even sit at the table to eat take out food in cartons. Her bags were still packed. This place was for derelicts. She was far from a derelict. Right now she had $17,000. She could go to any hotel on the Strip and that's exactly what she was going to do the moment she checked the messages on her answering machine.

Careful not to touch anything, Celia pressed the Play button. She smiled when she heard Birch's voice. The smile left her face as she listened to her husband tell her he was dining out with Sunny's therapist. "I should be home early, Celia, if you want to call. We had a good day today. My uncles work like Trojans. Sunny is really doing well, and so is Harry. That's why Libby feels she can leave them for a quick bite. All any of us have eaten for the past week is fast food. It gets to you after a while. Have you talked to Sage or Mom? I'll wait up till midnight my time. If I don't hear from you tonight, call me tomorrow. Hope the job's going well."

Celia erased the message and rewound the tape. "Dinner

with Libby Maxwell, eh. As if I care? Still, tomorrow I'll have to offer up a jealous protest, I guess.''

Bags in hand, Celia walked down the three flights of steps to her car. She threw the canvas bags into the trunk. "Riviera, here I come. Clean sheets, a clean bathroom, and Room Service. What more could a girl ask for?''

9

Fanny woke slowly, aware that she'd slept in her clothes. She rubbed her eyes until she was fully awake, a deep, gut-wrenching moan escaping her lips when she realized she hadn't been dreaming. It was all real. Marcus was in the hospital, and his chances of recovering were slim to none. Her children had deserted her, and she was alone. Had she dreamed that Billie and Bess were here? She strained to hear any sound in the house that would indicate her two best friends in the world had come to her aid. What could they do? What could anyone do?

Were the blinds and drapes closed, or was it dark outside? It must be evening since a night-light glowed in the hallway. When had she come home? Yesterday, today? What time was it? What day was it?

Fanny rolled over and buried her head in the pillow next to her. The pillow smelled like Marcus's aftershave lotion. She rolled over and swung her legs over the side of the bed. Maybe she should take a shower and add another towel to the pile on the bathroom floor.

Merciful God, who *was* this creature staring at her in the mirror? Fanny backed away from the vanity mirror to sit on the edge of the bathtub. Her head in her hands, her shoulders shaking, she cried. How had her life come to this? Weary to her bones, she stood and stared again at her reflection for a long time. Her fingers were clumsy when she opened the medicine cabinet. She looked at the array of prescription bottles lined up on the top shelf; some hers, some belonging to Marcus. Most were antibiotics and muscle relaxants. Somewhere, though, there was a bottle of sleeping pills John Noble had prescribed for her when Ash and Simon died. They were so strong she'd never taken any after the first one because it had left her groggy for days. She couldn't remember now why she had kept them instead of flushing them down the drain.

Fanny poked behind the talcum and Vicks VapoRub until she found the round squat container. Nine pills. Should she take them all or just half of them? Would taking all of them at once make them work quicker? Would she die with five as opposed to nine? Who cared? Why was she even worrying about the amount? She'd take them all and go back to bed. She'd go to sleep and never wake up. She brightened momentarily when she thought about seeing Ash again. He'd have a fit if she took the pills. He'd fought for his life like a tiger, and here she was taking her own life because she couldn't cope anymore. Ash would be ashamed of her.

The bright red pills in her hand, Fanny sat back down on the edge of the tub, tears rolling down her cheeks. Such a cheerful color. Red was a wake-up color. Why weren't these pills gray or some dismal brown color? She slid from the edge of the tub to the floor, hugging her knees, her head bowed. In her life she'd never been this tired, this weary.

"Listen, Fanny, this is shit for the birds. Pull up your socks and get moving. You're giving everyone the edge here. You know I taught you better than that. What the hell is a handful of pills going to do for you? Losers take the easy way out. I

*never thought you were a loser, Fanny. Me, yeah. Never you.
It's not time for you to come here. You were never a sniveler.
Are you listening to me, Fanny?"*

"Ash, is that you? Are you saying you don't want me there,
Ash? Did Simon tell you to say that to me? Or Sallie? I can't
do this anymore. So what if I am a loser. Why should you
care? You're there. I'm here. So what if I don't want to be
here anymore. Are you listening to me, Ash? So what, Ash?"

*"Because I care. You gotta be ready for something like this.
You still have things to do and places to go. I know all about
your future. This isn't your time, Fanny. Put those damn pills
back in the bottle or flush them. What gives you the right to
be so damn selfish? You have to think about the kids and
Marcus. I shouldn't tell you this, but I'm going to tell you
anyway. I never could keep a secret from you. They're getting
ready for him. Don't worry about the plug. He's coming on
his own. I'll take him under my wing. No pun intended. It'll
be okay, Fanny. Don't you trust me?"*

"Why should I trust you? Look what you did to me all those
years. I remember all those things. I remember everything. I
think you need to spell out what you mean. I want to be sure
I understand. Who's getting ready? I wasn't planning on pulling
any plugs. Why did you even say that to me? How do I know
it will be okay? Just because you sprouted wings doesn't mean
you know everything. I want some proof. How are you going
to do that, Ash?"

*"I thought we made our peace at the end. You know what,
Fanny, you love Marcus, but you aren't IN love with him. Both
of us know I'm the only one you were ever IN love with. It's
his time, Fanny. When it's your time nothing in your world
can stop it. Marcus is going to like it up here. You can rest
easy knowing I'm the one who will take care of him. Stop with
that martyr shit and get on with your life. I hate it when
you drag your feet. You need to wash those towels or they'll
mildew."*

"What else do you hate about me, Ash? I dream about you all the time. Why is that? Another thing, let me worry about my laundry."

"Fanny, Fanny, Fanny. I'm the father of your children and you were and still are IN love with me even if you won't admit it. I've been watching over you. I'm with you in spirit every hour of the day. I've watched you gradually lose your edge. You break my heart. You're starting to make mistakes that are going to do you and the kids in. You know what I'm talking about. Sometimes, Fanny, you are dumb as dirt. I told you not to get involved with Jeff. Why in the hell didn't you listen to me? Ruby is one thing. Jeff is something else. You can trust Ruby. I was wrong about her, but I wasn't wrong about Jeff. What's so damn hard about admitting you're wrong? The earth doesn't tilt on its axis, the oceans don't overflow. Life goes on."

"I didn't listen because I'm stupid just the way you said I was. What was I supposed to do, Ash? You up and died on me. You shot Simon. I have to live with that. That left a mark on me. Did you think about that before you pulled the trigger? I know you said you did it for me. Knowing that doesn't make it any easier. I didn't want to deal with problems. Hiring Jeff seemed like the logical thing to do. You always said the business stays in the family. I followed your rule. Jeff carries Thornton blood, so that makes him family. Why is Ruby okay and not Jeff? If I take these pills, I won't have to worry about him or anyone else."

"That's a dumb-ass attitude and not even worthy of discussion. Get rid of those pills NOW. Our kids need you, Fanny. You're screwing up. I hate it when you screw up. I want to believe you're perfect. Life is just too damn short to sweat the small stuff. You need to get on the ball and take charge. I want your word that you're going to get rid of those pills. I mean it, Fanny."

"Ash, wait, don't go."

"You don't need me, Fanny. You just needed to hear me tell you what you already know. When you need me the most, I'll be there for you. Listen. You made it bearable for me there at the end. I'm never going to forget that. I want your promise, Fanny, that you're going to do what I expect you to do. I want to hear the words. Say them. Out loud."

"I hate your guts, Ash."

"Ah, now that's the Fanny I know. Come on, flush those pills. All nine of them. I'm counting."

"I really do hate your guts."

"You wish. I miss you. It was good there at the end with us. It will be again when the time is right. It's just not your time right now. It is Marcus's time, though. Is there anything special you'd like me to do for him when he gets here?"

"Get out of my dream, Ash. I know this is a dream, and you aren't fooling me for one minute. If this isn't a dream, you better give me a sign right now. Besides, I always forget my dreams when I wake up. Just out of curiosity, Ash, exactly where are you? Are you, you know, *up there* or are you . . . ah . . . somewhere else?"

"It's not a dream. I'm right here. Open your eyes. You look like shit, Fanny."

Fanny opened her eyes. Ash Thornton was standing in the doorway, surrounded by a bright silver light. "Ash, you're walking."

"When I'm not flying. There is a lot to be said for this place."

"Do I really look like shit?"

"Yeah, but we both know it's a temporary thing. You were always good at fixing yourself up. How's Jake and Sunny, Fanny?"

"Don't you know? I thought . . ."

"There's a protocol up here that you have to go through. I don't have enough seniority yet. I got one shot, Fanny. I knew

you needed me, so I chose you. You can thank me by doing the right thing.''

''Jake's fine, Ash. He talks about you all the time. He's never going to forget you. We won't allow it. Sunny's doing great. Okay, look, Ash, I'm flushing the pills, all nine of them. Ash?''

''Yeah.''

''Thanks. You're right about me loving you. If you ever . . . *appear* and tell anyone, I'll deny it. Swear on Jake that you'll take care of Marcus. If I know that, I can let him go.''

''You have my word, Fanny.''

''Ash, are you happy up there. You know, really happy?''

''I miss all of you. I wish things had turned out differently. Yeah, I'm happy. When it's your time to come here, I'll be waiting, so don't be afraid.''

''Okay, Ash. What should I say? Have a good life? Enjoy your time up there? What?''

''Good-bye is just fine.''

Fanny woke. It took her a minute to realize where she was. She looked around, her eyes frantic. How long was it going to take before she stopped dreaming of Ash? Would the dreams ever stop? This one had seemed so real. She struggled to her feet remembering what she'd been about to do. She looked around for the sleeping pills. Where were they? She dropped to her knees to scour the white tile floor. There was no sign of the nine red capsules. Her eyes wide, Fanny lowered the seat of the toilet and sat down. Did she wake in her dream and flush the pills? Or did someone else flush them for her? Was that someone Ash? She looked at the vanity, at the empty pill bottle. She reached for the bottle and tossed it into the wastepaper basket under the vanity. She hadn't really lied to Ash. Normally she never remembered her dreams. For some reason, though, she always remembered, in detail, every dream Ash was in.

An hour later, her thoughts in turmoil, Fanny called the

medical center for an update on Marcus's condition. Satisfied that it was the same, Fanny showered, dressed, and had the table set in the kitchen. Bacon sizzled on the stove. Coffee bubbled in the pot. A bowl of golden scrambled eggs waited on the counter for Billie and Bess.

Fanny Thornton Reed was back among the living.

Ruby Thornton sat in her cluttered office, her mind whirling. The telephone glared at her. Iris was waiting for her call. What to say and how to say it so Iris didn't go into some kind of marital shock or whatever it was wives did when they thought their husbands were cheating on them. She'd stake her life, Thornton Chickens, and everything else she held dear, that Sage Thornton was a victim of some first-class chicanery. Did they still use the word chicanery today? Any minute now she was going to get a killer headache.

Family. Fanny was right about family when she said it wasn't all sit-down Sunday dinners, holiday get-togethers, smiles, and laughter. The phone was in her hand a moment later. She dialed Iris's number and wasn't surprised when Iris picked up the phone on the first ring. "Iris, honey, Sage stayed in the hotel last night. I saw him go up in the elevator. I followed Celia and she won tons of money last night. It was late when she left. I asked her to have a drink but she said she had to sub this morning. I called the school a little while ago, and she's teaching fifth-grade history. She didn't lie about that. Your husband looked incredibly tired and weary. That's it, sweetie. I'm going over to the offices because I need to talk to Billie about the costumes for the restaurants. I'll see Sage, and if I find out anything, I'll call you. Make some of those peanut butter cookies in case I decide to drive up the mountain this afternoon. Did you sleep at all? Then take a nap. I'll talk to you later."

She hadn't lied. What she'd failed to do was tell Iris all the facts because . . . seeing something didn't necessarily mean . . . what? Sage and Celia were not having an affair, of that she was certain. She'd simply evaded and avoided telling Iris everything she'd seen and suspected.

Ruby packed her briefcase. She looked around the office that had once been her father's. She hadn't changed anything. The furnishings were old, comfortable, and downright ugly. Why in the world did she ever think she was going to be able to leave here and do what she wanted to do? *Because hope springs eternal,* she thought. She'd worked nonstop for two days, putting the wheels in motion for Birch's free-range chickens, and it looked like the birds were going to fly. More money in the Thornton coffers.

Two years ago Fanny Thornton had walked into these very offices and said, "Ruby, I have a fabulous idea for you: fast-food chicken restaurants. Fast-food chicken! Think about it! You know, like those burger places, but chicken instead. People are becoming very health conscious these days. A couple of 'secret' recipes and it's off and running. Sunny's Togs and Rainbow Babies are always doing marketing studies to see what the latest trends are. Baby boomers, Ruby. They don't have time to cook. We're lucky they have time to shop for kids' clothes. That's one of the reasons we branched out into the catalog business. We have the names, Ruby. Millions of names. A restaurant in every city. Food priced right. A whole meal or a nutritious sandwich. I know just the right advertising firm for you too, Bernstein and Bernstein. They kicked us over the top. Think about it, Ruby. No matter what, those chickens aren't going to go away. All you need is a really clever name, some terrific costumes—and Billie can do those for you with her eyes closed—the secret recipe, and you're set. Write this down as I read it off to you. Ash always said when you take the time to write something on paper, it stays with you opposed to simply hearing it. Burger chains grew an average of 6.9% last year. The chicken chains saw revenues rise 10.9%. The reason for this is their dinners. Burgers have fat in them. Give your customers home-style food and you'll be a viable contender in the $7.5-*billion*-a-year quick-service chicken market.''

"Billion? Did you say billion?"

"Yes, I did. Ash would have been on this in a heartbeat. Start with the big cities. Put up small colorful buildings. Use plastic buckets or baskets that are every color of the rainbow. Women like things they can reuse. Different sizes of course. Special stuff for the kids. You can have special promotions and use our dolls the way the burger places do when they have giveaways. Remember one thing, Ruby. Mothers want something for their kids. Ash knew how to promote. I was the idea person. You're family now, Ruby.''

"Fanny, I wouldn't know where to start. It sounds . . . exciting. Billions, huh?''

"Yes, billions. It's pretty awesome when you stop to think about it. Colleges and universities have job fairs the early part of the year, so you'll be able to get in on it. Recruit the best of the best. That means you'll be paying for the best. Then you sit back and watch the money roll in. Unless you want to be a hands-on employer, which I heartily recommend. It will add a whole new dimension to your life and the business. What do you think?''

"I think, Fanny Thornton, oops, Reed, that you should allow your likeness to be cast in bronze. I think it's a great idea.''

Ruby sighed. Opening day across the country was thirty-eight days away. Just in time for the holiday season, when everyone was too busy to cook. She rifled through her briefcase one more time to make sure she hadn't misplaced Billie's or Sage's monthly reports. The last one she'd received was June. Her stomach flip-flopping, Ruby slipped into her coat. She needed to be aggressive. Business was business. Family was family. Was it a mistake to try to combine the two? A chill ran down her spine. Ruby shivered all the way out to the driveway. Inside the car, she turned the heater on full blast. If anything, she felt colder.

It was nine minutes past nine when Ruby opened the door to the offices of Sunny's Togs. She called a greeting.

"Ruby! What brings you to town so early?" Sage asked, giving her a quick hug. "I just put the coffee on. Billie seems to be running late this morning. Our receptionist called in sick yesterday, so we're kind of winging things. I guess you're getting nervous now that the countdown is on."

"Very nervous. So much hinges on the uniforms and the giveaways. Billie promised me she'd have something to show me three months ago but she . . . I guess she's busy with her own work. I feel terrible coming here like this, but you did cash my check."

Sage's jaw dropped. "Did you say three months ago?" He pointed to a chart on the wall opposite his desk.

"You're making me nervous, Sage. Is something wrong? We don't have a lot of time."

"I don't know, Ruby. That's the truth. You're right about the time element. Let me get you some coffee, and I'll bring you up to speed."

Ruby was spooning sugar into her coffee when the door opened. "Sorry I'm late."

"Not half as sorry as I am, Billie. Ruby's here. She wants an update, and she's entitled to one. What's going on?" To make his point Sage allowed his gaze to swivel to the chart on the wall. "We only have thirty-eight days left, Billie. Actually, we don't even have thirty-eight days, it's more like thirty-three since we have to depend on the postal system to deliver. Where are the samples?"

"What are you trying to say, Sage? Are you implying I'm not doing my job?"

"We cashed the check, Billie. Ruby's a client. You said you were on top of it all. So, show us what you have."

"It's not ready. I'm just one person. You approved the Thornton Chicken Basket with the parade of baby chicks on the handle. They're in production and will ship in ten days.''

"What about the uniforms, caps, and the chicks that cheep and fit in the pockets?"

"They're being worked on. Do you want me to hold a gun to their heads? I know they're behind, but there's nothing I can do.''

"Why didn't you tell me that, Billie? I could have recruited some women to help sew. I'm sure Fanny and Iris would have agreed to help. It's too close to our deadline to have to worry about this. That's just another way of saying I like things done on time. If you had just called me, Billie, we wouldn't be going through this now.''

Billie's voice was a low-voiced scream, "What do you want from me?"

"A production report," Ruby said, holding her ground.

"Do we have one, Billie?" Sage asked.

"No. Give me an hour, and I'll get one for you."

"Shipping dates, too," Ruby said. Billie paled at Ruby's businesslike tone.

"I'll be back in an hour." Irritated, Ruby slammed the door behind her.

"Let's hear it, Billie. Everything's going to hell around here. I'd like to hear from you personally, using your own voice, what you think is the problem.''

"If there was a problem, then I might be able to tell you. So what if I don't keep up with every little nit-picking detail. It gets done, doesn't it?"

"Ruby has every right to be anxious. Mom talked her into letting you handle those nit-picking details as you call them. Let's not forget that sizable six-figure check she paid us with, another to come when she's satisfied. It doesn't look to me like she's satisfied. On top of that, how many of the mini Bernie and Blossom dolls do you have ready to ship? Or is that another one of those nit-picking details?"

"Shut up, Sage. I have a headache."

"You're going to have more than a headache if you screw this up. Mom will yank your ass out of here so fast you won't know what hit you."

"That sounds like a threat to me, Sage. You're eating into my hour. Surely you have something to do. Oh, I forgot, I'm the only one who's responsible for what goes on here." The snarl in his sister's voice forced Sage to take a backward step.

"That's because you want your fingers in everything. Now when things are down to the wire, you want to delegate. Stuff it, Billie, and put your personal life on hold until The Chicken Palace gets off the ground."

Perspiration beaded on Billie's forehead. "Am I supposed to understand the meaning behind what you just said?"

"Billie, I would never ever think of interfering in your personal life. I think you know that. However, when your personal life starts to affect the family business, I have to start to wonder what's wrong. You've lost weight, your skin is . . . a funny color, you're nervous and twitchy. You're always going out to breakfast, lunch, or dinner, yet you've lost about twenty pounds. It doesn't compute in my book. You've been late every morning for the past month. You say you work late, but I came by the other night and you weren't here. Where were you, Billie?"

"That's none of your business, Sage. Keep up this inquisition, and I'm out of here."

"In the whole of your life you never talked to me like this. That's the part I don't understand. I'm your brother, Billie. If something's wrong, I want to help."

"If I need your help, which I don't, I'll ask for it. Now, if you don't mind, I have a ton of phone calls to make."

Sage shrugged. He managed to keep himself busy as he strained to hear his sister's low-voiced phone calls while he kept one eye on the clock for Ruby's return. He was about ready to jump out of his skin when Billie slammed down the phone for the last time. She stomped her way to the small kitchen area, where she poured a cup of coffee. She carried it back to her desk. "They can't meet the deadline. I told all of you it was a mistake to try to open 120 stores at the same time and expect things to run smoothly. No one listened to me. This is what happens when you overextend yourself and don't allow for contingencies."

"Is that what you're going to tell Ruby?"

"What else can I tell her?"

"What about the dolls?"

"We only have enough for opening day. The suppliers have been late. Rain checks might work. Rain checks bring people back, which in turn gives you a second shot at having them buy another meal. It's not the end of the world."

"Providing it's a two- or three-day loss. What kind of time are you talking about?"

"Sixty days," Billie mumbled.

"Sixty days! Ruby is going to bounce off the ceiling when you tell her that. You had almost a year, Billie. What is the problem here? Give me the goddamn list. We've been doing business with these people too long to put up with this kind of bullshit. They've always come through at crunch time. How'd you let this get away from you? You aren't overworked, Billie, so don't think about giving me that song and dance. Give me that list. Ruby's due back in fifteen minutes. Wait a minute. Who are these people? I never heard of half these names?"

"I switched up. These people gave better delivery and were cheaper."

"Better delivery! That has to be a joke, right? What exactly does cheaper mean?"

"It means I got more for my money."

"I don't think so. You did this without talking to me? I got it, they gave you a kickback and you took it, didn't you?"

"So what? I haven't had a problem until now. It was too much for them to handle."

"Then you should have gone back to our regular suppliers. You did pay them, didn't you? Don't tell me you stiffed them. How long were you going to keep this to yourself? Where's my cut of the kickback? Not that I would have taken it. It's your sneakiness that's getting to me. The others are going to feel the same way. God, Billie, what were you thinking of?" *Damn, I should have told her I know and offered to help.*

Billie ran from the room to lock herself in the bathroom. His face murderous, Sage made one call after the other. At one point he kicked the drawer of his desk so hard he was sure he had broken his toe. Ruby took that moment to enter the office.

"Give me the bad news first and the good news last."

"There is no good news, Ruby. Sit down."

There was nothing to do but tell Ruby the truth and hope for the best. He expected an explosion, the wrath of God, something. "All we need is Plan B. We have thirty-three days."

"I just happen to be in the business of trucking my chickens all over the country in refrigerator trucks. Your father bought an interest in the company when he worked for my father. Say what you will about your father, but that man had insight, foresight, hindsight, and male intuition where business is concerned. He actually liked the chicken business, but his true love was the gaming industry. So, what should we do? Do you have any ideas? More important, what are you going to do about your sister's problem? The rest of this stuff is secondary. Billie needs to come first. Your mother . . ."

"No! Mom doesn't need to know this. When the time is right, I'll talk to Billie. We have to give her a chance to get her head on straight. Today was an eye-opener for her. She'll act on it. Iris will help. She's good when it comes to a challenge. There's Chue and all the ladies in his family. Sunny might have some ideas. Hell, I'm willing to learn how to make those dolls myself. We have a lot of employees at the casino that constantly look for overtime or more hours. It's not the answer, but it's a place to start."

"Billie and Bess are back. They're with your mother. Would it be wise or unwise to pay them a visit?"

"A challenge is a challenge, Ruby. Go for it."

"And Billie?"

"I'll work on it. We all screw up at one time or another. I did. Birch did. Sunny did, and Billie was there for us each time. We can't do less for her now. I need to talk to Birch and Sunny and go on from there. I'm sorry, Ruby."

"Me too. If it's meant to be, it will be. That's my philosophy. If there's anything I can do, let me know."

"By the way, did you win anything last night?"

"Not a cent," Ruby said cheerfully. "What kind of night did you have?"

"My butt was whipped. I couldn't have made it up that mountain if my life depended on it. I had the most god-awful dream. Nightmare is more like it. When I woke up, I thought Mom had been in the room. I smelled her perfume everywhere. I even smelled it on me and was more tired this morning than when I went to bed. Is that weird or what?"

"I love your mother's perfume. Celia wears the same thing, doesn't she? It's so unusual, unique really." Later, Ruby swore she actually saw a lightbulb go off in Sage's head.

"I think you're right, Ruby. Now that you mention it, every time I'm near Celia my first thought is of Mom. That's weird, too. Oh well, tonight I'll get to sleep in my own bed next to my wife. Iris gives the best neck rubs, Ruby. I fall asleep even before she finishes. I haven't seen her or the kids for a whole day, and I miss them."

"You'd never do anything to jeopardize that little family, would you, Sage?"

"Never in a million years. Why do you ask? Oh, because of Dad, right? Nah. I had enough of that stuff growing up. I'm nothing like my father, Ruby. I thought you knew that."

Ruby smiled, the relief showing in her face. "Sometimes

it's nice to hear a man say the words. Do you think there's a man out there who might want me *and* my chickens?''

Sage laughed. "I'll start looking. Are you going to see Mom?''

"I'll stop at the medical center first. If she isn't there, I'll go to the house. I promise not to say anything about Billie. Don't wait too long, Sage.''

Sage raised his voice. "Bye, Ruby.''

When the bathroom door opened, Sage looked at his sister. "Sit down, Billie, we need to talk. Before we do that, I have something I want you to see.'' He slid the envelope Neal had given him across her desk. He wanted to cry at the stricken look on his sister's face.

Outside in the bright October sunshine, Ruby found herself humming a popular ditty she'd heard earlier on the radio on her drive in from the ranch. She should be upset with what had just transpired, but she wasn't. This was real family stuff, the nitty-gritty problems that attacked siblings from time to time. She was part of it now thanks to Fanny's insistence that she truly belonged to the Thornton family. By being part of the family, she had to take the good with the bad and work from there. An idea struck her as she waited for a traffic light to turn green. If she could put it into effect, she could save Iris a mountain of worry and wipe the misery from Sage's eyes. What it would do to Birch, she had no idea. Well, nobody gets it all. She'd read that somewhere just recently. Birch might even thank her someday. On the other hand, Birch might not thank her at all for sticking her nose into his private business. It was a chance she had to take.

The Chicken Palace needed a spokesperson. What better person than the newest addition to the family, the glamorous Celia Thornton? The female baby boomers would look at her svelte figure and know she couldn't cook and therefore relied on the family's famous chicken recipes. The male baby boomers would lust after Celia and the chickens she advertised. Celia would go on the road, first-class of course, making public appearances, meeting with town fathers and customers. A sweet deal if ever there was one. A generous salary, a bonus at the end of the year and her picture plastered all over the country would be all the incentive the greedy Celia would need. The big question was, how would it play out with the family? Time was of the essence now, with only thirty-eight days till the grand-opening events all across the country. She'd get on it the moment she left the medical center.

Ruby noticed an unusual quietness at the medical center as nurses walked around in their rubber-soled shoes. Their uniforms didn't crackle with starch the way they had when her mother was here. Nylon and polyester, she supposed. The nurses didn't wear caps anymore, either. She wondered why that was.

They were sitting quietly, knitting, all three of them. She knew they were making things for the twins Iris was carrying. Sitting in a waiting room like this was the best place to knit or crochet. Her own mother had made six afghans for her girls when Philip Thornton had his stroke. She herself had knitted mile after mile of nothing when her mother, Red Ruby, was here. She'd used all the stray yarn she could find, and, when that ran out, she'd bought odd lots and discontinued colors. The day her mother died one of the nurses told her she'd knitted five miles of nothing. She'd nodded and carried home the yarn. She thought she threw it in the attic, but she wasn't sure. Perhaps one day she'd be known as the woman who knitted five miles of nothing.

"How's everything?"

Fanny looked up. "Ruby! How nice of you to stop. I'm sorry I was asleep when you came by the house. It's been a difficult time. Is everything okay?"

"More or less. I wouldn't know what to do if things ran smoothly. A few snafus but nothing that can't be corrected. I wanted to talk to you about something. If this isn't the place or the time, we can do it another time. Has Marcus's condition changed at all?''

"No. This is fine, Ruby. What's on your mind?"

Ruby told them, leaving out the parts about Billie's problem, Iris's dark suspicions, and Sage's strange behavior. "What do you think? Will I be stepping over the line if I approach Celia?"

"In my opinion, no. My children, and that includes their spouses, haven't seen fit to confide in me. Celia certainly has a mind of her own and, as Sunny constantly reminds me, this is the eighties and women are out there making their way. I don't understand why Celia didn't join Birch in Atlantic City. The fact that she didn't leads me to believe she does what she pleases. It would be a marvelous opportunity for her, and it's very generous of you, Ruby, to include her in your plans.''

"Do you think I should ask Birch? He might not approve."

"I don't think it will matter if he does or doesn't approve," Bess said.

"No one likes to be left out. I think I would tell him," Billie Kingsley said.

"Fanny?"

"If it were me, I think I'd mention it. Sometimes Birch is very broad-minded. Other times he's so narrow-minded it makes you shiver. Birch has always tried to be fair. If it feels right, do it, Ruby.''

"What are you knitting? When my mother was here, I knitted five miles of nothing. It was a mishmash of color and mistakes.''

"Baby blankets. It gets cold on the mountain in the winter. Billie's doing the whimsical suns, Bess is doing the border, and I'm doing the center. If you have any time, Ruby, you could do the bumper covers.''

"I'd love to. What stitch are you using? Ah, I see. Okay. What's the lot number of the yarn?" Ruby scribbled in a small notebook. "I'll pick up the yarn on my way home. Is there anything I can do? Would you like me to fetch you some lunch?''

"No. We'll go out to lunch. Thanks for offering, though. Come out to the house, Ruby. I won't be spending the night here.''

"That's good, Fanny. I'm a phone call away.''

Ruby stared at the phone attached to the console in her car. Should she call Birch first or go to see Celia at the Golden Nugget? Birch, of course. She flipped through the pages for the number Sage had given her. Minutes later, Birch's voice crackled over the wire. "Thornton here.''

"Birch, it's Ruby. Listen, I'm sorry to be calling you at work, so I'll make it quick. For starters, we're on the road to free-range chickens. Secondly, how would you feel about me asking Celia to be The Chicken Palace spokesperson? I could hire a professional person, but I thought keeping things in the family was important. It will be a lot of traveling on her part and a lot of work. She's incredibly photogenic, so the commercials will be wonderful. I wanted to know what you thought before I asked her. Waitressing and teaching is hard work, not that this won't be. The pay will be a lot better, though.''

"It sounds like a wonderful opportunity. The decision has to be Celia's. I'm okay with it. Are things on schedule?''

"We're down to the wire. We ran into a few problems. Hopefully, all the glitches will be taken care of by the end of today. If not, we'll, what is it Sunny says, oh, yes, we'll suck it up and go on from there? How is Sunny?''

"She's doing great. This is the best thing in the world for her. She's not out here all day, maybe four hours or so. She has rosy cheeks these days. Harry feels useful, and he helps out as much as he can. I swear to God, Ruby, I will never, ever, take my arms and legs for granted again. How are Marcus and Mom?''

"Marcus is the same. Some people don't recover from severe head trauma, Birch. We're all hopeful. I just saw your mother, and she seems more with it if you know what I mean. Billie Kingsley and Bess are here, so that helps. John is in the middle of everything. How about you, Birch, are you okay?"

"The truth is, Ruby, I feel . . . great. I'm thinking of driving up to Vermont this weekend. They have some fresh powder. Sunny and Harry are up to the trip. Libby will be with us, so things should go smoothly. Sunny and Harry can 'lodge it' with hot toddies and a blazing fireplace while Libby and I ski. You'd like her, Ruby."

Ruby laughed. "I met her and I adored her. Give her my regards. Sunny and Harry, too. It was nice talking to you, Birch. The telephones work two ways you know."

"I'll remember that. Bye, Ruby."

"Bye, Birch."

A wicked smile tugged at the corners of Ruby's mouth. A ski trip. A lodge with hot toddies and a blazing fire. A winter wonderland. Togetherness. Sunny's earlier words rang in her head. "I can't wait for Birch to meet Libby. I know in my heart and my gut that she's his destiny. You know me. I'm never wrong."

"Oh, Sunny, I don't know if I want you to be right or wrong this time," Ruby muttered as she slipped the car into gear.

"Celia, what time do you get off?"

"Another thirty minutes. Can I get you something, Ruby?"

"Coffee would be nice. Do you like waitressing?"

"I hate it. I hate teaching, too. I have to eat and pay the rent. Birch . . . never mind. I'll get your coffee."

Ruby lit a cigarette and blew a perfect smoke ring. Celia returned with the coffee.

"Can you take a break?"

Celia looked around. "For a minute. Is something wrong?"

"No, not at all. I came here to offer you a job. Hear me out, okay?"

"Sure."

"So, are you interested?" Ruby asked later.

"Television commercials? Well, sure, it sounds exciting. Glamorous, designer clothes and limousines. A girl could get used to that real quick. What kind of year-end bonus are you talking about?"

"It depends on what The Chicken Palaces take in. I see it as a sizable amount."

"What's sizable, Ruby? You need to be more specific."

"Six figures easy."

"The lean side of six figures or the hefty side?"

Ruby leaned across the table. "For someone who's making thirty-five bucks a day subbing and another thirty in lunch-hour tips, I find this conversation very puzzling."

Celia leaned across her side of the table until their noses almost touched. "Listen, Ruby, I got burned once. I married a guy who's so wealthy it makes me dizzy, and he tells me I have to support myself and he's not about to share his trust fund. On top of that he beats me up and then goes off to Atlantic City to work for nothing while I bust my ass teaching ten-year-old snots and working my ass off serving hash to old people with white hair. What would you ask if you were in my place?"

Ruby sighed. This was definitely not the girl next door. This woman sitting across from her was jaded, cynical, and didn't trust anyone. "I'd say the middle range but it could go either way. There is an expense account that will require penny for penny documentation. I need your answer now so things can be set in motion."

"Okay, I'll take it. I should say I'll take it if Birch agrees. I'll call him the minute my shift is over. I've got eight more minutes to go. More coffee?"

"Sure." Let the little twit work for her money.

Ruby sipped at her fresh coffee and smoked a second cigarette while she waited.

In the lounge, Celia piled the change from her tips on the little shelf under the pay phone. Her voice was sweet and weary when Birch came on the line. "I know you're busy, honey, but this will take just a minute. I didn't want to make a decision until I talked to you. Ruby offered me a wonderful job. Oh, she did. Well, what do you think? I think it's great, too. It means I'll be on the road a lot. Ruby said it would all be first-class. The pay is great, and there's a bonus at the end of the year. I think it's going to be mostly weekend stuff. That means I won't be able to get to Atlantic City too often unless I'm somewhere close by. Are you sure it's okay, Birch? I know it's up to me. I can't take it if you aren't comfortable with me doing it. At the same time I want to help Ruby. Her back is really against the wall. I miss you, honey. I won't miss these two jobs though. Senior citizens don't believe in tipping. What have you been doing? How's Sunny and . . . Harry? Skiing in Vermont. You promised me that you would take me skiing so you could laugh your head off when I fell on the bunny slope. Oh, Libby is going, too. That's nice, honey. At least you'll have a partner. Of course I don't mind. See, Birch, when we share and explain things, life runs more smoothly. Have a good time, honey, and don't break any bones. I might not be calling for a few days if Ruby keeps me busy. I love you, Birch. You're the first thing I think about when I wake up in the morning and the last thing I think about before I fall asleep at night. You're my reason for living, and don't you ever forget it, even for a minute. Have a wonderful trip and give my regards to Sunny and Harry."

Celia walked back to the kitchen where she turned in her apron and headband. She tapped the kitchen manager on the shoulder. "I won't be back."

"I didn't think you would be," the manager sneered.

"For two bucks an hour plus tips, you know what you can do with this job, don't you?"

Celia held out her hand. "You owe me six dollars. Pay up."

The manager whipped out six one-dollar bills and slapped them into Celia's hand. She pocketed the money, a gleeful look on her face. She rejoined Ruby, who was paying her check.

"What did Birch say?"

"He said he thought it was a wonderful opportunity for me and to do it. He wished us both luck. He's going skiing in Vermont this weekend with Sunny, Harry, and their therapist. I forget her name."

"Libby."

"Yes, Libby. Birch loves to ski. He said he was going to teach me someday. I don't think I'd make a good snow bunny. I like warm weather, sunshine, and sand. I'm all yours, Ruby," Celia babbled, her opaque eyes glittering.

Ruby felt her stomach crunch into a knot. "Then let's get on with it."

"Was that Celia?"

"Yep. Ruby offered her the job as spokesperson for The Chicken Palaces. Big bucks and a super bonus at the end of the year. She's pretty excited. Traveling first-class is something she'll enjoy. I told her about our trip, and she was really enthusiastic about it."

"Then why the strain?" Sunny asked.

"We used to have this wonderful, carefree, easygoing relationship. I think it disappeared the moment we got off the plane. Sage acted weird from the moment he met us. Mom didn't take to Celia at all. I could tell. Everyone kind of stood back and . . . hell, I don't know what they were doing. Assessing us, I guess. I picked up on it and Celia did, too. I shrugged it off, and she didn't. She reacted, and then I reacted. Things got out of hand. To this day I can't believe I belted her around. Anger, frustration, rejection by my family for making a poor choice in their eyes. It got to me. I don't know if we can get back to where we were. Celia might have the right idea about putting space between us to see how we really feel. Personally, I think it's a mistake.''

''I just want to know one thing. Why did you trench in like that with the purse strings? You're so generous it's ridiculous. Come on, Birch, making Celia work at waitressing and subbing, that's not like you.''

''It is when I get the idea in my head that my wife is more interested in my money than she is in me. By the way, that idea is still with me. I think that's part of the problem.''

Sunny's voice was gentle when she said, ''Do you still love her, Birch?''

''I don't know. Jesus, I hate the word divorce as much as I hate the act. That would be the alternative. You don't stay with someone you don't love.''

Sunny's voice turned jittery. ''Maybe this weekend isn't such a good idea. It might give Celia ideas later on. I'm not saying she will think . . . I just know how bitter and angry I felt with Tyler.''

''Celia's okay with the trip. She knows Libby is going. She said she hopes we all have a good time. Celia does have some good points.''

''If you have second thoughts, it's okay with me and Harry.''

''No way. They have a dogsled run. You guys could do that. They have all kinds of stuff for disabled people. It's going to be a great weekend. Uncle Daniel told me we could take off Monday and Tuesday if we wanted to stay on. I'd like to. You and Harry are going to be tired from the trip and the excitement, so we'll lose one day until you regroup. I say we go for it.''

''Okay.''

''Did . . . ah, did Libby say anything about the trip?''

''She said she was looking forward to it and last night she went to the mall and bought a new ski outfit. She picked up outfits for me and Harry, too. We are going to shine, big brother. You have to pay her back, Birch. The bank hasn't transferred my money yet. Six hundred and forty-two dollars. She might need the money, so will you make out the check today?''

"I'll take care of it, Sunny."

"You know what, Birch. I love you."

Birch swallowed hard. "You know what, Sunny. I love you, too."

Sunny beamed her pleasure, her eyes moist with happiness.

10

"Oh, Birch, this is beautiful! How did you find this place? I always wanted to come to Vermont, especially in the autumn to see the change of leaves. Were you here before?" Sunny cried, her voice ringing with excitement.

"Uncle Simon brought Sage and me up here one weekend when we were in college. He loved it. That was the year Sage blew out his knee on the slopes. He swore he'd never go skiing again. What do you think, Harry?"

"I've never been in snow before. I lived in Florida and never left the state. I can't wait to touch it and feel it. I want to make a snowball. Seeing snow in movies and television isn't the same. Are you sure we'll fit in here?" His voice was so frazzled, the three of them clustered around, patting him on the back.

"Damn straight we belong here," Sunny said.

"Don't ever let me hear you say anything like that again," Libby said.

"You absolutely belong here," Birch said. "You are going to be catered to like never before. Libby and I made sure the activities are things you'll enjoy. The food's wonderful. There are fireplaces in the lobby and in every room. They have a wine cellar Dad would have been proud of. We'll meet up for breakfast and dinner. Lunch is kind of picnic style in the dining room. You guys can handle it."

The ever-practical Sunny said, "This must have cost a fortune."

"It depends on what you call a fortune. To me it was nothing if it gives you and Harry pleasure. I wanted to do it, Sunny. I owe you big time." Birch leaned over and whispered, "Having money means you can do good things for other people, like opening ski lodges before the season officially begins. You, Harry, and Libby are other people. Don't spoil our time here by equating everything with money."

"I see stars in Libby's eyes. I don't think she's ever had a vacation like this. I'm very grateful for her and Harry. You're right, it's nice to do things for other people who truly appreciate it. God, I hope we have a storm while we're here."

"Me too." Birch grinned. "Okay, let's settle in and make some plans. We'll meet here in the lobby in one hour."

"This is so nice of you, Birch. Sunny and Harry are like little kids when it comes to an outing. I don't think you could have done anything for them that would be better than this. It's hard to believe Harry has never seen snow. I want to thank you for all of us." Heat radiated up Birch's arm when Libby placed her hand on top of his.

"Okay, here's your key. Libby, your room is next to Sunny's on the ground floor, with a connecting door the way you requested. My room is on the far side of yours. Your bags will be right behind you."

Libby smiled and waved. Birch felt the urge to stamp his feet and burst into song. He remembered Sage heckling him about not being able to carry a tune. He clamped his lips shut and headed for the elevator.

Birch was the first one to return to the lobby, where a hostess handed him a cup of steaming tea. He threw his ski jacket over a bright plaid sofa and stared at the fire. He made a mental note to come back after the holidays if his uncles could spare him. Later on he'd take his charges to Hawaii. Sunny would love the ocean. He wondered what Libby looked like in a bathing suit.

"Mulling the problems of the world?" Libby asked.

"Kind of. I was making a mental note to myself to come back here. I thought about taking Sunny and Harry to Hawaii after the new year. You're invited of course. Have you ever been there?"

"It's on my list of places to visit someday. Maybe when I'm old and on a pension I'll go with some senior group. You know, a someday thing to keep you on your toes."

"We're ready," Sunny said, her voice full of joy and expectation. "Harry is about to explode, so let's get on with it. What's first?"

"You two are going for a sleigh ride. Real horses wearing real bells in a real sleigh with a real lap robe and a real thermos full of hot toddies. After that you're going sledding on real sleds with a steering mechanism. You have backup in front of you, on the sides, and behind you. Depending on how well you do, there is every possibility you can snowmobile tomorrow. With backup, of course."

"Honest. Oh, Birch, this is so wonderful. Isn't it wonderful, Harry?"

"I think I'm in shock," the soft-spoken Harry said. "You guys have to be the best people in the whole world. Your whole family is aces. I include you in the family, Libby."

"I think that's the nicest thing anyone's ever said to me," Libby said.

"What are you two going to do?" Sunny asked.

Birch waved his tickets. "We're hitting the slopes. We'll meet here around six and make an early evening of it. Tomorrow is jam-packed."

"Let's go, Harry. Don't break any bones, Birch. I forgot whatever first aid I knew."

"Don't worry, I remember *everything,*" Harry said.

"Harry's so smart he could be a doctor. If not a doctor, at least a nurse. He took every course there is. We're all safe with Harry." The love and loyalty in his sister's voice stunned Birch. Would someone ever say wonderful things like that about him?

"A penny for your thoughts, Mr. Thornton," Libby teased.

"I was wondering if anyone would ever say nice things like that about me."

Libby stopped in mid-stride. "Doesn't your wife say things like that?"

"No." Birch's voice was as cold as the air that blasted them when he held the door open for Libby.

"I hope I don't embarrass you, Birch. I haven't skied in a very long time."

"We're going to take it easy today. I want to see what you got before I subject you to the intermediate course."

"Oh ye of little faith. There is every possibility I might ski rings around you."

A worried look crossed Birch's face. Was she holding out on him? "Do you think so?"

"No, but it sounded good."

Birch laughed.

Settled in the ski lift, Birch asked, "Are you warm enough?"

"Toasty."

"I like your outfit. It matches your eyes. I really appreciate you taking the time to buy Sunny and Harry outfits. I love their excitement. Both of them make me feel so good. It's really strange how my life seems more complete when I'm around those two. I hesitate to use the word inspiration, but I can't think of one that's better. I gave Sunny the check to give you."

"She gave it to me. Thanks. The salesgirl guaranteed I would get at least one compliment. I got three."

"Three's good," Birch said. For some reason he felt flustered. He heaved a sigh of relief when it was time to slide from the lift.

"You go first. I'll be right behind you. See you at the bottom."

"I'm nervous."

"Don't be. Shift your mind into neutral and go from there. When you fly you're one with the plane. Skiing is the same. Go!"

At the bottom, Libby ripped off her goggles and grinned. "That was so . . . so wonderful! I'm ready to go again. God, I forgot how exhilarating skiing can be. How about you?"

Birch wanted to say he was so intent on watching her he hadn't had time to enjoy the run. He nodded. "Tomorrow our legs will let us know what we did today."

"Who cares? That's why they make liniment. I brought two bottles." Libby tilted her head to stare at the sun. "I bet we can make two more runs. Are you game?"

"You bet."

Birch watched his destiny settle into the lift chair, his heart in his eyes. He jerked his head to the side to stare at the blinding white snow. He wondered how a poet would put into words what he was feeling.

Libby smiled as Birch settled into the lift seat. Suddenly the late afternoon became brighter, warmer. Their shoulders touched. Then their knees touched. Warmth coursed through Birch. "I'm starving," he blurted.

"I was just thinking the same thing. Right now I think I could eat anything."

"Do you believe people can live on love?" Birch blurted. *Jesus, did I just say that?*

Libby tilted her head to the side. She appeared to be seriously considering the question. "Maybe in the beginning. Eventually one needs to chew. I think. Then there's the matter of water. One can live for a long time with just water. Of course you lose weight and become malnourished or is that undernourished? If you're looking for a one-word answer, mine would have to be no. What's your opinion?''

''I don't have one. Opinion that is. I don't even know why I asked the question.''

''Maybe it had something to do with Sunny and Harry. Although, I have to tell you, they both eat a lot.''

''I was thinking I wanted to kiss you, and those words came out.''

''Oh.''

''Get ready. Go!''

They were off the lift, face-to-face. ''I wasn't going to do it. I meant I was thinking about it.''

''Oh.''

''What would you have done if I had kissed you?''

Libby dug her poles into the snow with force. ''I would have kissed you back.'' In a flash the poles were uprooted and she was skiing down the hill like a pro. His eyes almost popping from his head, Birch gave a mighty surge forward.

They frolicked, they teased, they flirted as they swerved around trees and clumps of evergreens off the ski run. They reached the bottom of the run at exactly the same time; Libby swerving to the left, Birch to the right.

''That was very good,'' Birch said.

''For a girl is what you really mean?''

Birch grinned. ''You're almost as good as I am.''

''Tomorrow I'll strut my stuff. You up to the 'big' one?''

''Oh, yeah. I think I've had it for the day, though.''

''Me too. It was a long trip. I just want a hot bath and half a cow for dinner. I would be willing to settle for a whole chicken. How about you?''

''Lots of mashed potatoes, lots of gravy, lots of rare beef or well-done chicken. No fish. A big as in big, gooey dessert. Lots of coffee, the last one laced with brandy and then bed. Up at the crack of dawn, a big breakfast, eggs, bacon, pancakes, toast, juice, and lots and lots of coffee.''

Libby groaned. "Toast, grapefruit, and coffee. If we eat your menu, we'll be too stuffed to ski."

"I dream a lot," Birch laughed.

"About what?"

"This and that. Things. You."

"Oh."

"Do you dream?"

"Sure."

"What's in your dreams?"

"Things. Places. Sunny and Harry running a race. You."

"This isn't good, is it?"

"No it isn't."

"Something's happening."

"Only if we allow it. We need to disallow it. Is there such a word?"

"It doesn't matter. I know what you mean."

"Friends?"

"Absolutely."

Libby smiled as she reached for his hand. "What do you suppose that rich, gooey, big as in big, dessert will be?"

"Warm berry pie with soft ice cream, hot chocolate sauce, warm butterscotch syrup with whipped cream and slivered nuts. A cherry on top. My mother always put mine in a soup bowl. Everyone else got a regulation dessert dish." Birch guffawed.

They were still holding hands when they reached the lodge.

"Here they come. Here they come. Look, Harry, they're holding hands. I hope they had as good a time as we did."

Harry laughed aloud. The smile stayed on his face as Sunny expounded on the afternoon activities.

"It was great. The best. We even ran into a snow squall. Harry kept opening his mouth and swallowing the snow. We weren't the least bit cold. It was so . . . I don't know the words. What was it, Harry?"

"Intoxicating and invigorating."

"Yeah, yeah. I think it was one of the best days of my life. We're starving, how about you guys?"

"I was chewing the doorknob as we came in," Birch joked. "Let's split up, shower, change, and meet down here for a drink before dinner. The dining room has its own sofas and fireplace. We'll have a really nice evening. If we aren't too tired after dinner, we can watch a video."

"You and Libby watch a video; Harry and I are going to bed after dinner. We want to get up early to make sure we don't miss anything. Thanks again for giving us a great day," Sunny said as she blew a kiss in Birch and Libby's direction.

Birch clapped Harry on the back. "See you later."

Monday afternoon, three days after their arrival, Sunny and Harry watched the desk clerk post a snow advisory in huge block letters on a bulletin board behind the desk. "It's so early in the year for this much snow. I was reading the local paper last night and the article said they hadn't had this much snow, this early, since 1933," Harry said.

"It's kind of pleasant being socked in like this. Maybe the owners won't have to make use of those machines that make snow. I understand it costs a lot of money to operate them. What does snow advisory mean exactly? Just plain snow, a storm, a blizzard, or what?" Sunny asked.

"Ask," Harry said.

Sunny was frowning when she wheeled her chair next to Harry's. "The desk clerk said the advisory is for light snow. They update hourly. She said they're prepared to expect anything since the last storm. She also said the weather conditions were out of the ordinary for the past six months, and there is no way of predicting what the light snow will lead to. Maybe nothing. Maybe something. They're afraid the roads might get bad. Do you think Birch will want to leave? I hope not. I'd like to see a rollicking good storm."

"I think Birch will do whatever you want, Sunny. He's having as good a time as we are. I'm sure we'll stay to the last minute. I'm having a swell time, Sunny. For me this is like a dream coming true. Sitting on that snowmobile was the biggest thrill of my life. I didn't want it to end. I felt like everyone else for a little while. Did you feel like that, Sunny?"

"Yeah. Yeah, I did, Harry. The nicest thing was feeling young again. I don't ever want to forget what that was like. I don't want to cry over it anymore either. When something wonderful like this happens it makes it all bearable. I'm not going to say anything to Birch, though. He has to do the driving. If he decides we should go, we'll go. Is that okay with you, Harry?"

"Sunny, anything's okay with me, you know that."

Birch didn't mean to eavesdrop, but when he heard his name mentioned, he stepped behind a thick rubber plant, his eyes on the snow advisory, his ears on Sunny's conversation. He backed up until he was in the corridor, then advanced, calling out to Sunny. "Hey, did you guys see the snow advisory? How do you feel about staying to ride it through? I'm up for a good storm."

"Do you mean it, Birch?" Sunny cried excitedly.

"Hell, yes. We haven't made snow angels yet. Libby and I haven't tried out the snowmobiles either. I'll give Uncle Daniel a call and tell him we're staying on for the storm. How about you, Harry, can you handle a few more days?"

"Damn straight he can. Right, Harry?"

"Oh yeah. What's a snow angel?"

"You lie down in the snow and wave your arms. Then you get up without disturbing the snow and it looks like an angel left her mark. We can do it, Harry. I know we can. The trick is fresh powdery snow."

"It's settled then. I have to make some calls. I want to check on Marcus's condition, too," Birch said.

"Are you going to call Ruby?"

"I can. Do you want me to tell her something?"

"No, I want you to ask her if the new plane arrived. She ordered a special plane from Coleman Aviation, one of those special jobs spiffed out like Air Force One. Ruby goes first-class. She said she doesn't have anything else to spend her money on. Thad Kingsley was supposed to fly it into her this weekend."

"Who's going to fly it?" Birch asked, a stunned look on his face.

"You and Sage. She bought it for you guys. Sometimes, Birch, you're so dumb. Did you think Ruby was going to take lessons?"

"She bought a jet for us! That's mind-boggling."

"She's going to call it the love machine."

Birch choked on a mouthful of cigarette smoke. "I know that's a joke."

Sunny giggled. "You're right. It was a joke. She's calling it PAT. The P stands for Philip, her father and our grandfather. The A stands for Ash, her brother and our father. The T stands for all of us Thorntons. She told Jake he can learn to fly when he's seventeen. I just love her. Iris is crazy about her. Mom adores her. She's a Thornton through and through. At the end, Dad fell in love with her and said how sorry he was that they never got to be brother and sister. Hey, look, it's starting to snow."

"Order me a beer while I make my calls. We can all sit at that special table by the windows and watch the snow when I get back. Where's Libby?"

"Upstairs filling out our reports. She should be down any minute."

Birch's first call was to Celia. He wasn't surprised when the answering machine came on. He left a brief message. His second call was to Ruby, who picked up on the second ring. He explained the situation. "So, can you track Celia down and tell her we're going to be here a few more days in case she wants to get in touch with me. By the way, Sunny wanted me to ask you if Thad delivered your new plane."

"Saturday morning bright and early. It's a beauty if you're into airplanes. The Colemans gave me a real break on the price. It sure beats that plane we used to have, the one your dad said was put together with spit and glue. I'm keeping it for sentimental reasons, though. I bought the new one for you and Sage. I know how you two love to fly. Thad said it's state-of-the-art. Sunny and Harry will be comfortable when you take them on trips. I know what a hassle it is with the chairs and the dogs and all. I can't believe you didn't take the dogs with you to Vermont."

"Vacation time. Checkup time. They treat those dogs like humans. Libby and I are with them most of the time. They both carry beepers, and the people here are really good about it. We're the only guests. We think a storm is brewing, and we want to be on hand to see it. At least Sunny and Harry do. Ruby, I don't know what to say."

"Thanks works."

"How's Celia doing?"

"She's into it. She's incredibly photogenic. The commercials are going to be terrific. She's on the go from six in the morning until after ten. She's enjoying it all."

"Any news on Marcus?"

"He's the same. Your mother doesn't stay at the hospital sixteen hours a day anymore. She was worn to a frazzle. She does go, though, for three hours at a time. I think, and this is just my opinion, she's resigned to its going either way. She's been knitting these past few days, making Bernie and Blossom dolls with the help of Billie Kingsley and Bess. Are you all having a good time?"

"We really are. Just seeing Harry's face was worth the trip."

"Libby?"

"Libby?"

"Libby. You know, Sunny and Harry's therapist. Is she enjoying the trip?"

"Very much. She's fun to ski with. She took a couple of spills, but then so did I. We're all having a wonderful time."

"I'll give Celia your message. Give me the phone number in case she wants to call later this evening." Birch rattled it off and hung up. His third call was to Sage.

"I just wanted you to know we're staying on a few more days. Write down this number just in case. Sage, did you hear about the plane Ruby bought?"

"Yeah, this weekend. I went to see it. That's some bird. Dad would have loved it. When you get back, we'll take it up. It intimidated the hell out of me. It's like a palace inside. I knew the Colemans made super-duper planes, but this one is something else. Ruby christened it yesterday with a bottle of champagne. She waited for the paint to dry on the name. I thought that was kind of nice. Dad would have approved and so would Grandpa. When Ruby said she bought it for us I almost passed out."

"Yeah, me too. How's Billie? Did you . . . ?"

"We can do that when we take that bird up. Or, I'll find a better way."

"Is Iris there?" Birch asked, assuming the double talk was for her benefit.

"Yes."

"Is she okay? Billie I mean."

"No, but we're working on it. So much is involved. You know, money, that kind of thing."

"She tapped the trust fund and gambled with the money?"

"In addition to other monies that shouldn't have been used. It's under control for the moment."

"Whip her ass into shape, Sage. I mean it. Find a way to freeze that trust account. I know it can be done."

"I'm working on it. Speaking of freezing, how's the weather up there? I can't believe the weather reports I've been seeing of heavy snow and more on the way. The paper said some kind of freak cold front with a tremendous storm is headed for the New England states. Be careful, Birch. Iris is standing right here. She wants to say hello.''

"I'm watching it. I'd rather stay here and ride it out than be on the road. The van isn't a good snow vehicle." Birch did his best to work cheerfulness into his voice when Iris came on the line. When he hung up, the collar of his shirt was wet with sweat. The only thing that made him feel better was knowing level-headed Sage was in control of the situation. Loyal, dependable, best-brother-in-the-world Sage.

Birch returned to the main room of the lodge just as the receptionist posted the new snow advisory to read; HEAVY SNOW WARNING. Underneath, in smaller letters, the bulletin read, BY NOON TOMORROW.

Harry held out a bottle of beer. "Let's drink to the white stuff."

His eye on the snow advisory, his heart tripping in his chest, Birch held up his beer. "To the white stuff."

When the third advisory was posted an hour later, the desk clerk, who lived on the premises, spoke softly to Birch. "I sense the advisories are bothering you, Mr. Thornton. We're prepared. We have emergency generators, candles, firewood, heaters, and enough food to feed an army. We use CBs, and the rangers know we're here. The worst possible scenario is you all might put on a few pounds and get a heat rash from the fireplace. Most of our people have families down below and naturally they want to be with them when a storm comes. There is every chance this storm will blow over or pass us by. It happens all the time. Just this morning UPS brought us the latest videos and six new best-sellers."

Birch walked back to the fireplace. His heart was still tripping in his chest. From past experience he'd found when people were as cheerful as the desk clerk, there was room for concern. He likened it to an airline hostess assuring passengers things were fine when the pilot was approaching wind-shear problems. Maybe he'd made a mistake by staying on for Harry's sake.

"What's wrong, Birch?" Libby asked coming up behind him. Birch pointed to the snow advisory.

"Do you think it's a mistake to stay?"

"Not from Sunny and Harry's perspective. Look at them. They're loving this. They actually hope we get snowed in.

"I wouldn't worry. This is a popular resort. There are rangers and ski teams all over the mountain. Places like this have all the latest hi-tech equipment, and they're geared for emergencies."

"What if . . ."

"I don't play that game, Birch. Nine times out of ten the 'what ifs' don't come to pass. We learn to deal with problems when and if they arise. If you spend your life anticipating a disaster, you become one miserable human being. Sunny and Harry are not dumb. They know what could happen. They also know what to do if something does happen. We call it living life. Don't let them see your doubt. Right now you're our leader, and we expect you to lead us; to the dining room, to our rooms, to the game room, or just to the front door to watch the snow."

"How'd you get so smart? I'm not concerned for myself. I have to worry about Sunny because of Jake, and Harry because he's confined to a wheelchair. See, I stopped worrying."

"Dumb luck. Do you feel less anxious now?"

Birch shrugged. "Do you know what *really* makes me feel better?"

"I don't have a clue. I hoped it was my logic."

"That too. Sage is watching the weather forecasts. You have to do that when you live on a mountain. He's got something hooked up to his dish that gives him the weather conditions in every part of the country. Just knowing he's keeping his eye on things makes me feel better. From the time we were little kids we were able to home in on each other. I always know when he's in trouble and vice versa. Right now I know he's under some severe stress. The trick is knowing when you can help and when you can't. Whatever his problem is right now, only he can deal with it. If it were otherwise, I'd know. It's that simple.''

''Perfectly understandable.'' Libby's voice was wistful when she said, ''I'd give anything to have a sister or a brother. Sunny is the closest thing to a sister that I've ever had. Harry is the brother. I've had other patients, but those two touched something in my heart. I wish the dogs were here.''

''That's funny. I was just thinking the same thing. I believe, if we keep this up, we're going to spook ourselves. I think you're two beers down. You have to catch up.''

''I thought you'd never mention it.''

Birch signaled the waiter, his gaze sweeping over the man's head to stare out at the falling snow.

''Here he comes, our fearless leader,'' Sunny chortled. ''There's no one I'd rather be stuck in a snowstorm with than you three. We're going to make another toast to the white stuff.''

As one they chorused, ''To the white stuff!''

Sunrise was a beehive of activity as Chue's kids gathered up their coats, books, and playthings to carry home. Iris shooed her brood upstairs for their nighttime ritual as Sage shrugged into his jacket to walk the children home. Munching on a crunchy apple, he turned to his wife. ''We're going to talk when I get back. Don't go to bed, Iris. If you do, I'll wake you. This silence between us has gone on long enough. Please don't change the weather channel. I'll bring up the finished dolls from Chue's and seal the cartons. I don't want you doing any lifting or bending. Do you hear me, Iris?''

''Of course I hear you. Chue can probably hear you. Don't tell me what to do, Sage.''

"Okay. I'm asking you not to do any bending or lifting. Is that better?"

"It will do. Go. The kids are bundled up. We don't need any more colds. Kids perspire when they're bundled up and then go out in the cold. Their pores are open."

"Thanks for sharing that, Iris. You make me sound like an idiot. I knew that."

"Go already and don't slam the door," Iris snapped.

Sage clenched his teeth as he ushered Chue's giggling grandchildren through the door. A devil perched on his shoulder. He slammed the door so hard the kids roared with laughter.

Before leaving Chue's house, Sage loaded up the back of Chue's pickup truck with cartons of dolls. "This is, how do you say, a spit in the bucket," Chue said. "My family works continuously, but I fear we won't meet Miss Ruby's quota. My cousin and his family have closed their laundry. Their dolls will be ready to be shipped in the morning. Many other relatives will bring the cartons to your offices every few hours. Jake showed us how to work assembly-line style. It goes much faster. He is a very smart young man. What he does, Sage, is this. He looks at a problem, then asks himself how his grandfather would solve it. For some reason it always works for him. I do not understand that. Your father was not the problem solver of the world."

Sage smiled sadly. "The ideas are Jake's own. He just doesn't realize it yet. It's his way of keeping Dad alive in his thoughts. Sometimes I think Dad is an obsession with him. I appreciate all you and your family are doing. We'll make it up to you, Chue."

"There is no need. If I lived to be a hundred, neither I nor my family could ever repay your family for all you have done for us. It is our pleasure."

Sage felt flustered. Rarely did the old Chinese ever bow or revert to his old ways. He could count the times on one hand that it had happened and usually, if his memory was correct, Chue only did it in times of crisis. His stomach started to churn.

"My son-in-law will drive the truck to the UPS terminal in the morning when you're ready to leave. You will put the shipping labels on the boxes, yes."

"Yes."

Sage drove into the courtyard. Would Iris be in the kitchen or would she have gone to bed? When he saw her sitting in the rocker by the fireplace, he let out a sigh that could be heard across the yard. He carried the bulky boxes into the kitchen and stacked them neatly. Out the corner of his eye, he watched Iris working on the dolls in her lap. He had the cartons taped and labeled and a cup of coffee in his hand within fifteen minutes. He sat down opposite his wife.

"We need to talk, Iris. What's wrong?"

"What makes you think something is wrong?"

"Iris, I know you. For weeks now you've been acting strange. At first I thought it was your pregnancy and the fact that you're carrying twins. That's not it at all. I know you, Iris. We never had a problem talking things through before. You go to bed as soon as I get home. You feed the kids separately, and you stay in bed in the morning. We never see each other. We don't talk anymore. The house is a mess and what *was* that stuff you made for supper? Whatever it was, don't ever give it to me again."

"It was Hamburger Helper and Jake made it. As you can see, I've been busy. I'm trying to do my share for your family."

"If you're overburdened, let's get some household help."

"I don't want anyone underfoot. When this is finished, I'll try to live up to your expectations. I'm sorry if I'm less than perfect in your eyes. I'm sorry I'm getting fat, I'm sorry I don't look glamorous, I'm sorry the house is a mess, and I'm sorry dinner wasn't up to your standards. Maybe you should come home more and cook it yourself."

Sage stared at his wife, a helpless look on his face. "Iris, to me you are the most beautiful woman in the world. You are the mother of my daughter and you will be the mother of our twins. You are also a mother to Jake and Polly. To me that's the most important thing in the world. I'm not into glamour. You know that. As for the house, I don't care if it fills up with dirt. Help is just around the corner. The kids can do a little more if it's too much for you. They can stack the dishwasher, make their beds, and carry out the trash. We did it when we were kids. I can do the laundry if you don't have time. It's something else you aren't sharing with me. I feel it, Iris. Whatever it is I bet you shared it with Ruby. I had this strange feeling she was spying on me. Now, why do you suppose that is?''

"That's ridiculous. There is nothing wrong."

"Then why won't you look me in the eye? If nothing's wrong, let's go upstairs and make love." The panic on his wife's face brought Sage up short. *Christ Almighty, what the hell is going on here?*

"I'm not in the mood," Iris said coolly.

"Since when? You're as lusty as I am. Do I smell? Am I getting to look my age? What do you want me to do? You're breaking my heart, Iris, because I don't understand why you're withdrawing from me. I feel like I'm losing you, and I don't know why. Will you please say something?"

"I'm very tired. You sound like you have a guilty conscience and are trying to blame me for something. I didn't do anything. I sit up here on this mountain and do what I agreed to do when I married you. If that isn't good enough, then it's your problem, not mine. If you really want to do something, work on these dolls while I take a nap. I plan to work through the night. I don't want to let Ruby down."

Sage's voice dropped to a miserable whisper, "I guess what you're saying is it's okay to let me down but not Ruby. How did this happen? What the hell did I do? I know I must have done something to give you such an attitude. You don't even want to be around me anymore. Do you want me to move out? If that's what you want, I'm gone. I won't beg you to look at me, to smile at me, to talk to me. Where the hell do you get off treating me like this? I hope to hell this bullshit doesn't have anything to do with Sunny's kids . . .''

''You're being ridiculous. Are you trying to pick a fight, so you'll have an excuse to leave us? If that's your intention, I'll pack your bag for you.''

Sage slapped at his forehead. ''Where the hell did that come from?''

''You tell me,'' Iris snapped. ''I'm going upstairs to sleep for an hour or so. You can work on these dolls or not.''

''Do you want me to leave, Iris?''

''Is that what you want to do?''

''Hell no. I just want to know what's wrong? Why are we fighting? We never fought before. We had discussions, sharp words from time to time, but we never fought like this. You owe me an explanation since I'm not a mind reader.''

''I'm going to bed,'' Iris said.

Sage stared at the empty rocking chair for a long time as he racked his brain to figure out what was wrong with his wife. His fingers worked automatically, twisting and tying the yarn on the dolls that Iris had worked on earlier. He thought about calling his mother but nixed the idea almost immediately. Should he call Sunny and burden her with his problems? No. Birch wouldn't understand, or would he? With a wife like Celia, he doubted it. That left Billie, who was going through her own private hell at the moment and didn't need any extra problems. Ruby would be a good person to talk to but she was on Iris's side. Did he have a side? How could something so right go so wrong so quickly? He wished he could cry the way he had when he was a kid. He always felt better after a good cry when his mother gave him a cherry Popsicle. He was off the chair in a split second, rummaging in the freezer for the Popsicles Iris always stocked for the kids. He relaxed immediately.

"Sage."

"Jake, is something wrong?"

"Kind of. I know it's late but . . ."

"Want a Popsicle?"

"Sure."

"Lemon, lime, or cherry?"

"Cherry. I got a letter from my dad two days ago. He wants to know if me and Polly can visit him over Thanksgiving. He wants us to meet his other son. Iris said it was my decision. She told me I should talk to you."

"Do you want to go, Jake?"

"Yesterday I did. Today I don't. It was a nice letter. I think he wants me to answer the letter."

"He's your dad, Jake. That's never going to change. Iris and I adopted you and Polly, but that doesn't change who your dad is. Do you think it would be nice to meet your half brother?"

"I suppose so. Should I mention it to Mom?"

"I think I would. Your mom always gives good advice."

"I wish Pop Pop were here. He always had the right answers. I didn't do good on my history test today. I got a C- because I kept thinking about this and couldn't concentrate. Polly won't like going on a plane. I know she'll get homesick. She'll cry and then she'll throw up. Four days is a long time. I don't want to go."

"Okay. Do you want me to call your dad?"

"No. If it's my decision, then I have to tell him. Is it okay if I write the letter tonight? I know it's late, but I won't sleep unless I do it now."

"I think it's okay. You're sure about your decision?"

"Yeah, I'm sure. It's what Pop Pop would have decided. Is it okay to invite my dad for a visit?"

"Anytime, Jake. This is your home, and he's your dad. If it feels right, then you do it."

"That's kind of what I thought. The Popsicle was good. Thanks. You look sad. Is something wrong?"

"I have a lot on my mind."

"Boy do I ever know what that's like."

"I talked to your uncle Birch today, and he said your mom went snowmobiling with Harry and they had a great time. They went sled riding and had a real sleigh ride with horses with bells around their necks. Harry never saw snow before. Did you know that?"

"I didn't know that." Jake started to giggle and couldn't stop. "I'm trying to picture Mom and Harry on a sled. Who do you think steered the sled?"

"I think it had hand controls." In spite of himself, Sage grinned.

"I'm doing the right thing, aren't I, Sage? I don't want Mom or you and Iris to be disappointed in me."

"I told you, if it feels right, then it's right. Jake, Iris and I will never be disappointed in you. Nor will your mom. Never ever. Not even in a million years. Get going and do your letter. I'll mail it for you in the morning."

Sage poured himself a second cup of coffee before he adjusted the volume on the small portable kitchen television set on the counter. He listened to the ominous-sounding words of the weather forecast as his ruler traced the pattern of an approaching storm headed across the plains and up the East Coast, where a second storm, born in Canada, was heading in a southerly direction. The two storms, he explained, would meet up somewhere over the New England states. The ominous-sounding voice became more dire with each passing minute as Sage stared at the set on the counter. To drive home his warnings, the weatherman used his ruler to tap at colored masses floating and swirling on the map in front of him.

A headache started to wage a war inside Sage's head. He looked at his watch: 9:30. How fast did a storm move? Maybe he should call the station. What kind of weather stations did they have in Vermont? Probably the best, since the ski resorts made their living from snow. Freak snowstorms at the end of

October were something to pay attention to. A second war birthed itself inside his stomach.

A snowstorm was a snowstorm. He and Birch had lived through many of them when they were in college in Pennsylvania. The university had been closed on three separate occasions during blizzards. Both of them had considered it a lark at the time. This was different. He and Birch hadn't been in wheelchairs the way Sunny and Harry were. He'd feel a lot better if the dogs were with his sister and Harry. He continued to watch the colored swirls until his eyes started to ache. What time was it in Vermont? He looked at his watch again: 10:45. It was a quarter to two in the morning in Vermont. He should go to bed since there was nothing he could do. The war in his stomach met up with the war in his head, where they clashed. He should go to bed. He should also stop drinking coffee so late at night. He knew if he went up to bed, no matter how quiet he was, Iris would wake and come downstairs. He could sleep here in the comfortable rocking chair. All he had to do was close his eyes. But, if he did that, the demons that had been plaguing him these past weeks would invade his dreams.

Sage leaned his head back against the padded headrest. He was asleep within seconds.

Harry swung his legs over the side of the bed, careful not to disturb the covers or to make a sound. He pulled his chair close to the bed and, from long years of practice, hefted himself into the cushioned seat. His eyes still on Sunny, he waited a moment before he engaged the hand control that would allow him to move his chair backward. Satisfied that Sunny's breathing was normal and that she was sound asleep, he wheeled himself to the window. Mesmerized at the beauty outside the window, he gasped. He'd seen all kinds of beauty in movies and magazines but nothing compared to the wonderland he was now staring at. His shoulders slumped. A single tear rolled down his cheeks followed by another and still another.

Caught up in the beauty of the night, he almost didn't feel the light touch to his shoulder. "It's so beautiful it takes your breath away, doesn't it? It's okay to cry, Harry. I feel like crying myself. You want out there so bad you can taste it. I do, too. Let's do it, Harry! I can see us skimming across that snow in those snowmobiles. The snow and wind will be in our faces. It'll be the best thing in the world, something we'll probably never get to do again. I'm not afraid. Are you afraid?"

"Petrified would be a better word."

"I woke up a little while ago and heard the snowblowers. I bet they cleared a path to the utility barn, where they store the snowmobiles. There has to be a path. If the storm gets bad, it will be the only way to travel. The roads will be impassable. The mechanic in charge of the machines told me he gasses them all at the end of the day. We could whiz around for hours on a tank, Harry. No one will know. The mechanic might suspect when he sees the tanks are empty, but he went home with everyone else. I saw him getting into the shuttle bus. It's just plain old snow. The storm isn't supposed to hit until tomorrow around noon. It's two in the morning, Harry."

"What if something happens? We aren't like other people, who can get up and walk away. We could get lost." Harry's voice and tone said "convince me."

"The roof could blow off this lodge. The gas fireplace could explode. If there was enough snow, there could be an avalanche. There could be an earthquake. We know how to take care of ourselves. We'll do it by the book. If we don't do this, you'll always regret it. Am I wrong?"

"Probably. You make it sound so logical. If Libby finds out, she'll fry our asses. She might even quit, and where will that leave us?"

"She isn't going to find out. We're going to be very quiet. You and I are the last people anyone in this lodge would think of who would do something like what we're planning. You forget, Libby is falling in love with Birch, so she isn't going to do anything. Trust me.''

''I don't know, Sunny. If we do it, we'll be flouting everything they taught us at the rehab center.''

''Once. This is one of those once-in-a-lifetime things. Did you ever think you would be able to make a snow angel? No, you did not. You did, though. We can make another one. We'll be together. Nothing's going to happen. I thought you said you trusted me.''

''I do trust you. Most of the time. This is different. We could be playing with our lives. What if the storm kicks up?''

Sunny giggled. ''Then we kick back.''

Harry's face puckered in worry. ''Are you sure you want to do this?''

''Damn straight I'm sure. I want to do it for you. It's your decision.''

''Okay, but we're going prepared. That means flashlights, our battery-operated socks and gloves. We carry spares. Candy bars. If anything happens, we can eat the snow. Matches. Lots of matches. People always carry matches when they do things like this. And don't forget our Saint Christopher medals. I'm wearing mine.''

''I have mine on, too.''

''Should we leave a note in case something happens?''

''Harry, nothing is going to happen. Don't think negative thoughts. A note's good. We'll probably both feel better if we leave one. We'll be back before dawn, safe in our rooms and in bed. We'll tear it up when we get back. I'm psyched. Are you psyched, Harry?''

''I'm so excited, I can hardly breathe. I want your promise, Sunny, that we'll stay together. Swear you won't do anything screwy. I'm in charge. Agree out loud.''

''I swear. I agree. You're in charge. I'll stick to you like the peel on an orange. I'll write the note, too. What should I say in the note?''

''Say . . . let's see . . . say we went out to play in the snow.''

''That's good, Harry. It's the truth, too.''

Harry raised his hand and Sunny slapped it with all the force she could muster.

''To the white stuff,'' Harry said.

''To the white stuff,'' Sunny said.

11

Ruby stared out the window, seeing but not seeing what lay beyond the windows. The silvery glow from overhead told her there would be a full moon when the clouds released their hold on the sky. A full moon certainly explained the restless sounds of the chickens. For some reason the chickens, even though they were roosting, sensed the moon. The sounds they made spoke of uneasiness and were ominous to her ears. There had been a full moon the night her father was attacked by the turkeys, years ago.

Ruby turned to mix herself a stiff drink as she tried to ignore the barnyard sounds that seemed to circle the house and waft through the cracks in the window frames. The ice clinking in the glass in her hand, she paced the office, walking around the desk, the table holding the lamp, the cracked leather chair that still held an imprint of her father's form, a form that didn't fit her slim body. She'd tried cushions, extra padding. Nothing worked. She should have gotten a new chair, but it seemed sacrilegious to do so. It was easier simply to perch on the end of the flattened leather cushion than it was to throw out her father's treasured chair.

She really should clean up the office, paint the dingy walls, get some modern blinds instead of the green pull shades. She could do little things; hang some pictures, add some plants, refinish the old, scarred desk, put down a new floor, perhaps some slate or tile that would be easy to care for. Maybe a new comfortable chair with a footrest and a floor lamp set in one of the corners where she could read the latest periodicals. She set her drink down on the edge of the desk to make some scribbled notes. She finished the drink and fixed another.

The Wild Turkey, her father's favorite, went down smooth and easy. One more of these and she'd be swinging from the dusty chandelier shaped like a buck's antlers.

Ruby walked back to the window. It wasn't the full moon or the chickens' restlessness, it was something else that was making her jittery. Maybe she should make some phone calls. Iris might be under the weather. Sage was there. What could she do except hold Iris's hand? It was better for Sage to hold his wife's hand. Celia was home in bed, this she knew for a fact. The Chicken Palace's newest spokesperson had been dead on her feet after a hard day's work in front of the camera. Billie? It was possible, but unlikely, that the young woman had run afoul of her creditors. Still, it was a possibility.

Not bothering to think, Ruby picked up the phone and dialed Billie's number. "This is going to sound very strange, Billie, but I have the strangest feeling that something is wrong somewhere. I've discounted the full moon. I feel foolish calling everyone, but I won't sleep until I know everyone in my immediate circle is all right. I'm sorry if I bothered you."

Scratch Billie. Aside from sounding a little stressed, she was working, doing her best to uphold her end of their business deal. Marcus and Fanny. She called the hospital and was told Marcus's condition remained unchanged. She was told Mrs. Reed had left over an hour ago.

Ruby freshened her drink and added ice cubes from the small portable refrigerator under the counter. She dialed Sunrise. Sage's sleepy voice confirmed that things were okay on the mountain. Her list was whittled to Sunny and Birch. With the time difference, they were all probably snug and asleep at the lodge.

Damn, she was acting like a mother hen, and the chicks weren't even hers. Goose bumps dotted her arms as her stomach muscles tightened. Maybe it was Jeff at the casino and something terrible was going on. It was a far-out idea, but she couldn't discount it. She called Neal Tortolow's private beeper. A moment later her call was returned. "I'm not out of my mind, Mr. Tortolow, it's just that I'm having this . . . anxiety attack and can't pinpoint it. Mark it down to woman's intuition. Is everything all right at the casino? That's good. Okay, I'm sorry I took you away from the business at hand. Yes, I know there is a full moon. Fanny told me once all the weirdos in Vegas hit the casinos when the moon is full. I guess it's one of those little mysteries in life that will never be completely explained. Have a good night."

Ruby splashed bourbon into her glass. So what if she swung from the chandelier. Who was going to see her? No one. Maybe she should walk up to the house and go to bed. Sleep was out of the question, so why bother. It was easier to sit here and drink. If something was wrong, someone would have called by now. *Keep drinking, Ruby, and you won't know if anyone calls or not,* an inner voice chided. She started to pace again, her footsteps sluggish. She gulped at the drink in her hand as she rounded the desk for the sixth time.

Ruby was on her tenth round when the phone rang, startling her. The glass dropped from her hand as she fell over her father's chair to grab for the phone. "Fanny!" she gasped. "I'm so glad you called. Is everything okay? All evening I've had this awful, strange feeling like something is wrong somewhere. I called everyone to see if they're okay. Sage and Iris were sleeping, Billie's working, Celia's in bed, and Marcus's condition is the same. I knew you would have called if something was wrong. I didn't call Birch or Sunny because of the time difference. That's right, you don't know. They went to Vermont skiing. They left on Friday. I'm babbling here. I'm just so glad you called. You feel it, too? God, I can't tell you what a relief that is. I thought I was going out of my mind. At first I thought it was the full moon because the chickens are restless, but that isn't what it is. It's something else. I can't shake the feeling. If I figure out what it is, I'll call you back. One of my workers will pick up the dolls in the morning for shipment. We've really made inroads, and I can't thank you enough, Fanny. My heart swells every time you tell me that's what families are for. Call me if there's anything I can do.''

Woozy with the alcohol she'd consumed, Ruby stretched out on the old leather sofa her father had slept on more times than she could remember. She thought she could still smell his aftershave, the scent of him that was ''Dad'' to her for so many years. Tears blurred her vision before she wiped them on the sleeve of her blouse. She wasn't a crier—she never had been. She was tough, like her mother. At times she'd thought that was good. Now she wished she had more of her father's gentleness. Over the years she'd wished her father were more aggressive, more rough-and-ready. Still, she was thankful for his gentleness, his ability to see both sides of an issue and to be fair in his assessment of a situation. So many times she'd questioned that fairness, but, in the end, because her father said it was the best he could do, she'd accepted things.

Ruby's thoughts traveled to Texas and the only man she'd allowed into her private world—Metaxas Parish. She'd been introduced to him at the Cattle Barons' Ball shortly before her father's death. She'd attended the ball in Texas because the invitation had been sent to her mother by a friend who didn't know of her death. And there he was, bigger than life, the second richest man in the country. Of course she hadn't known that at the time. Older by fifteen years, brash yet gentle, she'd been attracted to him on sight, but he'd scared her because he was married. It didn't matter that Mrs. Parish lived in California and Metaxas lived in Texas. He was still married. He'd wooed Ruby with a passion, sending his private jet for her, offering what he called baubles and rags but which were priceless diamonds and furs, all of which she rejected.

In private, Metaxas was like her father, soft-spoken, gentle, and caring. In the business world he lived in, he was ruthless and power-driven. Once he'd shown up at her door in black tie, cowboy boots, and pearl white Stetson carrying a huge box with a gigantic red bow. Refusing to take no for an answer, he'd waited while she decked herself out in "the duds" and the "jools" he'd brought her. Before she knew what was happening, he'd whisked her away to his private jet. Their destination, Paris, France, where she allowed herself to succumb to his charms. It was the most glorious seven days of her life. And when it was over, like Cinderella, she returned to her pumpkin. She'd confided in her father because she didn't know what else to do. All he'd said to her was, "I want more for you than someone else's husband." The disappointment in his eyes was so great she'd packed and run. She didn't return until years later, when her father took ill for the second time.

Metaxas Parish, where are you? What are you doing now? Do you even remember me? Of course he remembered her. He'd pledged undying love the way she had. He'd offered her everything, the moon, the stars, untold riches. The one thing she needed, wanted more than anything in the world, his name and a flesh-and-blood family to call her own, was something he couldn't give her because his wife refused to give him a divorce.

In the beginning Metaxas had been stunned when he realized his wealth meant nothing to her. When she'd said to him, "How many houses can you live in at one time, how many cars can you drive simultaneously, how many planes can you fly at once?'' he'd stared at her, his face uncomprehending. He did understand her, though, when she said, ''God's been good to you, so you should start to give back like the Thorntons did and still do.'' Subscribing to a Dallas newspaper that was delivered by mail a day late, she was able to keep up with his philanthropic goodness these days. His endowments were mind-boggling. His A-List of friends started with presidents, queens, princes, and princesses, heads of states, governors, top-ranking politicians. Everyone in the world knew Metaxas Parish. In one guilty moment she'd confided to the entire Thornton family about what she considered her dalliance with Metaxas. They'd listened and not one of them had judged her. She loved them for their understanding. Once he told her he had the president's private phone number and was on a first-name basis. None of that mattered because no one in the world knew Metaxas Parish the way she knew him. Of that she was certain.

What would happen if she called him now? How would he act? What would he say in that slow drawl she loved so much? He'd probably say something like, ''Ruby honey, how's the big bad world treating you? Are ya'll calling me, sweet love, to tell me ya'll coming for a visit?'' Then his voice would drop to a bare whisper and he'd say, ''Sweet love, I remember our time in Paris. I remember every hour and every minute.''

Ruby's eyes filled with tears. If only life were simple. This time she poured liberally from the bourbon bottle, adding two nearly melted ice cubes. She marched to the window to take up her position again. She moved like a marionette with all the liquor she'd consumed. She craned her neck to look at the bourbon bottle and then at the clock. The night was still young, and she still had a half bottle of bourbon.

The night was suddenly quiet, too quiet. Even the chickens had stopped rustling in their roosts. It was too still, too dark with the big full moon hiding behind dark scudding clouds. Such a strange, weird night.

Ruby looked at the oversize clock on the wall. Five minutes

to eleven. Time for the evening news. She switched on the small television set perched on the side of her desk. She listened as Dan Rather expounded on the latest U.S. retaliation against Iran for their attacks on the Persian Gulf. She thanked God then for not having a son on foreign soil. Oliver North's face flashed on the screen. Was he a loose cannon or an American hero?

"I don't know, and I don't care," Ruby muttered as she added more bourbon and ice to her glass.

"Get on with it and give us the weather so I can go to bed," Ruby said to the face on the screen.

The world weather map flashed on the screen. "Cool and brisk in the morning, warming to the low seventies by afternoon," Ruby said, anticipating the weatherman's words. It took her a few seconds to realize the excitement in the weatherman's voice and to note that his words weren't those she anticipated. Instead he was elaborating on the battering the East Coast was receiving in the way of rain. The pointer moved upward as did the weatherman's voice. She listened to words like highs, lows, cold fronts, warm air as the pointer circled the New England states. The words, "freak snowstorm" jerked her upright from her position in the chair. High, gusty winds, freezing temperatures with a possibility of two feet of snow. "At this time, it looks like New Hampshire and Vermont will be hit the hardest. Connecticut and Massachusetts are expected to receive ten to twelve inches of snow before the storm is over. We're receiving some reports now of power outages, downed telephone lines and roads closed because of drifting. I repeat, this is the second snowfall of the season, and a freak storm at that. Stay tuned to this station for further details as they become available to us."

Ruby's hand shook as she added fresh bourbon to her glass. The last time she'd consumed this much liquor was when she walked away from Metaxas Parish.

She tried to visualize what twenty to twenty-five inches of

snow would look like at a ski resort. A ski resort that already had six inches of snow. Ruby's heart thudded in her chest when she envisioned Sunny and Harry in their wheelchairs. Were they safe? Of course they were. All resorts had ski patrols, police of some sort, and, of course, the rangers who patrolled everywhere. Ski resorts were prepared for things like this with generators, deep freezes, and firewood. They had their own plows and heavy snow equipment. The big question was, were they prepared for Sunny and Harry? God, she needed to think. Did Fanny know Birch and Sunny were in Vermont? She'd meant to tell her. She couldn't remember if she had or not. Did Fanny watch the late-evening news? Mothers were supposed to have a sixth sense where their children were concerned. Living on Sunrise Mountain, Fanny had seen her share of snow as she had when she lived in Pennsylvania. Fanny wouldn't attach any special significance to a freak snowstorm in late October.

Ruby tossed her drink down the sink and made a fresh pot of coffee in the small kitchen area off the main office. She needed her wits about her from this point on, and she wasn't sure why. She started to pace, lap after lap, until she was dizzy. When the coffee was ready, she gulped at it, scalding her tongue. She continued to drink the strong, bitter liquid until her brain started to clear.

What should she do first? Call the ski resort of course. She fumbled through the papers on the desk until she found the number Sage had given her. She placed the call, her heart racing inside her chest. "The phone lines are down, ma'am," the operator said. Ruby broke the connection.

Ruby's racing heart speeded up. Call Sage or Fanny? Fanny had other things on her mind these days. Sage was tuned to his brother. Was she the only one in the world concerned? If so, why was it so? She was only an aunt from the wrong side of the blanket. Would anyone thank her, not that she was expecting thanks, for waking them in the middle of the night to tell them a storm was battering the New England states? Her clenched fist crashed down on the desk. "Like I really care what anyone thinks," she mumbled. She reached for the phone just as it rang. Nobody ever called her at 11:15 at night. Fanny? Sage? Metaxas? Oh, yes, in my dreams. "Hello," she said, her voice strangled-sounding.

"Aunt Ruby. Listen, I know I'm going to sound like an overanxious parent, but I just saw the evening news. I feel like I'm going to explode. Did you see the weather report? I dozed off and woke up just as it came on."

"Oh, Lord, Sage, I've been sitting here wondering if I should call you. All day I've had this . . . ominous feeling. Even the chickens are restless. At first I put it down to the fact that there is a full moon. I tried calling the resort in Vermont, but the phone lines are down. I tend to think that happens when there is a storm in those parts. I was debating calling the ranger station when you called. I'm sure we would have heard something if there was a serious problem."

"How, if the lines are down? I have a really bad feeling about this. I always know when Birch is in trouble. He's in trouble. I know it. I sense it in every bone in my body. I feel like I should be doing something, but I don't know what. I wanted to call Mom but decided not to alarm her. I'm hoping I'm overreacting. For whatever it's worth I've been out of sorts all day myself. Part of it has to do with Iris. By the way, I engaged the services of a . . . never mind, it's not important," Sage said when he remembered Celia Thornton was the spokesperson for the Thornton chain of Chicken Palaces. "Is your new plane gassed and ready to go?"

Ruby's heart turned over in her chest. "I . . . told them to keep it that way. Dad always kept the plane cleaned, gassed, and ready to go at a moment's notice. When they sent me away to school I got sick a lot in the beginning. Dad was always there before it got dark. He brought your father with him once, but Ash didn't know who I was at the time. I had appendicitis.

When I finally got to meet him face-to-face before he died he said I looked familiar and even asked if we'd ever met. I lied and said no. God, why am I telling you this? It isn't important in the scheme of things. The answer is yes, the plane's ready. If you're thinking what I'm thinking, you better forget it. I'm certain the airport is closed. I don't even know if Vermont has an airport. Do you know?''

"They have a small airport. A lot of single-engine planes fly in and out of there. My dad could have set that plane down on a dime in weather conditions you'd only see in your worst nightmares. He was that kind of pilot. Hell, he was an ace during the war.''

In a jittery-sounding voice, Ruby said, "Are you that kind of pilot, Sage?''

"Probably not. I'd give it my best shot. Something's really wrong, Ruby. I want you to trust me on this.''

"I do because I feel just the way you do. Don't those places have CBs or two-way radios? What do they call those things? Truckers use them and have strange names.''

"I'm sure they do. It's not good enough. What if Birch got caught in the storm and lost his way? He could freeze to death. He's lived too long in hundred-degree temperatures in Costa Rica. He's no survivalist. When it comes to snow and freezing temperatures, not too many people are.''

"We need to be logical here, Sage. If that were the case, the lodge would send out the ski patrol to find him. Using their CBs or whatever you call those things they talk on. I'm switching the television to the weather station. You do the same. You call me when they do the next update. I don't want to call and wake Iris.''

"Ruby, do they ever find people in snowstorms?''

"All the time," Ruby lied.

"Are they alive?''

"Of course," Ruby lied a second time.

"You're lying, aren't you?''

"Yes. The will to live is very strong, Sage. People have survived horrible horrendous things against all odds. Look, we're probably worrying for nothing. All four of them are probably snug in their beds. Let's face it, we at least know Sunny and Harry are safe. It's the middle of the night in Vermont. I think you and I both reacted to the term 'freak storm' and then both of us ran with it."

"One last question, Ruby. If I decide I want to go there, will you let me take your plane? It's a lot to ask."

"Let me ask you a question, Sage Thornton. If I let you take my plane, can I go with you? Dad gave me flying lessons one year as a birthday present. He kept a Cherokee at Logan Airport for me. I never got my license, though. Dad had his stroke. Sallie moved him to the mountain. Mom got sick, then Dad passed away. Life just got in the way. I might be some good to you."

"Okay, it's a deal. I'll call you after the next weather forecast."

"I'll be waiting." Ruby broke the connection and called the main house. "Edna, I want you to pack me a bag. This is what I want, my long underwear, my fur-lined boots, some flannel shirts, and those heavy wool slacks. Bring my shearling jacket, a wool hat, some gloves, and extra wool socks. Bring both pairs of boots. Fill that huge jug with coffee and make it strong. Make a bunch of sandwiches, thick ones. Add some fruit. Pack up all the flashlights and extra batteries. Look in the garage for the flares. The box is marked. I think we only used half of them when we marked the runway during that dust storm when the pilot was bringing in those baby chicks. If there is an extra one, bring it too, and lots of cigarettes. Two bottles of that fifty-year-old brandy will do nicely. Don't forget anything, Edna."

What in the name of God was she contemplating? Only a fool would do what she knew Sage was planning. What was even worse, she was planning to go along with his outrageous plan. They were both fools.

Ruby's hand snaked out to the phone. What she was about to do was probably another mistake. Later she could blame it on the bourbon even though she was now stone-cold sober. She dialed the number from memory, not because she dialed it often but because, like now, she'd dial the number and break the connection just as the phone was about to ring at the other end of the line. How many times had she done that? Hundreds? Thousands? Probably thousands. She sucked in her breath and held it for a long moment before she let it out with a loud swoosh. She looked down at her trembling hand. The last time her hand had trembled like this she'd been in bed with Metaxas Parish doing wild, wonderful things that she still dreamed about. Her shaky hand balled into a clenched fist. She banged the desk so hard everything scattered, pencils and pens skittering to the side and rolling on the floor. The small, portable television teetered a moment and then was still. Coffee swished upward to splatter everywhere. "So, who gives a good rat's ass," she muttered.

The voice was deep, resonant, even at this time of night. Often the voice sounded like a mixture of gravel and molasses. She would know it anyway even if the owner was across a crowded room and whispering. "Metaxas, this is Ruby Thornton."

"Sweet love, is it really you? Darlin' girl, I still dream about you and wonderful dreams they are. Ya'll having a change of heart where ol' Tex is concerned? Heard about your new venture. Ah wish you the best, li'l gal. So when are ya'll coming for a visit? My plane is gassed and I can be there before you blink if it's me ya'll want to do the visitin'," Metaxas drawled.

"I've been thinking about redecorating these offices. Sprucing the place up if you know what I mean. Some pictures, some plants, a new floor, maybe a chair with an ottoman. New window treatments, that kind of thing. Bright colors. The chicken business is booming. We're about to go with free-range. Maybe you should think about doing something like that with your cattle. You always say you want to be ahead of the pack. Our kickoff for the fast-food palaces is right on schedule. Promotion started a week ago. It's a billion-dollar industry.'' Her voice was as jittery and shaky as her hands.

''That's a powerful amount of money. Decorating is something ladies do when they don't have anything else to do. Or else they sell real estate. I'd like to think you were pinin' for me. Now if you'd marry me, we could combine our little empires and control the beef and chicken markets in this country. Forget giving them Colemans a piece of the action. They got enough money with all their electronic and aviation sidelines. They're only distant relatives anyway.''

''You told me you hate chickens.'' Ruby immediately picked up on the word marry. She drew in a deep breath. ''You aren't free, Metaxas.''

''Sweet love, I am now. Colette up and asked for a divorce a year ago. She said she don't want none of my holdings. Now, don't that beat all. I was prepared to split things right down the middle. He's an artist fella who travels all over paintin' strange things. Bohemian, Colette called him. I bought a hundred pictures, sight unseen. She agreed to that. I'd be mighty pleased to send them to you for your decorating spree.''

Ruby gasped. ''You're free!''

''Will be in two more weeks. I was planning a little trip your way. Was going to set my whirlybird right down in your chicken patch and surprise you.''

''You can't do that. It will scare the chickens. We don't have a patch. We have a yard, like in barnyard but big. You have a helicopter?''

''Hell, little love, I have a dozen of them. You want one? I can have it there by morning.''

''No. I . . . I just bought a jet. I'm keeping Dad's old plane, though. Sage and Birch like to fly. I bought it for them.''

"That's mighty nice of you. Okay, sweet baby, enough of the polite talk. Why did you call me at this time of night? Are you in trouble?"

"I think so. I just want to tell someone in case . . . you know, let . . . there is nothing you can do. Do you still want to marry me?"

"Do birds want to fly? Didn't you just hear what I said?"

"I didn't hear you say, 'Will you marry me, Ruby?' "

"I was going to do that in your barnyard after you give me the tour. On my knees. Chicken poop and all."

"Really."

"What's your answer going to be?"

"I need time to think and can't rush into anything. I'm not signing any prenuptial agreement."

"Didn't ask you to, did I? Does that mean yes?"

"No, it doesn't mean yes. It means I'll think about it. I don't have a dress. Finding the right dress and shoes could take a long time."

"Sweet love, we could do the honors in the buff. That takes care of that problem right off. I'd like to know so I can make some preparations. We want to merge right away. We can set Wall Street on its ear."

Ruby's voice turned testy. She realized her voice was back to normal, and her hands weren't shaking. "It sounds to me, Metaxas, like you want my chickens more than you want me."

"A long time ago you told me it was a package deal. Your exact words were, 'Love me, love my chickens.' Do you *ever* eat beef?"

"No. Do you *ever* eat chicken?"

"No. It pays to be up front with things like this. We'll hire two cooks, one to cook for me and one to cook for you. Things always work out. You calmed down now? You sounded like a pregnant filly at the starting gate."

There was a smile in Ruby's voice when she said, "Pregnant fillies don't run."

"Exactly. My ears are open, sweet baby. What can I do for you?"

"Just listen." The words exploded out of Ruby's mouth like bullets. "I'm ready. I'm just waiting for Sage. I'm sure the airport's closed. I need you to call somebody so we can use the runway. I don't know how that works. I'm sure Sage does. If my brother could land on a flight deck or on a patch of cleared ground in the jungle, then my nephew can land in snow. You have my word that we absolve everyone of any kind of liability. Will you do it, Metaxas?"

"Of course I'll do it. It goes without saying it's a damn fool thing you're planning on doing. You don't even know if there is trouble. You could get yourself killed on a hunch. Where does that leave me?"

Ruby burst out laughing. "Alone without my chickens. It's not a hunch or a whim. It's my gut instinct and the instinct of my nephew who knows his twin is in danger. That's enough for me. You've done worse things with less to go on, Metaxas."

"That's true, but I'm a man."

"What the hell do you think my nephew is? Don't go giving me that 'Me Tarzan you Jane' crap. This is the eighties. We women have been liberated for a long time. We had this discussion once before, Metaxas, and I thought we both agreed that the only thing you could do that I couldn't do was stand up and pee in the bushes. And the only thing I could do that you couldn't do was deliver a baby. Put those things side by side and there isn't a woman in the world who would want to pee in the bushes. I rest my case."

Metaxas's low rumble of laughter tickled Ruby. He'd laughed like that in bed. "I'm going to follow you," he said. "If the people I'm going to be calling know I'm going to be landing first, your chances are better. I can leave right now. We'll probably meet up within the hour of landing. I don't want to brag, Ruby, but I can set my plane down on a lily pad without damaging the petals. I've been skiing in Vermont more

times than I can remember. I could find my way on the Molly
Stark trail blindfolded. Assuming we're going anywhere near
the trail that is. As a point of reference the airport is close by.
That doesn't mean we'll land at the airport. Trust me, sweet
baby.''

''Then you're my man. I think I will marry you after all.''

''In the buff or in a dress?''

''You name it. If we pull this off, I'll be up for anything.
You could have told me about Colette.''

''I could have. I didn't know for sure if she'd change her
mind or not. You being a woman of principle, well, I didn't
want to get you all fired up and then have to fizzle out. I want
you to swear you'll hang those pictures someplace where they
can be seen. That's a big part of our divorce settlement.''

''I promise.''

''Ruby, have you given any thought to how you're going to
reach the lodge once you land? How far is it from the airport?''

''I don't know. Sage knows, though. He used to go skiing
there with Birch and my brother Simon. Snowmobiles? Can
you arrange that?''

''Of course I can. I can do whatever it takes as long as
I know what is going on. This cannot be a Mickey Mouse
production.''

''Are you going to fly alone, Metaxas?''

''I'll bring one of the guys with me. Maybe I'll bring my
whole flight crew. I'm going to hang up now, Ruby, and get
my show on the road. I'll see you on the ground. You're sure
now that you want to marry me?''

''Damn straight,'' Ruby said smartly. ''I'm hanging up now,
Metaxas, an updated weather report is coming on. I . . . I guess
I'll see you, in what, five hours?''

''More like six. Dawn. Eight or nine East Coast time.''

''Bye, Metaxas.''

''Bye, sweet love.''

Ruby flopped back on the chair, her eyes glued to the small

screen. The bottom line to the five-minute update was that the freak snowstorm was increasing in intensity and there was no way to predict the exact accumulation of snow. The National Weather Service was issuing a blanket order for the state of Vermont, warning all residents to stay indoors and not take to the roads. Ruby felt herself crumbling. She jerked upright when the phone rang.

"I'm on my way. I'm not waiting, Aunt Ruby," Sage said.

"I'm ready. Sage, I called Metaxas Parish. He's going to make all the necessary calls. He'll clear the way for us. He's leaving now. He'll probably get there before we do. He said . . . he said he'll see us on the ground. He also said he can land his plane on a lily pad without damaging the petals. He asked me to marry him. I said yes. We can do this, can't we, Sage?"

"We're going to try like hell. I'll meet you at the airport in fifty minutes. Be on time."

"I'm out of here right now. Do you want me to call anyone?"

"I woke Iris and told her. She'll call everyone in the morning. There is nothing they can do. It's better that just you and I go. If you don't agree, call whomever you want. I don't think I'd call Mom, though."

"I'll stop by Celia's and tell her. She might want to come along."

Sage snorted. No words were necessary.

Ruby hung up the phone and turned off the television. She checked the back of the Range Rover before she climbed behind the wheel. All her bags were neatly stowed in the cargo area. High beams flashing, Ruby tore out of the parking area, cell phone in hand. She dialed Celia's number three different times, letting the phone ring and ring. Each time the machine came on she said, "Call me, this is an emergency." After the sixth call, Ruby called the main number of Babylon and asked to be put through to Neal Tortolow. When she heard his voice, she identified herself and explained the circumstances. "By any chance have you seen Celia Thornton tonight?"

"As a matter of fact I just saw her heading for Jeff's office."

"I'm going to give you this number to give her. Tell her it's an emergency and to call me right away." Ruby rattled off the number. What was it Celia had said when she dropped her off at the apartment? Oh, yes, she was dog-ass tired and going straight to bed. What Ruby should have asked was to whose bed?

Jeff Lassiter's face was ugly with anger when he slammed the door behind Celia's back. "What the hell is this? You were supposed to be here at nine. I had everything set up down the Strip. It's eleven-thirty now. If you don't want to wear a watch on that skinny arm of yours, put it on your ankle. Or is it true what they say about dumb blondes and you really can't tell time? Your mistake, Celia."

"Don't talk to me like that. In case you haven't heard, I've been working. Hard. I know you know, because you say you know everything, that I'm the new spokesperson for Ruby Thornton's chicken empire. There was no way I could turn that down. So I'm late, so what. That doesn't give you the right to talk to me like that. Just watch it, Jeff, or I'll slam you to the wall, and you won't even have this office to diddle around in."

"Just try it. We had a deal. You might be able to pull crap like this with your in-laws but it isn't going to work with me. Don't forget, I have those pictures."

"So you have pictures, so what?" Celia hoped the jolt of fear she was feeling didn't show in her eyes. *Damn it, why didn't I keep those pictures myself?* she thought. Obviously her fear showed, because Jeff was smiling. She wet her lips trying to stare him down. She was the first to look away. She seethed inwardly, knowing Jeff now had the upper hand.

Celia was about to leave when a knock sounded on the door. She ignored Jeff's warning look and opened the door. "Mrs. Thornton, I have a message for you. Miss Ruby Thornton asked me to give you this number. She wants you to call her immediately. It's an emergency of some kind.''

Celia's mouth tightened into a thin line. "Call her back and tell her I'm not here."

"I can't do that, Mrs. Thornton. I already told her you were here. She called just as you walked back to the office."

"Then call her and tell her you were mistaken or that I just left."

"I'm afraid you'll have to do that yourself. I'm not going to put myself in a position where I have to lie for anyone. For whatever it's worth, it sounded pretty important."

Celia snatched the paper out of Neal's hand, slamming the door shut in his face at the same time. She stalked her way to Jeff's desk to pick up the phone. She took a moment to compose herself, her mind racing to come up with a lie Ruby would believe.

Celia's voice was tired but sweet when she said, "Ruby, it's Celia. Is something wrong? I was so wired up I couldn't sleep, so I thought I'd come here to the casino for an hour or so and have a nightcap. I've been a night owl for years. Birch said he thinks I have vampire blood in my veins." She emitted a little laugh that sounded nervous to her own ears. "Yes, yes, I'm listening."

Lassiter pressed the button on the speaker phone. Ruby's agitated voice poured into the room.

"Did I hear you correctly, Ruby? Sage *thinks* something is wrong. It's that twin thing everyone talks about. He wants to fly your brand-new multimillion-dollar plane to an airport that's closed and you're going with him all because he *thinks* some-thing *might* be wrong. You want to know if I care to go along on the trip. I'll pass, Ruby. Birch told me many times he was a Boy Scout. Ski resorts make their living off snow. Every Sunday in the newspaper they have stories about the latest equipment they have when storms like this crop up. They have generators, deep freezes stocked with food, endless supplies of firewood, gasoline-powered snowblowers. They have all kinds of medical stations and units, ski patrols and, of course, the rangers. What can you and Sage possibly do that they aren't doing except endanger your own lives and the life of that brand-new jet you just bought?''

''I had to ask, Celia. It was a courtesy. Sage and I are willing to take that chance.''

''Well, I'm not. Those weather forecasters blow everything out of proportion. For the past three days I've heard our own weatherman predict rain. I haven't seen a drop so far. They prey on people's fears and it fills up the airtime. Birch is very good at looking out for himself. Have a safe trip. I'll keep up the work schedule tomorrow. By the time you get back the commercials will be wrapped and ready to air. The blowup ads are supposed to be ready for the print media late tomorrow. Have a safe trip and give Birch a kiss for me.''

''Talk about a loving wife,'' Lassiter sneered.

''I can see the evil shining in your eyes,'' Celia sneered in return.

''What you're seeing is your own evil reflected in my eyes. You better get moving, sweetie. Tomorrow morning is going to be here before you know it. How are you going to cover those bags and dark circles under your eyes?''

''You let me worry about my dark circles. For your information, I do not have bags under my eyes.''

Jeff's laughter followed Celia out the door. She was halfway across the casino floor when Neal Tortolow caught up with her.

''Mrs. Thornton, wait a minute. Can I offer you a ride to the airport?''

''Don't be ridiculous. I'm not flying into any freak snowstorm because someone *thinks* something *might* be wrong. How asinine can you get?''

Neal blinked. ''What if something *is* wrong?''

''That's why they have trained people at those places. I don't think being a Boy Scout is going to cut it in a situation like this. Trained professionals are what is needed. All Sage and Ruby are doing is endangering their own lives. By morning everything will be fine, you'll see. Those weather forecasters are lunatics.''

"It takes one to know one," Neal muttered.

At the airport, Sage did his last-minute check. ''I'm on my way, Birch.'' He crossed himself as he taxied down the runway. Three minutes later he was airborne. ''Just hang in there, big brother, I'm coming as fast as this bird can fly.''

"Amen," Ruby said.

12

Fanny stirred in the recliner. In her half sleep she knew the television was still on, knew the wind outside was stronger than before, knew she felt cold, knew the fire was low, knew that Billie Kingsley and Bess had gone to bed. She squirmed as she fumbled for the afghan she'd knitted in two days while sitting at the medical center waiting for a change in Marcus's condition. She struggled to wakefulness as she tried to concentrate on the words bouncing off the television and, at the same time, challenging herself as to the color of the afghan she'd recently completed.

The cold won out. Tossing the colorful covering aside, Fanny staggered over to the fireplace, still groggy with sleep, to toss two large logs on the dying fire. The bark took flame immediately, sending a shower of sparks up the chimney. On her way to the bathroom she noted the color of the afghan: three different shades of daffodil yellow. Oliver North in full-dress uniform glared at her from the screen. What exactly did a loose cannon mean? Ash would have known. She'd seen the marine's face earlier on the six o'clock news and then again on the ten o'clock news. She decided she didn't care what he looked like and didn't care if he were in his skivvies or full dress. Loose cannons or patriots weren't in her thoughts these days. Let someone else take charge of all the wrong or right doing that was going on in the world. For one split second she felt like throwing the brass lamp at the television. It occurred to her then, in the next split second, that all she had to do was press a button. Oliver North would be erased forever or until she turned the set back on. She could, of course, read the *TV Guide* to select an inane game show or cartoon or even a late-night rerun of some sort. Marines didn't spout off in game shows or reruns of *Gilligan's Island*. Or did they? Not wishing to take a chance, Fanny pressed the remote.

She was in the kitchen now. How neat and tidy it looked. Someone had watered the hanging plants and herbs on the windowsill. The red-and-white-checked dish towel was neatly folded on the side of the sink. Marcus always wadded it up into a ball and tossed it in the sink. She herself always hung it on the oven door. Green-checkered place mats were on the table. They didn't match the red-checked cushions or dish towel. Maybe the red ones were in the laundry. She'd always been partial to the color red. Marcus liked varying shades of blue. They'd argued over the kitchen colors when she'd finally convinced him that blue in a kitchen was depressing. Her ironing board cover was red-and-white-checked. It seemed to make the ironing go faster, not that she ironed much these days. Color coordination was the name of the game.

Fanny fixed the coffee basket, plugged the pot in, and sat down to wait. She wondered if black coffee ran in her veins. If it did, so what? What would they give her if she ever needed a transfusion? Coffee or blood? She walked over to the sink to stare out at the night. How light and bright it was. A full moon. When she lived on the mountain, she'd loved to sit outdoors, even in cold weather, and stare up at the silver moon. Suddenly she wanted to cry and didn't know why.

What would she do with her life if something happened to Marcus? She was too young to wither on the vine. She'd done her stint with Rainbow Babies and Sunny's Togs. The challenge was gone. Ash was gone. Simon was gone. Suddenly she longed for Sallie to put her arms around her, to talk to her, a mother to daughter talk. She needed to wallow, to cry and wail and have someone tell her things would be all right. "It ain't going to happen, Fanny. You're on your own," she muttered.

Fanny trotted back to the den for the afghan. Carrying it and a mug of coffee, she walked out to the patio to settle herself in one of the wooden lounge chairs Marcus had made in his workshop. She smiled ruefully when she sat down. The left leg was shorter than the right leg. When he wasn't looking, she'd used wood glue and stuck a small piece of wood she sanded down under the leg. It worked until Marcus sat on the chair. He'd added the repair to his list tacked on the garage door. She longed for Daisy to cuddle with. She belonged here with her. Tomorrow she'd go to the mountain and bring her, Growl Tiger, and Fosdick back. Life was going to go on, she needed to get back into her groove. It was time for Billie and Bess to go home, too. They had wet-nursed her long enough, pulled her through the worst days. Now it was up to her to follow through. She'd tell them at breakfast.

It was terrible to feel alone, to feel you had outlived your usefulness. Was that the way Sallie felt at the end? Sallie had given up everyone and everything. Ash hadn't, though. Ash had savored every single minute of his life right to the end. If ever a person was meant to live forever, it was Ash Thornton.

Ash always said, make everything in your life work to your advantage. The only problem was, he'd never told her how to do that. When she'd asked him, he'd stared at her, and said, "Fanny, there are some things in life you just have to figure out for yourself." Then he said, "I'm not going to be here forever to keep my eye on you. When it comes down to the wire the only person you can depend on one hundred percent is yourself.'' Why was she remembering all Ash's little homilies tonight? Was something going to happen tonight? Was the full moon spooking her? She thought about Ruby and the strange conversation they'd had earlier. Nothing was going right. Why was that? Ash would say, open your mind, explore, demand explanations. Don't settle for maybes, what ifs, and excuses. Get to the bottom of things. Don't depend on anyone but yourself. ''What I need to do,'' Fanny muttered, ''is to stop thinking about Ash like he's still alive and in my life.'' The clock in the kitchen chimed. Midnight. The witching hour.

Fanny set her coffee cup on the ground. Snuggling beneath the daffodil afghan, she was asleep within seconds, the bright moon painting her sleeping form a sparkling, silver color. Almost immediately a barrage of sound heralded Ash Thornton's arrival. She ran, the sound following her. ''Leave me alone, Ash, I need to find my own way,'' she shouted over her shoulder. The sound followed her as she ran among the cottonwoods to seek shelter from the blaring horn.

''You made a mistake, Fanny, when you gave Jeff my wings. They weren't yours to give. I wanted Jake to have them some day. I had a message inscribed on the back just for him. That was a shitful thing for you to do, Fanny.''

''Then you should have told me to save them for him. I didn't know anything about the message. How could I?''

''I shouldn't have to tell you something that's so important. It's common sense. Jeff Lassiter was the last person in the world you should have given my wings to. He made a goddamn key ring out of them. A fucking key ring, Fanny! Why didn't you give him Simon's wings? Get them back, Fanny, and attach the clasp for Jake.''

''I'm not an Indian giver, Ash.''

''Then steal them. They belong to Jake. Never Jeff. The minute I take my eyes off you, you screw up. I don't tolerate

screwups. Don't cry. Crying won't solve anything. You do what you have to do in this life because no one else is going to do it for you. I told you that a hundred times. Why don't you listen?''

"Because I'm sick and tired of listening to you. Sometimes you lie, Ash. It's hard for me to know when you're telling the truth. I'll find a way to get them back so there is no need to talk this to death. Let's face it. Your character wasn't exactly sterling when you were on this earth."

"That was back then. I'm platinum now, baby."

"I want to know about Marcus. I don't know what to do with my life. I'm marking time. I'm not doing anything constructive. I'm not contributing. Can't you ask them to, you know, rescind the order or whatever it is you do up there to change things?"

"I'm not one of the chosen few, Fanny. No one asks for my opinion. I can only tell you what I observe."

"I think you're nuts, Ash Thornton. I'm nuts for listening to you. I know this is a dream. You know it's a dream. You aren't real. You're dead. This is my subconscious working overtime because I'm on what you always called overload. You're sneaky, Ash. I'm afraid to go to sleep because I know you're going to stalk me. I'm so tired."

"Fanny, Fanny, Fanny. I have no control over things. Your subconscious wants me here. Even up here I have a hard time understanding that since you said you hate my guts."

"Sometimes I do. Not all the time. How did you know I gave Jeff your wings? I'll find a way to get them back. I refuse to take all the blame for that. You should have told me, put it in writing, that you wanted them to go to Jake. Your will was not very explicit. Things like that should be put in a will, so everyone understands what they're supposed to do."

"I relied on you."

"Get off it, Ash. Tell me this, why am I feeling so . . . antsy this evening? I don't want to hear anything about the full moon either.''

''You should have paid attention. You're wallowing in your own self-pity. That's a dangerous thing to do because you miss what is going on right in front of your eyes. Your ears, too. You tell me what you suspect, and I'll tell you if you're right.''

''Ruby was upset because the chickens were restless. I sensed fear in her. It rubbed off on me. I was feeling something too, though. I just can't pin it down.''

''The chickens always get restless when there is a full moon. I think every weirdo in Vegas showed up at Babylon when the moon was full. It's one of those either-or things. Translated that means either you pay attention or you don't.''

''That only leaves Marcus and the kids. Is it Marcus's time? Is it the kids? I don't even know what they're doing these days. Ruby told me Birch and Libby took Sunny and Harry to Vermont skiing to that resort Simon used to take them to. I should have known that, Ash.''

''Yes, you should have.''

''Are they in trouble, Ash?''

''Yes.''

''There is all kinds of trouble, Ash. Minor trouble, big trouble, and serious trouble. Which one is it? Answer me, Ash. You can't lay something on me like this and then float . . . sail . . . fly away. They're your kids, too! Come back here! I want an answer, Ash, and I want it right now!''

Fanny woke with Ash's name on her lips and sweat dripping down her face, the afghan wadded up under her chin. Disoriented, she staggered into the kitchen, where she refilled her coffee cup. She carried the heavy mug, the afghan dragging behind her, into the living room, where she switched on the television set, turning the volume low. She watched aerial maneuvers of an old war movie, realizing Ash used to do the same thing these pilots were doing. Her heart thudded in her chest. She reached for the remote, flipping through the channels.

She whipped past the weather channel, then switched back when she heard the words "New England states." She stared, mesmerized, at the swirling snow and the weatherman's horrific words. A second later the portable phone was in her hand and she was punching out Ruby's number at the ranch.

"Edna, this is Fanny Reed. I'm sorry to wake you. Is Ruby there?"

"No, Miss Fanny. She took the airplane on a trip. I packed her things myself. Your boy went with her. I think he's flying the plane. Where did they go? Miss Ruby didn't say. It must be somewhere that it's cold with snow. I don't think Miss Ruby will mind me telling you she wanted her long underwear, her boots, warm clothing, and lots of flashlights and those flares that were in the garage. She told me to pack plenty of brandy and cigarettes, too. I saw the truck leave about twenty minutes ago. When I asked her how long she'd be gone she said, 'You'll see me when you see me.' You might be able to catch her at the airport."

Her insides shaking, Fanny called information for the airport number, her fingers drumming on the end table as she waited for the operator. She repeated the number twice before she dialed it. They transferred her five times before she reached the person who told her the plane had just taxied down the runway and was now, this second, airborne. "I'm not at liberty to tell you the pilot's flight plan, ma'am."

Fanny slammed the portable phone on the coffee table. She picked it up again and dialed Sunrise. She wasn't surprised when Iris picked it up on the first ring. What did surprise her was her daughter-in-law's frosty tone of voice once she identified herself.

"Where did they go, Iris? Why didn't someone tell me? What's going on?"

"I probably know as much as you do, Fanny. Sage woke me up and said Birch was in trouble and he was going to

Vermont. Ruby called Metaxas Parish and he's flying there too.''

''Metaxas? Did Birch call? How . . . why?''

''There's a terrible storm at the lodge where they're staying. Sage said Birch is in trouble. It's Sage's instinct. No, Birch didn't call. Sage flew Ruby's new plane. He is certified to fly that type of plane but he has never flown a plane like it on his own. Ruby went with him. She's his copilot. She doesn't have a license so what does that tell you? That's all I know. Metaxas won't let anything happen to them. We all know how much he loves Ruby. Maybe this . . . whatever this is, will bring them together.''

''Why didn't you call me?''

''Fanny, why haven't you called us? The phones work two ways. I allowed for Marcus's accident, but you can't tell me you couldn't find five seconds in your day to make one phone call. I haven't heard from you since Celia got here. I also suspect Sage is having an affair with her. That's just in case you're interested. What do you think of that, Fanny?''

''What I think is you're out of your mind with worry about your husband and your pregnancy. Sage would never do what you just suggested. I know my son. I want you to know I resent what you just said. How could you even think such a thing about Sage? He and the others made it very clear they didn't want to discuss anything with me. They let me know right up front. It was their way or no way. I had to accept that.''

''That's because you made a very stupid mistake, Fanny. Even I knew it was a mistake. Family comes first. You always preached that to Sage and the others, and Sage preached it to me. Then you up and do something stupid that negates those same preachings. You should have listened to your children, Fanny. Because you didn't, Sage is off in a plane he's not familiar with, trying to aid his brother because he thinks he's in trouble. He could crash that plane and die. Your last memory of him will be that day in your kitchen when you turned on him in favor of Jeff Lassiter. How are you going to handle that, Fanny?"

"Iris. . . . I never heard you talk like this. You're making me sound like the enemy."

"Right now you are the enemy. I didn't want Sage to go. He didn't listen to me. He would have listened to you, though. He turned to Ruby. Ruby took over your job, Fanny. She's been your stand-in for a long time now. I bet you didn't even notice."

"Marcus . . ."

"Before Marcus. The world doesn't stand still because someone had an accident. I hope and I pray every night that Marcus will recover. There is nothing else I can do. Life has to go on whether we like it or not. There were a lot of things you could have done that you didn't do. Your whole family is fucked up, Fanny. You don't know the half of it. Excuse my language, but it's how I feel right now. I don't have anything else to say, so I'm going to hang up and watch the weather channel. Maybe you should do the same thing. Before I hang up, I'm going to give you something to think about. Ruby asked Celia to go with them and she said no. If I hear anything, I'll call you."

A look of pure horror on her face, Fanny could only stare at the pinging phone in her hand as a headache banged away inside her head.

Out of control.

Helpless.

Alone.

Danger.

She would not cry. She absolutely would not cry.

Pull up your socks, Fanny. You really didn't have a clue, did you? This isn't the end of the world, you know. It's close, though. You can't coast through life no matter how idyllic you think that life is. You can't rest on your laurels either. Do you know why that is, Fanny? Resting on your laurels is just an expression. If you rest, somebody else gets the bead on you

*and you lose it. You can't ever lose the edge that makes you
who you are. You lost it once with Sunny because of Simon. I
made sure you got it back. I'm not with you anymore, Fanny.
You're on your own now. Get that edge back before it's too
late. You're the only one who can do it. If you don't get on it,
you're lost.''*

Fanny whirled around. She wasn't sleeping this time. She
wasn't dreaming either. "Ash?" she whispered. When there
was no response, and she knew there wouldn't be, Fanny beat
her clenched fists on the arms of the chair. Ash was right, she'd
lost the edge.

You're the only one who can do it.

Fanny gritted her teeth. "I can do this. I will do this."

Where to start? Ash was right. She didn't have a clue. Or,
did she? Ash wanted his wings back. That was a place to start.
Steal them, he'd said. "I can do that." Iris had said Celia was
having an affair with Sage. "I can take care of that, too." She
did have a place to start after all.

"Thanks, Ash."

"Anytime."

Fanny jerked around. All she could hear was a low, throaty
chuckle that at one time had heated her blood and made her
pulses sing. She smiled as she ripped off a salute that would
have pleased a five-star general.

Back among the living.

With a mission.

The time was one o'clock in the morning.

Five more hours till the world woke.

Five hours to form a plan.

Things were going to be all right. Ash would have told her
if something was going to go awry. Still, Fanny kept her eyes
on the television screen as a plan began to formulate in her
mind.

Thanks to Ash, her edge was almost within her grasp.

* * *

The two wheelchairs rolled silently down the carpeted hallway to the main room of the lodge. The room was dark, the only illumination coming from the fireplace. Fed by propane gas and thick logs, the fire burned slowly. Very little warmth could be felt in the room. "It feels kind of like church, doesn't it, Harry? It's so quiet and still. I can even smell beeswax. They must use it on the furniture. It's so white outside. Isn't it amazing that rain and sleet make noise but snow doesn't? It's truly soundless. It's supposed to be like this on Christmas Eve. It never is, though."

"Sunny, very rarely do I think about the past. No matter what, we can't get it back. Just once, though, I'd like . . . I'd like to jump up and *RUN*. Before we go out those doors, I want us both to understand, and to agree, that something could happen to us. I'm willing to take the chance for myself. My motor skills are better than yours. I can't make that decision for you, Sunny. You have to think about Jake and Polly."

"Nothing is going to happen, Harry. We're going to stick together. We could talk ourselves out of this if we keep this up. Let's do one last-minute check before we open those doors."

Harry rattled off the items from the list he withdrew from his pocket. Sunny ticked each one off. "Okay, Harry, let's go."

Their wheelchairs side by side, they managed to get the door open without a problem. Harry wheeled his chair backward to hold the door open for Sunny. She scooted through as a gust of snow hit her head-on. She laughed as she steered her chair to the side to allow room for Harry. "Put your goggles on, Harry."

"I got them on, Sunny. They should make these things with wipers. It feels great. It's really coming down. I bet there is twelve inches of snow out here. It's drifting, too. Get behind me, Sunny, so your chair shoves mine. Even though they blew this path clear, it's drifting. We need all the power we can get out of these chairs to get us to the barn. Are you okay? Do you love this?''

''I love this, Harry. I really do. Keep going, don't stop.'' She was shouting, her voice carrying on the wind. She had no way of knowing if Harry heard her or not.

In the lead, a violent gust of snow slammed against Harry, pushing his chair backward, Sunny's chair sliding behind him. His chair tilted as he grappled with the padded armrests, trying to rock the chair toward the left to right it. Sunny swerved her chair, ramming it against his. She moved the control to reverse and then back to forward until Harry's chair was moving forward. The wheelchair races they had at the center were proving to be invaluable now. The makeshift obstacle courses on the center grounds would help both of them if Harry didn't forget all he'd learned. Harry waved his arm to indicate he was okay.

Sunny snuggled deeper into her jacket, shrugging the muffler up to her nose and chin. She felt a moment of panic when she realized her chair was slowing down. They'd charged the batteries earlier, but the manufacturer probably hadn't allowed for such a strenuous terrain. She made a mental note to write them a letter about the chair's performance.

Harry turned around. ''I'm losing juice, how about you?''

''I'm slowing down, too. Can you see the barn? It's not that far from the lodge.''

''I think I can see it. We still have some ground to cover, and the snow is getting deeper. My wheels are caking up with snow.''

''So are mine. What should we do?''

''Turn off the battery and propel it.''

''I can't turn the wheels, Harry. I'm stuck in the tire grooves you made. Can you move your chair?''

''Some. We don't want to use all our energy to slog a few inches. I think we're a little more than halfway. We both have upper-body strength. If we slide out of the chairs and get on our knees, we can shove the chairs forward. I'll wiggle behind you and push you since I have more strength. The chairs will take the brunt of the battering. Do you agree?''

Sunny was already out of the chair crawling forward as Harry crawled backward.

Exhilarated, Sunny shouted, ''It's working, and we're making better time. I see the barn. Are you okay?''

''I'm okay. Don't talk. Just keep moving.''

''The snow's getting deeper, Harry. The drifts are up to my chest. The chair won't go through. Stop. We need to think this out.'' Sunny sat down in the snow. ''We should leave the chairs and belly-whop the rest of the way. We can't get hurt. The snow is soft. I'm game if you are. We're about five hundred feet from the barn. Think of it in terms of swimming, Harry. We won't have to exercise for a month. I'm a better swimmer, so I'll go first.''

Harry felt his first moment of panic as he pushed his chair aside. The chair meant safety, and he was giving it up. He wondered how long it would take for the drifts to cover it. He could feel his heart take on an extra beat. The snow would obliterate all traces of them. He was on his own now, as was Sunny. *Don't think,* he cautioned himself. *Just do what Sunny's doing. The barn's in sight. You can do this. You will do this because you are capable of doing it.* Oh, yeah, in water. This was snow. Thick, heavy snow. Deadly snow. He risked a glance backward for one last look at his and Sunny's wheelchairs. He couldn't see them.

''How much farther?'' he shouted.

''I don't know,'' Sunny shouted back. ''I told you not to look. Just keep moving forward. You lose momentum if you stop.''

She was right. Sunny was always right. He flopped forward with all the strength he could muster. His face came down on the heel of Sunny's boots. Stars ricocheted inside his head. Had he broken his nose? He felt something warm on his upper lip. Blood, he surmised. He brushed at it with the sleeve of his jacket before he gave another violent surge forward. He repeated his efforts until he was dizzy. He didn't stop. He knew instinctively if he stopped, he'd never move again. He wanted to scream, to bellow, how much farther, when Sunny gasped. "Just a few more feet, Harry. I can see the barn door. Don't stop."

Every bone in his slender body protesting, Harry sidled up next to Sunny. "We made it, thanks to you."

"No, Harry. You did the first half. I did the second half. You sound funny. What's wrong?"

"I think I broke my nose."

"In the snow?" Suddenly she started to laugh. "That's the funniest thing I ever heard. We have to make sure we log that ditty in when we get back to the center. Listen. We have to figure out how we're going to open the door. If you cup your hands together and if you think you can hold my weight, I can put my knees in your hands. I should be able to open the door that way. Closing it might present a problem. Don't worry if I fall. I'll land in the snow."

"The door's on hinges. It swings shut by itself. I noticed that the other day. Okay, climb on."

Her hands on Harry's shoulders, Sunny pulled herself closer. Harry reached for her waist to help her into the deep well he made with his arms. He almost fainted when he heard the door swing open. Together they rolled over and over until they were on the dry concrete inside the barn. The huge door closed with a loud bang.

Safe.

Both lay quietly on the concrete, their breathing rapid and coarse-sounding.

"It's dark as hell in here," Sunny said a long time later. "There is a lantern on each post. I saw them the first day we were here. We'll have to do the knee thing again, but first I have to get my bearings. How many times did we roll over?"

"Four I think."

"That means one of the poles should be off to my right. Light a match. We can't afford to use up all my energy. I don't mind telling you I'm going to need some time to rest before we go out on those snowmobiles."

"We'll eat one of the candy bars and one of the oranges. That will fix our blood sugar. We'll save the rest. How are your battery packs?"

"My feet are still warm. The ones inside my gloves are okay, too. We probably have two more hours on each pack. We got here, Harry! Isn't it amazing? How's your nose?"

"It hurts like hell. I'm not going to worry about it. When we get out in the snow, it'll probably freeze up. Okay, look quick because the match is probably going to go out since it's drafty in here."

"Okay, I see it. Five rollovers should do it. Harry!"

"What?"

"We left our gear in the wheelchair pockets. The only thing I have on me is the battery packs and the candy bars. You have the oranges and your battery packs. You do, don't you?"

"Just the oranges and the packs. We left them behind? How could I have been so stupid?"

"It was easy. I didn't think about it either, so that makes both of us stupid. We can stay here and not take the machines out. Someone will come and get us in the morning. How many matches do you have left?"

"A whole pack."

"I'm going to roll over; follow me and count. Five rolls straight across and then two down in a straight line. I'll probably smack right into it."

Twenty minutes later there was light in the barn. The matchbook held only three matches thanks to the draft in the barn. Sunny and Harry huddled close, with their backs to the pole holding the lantern.

"I think, Harry, a twenty-minute catnap would be a good

idea. You sleep first, and I'll watch the lantern. After I wake up, we'll eat the orange and the candy bar. After we do that we'll decide if we want to finish what we started. We need the rest. We got this far, Harry, and we took care of ourselves. It's a dumb thing we're doing to other people but not us. We panicked back there. One of the most important things they taught us was not to panic. So what do we do? We panic. That's not going to happen again. I'll wake you in twenty minutes. The sound of the wind is hypnotic. When we lived on Sunrise, I prayed for wind to rock across the mountain.''

Sunny looked down at Harry. He was already asleep, snoring lightly. She herself was exhausted but she wasn't so tired she would fall asleep on her watch. She spent the time humming a lullaby Jake loved when he was a baby. Her gaze swiveled around the cavernous barn. Storage cabinets were everywhere. They probably held blankets, flashlights, and all the things they'd left behind in their wheelchairs. She could use up the twenty minutes rolling and sliding around to get what they needed if Harry still wanted to go out on the snowmobiles.

Prodding, picking, and poking, Sunny tossed flashlights, crackers, matches, a bottle of brandy, a small first-aid kit with a snow-white cross on the front and two tightly folded blankets. As an afterthought she threw a third blanket and a second package of graham crackers onto the pile. She eyed her treasure. She was about to close the cabinet when she saw the neat row of green-and-red portable shovels. She tossed two of them on top of the blankets. Opening her jacket, she stuffed as much as she could inside and zipped up the jacket. She slid on her rear end back to where Harry was sleeping. She piled everything neatly to the side before she rear-ended her way back for the rest of the things.

Eight minutes until it was time to wake Harry. Sunny spent the time staring at the long line of snowmobiles. She knew there was something wrong, but she didn't know what it was. Then it hit her. The machines were on a track. The same kind of track used at carwashes. Electric tracks. "Shit!" she said succinctly. Now what were they going to do?

Sunny rolled over and over until she came to a stop by the line of snowmobiles. Maybe there was a generator somewhere. They had generators on Sunrise and at Babylon. Her father had shown her how to use them. "You turn on the switch, Sunny." She giggled. It was that simple. Where was it? She fished around in the pocket of her ski jacket for one of the packs of matches. Cupping her hands, she managed to get a five-second look before the match went out. The generator was right where it was supposed to be; at the far left of the last snowmobile on the track. Two switches. A black one and a red one. She surmised that since the track ran under the barn door, one switch must be for the track and the other one must be for the door.

Rolling over twice, Sunny was able to see into the snowmobile. Some were two-seaters. Others were single. A double was the first in line. The second was a single. Harry could take the double and the gear. If they decided to go ahead with their plan.

"Wake up, sleepyhead," Sunny shouted as she rolled her way over next to Harry.

Harry bolted awake. "Is it still snowing?"

"The wind is shrieking. It's hard to see through the windows. My guess would be yes, and harder than before. Look what I found, Harry. I also discovered another problem but I also solved it. The snowmobiles are on a track like they have at carwashes. That means it's electric. However, there is a generator, and guess who knows how it operates. Me. You ponder all this while I take my nap. Whatever you decide will be all right with me. How's your nose?"

"It hurts like the devil."

"Roll over by the door and scoop up some snow and make a snowball. Hold it on your nose for a while. The snowmobiles are on a track that leads to that far door, not the door we came in. I can see the snow on the floor from here. Don't forget to wake me up, Harry.''

A second later Sunny was asleep, sliding down the mountain with Jake and Polly in front of her on an oversize sled, her father behind her in a fat black inner tube.

''Are we going faster than the wind, Mama?'' Jake asked, clutching her arm with all the strength in his small body.

''We sure are. Look at Pop Pop. He's laughing so hard he's going to fall out of that tube,'' Sunny squealed.

''More, more, more,'' Polly chortled.

''Can we do it again, Mama?''

''Sure. As many times as you want.''

''Will we always do this? Will your bad leg get to be a good leg again?''

''I don't think so, Jake. Next year Chue will do this with you.''

''Will you be sad, Mama? Will you cry?''

''I might be a little sad, Jake. I'll smile when I see you on your sled with Chue. If you're happy, Mama will be happy.''

''Will you always be happy, Mama?''

''I hope so, Jake.''

''I like to hear Pop Pop laugh. Do you like to hear him laugh, Mama?''

''I love to hear Pop Pop laugh. When I hear you laugh I feel happy. I don't want you ever to be sad. Sometimes things happen, and they make us sad. We wear a sad face for a little while, but then we have to put on our happy face and get on with the business of living. You know, make the beds, cook, do the dishes, the laundry, pick up toys, things like that.''

''I like the snow. I like it better than swimming.''

''I do too. When I was a little girl, I played in the snow all the time. Do you want to make snow angels when Chue drives us up the mountain? Pop Pop looks tired, so maybe we should make our snow angels and go inside for cocoa. You can put the marshmallows in the cups. Okay? What are you doing, Jake?''

Jake squeezed his eyes shut. ''I'm making a wish. Wishes are good, aren't they, Mama?''

''Wishes are very good, Jake. What did you wish for?''

''I made two wishes. I wished that Pop Pop would never go away, and I wished your bad legs get good so you can play in the snow. Is that a sad wish or a happy wish?''

''It's a happy wish,'' Sunny said, tears streaming down her cheeks.

''Will my wishes come true, Mama?''

''You'll just have to wait and see.''

''Sunny, wake up.''

''Are the twenty minutes up already? Did anything happen?''

''I peeled the orange and opened the candy bar. I did the snowball thing, and my nose feels a little better. Were you dreaming?''

Sunny reached for her half of the orange. ''I was dreaming about the last time I took Jake and Polly sled riding down the mountain. My father died the next year, and we never got to go again. Chue would bring us back up the hill in the truck. Jake made a wish that day that I would get to play in the snow again. I wonder if that dream was an omen or something.''

''We were talking about Jake and Polly earlier. You dreamed about them because they were on your mind. This is a good orange. Here's the candy. I've been thinking. I think we should replace our battery packs now. We've used up quite a bit of time on the ones we're wearing. If we're going, let's start fresh. What did you decide?''

''We came out here to play in the snow. So, let's go out and play. We'll take the snowmobiles out and ride them for a little while and come back. The barn seems colder to me, so that must mean the temperature is dropping. We'll go in a straight line and turn around at some point and follow the tracks back. How does that sound?''

"It sounds okay. Have you given any thought to how we'll get back to the lodge?"

"I say we drive the snowmobiles right to the front door."

"That's a great idea, Sunny."

They were children then as they packed up their orange peels and candy wrappers, stuffing them in their pockets. The battery packs were opened and changed. They were suited up and in the snowmobiles twenty-five minutes later.

Hard, driving wind slammed into them as the snowmobiles slid off the track and onto the snow. If the door made a noise when it closed, neither one heard it. In the lead, Harry turned on his light, Sunny followed suit. It seemed to Sunny that Harry catapulted ahead of her into the swirling snow. She panicked when she lost sight of his headlight. She opened her mouth to shout for him to slow down, but her mouth filled with snow. She clamped her lips shut and increased the speed on her machine until she was directly behind Harry, whose machine had a high-pitched whine that irritated her. Her own machine sounded sluggish and definitely wasn't performing the way Harry's was. When she started to fall farther behind, she sounded the horn. Harry turned his machine and headed toward her, his headlight blinding her.

"What's wrong?"

"I don't know. The engine doesn't sound like yours. You were so far ahead of me I was afraid I'd lose you."

"Check the gas."

"Give me one of your flashlights. God, Harry, it's on E. Check yours."

"I have half a tank. Come on, get in this one. Push the stuff on the floor. Hold my arm, and I'll boost you over the side. Hang on now. Maybe it's better we're together anyway. Ten more minutes and we'll head back."

"Can you see better with or without the light?"

"It's an either or. I think I'll turn it off. Buckle up, and let's go!"

"Don't go too fast, Harry. We don't have any visibility. You could hit a tree or an outcropping of some kind." There was pure fright in Sunny's voice when she said, "Harry, I can't see my snowmobile."

"It's right there, Sunny. The snow can't have drifted that quickly."

"It did, Harry. Can you see the tracks?" To make her point, Sunny flashed the light she was holding. "They're gone, Harry. The tracks are gone!"

"They can't be gone. Five minutes haven't passed. You aren't shining the light in the right place, Sunny."

"Then you try it, Harry." Sunny cringed, hating the fear she was hearing in Harry's voice.

The beam on the powerful flashlight arced to the right and left. All that they could see was swirling snow that drifted as fast as it hit the ground. All signs of the snowmobile and the tracks both machines made earlier were gone.

Harry wiped his gloved hand over his goggles. "It's impossible, but you're right. We're turning around and going back."

"Harry, you turned around when you came back for me. We're headed in the right direction now."

"Don't you remember, Sunny, I turned around again after you got in? We were already skimming over the snow."

"Harry, are you sure? We need to be sure here before we get ourselves lost. I think I'm losing my voice from all the shouting."

"I'm not sure, Sunny. You aren't sure either."

"You're right, Harry. I turned around to look at my machine. But, didn't you swerve and turn around when I called your attention to the fact the tracks were obliterated?"

"I can't be sure. I think it was sideways. We could be going east or west for all I know."

Panic coursed through Sunny. "What . . . what should we do, Harry? You're using up all the gas. We need to make a decision."

"You make it, Sunny. My vote would be to go straight."

"Okay, let's go straight. No, no, turn and go the other way. Wait, that doesn't feel right either. Oh, Harry, nothing feels right. I'm scared."

"That makes two of us. We're going straight. Cross your fingers and say a prayer."

"Does it feel like we're headed back to the barn, Harry?"

"Yeah," Harry lied.

"You're lying aren't you?"

"Yeah."

"What's going to happen to us?"

"I don't know, Sunny."

13

"Talk to me, Ruby. I need sound, noise, something to take my mind off what we're doing. I gotta tell you I'm piss-assed scared. I don't know if I'm capable of pulling this off. How in the damn hell did you talk that Texan into doing this?"

"Sage, I've been talking nonstop since we became airborne. I don't even know what I said to be honest. Like you, I wanted to hear sound. I thought you'd be tired of hearing me babble by now. You didn't even hear me. You're so caught up in worry you just now realized I'm here. Listen to me—if you weren't scared, there would be something terribly wrong. As for Metaxas, he doesn't know the meaning of the word fear. As you know, according to all the books, there's nothing to fear but fear itself."

"Worried is more like it. What we're doing is incredibly stupid. I know it, and you know it. Metaxas knows it, and he's out there, ahead of us somewhere."

"I've always believed it's better to try to do something than sit around and do nothing. Your father said I was a mover and a shaker like he was,'' Ruby said, her voice going from a high-pitched wail to a subdued whisper.

"My dad was a mover and a shaker all right."

"You need to forgive your father, Sage. We don't live in a perfect world, so things go awry. Your father's destiny was carved out for him the day he was born. He played out the hand he was dealt the only way he knew how. If we lived in a perfect world, he would have been a perfect father and you kids would have been the Brady Bunch. You're a better person because of the hand your father was dealt. That's how I see it. I was bitter, too. Ash told me I had the best of the deal, and, you know something, he was right. The best part of your father's saga was that he made things right in the end. Some people don't get to do that. The last few years of his life were his happiest. When your mother needed a break she'd call me and I'd go to the mountain and stay with him for a few days. He balked at first, but I wore him down with my persistence. We became close, and he confided many things to me. It worked for both of us because I didn't judge him, and he didn't judge me."

"Why do you suppose he kept Jeff a secret? That had to be the lowest blow of all to Mom. To all of us when we found out. Even Grandma Sallie knew."

"For the same reason my father kept me a secret. Some small part of your father and your grandfather knew it was wrong, and that same small part of them didn't want to hurt anyone else unnecessarily. Stop and think about it. If Ash had told you kids and your mother about Jeff, all of you would have been devastated. He didn't think any of you would have been able to handle it. I think he was right about that. My own father used the same kind of reasoning. What neither one of them took into consideration was how deep the hurt went for me and for Jeff, too, I would imagine. It hurt to my soul. I spent years in therapy trying to get a handle on it. I used to rant and rail from time to time. I said some bitter, ugly things to my mother and father. They'd get tears in their eyes and their shoulders would slump and that would be the end of it until I boiled over again. It was what it was. Nothing can ever change the past. That's what was hard to accept. It's baggage that needs to be left behind in the past. I understand it better, but to this day I still have a hard time with it.''

"I did love him, Ruby. I didn't agree with the way he did things, but I did love him. He did tons of good things that people didn't know about. Then he'd go and do some piss-ass thing that didn't count for beans and blow his horn. I never could figure that out. Our family was never peaceful. There was always some crisis in our lives. Even when Birch and I went East to school we knew something was going on between Mom, Dad, and Simon. It followed us. Birch tried to run. Hell, he went halfway around the world for all the good it did him. You can run, but you can't hide. Birch didn't know that for a long time. He knows now, though. What is your opinion of Celia, Ruby? By the way, in case you're interested, we passed Hartford, Connecticut a little while ago.''

"What's it known for?"

"I have no idea. Paul Newman and some kind of spaghetti sauce. Maybe popcorn. I went to school with a kid from Hartford. So, what's your opinion of Celia?''

Ruby sucked in her breath. Lie or not to lie?

"Celia is a beautiful young woman."

"I didn't ask you if she was beautiful. I asked you what you thought of her."

"She's family now, Sage. I thought we valued loyalty above all else.''

"We do, and that's why it does matter, Ruby."

"Maybe I should ask you what you think of her. In some respects, Sage, I'm still an outsider. I applied for my wings but I'm not sure they've arrived, if you know what I mean. I love it that you kids have accepted me. I'm only a stand-in for your mother at this point in time. Do you know what I mean?''

"Yeah, I do. Celia scares me, Ruby. The minute I locked eyes on her at the airport the day they arrived she scared me. I had this scary, creepy feeling. I swear to God I looked into her eyes, and I thought I could see straight through her head. Her eyes are translucent. Didn't you ever notice that? I felt . . . you're going to laugh when I tell you this, but I felt like she was *evil.* I couldn't bring myself to hug her or kiss her cheek. I was damn lucky I managed to shake her hand. I haven't changed my feelings either. Sometimes I think she stalks me. She's a game player, and I think she's tied herself into something with Jeff Lassiter. I know this for a fact because Jeff put her up in that special room my father kept at the casino. I had her booted out when I found out. She knows I'm responsible for that. She charged up a storm and then paid off the charges with casino winnings. My gut tells me she doesn't love Birch. That's the bottom line. So, I guess my next question is, why did you hire her, of all people?"

"My back was to the wall, Sage. Billie . . . I'm not blaming anyone, I just didn't have many choices at the time, and it was down to the wire. Too much money was invested to let it wither on the vine. We signed a contract. I can pull it anytime I want. For whatever it's worth, she's been doing a good job. She's incredibly photogenic, and she speaks well. We can rerun the commercials till the end of time as long as we pay her a residual. We can always hire someone else to do the live interviews as time goes on. I thought I was doing the family a service by hiring her. Fair is fair, Sage. Birch brought her here, cut off her funds, and then left her to flounder. Birch was okay with the job offer. At least he said he was. Again, it's what it is."

"Well, I want it on record that I don't like her, and I don't *trust* her."

"Are you telling me this because you think we . . . you might not make it? Just how fast are we going, Sage?"

"About 600 knots ground speed. We're inside the jet stream, so we're picking up about a hundred more miles an hour. Flying west to east the predominating winds in the jet stream are 100 to 150, but then you know that. Our ETA is another hour from now. I wasn't thinking clearly when I told you five to six hours. Metaxas will be landing soon if it's possible to set down. Someday I want you to tell me how he got clearance for you to be my copilot when you don't even have a pilot's license.''

"Someday.''

"Dad was a member of the Mile High Club. Did you know that, Ruby?''

"Hell, yes, I knew that. He gave me his pin and patch as a joke. I guess having sex at 5000 feet is supposed to be some kind of major accomplishment. My personal opinion is it's stupid. What is your feeling?''

"Stupid is as stupid does. Once Birch and I sneaked his pins and wore them to school. We thought we were hot stuff until we found out no one knew what the damn pins meant except the principal. He called Dad, who was appropriately pissed off. In private he thought it was a hell of a joke. Mom gave us kitchen duty for sixty days when the principal called her. That meant washing and drying the dishes, setting the table, clearing it, sweeping and scrubbing the kitchen floor, on our knees, and taking out the trash. We had to peel all the vegetables, too. If we couldn't see our faces in the shine of the pots, we got a week added onto the sixty days. Mom made up these little pins that were really buttons and made us wear them.'' In spite of himself, Sage chuckled.

"What did the pins say?''

"Kitchen God 1 and Kitchen God 2. I was the two. Birch claims to have Mile High status, but he refused the pin and patch because he swore Mom would think up something worse than the Kitchen God stuff. We were on our honor to wear them twenty-four hours a day.''

"Did you?''

"Yeah, but we made up some lie about what it *really* meant.

All of our friends wanted one of those pins. It was kind of funny at the time.''

''What is our flight level, Sage?''

''We're at 39,000. We'll be descending soon. We'll pick up the snow around 25,000 feet. See if you can raise Metaxas? Do you really love that guy, Ruby?''

''I do.''

''Then why'd you ask me to look for a husband for you?''

''I was feeling old, vulnerable, you name it. I never, ever, thought Colette would give him a divorce. I got tired of eating myself alive over something that could never be. Shhh, I think I might have him.''

''Sweet baby, is that you?''

''I've been called a lot of things in my day, Metaxas, but never sweet baby.'' Sage grinned at Ruby. ''Your sweet baby is right here doing what she's supposed to be doing. How's it looking?''

''Bad, boy. Give me a fix on where you are.''

Sage rattled off the information.

''I'm thirty-eight minutes ahead of you at 23,000. This baby is a killer, boy. Everything is closed up tight. I got one angel on the ground I'm going to owe big time if he comes through. He's all we have going for us. There is some kind of flashing light out there that's iridescent. Don't know where the hell it's coming from. Tomorrow neither one of us will have a license.''

''That bad, huh?''

''Worse.''

Ruby licked at her dry lips. Her tongue felt thick and swollen in her mouth. She wanted to say something, but the words wouldn't move past her lips.

''Sage, tell my sweet baby I love her.''

''She heard you.''

''Tell him . . . tell him I'm giving up the chicken business,'' Ruby gasped because she couldn't think of anything else to say.

"Don't go getting carried away here, Ruby," Sage hissed. "Just tell him."

"Metaxas, Ruby said to tell you she's giving up the chicken business."

"Sweet baby love, ya'll doing that for Metaxas. Ya'll just made my day. I gotta ask why? We're dropping down to 21,000. No visibility. That strange light is ahead of us. I'm picking up some strange static. Maybe my angel on the ground is trying to make contact. We're signing off now."

"She's allergic to chicken feathers."

Sage shuddered at the sound of Metaxas's laughter.

Ruby started to cry. "I just know that fool man is going to get himself killed. I just know it."

"Ruby, I need you to be quiet now."

"We're at 36,000 feet; 35,000 feet; 34, 33, 32, 31, 30, 29, 28, 27, 26, 25—and I see snow all around us—24,000 feet, 23, 22, 21. Metaxas was right. There is no visibility—20,000, 19, 18,000 feet."

Sweat dripped down Sage's face. He knew his hair was plastered to his head in wet strands. In his life he'd never been this scared. He wondered if he'd ever see Iris and the kids again. *Please, God, help me.* If he were at 16,000 feet, Metaxas must be down to around 7,000 or 8,000. *I can do this. I will do this. Oh, yeah. Please, God, help me.*

"Will I do? The Almighty is kind of busy right now."

"Dad!" Sweat trickled into Sage's eyes. He swiped at it with his sleeve. What was happening here? Was something going to happen? Was his fright and panic taking over, causing him to hallucinate?

"It's me. Wings and all."

"I need help. My God, is it really you? I don't know if I can do this. Help me. Are you real? Am I sleeping? Am I wigging out?"

"Everything is A-okay. All you need to do is keep your wits

*about you. I don't think you ever asked for my help before,
son. As I recall, you were the defiant one.''*

"That's because I was afraid you'd say no. It was better to
muddle through than risk a no from you. Where are you?"

*"I'm on your left wing. How many times did I tell you a
good pilot is only as good as his wingman?''*

"Two thousand at least. Are you going to make sure I land
safely, Dad?"

*"You're going to do that yourself. I'm just here to guide
you. I really don't think you needed to tell my sister about the
Mile High Club.''*

"I'm at 13,000 feet, Dad. Zero visibility. Zero, Dad! Where
the hell is Metaxas?"

"Sage, who are you talking to?" Ruby asked through
clenched teeth. "You're going down too fast. Too fast, Sage.
Stop mumbling. Who are you talking to?"

"Dad. Shhh, I can't hear him if you keep shouting."

"Your dad? Where . . . where is he, Sage?"

"On the wing. If you look out, you can see him. He's covered
with snow and he's the one making the bright light. Do you
think he can feel the cold?"

"Sage . . ."

"You okay, son?''

"I'm fine, Dad. I never thought you'd be my wingman.
Never in a million years. How am I doing?"

*"You're at 8,000 feet. Did I ever tell you the ultimate high
for a pilot is coming in low and fast? Better than an orgasm.
Don't do it, though. Listen to me and I'll get you down right
behind Metaxas.''*

"Maybe you should be helping him, Dad. He's going to
slough through it first. Yeah, yeah, you told me that the same
time you told me gold wings and navy whites will get you in
any woman's bed. Metaxas isn't as good a pilot as you are . . .
were. How do those wings feel? What are they made of?"

"Chicken feathers," Ruby chirped, her face whiter than the snow outside the plane. "Seven thousand feet."

"Metaxas is flying blind. He just ripped the tops off some three-hundred-year-old pine trees. He didn't listen to me. I can do two things at once you know. That means I am helping him. To answer your question, I never asked what the wings are made of because I don't care. Hard right, Sage. I said hard! We're doing just fine, son. Easy on that throttle. You're at 5,000. Ease back. Zero visibility. You're doing fine, son. Don't expect any transmission. Parish's radio is out. He's going down, and he's coming in too fast. There is no angel on the ground. You need to know that, Sage."

"But, Metaxas said . . ."

"I know what Metaxas said. There is a man on the ground, but he lost his radio contact. I told you he was flying blind. He went down with nothing but his guts churning at 100 knots an hour. I helped a little. Two thousand. Easy does it. I'm going to leave you now, son. If you follow the light, you'll make it."

"Dad, wait! Dad!"

"Where's that light coming from?" Ruby shouted. "My God, it's like daylight. Metaxas must have some really good flares. I bet they're weather balloons or something like that. One thousand feet, Sage. Can you see his plane?"

"I can't see past the bright light. Hold on, Ruby. Five hundred, four, three. Chicken feathers, my ass. My old man would never wear something as tacky as chicken feathers," Sage grated.

"I see the flares. They're red, Sage. What *was* that light? Where did it come from? Are you all right? Can you see Metaxas? What happened to the light?"

Sage felt dizzy as the breath exploded from his body in a loud sigh. Shaking, he craned his neck to look out the window at the swirling snow. He was almost afraid to stretch his neck farther to see the wing of his plane. He blinked when Ash

Thornton raised his thumb in a jaunty salute. *"I couldn't have done it better, son. You're as good as your old man. You can take that one to the bank. See you around."*

"Dad! Dad, wait! Hey, Dad!

"Did you see him, Ruby? He was right there. He gave me his famous thumbs-up. Tell me you saw him. Please, Ruby, you did, didn't you?"

"No, Sage, I didn't."

"He said . . . what he said was . . . I was as good as he was. He said that, Ruby. I swear to God he said that. We both know there is no way in hell I could have brought this plane down in one piece. I was flying blind. He said Metaxas sheared the tops of some three-hundred-year-old pine trees. You don't believe me. I can see it in your face. I know what I saw. You saw the same bright light I saw."

"Sage, if thinking you saw your father helps, then I'm willing to concede that you *think* you saw him. It was all in your subconscious. The weather service shoots off those balloons all the time. We're on the ground, and that's all that matters."

"What do you think the odds of that happening are? We're from the biggest gambling Mecca in the world and no odds-maker would have touched this one. You know it, and I know it. It helps to believe."

"Yes, it does. I see lights coming our way, Sage. Secure the plane, and let's hit the ground. I'll get our gear and open the door. I'll fly with you anytime, Sage."

Sage offered up a shaky grin. "I didn't do it myself, Ruby. Someday I hope you realize that." Ruby nodded, her eyes on the wing of the plane. She gasped when she saw a form outlined in a bright light. Words that sounded as though they were coming from outer space circled her. She reached out to grab hold of the doorframe leading off the cockpit deck. *"Sage was right. I'd never wear chicken feathers. You owe me an apology, Ruby. I'm waiting."*

"I . . . I . . . A man of your class and distinction would only wear pure down. My apologies, Ash.'' Ruby's knees crumpled as she tried to grapple with what she'd just seen and heard. Sage caught her.

''I told you. Oh, ye of little faith.''

''We've just come through one of the worst experiences of our lives. It's natural for us to hallucinate. You spooked me, Sage, and I spooked you. We aren't going to talk about this anymore, okay?''

''Okay. Here comes your sweet love. I can't see him, but I can see the high-powered light he's holding. Bundle up, Ruby. We actually landed at the damn airport. That's something else the oddsmakers in Vegas wouldn't touch.''

Sage opened the door. A violent gust of wind drove him backward as stinging snow battered its way through the open doorway. ''We have to back out and fall to the ground. The big question is, who's going to shut this door?''

''Sweet love, you made it,'' Metaxas Parish said, catching Ruby as she dropped to the ground. Within seconds she was covered with snow. ''Guess the young pup that flew you here knows a thing or two after all.''

''More than a thing or two. How did you do it, Metaxas?''

''I'll be dipped in oil if I know. Some guy talked me down. After I sliced off the trees. I'll have to make good on those. We had some kind of effervescent light or something. The guy knew his stuff, though. He was a wise-ass, too. Called me a powder-puff pilot. I set him straight in a hurry. I asked him what his name was, and he said Major would do just fine. I don't know if it was a title or a name.''

''Guess it was your angel on the ground.''

''No. He had no radio contact with us. He did set up the flares, though. We came in blind the same way you did.''

''I think it was Ash. Don't laugh, Metaxas. Sage talked to him all the way down. He said he was sitting on the wing the whole time.''

''Sweet love, you don't see me laughing now, do you? Pilots

experience all kinds of things that seem real. Flying has always been an ethereal experience for me. Why don't we just say we had some kind of well-meaning intervention and let it go at that?''

''That sounds good,'' Ruby said as she mashed her body against his. ''We brought stuff, flares, food, cigarettes, and brandy.''

''We did, too. We need to gather round now and make a plan. I have no way of knowing where we are exactly, other than a runway of some kind. We're going to have to go on foot to locate those snowmobiles. That means we go in a single file. I was only able to scare up four men, so that makes us a parade of seven. We're looking for the Molly Stark Trail. The key word is *togetherness.*''

''We can do this, can't we, Mataxas?'' Ruby asked.

''I didn't come all this way to fail, sweet love. If they're out here, we'll find them. Trust me.''

''I do. What is the temperature, do you know?''

''Single digit. Maybe minus. It doesn't matter because we can't change it. I don't think I've ever seen this much snow in all my life.''

''We could die out here,'' Ruby said, her teeth chattering with cold.

''Not likely, sweet love. When it's my time to go, I plan to be in my own bed.''

The high-powered light in one hand, compass in the other, Metaxas huddled with Sage. ''This is the way I see it, Sage. Tell me if you agree.''

Jeff Lassiter popped the cap off a bottle of Budweiser. He stretched out his legs before propping them on the coffee table that was littered with other beer bottles, peanut shells, and scraps of paper. He pressed the Play button on the remote control, not because he wanted to watch television but so there would be noise in the penthouse apartment.

He'd moved in today because he couldn't stand living with his mother for another minute. The stifling heat, the smell of arthritis liniment, the game shows, and the cat hairs were driving him crazy. He'd engaged the services of a home health aide who came in three times a day to help his mother. It freed him up to do as he pleased, and it pleased him to take advantage of the penthouse living accommodations that came with his contract.

Now that Neal Tortolow was running the casino and he'd been reduced to a figurehead, just the way he'd planned, he was having the time of his life. He hadn't counted on Celia Thornton, though. She was definitely a plus as long as he could keep her in line.

Jeff picked up the paper and grinned. If only they knew how close he was to his category killer. The jackpot was building daily for the birth of the killer, and he was the one who was going to have it. The industry was still touting the event as the seeker of the Holy Grail. He eyed the bottom line on the article in the paper and laughed aloud. The reporter was likening the secrecy of his project to that of the Manhattan Project with the determination of a race to the South Pole.

Jeff found himself frowning. The eternal betting truths were that gamblers tended to stick with games that were nonthreatening and packed a potentially large payout. He wondered if anyone in the industry with the exception of himself realized the mantra is "evolution, not revolution." He was relying on his own brainstorm to mix the deadly combination of inherently addictive quality of the slot machine's intermittent rewards with a game that got progressively harder as the player's skill increased. It was going to fly. He could feel it in every bone in his body.

Relocating his project to an empty building at the end of town was a blessing he hadn't counted on. The Thorntons couldn't do a damn thing about it now. His crew of engineers, software designers, graphic artists, and Ph.D. mathematicians were working round the clock. All he had to do was show up every Friday morning with an envelope full of cash. Cash that Celia and a few select friends delivered, minus their commission. No paper trail. Celia could of course blow the whistle, as could the others if things got sticky. But then, why would they kill the golden goose. He thought about the complete dossiers he'd collected on ''his people,'' a trick he'd learned from his father. His smile stayed with him. He made sure the select few sent the Internal Revenue Service their check each Monday morning. Hell, most of the select group would probably get a healthy refund come next May. They might even thank him when their refund arrived.

To date only two states had legalized gambling, Nevada and New Jersey. In two more years, if his calculations were accurate, and he had no reason to think otherwise, other states would legalize and cut down his odds. The two years were a cushion he wasn't going to need. Six more months, and he'd be the proud possessor of the Holy Grail of Las Vegas, Nevada, at which point he'd take his show on the road. Just the way his old man would have done. Yes, sir, The Emperor of Las Vegas, wherever he was, would have to give the devil his due. He absolutely had the same insight, foresight, and hindsight as his old man had. *Review all the angles, play every card you're dealt, and don't lose your edge. Well, Daddy dear, my edge is razor-sharp.*

A frown built between his eyebrows as his gaze fell to his key ring on the coffee table. His old man's gold wings. He reached for them, his thumb and forefinger caressing the burnished gold. Why hadn't his father given him the wings? Why was it Fanny Thornton who had given them to him? Didn't his father think he was worthy of them? Wasn't he good enough for something so personal? Why didn't his father's *real* sons want the wings? He decided at that moment his father's aviator's wings were the thing he treasured most in his life. Not his new sports car, not his bulging bank account, not his project. If he were offered his weight in gold for the wings, he wouldn't part with them.

Jeff slapped his knee with glee. His foot snaked out to tap the line of beer bottles on the coffee table. He watched as they teetered, then toppled over the side. He slapped his knee again, howling with laughter. "That's just what's going to happen to you Thorntons. You're going to teeter and topple over.

"C'mon, Celia, where the hell are you? It's 4 A.M." The words were no sooner out of his mouth than the phone rang.

"Open the elevator. I'm coming up from the garage."

Jeff walked over to the front door. He pressed the release button on the penthouse elevator. Five minutes later, Celia Thornton walked into the apartment.

"Was it a good night?"

"Absolutely." Celia tossed a straw purse on the table. "I'd like a drink."

"Help yourself. Ah, you did do well. I see you took your cut."

"Right off the top, honey. Here's to money, money, money!" she said, holding her glass aloft. "Switch on the weather channel, Jeff. I do believe my husband is lost in a snowstorm in Vermont. I'd like to see what his chances are."

Celia sat down next to Jeff on the sofa. "Do you mind if I sleep here tonight? I have to be up at six and out of here by 6:45. There is a spare bedroom, isn't there?"

"There's two spare bedrooms. If you have to be up by 6:45, there doesn't seem to be much point in going to bed. We could use that hour doing . . . other things."

"If by other things you mean sex, forget it. I'm married."

Jeff hooted. "C'mon, you were on the make from the minute you got here. I see the way you flaunt yourself. That's no granny dress you're wearing, baby. The big question is, what are you wearing under it?"

"Nothing."

"You seem to forget I saw you in the buff. I tease myself with those pictures every night before I go to sleep."

Celia's eyes narrowed. "Don't tell me you're one of those people who get it off by looking at dirty movies and pictures."

"Sometimes. You look like the type that carries a dildo around in your back pocket."

"Looking like it and doing it are two different things. On second thought, I think I'll just take a room for the rest of the night."

"Hey, come on, what's a little roll between the sheets? It can mean nothing or it can mean something. Let me put it to you another way, Celia. I'm horny as hell, and you owe me."

"I don't owe you my body, Jeff."

"You owe me your soul. Peel it off, toots."

"I will not."

Jeff's arm whipped around Celia's back. The sound of the zipper going down was so loud in the room it drowned out the weatherman's voice. "Are these babies real or are they silicone?" Jeff asked, cupping Celia's right breast while he held her left shoulder firmly in his free hand. "Why fight it, Celia? We're going to do it, so relax and enjoy it. Or are you one of those cold fish who *pretends?*"

"That question poses one for me. Are you the kind of man who has to force or trick women to have sex with you? I haven't seen any women hanging around you, and that poses still another question. Are you a switch hitter? I have seen a lot of pretty young men working for you."

Celia took the slap high on her cheekbone. A second later she was on the floor with her arms pinned down, Jeff on his knees looming over her. "Get off me. I said no. Don't do this." She struggled, but was no match for Jeff's strength. She heard his zipper go down, felt him shrug loose of his trousers. She tried to clamp her legs shut, but his knee pried them apart. Every obscenity she knew rolled off her lips. When he entered her, she screamed and kept on screaming until he loosened his hold on her arms long enough to whack her jaw. The moment he exploded inside her, she shoved him off her, reaching for a cut glass bowl on the coffee table. She brought it down on his head with all the force she could muster. She rolled out of the way, reaching for one of the beer bottles that she broke on the edge of the coffee table. "Come one step closer, you son of a bitch, and I'll gouge your eyes out. You're bleeding. Profusely. Head wounds always bleed. Did you know that? This is just a guess on my part, but I'd say you probably need . . . say seven, maybe eight stitches. I don't think Mrs. Thornton is going to appreciate all this blood on her nice beige carpet. Blood doesn't come out. Sometimes with club soda but as a rule, no. If you ever touch me again, you four-eyed bastard, I'll stalk you and slice off your balls. Do you understand me? I might go down, but you'll go down with me and where will that leave you?"

Celia moved across the room out of Jeff's reach. She pulled on her dress. She was surprised that she was still wearing her spike-heeled shoes. The broken beer bottle still in her hand, she walked closer to where Jeff was lying. Her voice filled with venom, Celia said, "Now I know why your father didn't want you to have the Thornton name. You're a disgusting little weasel, and he was ashamed of you. I hope you bleed to death, you slimy bastard."

Twenty minutes later, Celia Thornton locked the door of Room 2222 and headed straight for the shower, tears rolling down her cheeks. She wasn't crying because Jeff Lassiter raped her. She was crying because of the darkening bruise on her face.

Sunny tugged at Harry's sleeve. She was hoarse with all the shouting she'd done earlier. "We're lost, aren't we, Harry?"

"Yeah, we are. We're almost out of gas, too. The battery's

about gone on the light. I'm hoping to see some kind of stand of trees, anything that will give us a little shelter. Maybe we can rig up something with the blankets around this machine. I'm just talking, Sunny. It's all my fault. I never should have let you come out with me. Just because I'm a horse's patoot doesn't mean I had the right to take your life in my hands."

Tears burned Sunny's eyes. She knew if she cried, the tears would freeze on her lashes. Maybe her eyeballs would freeze. She took a second to wonder how that would feel. She knew whatever she said would be carried away on the hurricane-force winds. She patted Harry's shoulder to let him know she understood and wasn't blaming him.

Would they ever be found? Weeks from now? Months? The spring thaw? It must be almost four or five in the morning. That meant it had been snowing for more than twelve hours. How long did storms like this last? A day? Two days?

Sunny tugged at Harry's sleeve again and pointed to what looked like a small crop of evergreens. Harry turned on the snowmobile's light as he steered the machine to where Sunny was pointing. A feeling of light-headedness swept over Sunny when Harry cut the engine of the snowmobile. She didn't know which was worse, the high-pitched whine of the snow machine or the shrieking, howling wind surrounding her.

"Maybe we can make an igloo. Sage makes them with the kids in the winter all the time. We're still warm enough. Let's try, Harry. There is a little shelter here. That awful wind doesn't seem as strong in here. We have the blankets. I brought three and at the last minute I threw in two of those collapsible shovels. We'll have to work fast. We're going to make it, Harry, I know we will. We can't just sit, though. It will be light in a couple of hours. Birch will find us. We're going to think positively. You slide out first and catch me when I go over the side. We'll slide backward and work from there. The snowmobile will be by our front door if we get this igloo built. It will take the brunt of the snow and wind. My battery packs are still a little warm. We have another fresh one and a little time on the one we changed. We'll be okay, Harry. If something was going to happen, I'd feel it. Women sense things. Okay, here's your shovel. We build a high pile of it, pack it down, and then carve out a door and a space inside just big enough for us to sit up. It's the only thing I can think of. If you have a better idea . . .''

"No. We'll do it your way. It must be the same principle as building a sand castle. Lord. It's cold."

"Harry, are you all right?"

"I'm just scared out of my wits."

"Me too. We can't think about that, Harry. We have a project we need to work on right now. We have a completion time. We need to pretend we're back at the center and Libby is monitoring us. I say it's going to take us every bit of two hours to build the igloo because we're going to stop for breaks. Let's get to it. The cold air is searing my lungs, so we won't talk anymore. Okay?"

Harry nodded.

"I can do this. I know I can do this. I have to do this. I have to do it for Jake and Polly," Sunny murmured.

"What about me and your mother?"

"Dad?"

"It's me, kiddo. It's cold as a witch's tit, isn't it?"

"Oh, man, I really screwed up this time. I can't even remember if it was my idea or Harry's idea to come out here. I thought we could do it. I hate my limitations. I just goddamn hate them. I don't know how you did it. I'm dreaming, and that's why you're here. I dream about you so much. I can't figure out why that is. How come you're here? Is it time for me to die?"

"Of course not. I told you I'd look out for you. I have to admit this wasn't one of your better ideas. The igloo is a nice touch. I probably would have thought of it eventually. I like the way everyone looks out for each other. Was it always like that when you kids were growing up?"

"Yeah. We couldn't depend on you. Mom was busy being

mother and father and doing her own thing. It's okay. You made up for it those last few years with Jake. How's Grandma Sallie? This is stupid. I'm talking to myself. I know you aren't here. I'm just thinking, dreaming this so the work goes faster. How's it going up there?''

"Your grandmother is fine. It's peaceful. I had a hard time adjusting at first. I wanted to go go go. There is no place to go."

"So what do you do?''

"Watch over all of you. Let me tell you, kiddo, it's a full-time job. None of you have your shit together. Your mother was on overload and ready to take a handful of pills. I had to put a stop to that in a hurry. Tomorrow I have to pay your sister a visit and straighten her out. Sage is a hell of a pilot. He's almost as good as I was."

"It sucks, doesn't it?'' Sunny giggled.

"Yeah it does. Sunny, listen to me very carefully. Do not go to sleep. Do you hear me?''

"Why are you yelling at me? Is it because of the storm?''

"What did I just say, Sunny?''

"You said not to go to sleep. I heard you. I won't go to sleep.''

"Promise me. Don't let Harry sleep either.''

"I promise. I am really tired, though.''

"Sunny, listen to me. This is what I want you to do. I want you to build a domino bridge in your head. The kind we used to build when you and the twins were little. I want you to picture those black-and-white tiles as slats on a bridge. It's going to take 3,254 of them to get you to the front door of the lodge. When the bridge is all done, when you've counted 3,254 tiles, then you can go to sleep. I'm going to be watching you and listening to you count. Did you understand what I said?''

"I understand, Dad. I'm not stupid.''

"I know you're not. But, you are tired. If you fall asleep, you'll freeze to death.''

"Where are you going, Dad?"

"To help Sage."

"What'd he do now?"

"If I told you, you wouldn't believe me. Start counting."

Sunny sighed. The only thing she wanted to do was sleep. Building a bridge of dominos in the middle of a snowstorm was the stupidest thing she ever heard of. "Harry, listen to me. We're going to build a bridge. I was just talking to my dad and ... I know that sounds stupid, but I was talking to ... *someone*. Repeat after me ..."

The small group huddled under the wing of Metaxas Parish's plane. "I'm better off drawing you a quick map in the snow than trying to show you the map in this wind. Now, this is where we were *supposed* to land. That guy, Major or whatever his name was, said we were off course. According to him, we're over here. That means we have some tough climbing to do. It looks to me like there is twelve inches of snow on most of the ground and some twenty-inch-high drifts. I'm no weatherman, but I'd say an inch to an inch and a half of snow is falling every hour. The air doesn't feel like there's going to be any letup soon, so there is no point in waiting for a more opportune time. What I do know for certain is the temperature is below freezing. What we have to do is get to the top of the tree line. Put your scarves over your mouth and don't talk. We'll rest every twenty minutes. If anyone has anything to say, say it now. No. Okay, let's get cracking. Sage takes the lead, I'm next, and Ruby is behind me. You guys, one on each side of Ruby and two behind. Stay tight."

Sage struggled to take a deep breath. He lost the struggle and was forced to take little puffing breaths that left him exhausted. He knew he was climbing because his legs protested each step he made in the thigh-high snow. His heart labored each time he pulled one foot out of the snow. He stumbled and landed facedown. He cursed ripely, the snow blistering his face. What the hell happened to his damn scarf? He was on his feet again, his mouth full of snow, trudging forward. At the rate he was going he would be lucky to make a tenth of a mile in an hour. Impossible. He wanted to call out to Metaxas to see how he was faring. He negated the idea immediately. Calling out would take energy and time. He had to hunker down and keep moving. Maybe what he needed to do was come up with something he hated and feed off that hatred so it would keep him moving. The only problem was, he didn't hate anyone or anything. *Oh, yes, I do. I hate this goddamn fucking snow. I hate these goddamn fucking drifts that are up to my thighs.* His knees buckled and he was facedown again. *There has to be a better way. Snowshoes. Why hadn't anyone thought of snowshoes? Probably because they wouldn't work in snow like this,* he answered himself.

A violent gust of wind slammed into Sage, driving him backward. He rolled over twice before he landed on his back in a deep drift, losing all the momentum he'd gained. He cursed again with words he hadn't used since his college days when he'd tried to blend in with the rough-and-ready crowd on his dorm floor.

"Up and at 'em, boy. No time to play in the snow," Mataxas bellowed.

"Go to hell," Sage said as he struggled to his feet.

He trudged on, his breathing labored. If he survived this night . . . morning or whatever time of day it was, he would devote the rest of his life to never, ever, setting eyes on snow again. He continued to curse as he struggled to pull his foot out of a snowdrift. The effort left him exhausted. He wondered what time it was. Surely it must be close to dawn. Perhaps things would improve with daylight. Even he knew it was a stupid thought. For some reason his head felt heavy, his eyes heavier still. His eyelashes were frozen, and snow was piled high on his ski cap. If he pulled the ice off his eyelashes, would they come out by the roots? What would he look like without eyelashes? Iris loved his eyelashes. She said they were thick, double what most people had, and curled upward. Eyelashes any girl would kill for, she'd said. Birch had the same thick eyelashes. Girls, women, grandmothers always commented on his and Birch's eyelashes. Here he was contemplating pulling them out. "Like hell," he muttered.

Numb with cold, Sage squeezed his eyes shut and plunged forward. He was beyond all feeling, his thoughts wild and chaotic. He needed to go to another place, another time. A place that was warm and safe. He tried to think as his gloved hands pawed at the snow in front of him.

He was eleven years old walking next to Birch in the desert, sweat dripping down his face. His St. Louis Cardinals baseball hat was yanked down low on his forehead. "I hate this *mission.* I want to go home," he snarled.

"Me too. Let's sit down and rest. I need a drink," Birch said.

"We can't sit. Dad gave us a deadline. He said we had to complete this mission in four hours. He's waiting."

Sage rebelled, his heavy work boots digging into the sand under his feet. He looked around for a tree or some scrub that would afford him a little shade. There was nothing. Defiantly he sat down, Indian fashion. "My legs hurt, my arms hurt from carrying this backpack. I don't even know why we're carrying all this junk. I'm boiling hot."

"We have to survive. Dad said so. He's testing us on this mission. Do you want to disappoint him?" Birch demanded.

"I don't care if he's disappointed or not. Mom doesn't care if we know how to survive in the desert. I'm never coming out here again, so I don't care. Nobody else's father makes them go on *missions.* Me and you aren't in the navy. My blood's boiling, and my eyeballs are on fire."

"You're whining, Sage," Birch said, his lower lip trembling. "Are you going to cry?"

"I can't cry because my eyeballs are so hot they're drying my tears. I'm going home. I'm not going on this mission. So there!"

"We can't go back. It's too far. We only have another hour, maybe a little more, till we get to the end. Think how good that cold soda pop is going to taste. We can do this, Sage. We practiced going up and down the mountain. Let's go, Sage. The sun is getting hotter."

"Kiss my ass, Birch," Sage said with an eleven-year-old's bravado.

"If I kiss your ass, will you get up and move? Pull down your pants. We're frying out here. Sunny could do this with her hands tied behind her back and blindfolded."

"Shut up, Birch. I don't want to hear how good Sunny is. First of all, she isn't stupid. We're the stupid ones because we're here. I don't see Sunny, do you?"

"She could do it. She'd beat Dad at his own game. He knows it, too; that's why he didn't make her come with us. He wants us to be tough like her. I heard him tell Mom we were sissy wimps. He said he won't tolerate that in a son of his. He made Mom cry. She said we were sturdy, strong boys, and she called him an asshole. To his face."

"He is an asshole, Birch. I hate him. Don't lie and say you don't either. I'm going home. I don't care how far it is. You can stay and finish this shit mission or you can come with me."

"Sage, it's twice as far."

"Then that's *our* mission. I say we can make it. My tongue is bigger than my mouth. How do you suppose that happened?"

"Take a drink."

"I don't want to take a drink. I just want to go home. Shhh, what's that noise?"

"Oh, jeez, it's a rattler. Oh, no, it's three of them. Oh, shit! Don't move."

"Shit is right. I can't remember, what are we supposed to do?"

"We're not supposed to panic, Sage. When you panic fear takes over, and you lose the battle. Dad told us that a hundred times. Don't move your feet. Sit just the way you are, and I'll get the shovel out of your backpack. I tied mine to my belt a while ago. When you have it in your hands and I have mine in my hands, we'll strike. We'll get two of them, and the other one will go away."

"I know what to do if we get bitten."

"That's good because I forgot," Birch said. "On the count of three, you slide backward and strike downward. Go for the head."

"One. Two. Three! Yoweeeee! We got them! We killed them! There goes the other one. We did it! We did it!" Birch screamed at the top of his lungs.

Sage forgot his pain, his discomfort, his dry mouth, and his burning eyeballs as he gouged out a hole in the sand. Birch buried the heads of the two rattlesnakes. He bent down to pick up the snake Birch had killed. "Put it around your neck. That's what I'm going to do with mine. When Dad finds us, he'll see we're survivors. If he doesn't like it, then he can kiss my ass, too. So there!"

Birch linked his arm with his brother's. "Yeah, he can kiss my ass, too. If Mom heard us, she'd put soap in our mouth. Bill Waters says 'fuck' out loud all the time. Did you ever hear him? He calls his dad his old man. He's allowed to do anything he wants to do. He never gets punished."

"Does he know how to survive? Could he kill a snake? I don't think so. I hate him. He's dumb as dirt and as ugly as this snake I just killed. I wish I were in the pool with Sunny dunking me. I wish I had an ice-cold cherry Popsicle. I wish my underpants were full of ice cubes. What do you wish, Birch?"

"I wish Dad was here to give us a ride home in the Jeep. I wish I was covered from top to bottom with Mom's homemade banana ice cream. I'm glad you're here, Sage. It's good that we can always count on each other. Bill Waters doesn't have anyone he can count on. That's why he's a big bully. It's good that we're twins. I think old Bill is jealous of us.''

"Dad's going to be rip-roaring mad when we don't show up at that spot he marked on the map.''

"Yep." Birch whipped his arm around his brother's shoulder. "Maybe he'll see that there is more than one way to survive. He won't speak to us for about two months, you know that, don't you?''

"Yeah. So what?''

"As long as we have each other and Sunny in our corner we'll do okay. Let's swear now that we'll always help each other and listen to what our heart says, okay?''

"I swear," Sage said solemnly.

"I swear, too," Birch said just as solemnly.

"Let's give these rattlers to Sunny as a present.''

Birch grinned. "That's a great idea. She'll love them.''

"Jeez, I'm hot. I bet our blood is almost boiling. I think I can hear it pumping in my body. Which is better, being hot or being cold?''

"I've never been as cold as I am hot. How do you think ice cubes in your underwear will feel?" Birch asked.

"Really good. Better than good.''

"He won't acknowledge the snakes.''

"I know. Sunny will though. Let's do that ice-cube thing when we get home to see how it feels," Sage said.

"Okay. Keep going. We're gonna make it, Sage.''

"I know we will because we aren't sissy wimps. He's going to punish us pretty bad for disobeying a direct order.''

"So what?" Birch said.

"Yeah, so what? I think cold might be better.''

"Nah. When you're cold, you can't get warm. When you're hot, you can cool off," Birch said. "Maybe someday we'll get to test the cold thing. Dad might take us to the mountains and make us trudge in snow. We'll remember this day then. That's when we'll really know."

"I hope that doesn't happen, Birch. Cross your fingers and say, 'I hope that never happens.' "

Birch did as instructed. "If it does happen, I hope we're together like we are now. What would be even better is if Sunny is with us. Let's hold out for Sunny if Dad decides to do the mountain thing."

"Okay."

14

Fanny Thornton Reed walked over to her car parked in the driveway, coffee cup in hand. Another few minutes and it would be light out. A new day. The urge to slam her fist through the windshield was so strong she backed away. She returned to the small front porch, to the His and Hers rocking chairs Marcus had insisted they buy. She sat down to finish her coffee. When the cup was empty, she would climb into the car and drive to the medical center, where she would sit in the waiting room and knit. "I'm sick and tired of knitting. I'm sick and tired of going to the medical center. I'm sick and tired of everything and everyone. I'm damn sick and tired of feeling like this," she mumbled.

"Then do something about it. You're whining again, Fanny. When was the last time you did something worthwhile? Something that made a difference in someone's life?"

"Are you here again, Ash?"

"What do you think?"

"I think you're nuts is what I think. You're dead, so stop

minding my business. So what if I'm sick and tired of things? I'm entitled to feel the way I feel. What would you say if I told you I plan to go to Calcutta to join up with Mother Teresa?''

"I'm not touching that one. Did you get my wings back yet? That was a direct order, Fanny."

"Screw your orders, Ash. I don't have to listen to you anymore. I'll do it when I'm damn good and ready. It was my mistake, and I'll take care of it.''

"When?"

"When I'm ready. Let's get down to business here. When is it . . . what I mean is, when is Marcus . . . if you're going to take him then take him. I can't stand this.''

"There's been a change in plans. I came to tell you. He got a reprieve."

"What exactly does that mean? If he isn't going to die, that means he's going to live. That's what you're saying, isn't it?''

"You need to make plans, Fanny."

"Why? What kind of plans? If you can't talk sense to me then go away.''

"I wish I were there to help you, Fanny."

"I don't need your help, Ash. When were you ever around when I needed you? Never, that's when.''

"You are so cold and bitter these days, Fanny. Where's the old Fanny I knew and loved?"

"You killed her. You ruined her life. If I could have one wish, it would be that I never had gotten off that bus in Las Vegas. I should have kept right on going.''

"You don't mean that. You're upset because things aren't going right. In the end, what will be will be. You can't swim against the tide, Fanny."

"What am I supposed to do?''

"Pull up your socks and set a steady course. Get my wings back. I'm getting tired of telling you what to do. I hear a car. I think you're getting company."

"Don't go, Ash. I want you to explain about Marcus.''

"I have to go, Fanny. The kids need me."

Fanny snorted. "Like you were ever there for them."

"I'm trying."

"Guess what, Ash, so am I."

Fanny shook her head to clear her thoughts. Would she ever in this lifetime be free of Ash? She looked up when a car door slammed.

"Mom? Mom, I . . . Oh, Mom . . ."

"Billie, honey, what's wrong?"

"Everything. Oh, Mom, I'm so glad you're here. I wanted to come out here so many times. I need . . . Mom, I screwed up. Big time."

"Then we'll just have to unscrew whatever it is. Do you want to go inside and have some coffee?"

"No. I like sitting out here watching the sun come up. You and I used to do that a lot when we lived at Sunrise. Do you like it here? It's so different living in the desert after Sunrise and then the penthouse. I've been gambling, Mom. Not just a little either. Before I knew it, I was hooked. I've used up half my trust fund. I cut corners. I betrayed the company, Sage, and Ruby. Ruby was really nice about it, but she was angry. She had every right to chew my head off. Sage . . . Sage looked so . . . disappointed in me. I've been lying, cheating, and stealing. Me Mom. I'm sick inside. I don't remember the last time I slept through the night or when I had a good meal. Sage said I looked like shit, and he's right—I do. I broke Dad's cardinal rule. I know he's up there somewhere shaking his head at what I've done. I'm not even a good gambler. I wore disguises, Mom. I tried to cover it up a hundred different ways. Someone took pictures of me and gave them to Sage. I wanted to die. I need you to help me, Mom. I know you have other things to do and Marcus is in the hospital. I need *you*, Mom."

"I'm here, Billie. For starters we're going inside. You are going to shower and change into fresh clothes. Go through my closet. We're pretty much the same size. Then I'm going to make you a big breakfast. After that we're going to the medical center because I have this strange feeling something is going on where Marcus is concerned. We'll talk on the way and figure out the best way to deal with your problem.''

''Are you mad, Mom?''

''With myself. I always thought your father and I were lucky when none of you developed gambling fever. If your father had a particular fear, that's what it was. In regard to everything else he was totally fearless. It was inevitable, I suppose. I'm angry with myself that I didn't see what was happening to you, honey.''

''Mom, if I told you the lengths I went to conceal what I was doing you would be so disgusted with me you'd break down and cry. I can't seem to help myself. You have to help me.''

''Billie, I can't do it for you. You have to want your life back. In order to do that, you are going to have to fight this addiction. After your father died I found out all the good things he did. Do you know he helped to fund an organization for people like you? It's on the same lines as Alcoholics Anonymous. You go to meetings, you have sponsors, you join support groups and discuss your addiction and, Billie, it *is* an addiction. The casino still funds the organization and will continue to do so. Sometimes I marvel at his insight, at the way your father did things. It was almost as if he *knew*. I still dream about him. We carry on these imaginary conversations. I always feel so much better after I have one of our . . . little talks. I don't tell that to too many people, Billie.''

''I didn't get one minute of pleasure out of it. I always had the feeling Dad was watching me. Then I'd get belligerent and hit the tables big time. Defiance was my middle name. I started after Dad died. I do have an appointment with a shrink tomorrow. I decided that was the place to start.''

''It's a very good place to start. It shows you're still in control and that you want to get a handle on it. It's not going to be easy. You realize, don't you, Billie, that you have to repay the firm and make good on everything. Will repayments wipe out your trust fund?''

''Just about, Mom. I'm prepared for it all. I'll have a very small nest egg left. It won't get me far in this world, but it's better than nothing. Some people don't have any kind of savings at all. They gamble away their houses and their lives, and then they cry. The thing that makes me feel the worst is I didn't listen to Dad. This may sound stupid to you, but I think it had something to do with him never remembering my name. I'm not blaming him. I take full responsibility for what I did. Do you know they have special classes in the schools now? It's a major thing for young people today. It's a question of probabilities. A person stands a one-in-two-million chance of being killed by lightning. The odds of me winning a jackpot are one in 12.3 million. I knew that, Mom, and I still hit the tables. That doesn't say much for me, does it? God, Dad must be spinning like a top over this.''

''Billie, he's the one who fought with the school board to put the gambling classes in the schools. No one in the family knew any of that. All these strangers kept coming up to me at his funeral to tell me the wonderful things he did anonymously. In many respects he was more generous than Sallie was. I guess it was his legacy to us.''

Billie buried her face in her hands and howled her misery. All Fanny could do was whisper and croon to her daughter the way she had when Billie was a little girl. ''Let's get that shower while I make us some breakfast. I imagine Billie and Bess are up by now. I'm going to tell them they can leave today. It's time for me to take charge of my life too.''

''I didn't even ask how you were, Mom. I hate it when we're all on opposite sides. You made a mistake, though, where Jeff Lassiter is concerned.''

''Yes, I know. I need to find a way to make that come out right. I have to come up with a way to get his key ring so I can steal your father's wings. I gave them to Jeff, and your father meant Jake to have them. I didn't know that at the time.''

"How do you know it now?"

"Your father told me. In one of those bizarre dreams I have. He had something engraved on the back for Jake. Jeff will never give them back. He had the wings made into a special key ring. I have a feeling, and, honey, it's just a feeling, but I think those wings make Jeff feel like your father. You know, brash, cocky, arrogant, cock of the walk. Like The Emperor of Las Vegas. It's a mind thing. I could be wrong, but I don't think so. I have this feeling that if I get those wings back, he'll deflate.''

"Did Dad tell you that, too, or did you dream it?"

"Uh-huh. Bacon and eggs or pancakes?"

"Both."

"Coming up in twenty minutes."

Her back to the kitchen doorway, Fanny heard her friends before she saw them. "You're leaving, aren't you?"

"It's time. Bess and I were watching out the window when Billie arrived. We both think you're ready to stand on your own," Billie Kingsley said as she wrapped Fanny in her arms.

Fanny nodded. "Do you have time for breakfast?"

"No. Bess is going to drive me to the airport. I'm a phone call away. You know our motto is the same as the Postal Service, rain, snow, sleet, we'll be here. All you have to do is call."

"Bess . . . I'm so sorry about that wonderful trip around the world."

"Don't be. Two days away from home and I start to get itchy. John's worse than I am, but he won't admit it. I'll call you later today."

"Okay. Be careful driving home."

The kitchen was so silent, Fanny cringed at the sound the eggs made when she cracked them on the edge of the bowl. Her shoulders slumped.

"Mom? What's wrong?"

"A lot of things. This is going to sound strange coming from me, but I really and truly miss your father. It's as though I'm tied to him with this invisible, unbreakable cord. Even now I feel that cord being pulled. A part of my heart will always belong to him. It doesn't make sense. Here I am married to Marcus. I was divorced from your father. I married his brother, and then he died the same day your father did. Do I grieve, do I fall apart? No. What do I do? I go out and get married for the third time. All I do is question myself. Why, why, why? I thought I loved Marcus. Maybe I just think I love him. Simon was a jackal, and I thought I loved him, too. Even on your father's worst day I still loved him."

"Maybe you're a one-man woman, Mom."

Fanny smiled as she scooped eggs onto Billie's plate. "You could be right. Now, let's talk about you and what we're going to do to help you."

"I wonder what time it is in Vermont," Billie said.

"Why did you ask that?" Fanny asked sharply.

Billie shrugged. "I don't know. The words just came out. Aren't they having some kind of freak snowstorm or something?"

"Your brothers and sister are there. Sage flew Ruby's new plane there last night. It's been in the back of my mind all morning. By morning I mean since midnight."

"Put the weather channel on and see what's going on," Billie suggested.

Fanny switched the channels until she saw swirling white snow cover the screen. She drew in her breath.

"Wow!" Billie said.

"Good Lord, how . . . how could Sage land a plane in those conditions?"

"He couldn't. No airport would give him clearance. Providing there was an airport that was open. I'm sure he turned around and headed back."

"Metaxas Parish flew out of Texas first. They were going to meet up on the ground."

"Then Metaxas turned around, too. Look at that snow, Mom. Only a fool, and Sage is no fool, would try to fly in that kind of weather. Metaxas didn't get to be the second richest man in the country by being a fool either. Stop worrying."

"Okay. Let's talk about you, honey."

"That's why I'm here, Mom. I knew if anyone could help me it was you."

The small travel clock buzzed. Celia rolled over, her arm reaching out to press the small button on the back of the clock. She rolled back over, realizing she felt awful. Not just awful but shitty awful. She bolted for the bathroom, her stomach heaving with each step she took. Her eyes watered as she strained to throw up in the bowl. When nothing came up, she whirled around to stare at herself in the bathroom mirror. The words "dry heaves" ricocheted inside her head. Pregnant women experienced dry heaves. Pregnant women felt dizzy and disoriented early in the morning.

Celia sat down on the edge of the bathtub as she tried to recall the date of her last period. She *couldn't* be pregnant. Stress could delay one's period. Her best guess was that she was two weeks late. From her perch on the edge of the tub she could see her reflection in the oversize bathroom mirror all hotels seemed to favor. She looked like she'd partied for seven straight days. Her eyes were puffy and her right cheek was black-and-blue. She'd seen peanut butter and jelly sandwiches that looked the same way her face looked. Makeup would help, but it couldn't obliterate the puffiness and the deep purple half-moons under her eyes. My God, what if she was pregnant. Her fledgling career would come to a grinding halt just as it was getting ready to take wing. Her hands went to her flat belly. What would she look like when her stomach started to grow?

A beached whale, she answered herself. She shuddered when she remembered how the women in Costa Rica grunted, squeezed out their babies, rested for sixty minutes, and then went back to work. Those women had babies every year. Babies ruined your life. When you had a baby, you weren't free to do as you pleased. What would Birch say? He'd probably be happier than a pig in a mud slide. Birch loved kids. He adored his nieces and nephew. "I hate drooling, slobbering, rambunctious kids," she snarled to her reflection in the mirror.

Maybe one kid wouldn't be too bad. She could insist on a baby nurse and a full-time housekeeper. The family wouldn't cast her aside if she were pregnant. Birch's mother was very family-oriented. Another heir to the Thornton coffers would definitely solidify her position. She could play on Ruby's heart-strings, too. Ruby was filthy rich. She'd ask Ruby to be the godmother and name the child Ruby if it was a girl and Reuben if it was a boy. Ruby would eat it up and ask for dessert. Ruby would be a wonderful ally. All she had to do now was to make nice to everyone. Oh, yes.

Celia's face turned ugly when she thought of Jeff Lassiter and the pictures he'd taken. Where did he keep them? Somehow she had to get them back. But, how was she going to do that? If the pictures became available to even one member of the Thornton family, she might as well pack her glitzy gowns and head for the nearest women's shelter, if there was such a thing in Las Vegas.

Celia stood up and peeled off her tee shirt. She stared at her slim, rounded body. Soon her breasts would sag, her middle would expand, and her ass would broaden. Her ankles would swell, and so would her hands. The sharp planes of her face would fill in, and she'd look like a butterball. Well, that's why they had diets and gymnasiums. The thought didn't make her feel one bit better. When she was dressed, made up, and had a cup of coffee in her hand, she might be able to think more clearly.

While the shower pelted her, Celia formed Plan A, Plan B, and Plan C in her mind. A girl always needed backup and her ex-con friend Solly could always be brought in if it looked like she needed Plan D. For starters, though, she would find time today to go for a pregnancy test at the first lab she could locate. Following the test and what she knew would be positive results, she would call Birch and inform him of his new status of father-to-be. She thought about things like dark clouds, baby bottles, silver linings, and million-dollar bank accounts.

This new day would be whatever she wanted it to be. Jeff Lassiter was the only glitch on her horizon. She simply would not allow a blemish on this new horizon. No way, no how.

Birch Thornton yanked at the covers. Sometime during the night he must have kicked off the down blanket. He waited now for his body heat to warm the bed. What he should have done was throw some logs on the smoldering embers. He debated a moment. What the hell, he was freezing now, how much colder could he get? He sprinted from the bed and tossed three huge logs any old way onto the grate. Shivering, he raced to the bathroom and then back to bed. There would be no more sleep for him. The digital clock on the small radio the lodge provided told him it was 5:10. Three hours till breakfast. He eyed the small coffee machine on the dresser. When the room warmed up he might consider making coffee.

He yanked at the pillows to prop them up behind his back. He was never one to laze about in bed. Normally the moment he opened his eyes he was so wide-awake he just got up and started the day. He twiddled his thumbs as he stared at the empty length of bed next to him. He thought about Celia and their marriage for the space of a few seconds. Then his thoughts switched to Libby in the next room. Libby was real and warm, with the nicest crinkly smile that said she allowed him into her world. He felt something for her that he couldn't deny, something he wanted to pursue. He knew in his heart that he was capable of being unfaithful with someone like Libby. Did that mean he was like his father?

Birch was jolted from his thoughts when an evergreen branch whipped across his window. Shit, he'd forgotten about the storm. He threw back the covers and walked over to the window to open the drapes. Good God! The snowdrifts outside were halfway up his window. He listened to the howling wind as he strained to see past the window-high drifts. How much snow was out there? A foot? Two? He yanked the drapes closed and walked back to his bed. The room was too warm now for sleep, and he was wide-awake. Libby's fire was probably out the way his had been. He eyed the connecting door. Maybe he should make coffee and knock lightly on her door. If she answered the door, he would make up her fire, then invite her into his room where it was warm until her own fire took hold. Sunny and Harry had each other in their king-size bed and Sunny's tongue would blister him if he so much as dared to knock. Sunny always was and probably always would be a bumble bee when it came to privacy. More so these days because she didn't want anyone to see how difficult it was for her to get ready for the day.

When the coffee was ready, Birch tapped lightly on the connecting door. Libby opened it immediately. "Is something wrong?"

"No, not at all. I was wondering if you wanted some coffee. My fire was almost out, so I woke up."

"Mine too. It's toasty now. Coffee sounds good. What are you using for cream?"

"That powdered junk. It's better than nothing. Your room or mine?"

"Yours. I just threw my logs on. It's going to take a while for those logs to catch fire. If you don't mind, I'll close the door. It will warm up faster that way. Did you look outside?"

"The drifts are up to the windows. I've never seen snow

like this. Harry is going to be so happy when he wakes up to all this snow.''

''Harry is a real sleepyhead. He can sleep for fourteen straight hours. I find that remarkable. Sunny's a good sleeper, too. Part of it relates to their medication. Were you thinking of waking them?''

''Not me. Sunny's whole day would be ruined if I woke her. I'm sure they'll both be up in time for breakfast. I hope it isn't cold cereal.''

''If it is, we'll revolt. I'm pretty handy in the kitchen.''

''Me too. What's your specialty, Libby?''

''Ham omelet with a little onion, a little cheese, and some diced tomato. At the end I add a few slivers of fresh garlic, just enough to give it flavor, and then I throw out the garlic. For the benefit of other people. I happen to love garlic and onions.''

''I do too. My mother always said frying onions, green peppers, and garlic made the best smell in the world. Our house always had the best smells in it. Mom would keep orange peels and cloves in a little pot on the pilot light. I used to love coming home from school, hungry as all get-out, and walk into our kitchen for homemade cookies and chocolate milk. It's one of my best memories. What is yours?''

Birch stared at Libby as she answered. He barely heard the words because he was so intent on how wonderful she looked so early in the morning. Her hair was pulled back into a ponytail, but some of the wispy bronze curls framed her face. Her bathrobe was old and frayed at the sleeves but it looked warm and comfortable. Slipper socks that went halfway up her legs looked just as worn and warm. He wondered what she had on underneath. To his own chagrin, he asked.

''A flannel nightgown. You haven't heard a word I said, have you?''

''Actually, no. I think I'm falling in love with you.''

"Don't say that, Birch. I shouldn't have come in here. I thought we agreed . . ."

"Yes, we did. Nobody ever told me how to turn off feelings. Do you know how? If you do, tell me."

Libby's voice was so sad, Birch felt his eyes start to burn. "I didn't sleep much. In fact, I didn't sleep at all. I kept thinking about us. There is no us, but that's how I was thinking. When we go back, I'm going to hand in my resignation. I don't think I can be around you and not . . . what I mean is . . . damn it, you know what I mean and what I'm trying to say. When I go to bed with someone it has to be because it feels right and means something to me. I'm not a one-night-stand person, and I can't sneak in and out of motels for . . . trysts. That's not who I am. You're married, Birch. If we . . . if we give in, we'll both hate ourselves. At least I will."

"You can't leave. What about Sunny and Harry?"

"I'll make sure my replacement is someone they'll both be comfortable with. The three of us discussed the possibility I might leave someday. It will be an adjustment for both of them in the beginning, but Sunny and Harry are realistic. It's the way it is."

"Jesus. Why do I suddenly feel like some lowlife?"

"I don't know, but if it's any consolation, I feel the same way. The flip side of that coin is we hardly know one another."

"I know all I need to know. My grandmother Sallie met the man she loved more than anything in the world at a funeral. She said the minute their eyes met, she knew she was staring at her destiny. That's how I felt when I first met you. My grandmother was married then, too. I'm not saying that was right. It wasn't. I'm trying . . . to . . ."

"Justify us going to bed together?"

"Yes."

"I didn't even brush my teeth," Libby said.

"I didn't either," Birch said, reaching for her hand.

Libby's shoulders sagged under the plaid flannel robe. "Are

we talking about just this once so we have a memory when we're old and rocking on some front porch in a retirement home?''

"Hell no. I'll get a divorce. I don't love Celia. I don't think I ever loved her.''

"I can't be the reason for your divorce. That's not who I am. It's not who you are either. People have to work at a marriage. I've seen so many marriages go bad because it's so easy to get a divorce. Then those same people marry someone like the person they just divorced and the same thing happens all over again. We shouldn't even be having this discussion. I'll go back to my room and lock the door. We'll meet downstairs for breakfast and pretend we never had this encounter.''

Birch's voice was hoarse when he said, "I don't want to do that. I want to carry you over to that bed and make love to you.''

"I want that, too, but we can't allow it to happen. The longer we talk about this, the worse it is for both of us.''

"No. No, I'm not going to let someone else control my life. I want you. You want me. I'm going to get a divorce. I want you to believe that.''

Libby stared at Birch, aware of how tormented he was. She tried to square her shoulders, willed her backbone to stiffen. She failed. Tears trickled down her cheeks. Her voice was little more than a whisper when she spoke. "Just this once. Then I'm out of your life. If you agree to that, we can . . . what we can . . .''

"Shhh. I'm not agreeing to anything except to loving you. We'll find a way to make it work. I swear we will. I want you to trust me.'' He kissed away her tears. She crumpled beneath his touch, all her protective instincts rebelling against the idea.

"I need you,'' Birch whispered. "I've wanted you since the day I met you. All I did was look in your eyes, and I knew we were meant for one another.''

The intensity of his emotions frightened her for a brief second, but her own need seemed so urgent that she nestled herself against him. "I want you to make love to me," she whispered in a low, throaty voice he'd never heard before as she began to trail kisses along his jaw and down to the curve of his neck.

Birch moaned. "Libby, Libby," he said as he brought his mouth down on hers, tasting the sweetness of her lips, drawing from them a kiss so steeped in passion he released her, his dark eyes searching hers in wonderment.

Libby watched Birch's thick, dark lashes close, heard her own breath in ragged little puffs as she lifted her head, her mouth searching for his.

Birch leaned forward, his hands feverish as his lips met hers in a scorching, searing kiss. The kiss was long, deep, and yearning. She drew away, her mouth trembling.

He picked her up, carrying her to the bed, where he nestled her between the thick, downy pillows. He sat beside her, his fingers tracing the curve of her cheek, down to the ridge of her jaw. He whispered words he later couldn't remember, words Libby had to strain to hear as she stretched out her arms to him.

The scent of him was clean and manly. The stubble of his beard scratchy against her face. She heard him mutter something about too many clothes as he shrugged out of his robe and the bottom of his pajamas. She did likewise, her gaze never leaving his face.

Birch felt his hands tremble as he touched the satiny skin of her shoulders and breasts. In the whole of his life he'd never experienced such intense feelings. He could feel himself feeding on the sight of her. The urge to paw the ground, to bellow like a bull was so strong he grabbed her to him, crushing her against him.

Libby felt her breath quicken as her pulses began to pound. She gently withdrew and rolled to the side, lifting herself into his arms, fitting each curve against his body, pressing him close to her. She drew in her breath when she felt his hardness. Her hands were as feverish as his as she once again rolled over, her grasp on his waist secure. "Love me," she whispered.

Caught up in her passion, Birch found himself matching his own responses with hers as he sought to fill her needs, which were echoed in him. He wanted all of her, all at once. He caressed her hips, her leg, her flat belly knowing she was opening herself to him.

Libby rotated her hips against him with urgent, searching motions. She felt the hardness of him jolt against her thigh, and then her world exploded as he entered her. She threw back her head, lost in the tide and ebb of sensations she knew she would remember for all her days. Suddenly she cried out his name as she climaxed beneath his touch.

Drenched with each other's sweat, they rolled over together, their slick bodies glued to one another, wonderment registering in both their eyes.

"I want to fall asleep like this and know when I wake you'll be in my arms," Birch whispered against her damp cheek. She nodded, her eyes already closed, but not in sleep. She held her tears in check until she was certain he was sleeping.

Libby moved slightly, her head against the pillow as she stared at the man who had just made her come alive. How was she going to walk away from him? How could something that felt so wonderful be wrong? How vulnerable he looked in sleep. She wanted to move closer, to smother his face with kisses, but was afraid he'd wake.

In spite of herself, she leaned over and kissed him until his eyes opened. "Now," she whispered, "I want to make love to you."

"I'm waiting," he whispered.

When the room grew light and the fire was almost out, they looked at one another, their faces alight with love. "I'll wash your back if you wash mine." Birch grinned.

"Just my back?" Libby teased.

Birch pretended horror. "That's where I'm going to start.

Where I finish, will be anyone's guess. One bar of soap or two?''

"I want my own. I'm going to lather you from top to bottom and save the middle for last. Is that okay with you?"

"Absolutely."

A long time later, Libby said, "It's quarter to eight. Should we head for the dining room or should we knock on Sunny's door?"

"I say we let them sleep. We can't go out. There isn't much to do in the lodge except eat, look at the fire, or watch an old movie."

"I rather thought they'd be up by now. Harry was so excited about the snow, I kind of thought he'd be up staring out at the white stuff. One knock. If they don't respond, we'll go downstairs. Okay?"

"Okay."

Precisely at eight o'clock, Birch and Libby closed the door of Birch's room. They walked the short distance down the hall to Sunny and Harry's room.

"The door's open, Birch. They must have gotten up early and are in the dining room waiting for us. The bed's made and the fire is out. They both need to be warm. I wonder if they slept in their clothes. They even made the bed. They do that, you know. Harry does one side, and Sunny does the other. Usually, though, it's not this neat. It looks to me like the fire's been out for a long time. There aren't any red embers."

"Here's a note," Birch said as he snapped on the light.

"What's it say?" Libby asked, craning her neck to read the note over Birch's shoulder.

"Jesus Christ! They went snowmobiling at two o'clock this morning. They never went to bed, and they weren't here to keep the fire up. Six hours!"

"Don't panic. They might be in the dining room or the great room, where it's warm."

"You don't believe that any more than I do,'' Birch shouted

as he raced down the hall. He was aware immediately of the silence, the emptiness, of the smell of perking coffee and cinnamon.

Sunny and Harry were nowhere in sight.

The storm outside was still raging when Birch ran to the heavy front doors. He pulled them open, gale-force winds driving him backward. He was covered in snow in a matter of seconds.

"They must be here somewhere. They wouldn't go out in this storm," Libby said, her face ashen. "Sunny would never do something so foolhardy. Harry wouldn't either."

"Trust me. They're out there. They probably figured the barn where the snowmobiles are kept is just around the corner, and they could make it there in their chairs. Their wheelchairs are gone. They're out there, Libby. Get dressed. We have to look for them. Better yet, you bring my stuff while I talk to that night manager and have her call the rangers."

The manager's face drained of all color when Birch told her what he suspected. "You have to raise the rangers. We're going out, but I'd like to know someone is looking out for us. You know, backup."

"Mr. Thornton, I don't think your sister would be foolish enough to go out in this storm in a *wheelchair*. I don't think you should attempt anything until I speak with the ranger station."

"If you were the one out there in a wheelchair, would you want me to wait for a ranger?"

"Well, no, but . . ."

"There are no buts. They left at two o'clock. It's eight now. That's six hours. Anything could have happened to them in six hours."

The manager's face got whiter at the thought of the liability involved. She tried the ranger station again, with no results. The look on her face went from helpless to hopeless.

"How long does a tank of gas last in a snowmobile?"

"About an hour and a half if it's full. Speed has something

to do with it. Clarence didn't fill the tanks yesterday because he wanted to catch the shuttle down the mountain. He has a family, and he wanted to be with them. I told him it was all right to leave. Some of the tanks were nearly empty. Clarence gave me the work sheets before he left. Only six of the machines had a full tank."

"Is there any place they could take shelter if they ran out of gas?"

"There are what we call two line shacks, where we keep emergency supplies for the ski patrol. I can show you on the map. It's unlikely they made it that far. There wasn't enough gas in their tanks. There is a possibility your sister and her friend are still in the barn. If they had the presence of mind to check the gas tank. Clarence always puts a yellow magnet on the tank when he fills it up. I have no way of knowing if your sister realized the meaning of the magnet. Their wheelchairs were kept in the barn when they took out the machines yesterday. Clarence might have explained the way it works, but I can't be sure. Start there, Mr. Thornton. I'll keep trying the rangers. Stay close to the building, and you'll be able to see the barn. I'm sure that's the way they went. The walkway was cleared by the snowblower around dinnertime last night. Good luck."

Libby was muttering to herself as she pulled on her fur-lined boots.

"This is not our fault. Making love has nothing to do with this, Libby, so don't start blaming yourself. Even if you had stayed in your room and I stayed in mine, we would just now be meeting up down here. Neither one of us would have checked on Sunny during the night. Don't go packing any bags for a guilt trip. Okay, are you ready?"

"I'm ready. What do you feel, Birch? Tell me the truth."

"I don't feel anything," Birch said grimly. "Stay right behind me."

"Don't you worry about that," Libby said. She adjusted her snow goggles.

The wind howled and shrieked as the snow battered them. For every three steps they took forward, the wind drove them back two steps.

Heads bent, they trudged forward. What would normally have been a five-minute walk to the barn took them forty minutes just to the place where Birch fell over Harry's wheelchair. Libby fell against him, sliding forward to land against Sunny's chair. She started to paw through the snow, shrieking and crying that Sunny and Harry were buried in the snow.

"No, they're not here. Look, Libby, neither Harry nor Sunny is stupid. The barn is right there. They would have seen it outlined in the snow. We need to think like them right now. Going back to the lodge would have taken them too long. I think they opted for the barn and either crawled or bellywhopped. Maybe they used their rear ends to bounce along. They're not here. I know they're not," Birch shouted to be heard above the wind.

Twenty minutes later, they arrived at the barn. "The door's open. I was right. They made it this far. Can you make it, Libby?"

"I can make it. My question is, how in the name of God did they do it? We have legs and feet and right now I can't feel mine at all."

"I don't know."

"Sunny! Harry! Are you in here?" Birch and Libby shouted over and over, their voices echoing in the cavernous barn.

"Look. They managed to light one of the lamps. That took some doing on their part. It shows they were thinking and had their wits about them. Shine your light around, Libby, so I can find the oil to replenish the lantern. Ah, here it is."

"Two of the snowmobiles are gone from the track!" Libby cried, her voice full of anguish.

Birch could feel his heart thundering in his chest. He had to do something. "I say we gas up these machines and begin our search. There's a lot of emergency gear in here. Let's hope they had enough sense to take some of it with them. My gut says they did because things are less than tidy on the shelves. The messiness tells me they were grappling for things that were higher up because everything else is incredibly neat and precision-aligned."

"God, I hope you're right, Birch."

"I know I'm right," Birch said with more confidence than he felt. He put his arm around Libby's shoulder and pulled her to him. "One more time, Libby, this is not your fault, and it isn't my fault. I'm going to light the rest of the lamps. Hopefully, if they aren't too far away and the snow lets up from time to time, they might see a flicker of light. We don't have anything to lose by lighting them."

"I agree. The snowmobiles don't need gas. The magnets are on the tanks. Harry and Sunny were the only ones using the machines. These six are gassed and ready to go."

"Shit!" The single word exploded from Birch's mouth. "You'd think a place as modern and sophisticated as this would have a horseshoe track that would bring the used machine to the rear instead of back to the starting point."

"We need to think like Sunny and Harry. I'll be Sunny and you take Harry's part. Which way would they go? Which one would take the lead? Sunny was talking about the Molly Stark Trail yesterday. She was reading one of the brochures. I remember her commenting on the landing strip and the fact that the trail was only a mile and a half from the lodge. She said if a skier got lost, they just had to find the trail and they could make it back here. She wasn't speaking to me directly but to Harry. She probably said more but I didn't hear it."

"We'll strike out in the direction of the trail. This map they have on the wall is clearly marked. With only one lantern it's doubtful either Sunny or Harry saw it. I almost missed it myself. I'll take the lead. Stay close behind me."

"Birch, they could have gone in a hundred different directions."

"I know, Libby. We'll do our best. My gut tells me they didn't get too far with the small amount of gas they had in the machines."

"Several miles at least, Birch. If their machines died on them, it's anybody's guess what they did."

"No negative thoughts, Libby. Are you ready?"

Libby adjusted her goggles. She nodded.

Not bothering to look for the mechanism that operated the tract, Birch pushed his machine off the track out into the snow. He started the engine before he went back to the barn to push Libby's machine outside. The last thing he did was to close and latch the monster double doors.

His heart thumped and thudded in his chest the way it had when he was little and watching a horror movie on television. Back then he had Sage to cling to. He wondered at that moment what his brother was doing. Probably riding down the mountain in the late-fall sunshine. Iris would have cooked what she called a he-man breakfast for him. She would have kissed him good-bye at the door and waved until his car was out of sight. Sage would be clean-shaven, dressed in his white shirt, tie, and business suit, listening to a Bob Marley tape on the ride down the mountain. Sage always was a lucky son of a bitch. He wished his brother was riding the snowmobile behind him instead of Libby. Right now Libby was too emotional. What he needed now was Sage's cool, level head.

Some things were just not meant to be.

15

Fanny sat in her parked car in the underground casino parking lot, smoking. Time this morning seemed ominous somehow. She felt disoriented, unsure of what she should do next. Being with Billie and listening to her problems had drained her, leaving her feeling listless and somehow angry. She wished for coffee, for a comforting friend, someone to tell her it was okay to break and enter and steal her dead husband's aviator wings. She should be home listening for the phone to ring. What if something happened to Sage while she was doing Ash's nefarious bidding? If she were at the hospital, she could turn the television in the waiting room to the weather channel. "And what good will that do me if the phone rings in my house?" she muttered. She fired up another cigarette. One of these days she had to quit smoking and cut down on her coffee intake.

Fanny leaned her head back against the headrest of the driver's seat. Billie a gambler. How was she ever going to come to terms with that?

"*I kept telling you you were losing your edge. Now, do you believe me?*"

"I can't believe you're here again, Ash. Is your afterlife's work following me? Why can't you leave me in peace? I'm not in the mood for your snide comments today."

"*Get out of this garage. Do you have any idea how many weird people hang out in places like this? Why do I have to do all your thinking, Fanny? Let's get with the program here.*"

"I'm here to get your wings back, Ash. I'm going to break and enter and steal them just the way you want. I should be at the hospital. I should be with Billie. Instead I'm sitting here in a parked car trying to figure out a way to break into my own apartment and all because I'm listening to a dead man give me orders. Go away, Ash."

"*I'm tired, Fanny. Those kids of ours have given me a run for my money. How the hell did you do it all those years when I wasn't there to help you?*"

"It was hard, Ash. Some days I didn't think I'd make it. It all worked out but it did take its toll. I don't regret one minute of my life. That's not quite true. Some days I do. Do you know about Billie?"

"*Of course I know about Billie. She learned a hard lesson, Fanny. I preached till I was blue in the face. Where was she while I was doing that?*"

"Probably hiding while she tried to figure out why you could never remember her name. How could you forget your own daughter's name? That was unforgivable."

"*Yes, it was. I can't change the past.*"

"You were a shit, Ash," Fanny said vehemently.

"*Yes, I was.*"

"I like it better when you argue with me. It's easier to hate your guts that way."

"*Where you're concerned, Fanny, hate is just a word. It isn't in you to hate anyone. That's a commendable trait. Billie's going to be fine. Trust me on that one.*"

"That one? Does that mean the others are in trouble? Earlier you said you had to help the kids. Ash, don't do this to me. Are they okay? Should I go home to listen for the phone? I don't think I could bear it if something happened to them. Are you watching over them? Ah, what can you do, you're dead!"

"I didn't say I could do anything. I said they needed me. Like you need me. When the day comes, and it will come, Fanny, when you no longer need me, I'll be gone forever."

"I don't want that, Ash. I feel closer to you now than I did when you were alive. I wonder if I'm losing my mind. Maybe I'm having a nervous breakdown. All I want to do is cry. That's a sign of depression. Maybe I already lost my mind and I'm too stupid to know it. You used to call me stupid a lot, Ash."

"That's because I was jealous of you. The kids are in trouble. If they remember the things I tried to teach them, they'll be okay. They have more of you than me in them. Right now I don't know if that's good or bad. They aren't kids anymore."

"If they need you why are you here? I can do what I have to do by myself. I don't need you here pep-talking me."

"All you have to do is cut me loose, Fanny."

"I can't do that. Why can't I do that, Ash?"

"We'll talk about that later. Get those wings back, Fanny."

Fanny's voice was honey-sweet when she said, "Ash?"

"Yeah."

"Kiss my ass."

"Ah, if I could, I would. Move!"

"I hate your guts!"

"You keep saying that. Is it okay to leave?"

"Go and don't come back," Fanny shouted.

"Okay."

"Will you look after the kids, Ash?"

"Fanny, Fanny, Fanny. What do you think?"

"I love you, Ash."

"I know. I love you, too, Fanny."

"Do you really, Ash? Truly?"

Fanny looked around as she waited for Ash's response. She sighed deeply. "Life goes on, Ash. A person can't live on memories. Thanks for . . . whatever." She waited a moment to see if there would be a response. There wasn't. She sighed again as she climbed out of the car.

Fanny glanced at her watch as she weaved her way across the casino floor to Neal Tortolow's office. She knocked softly and entered when the door opened.

"Fanny! What brings you here so early in the day? Is something wrong?"

"There is always something wrong, Neal. First things first. I want to apologize to you. Things were mixed up in my mind. Ash always preached to me that business stays in the family. Blood ties, that kind of thing. I thought . . . hiring Jeff was the right thing to do. I couldn't have been more wrong. I'm grateful to my children that they made it right. You might not be part of my blood family, but you are part of my extended family. I don't know how I could have forgotten that. I just want you to know I'm sorry."

"Apology accepted. How about a nice cup of coffee. It's just the way you like it."

"I'd like that very much. I need your help, Neal."

"Name it and you got it."

Fanny explained about Ash's wings. She waited for Neal's reaction.

"Let me be sure I understand this. You want me to call Jeff down here and tell him you want to meet with him in the conference room. You are then going to go to the penthouse and steal his key ring."

"At first I was just going to take the wings, but then that would point the finger to me. The whole key ring will be better. I'll leave the keys somewhere and they can be put in Lost and Found. The wings belong to Jake. I didn't know that. Ash had something engraved on the back of the wings for Jake. I have to get them back.''

''Okay.''

''You'll make the call?''

''Of course. Ash used to talk about those wings all the time. He treasured them more than anything. I knew they were meant for Jake. Lassiter made such a point of showing me and everyone else those wings every chance he got. It used to make me sick the way he'd fondle them. I never understood why you gave them to him.''

''I made a lot of mistakes, Neal. It was a bad time for me. When Ash died, I thought I was clearing up loose ends. My own children had so much. Birch and Sage didn't want the wings, so I thought Jeff would want them. You know, a tangible thing from his father. It seemed like the thing to do at the time. If I thought Jeff would willingly part with those wings, I'd go to him up front. I know he won't. I know it as surely as I know I have to keep breathing if I want to continue to live.''

''Okay, let's do it. He'll take the elevator to the main floor. I'll meet him and tell him you're in the ladies' room. Don't take too long. He and I aren't exactly friends these days, and he might get suspicious.''

''Just keep him down here.''

''What is your reason for asking him to meet you?''

''Reason? Oh, I'll think of something. I'll take the elevator to the second floor and the penthouse elevator from there. I still have my card key.''

''Good luck.''

''Thanks.''

Fanny waited five minutes on the second floor. The minute she saw the private elevator stop on the ground floor she pushed the button to bring it to the second floor. She didn't realize she was holding her breath until her lungs protested. She exhaled, the sound exploding in the elevator.

Her knees were like wet noodles when she exited the elevator.

Jeff's door opened to her touch. That had to mean he had left his keys behind. She blinked at the mess in the living room. Beer bottles were everywhere. She wondered if Jeff had had a party the night before or if he was the one who consumed all the beer. Where would a person like Jeff put his keys? She herself had always tossed them on the foyer table. She ran to the small hallway. The table was bare.

Ash, Sage, and Birch always emptied their pockets at night and threw the contents on the dresser. She raced to the master bedroom. The dresser was as bare as the foyer table. Maybe they were in the living room, where the mess was. She pawed through the newspapers, the dry food cartons, and loose papers. There they were. Ash's aviator wings attached to a massive key ring. In her hurry to grab the keys she disturbed the contents of the table. Colored pictures slid across the table. She took a second to look and then gasp. Horrified at what she was seeing, she started to shake. Sage and her naked daughter-in-law! Polaroids meant there were no negatives. *Take them,* her mind screeched. She swallowed, her mouth dry, her tongue thick.

What was Jeff Lassiter doing with pictures like this? What was her son Sage doing with Birch's wife? God in heaven! Fanny jammed the pictures and the keys to the bottom of her bag and ran to the door. As she fumbled with the door handle she broke into a drenching sweat. She had to get out of here. Now. She ran to the elevator and jabbed at the down button on the wall. Once inside she almost collapsed. Sage with Celia. Impossible. Trick photography. In a million years she'd never believe what her eyes had seen. Never, ever.

Eyes wide, nostrils flaring, Fanny ran from the elevator on the second floor to the stairwell. In the dim concrete stairwell, she leaned against the coolness of the wall as she tried to bring her labored breathing under control. She needed to be calm and cool when she met with Jeff. What *was* he doing with those obscene pictures? How long would it take before he noticed they were missing? Blackmail? Would he call the police?

Fanny walked out of the stairwell onto the main floor. She walked as fast as she could to the conference room. She opened the door to see Jeff pacing around the table. "I'm sorry I made you wait, Jeffrey. It was my intention to ask you to have breakfast with me—I need to talk to you about several things—but I've just had a call. I have to go to the medical center right away. Perhaps later in the week if you aren't too busy."

"Of course. Can I drive you?"

Drive. One needed car keys to drive. "Oh, no. Thank you anyway. I think best when I'm driving. I'll . . . what I'll do is . . . call you. Yes, yes, I'll call you later. Later in the week. Excuse me," she called over her shoulder as she ran from the room.

On the way to the medical center Fanny ran a red light and then traveled a mile on the shoulder of the road, horns blaring from every direction. When she finally skidded to a stop in the parking lot, she collapsed against the car door, her elbow jarring the horn. The sharp blast left her cowering in the seat. She had to get out of here. The rest room at the medical center in the privacy of a stall would be a good place to open her purse. How long would it take Jeff Lassiter to discover the missing pictures? How long before he discovered his keys were missing? Would he tie her visit to the missing items? If everything Ash said about Jeffrey was true, then of course he would suspect her. Proving it would be something else entirely.

Fanny caught a glimpse of herself in the plate-glass window of the medical center. That haggard, bewildered person couldn't be her. Where the hell was Ash? He should be here, pep-talking her. She snorted her displeasure as she whipped around the corner to trot down the hall to the waiting room, which seemed like home these days. She needed to sit down with a cup of coffee and a cigarette. First, though, she had to go to the ladies' room.

Fanny raced to the handicapped stall at the end of the row. She bolted inside and slid the lock home. The sound was so comforting she wanted to cry. The small shelf on the wall was perfect for lining up the junk in her bag. The first thing she did was remove the gold wings from the key ring. Without stopping to think, Fanny slid the cold, shiny wings down her bra. She wadded up the key ring in loose toilet tissue and placed it in the trash basket. She withdrew the obscene pictures and stared at them, getting sicker by the moment. Should she tear them up and flush them down the toilet? Should she keep them as evidence? Evidence of what? Maybe she could hide them. Where? In the lounge. There were pictures on the wall. Behind one of the pictures until she could decide what to do with them.

"Make it quick, Fanny. He's on his way. He put two and two together. I'm only telling you what you already know."

"This is the ladies' room, Ash. I know I didn't invite you here. Get out. I need to think. I got the wings. These pictures ... He saw right through my little act. I know he did. He's probably going through my car right now. What should I do, Ash?"

"Stash those pictures. They aren't real, you know. I might have done something like that in the old days. Neither Birch nor Sage would do something like that. Sage would never allow that to happen. You need to believe that, Fanny."

"I do believe it. You don't have to tell me anything about *my* son. Our son. Jeff's coming here. I know it. I just know it. He'll find a way to get my purse. Oh, God, this is ... this is the worst thing I've ever experienced in my life."

"If that's what you believe, then make it easy for him. You have the wings. You got rid of the keys. Now, hide the pictures and go out to the waiting room. Do it, Fanny. Do it right now."

"I'm doing it, Ash. Watch me. See, I ripped the backing

just a little. I'm sliding the pictures down inside. Now I'm hanging it back the way it was. Your mother hung these pictures, did you know that?''

"Take a deep breath, act like nothing happened. Light a cigarette. You can quit another day. Toss your purse on the floor by the chair and walk over to the nurses' station. Act unconcerned, Fanny."

"Okay, okay."

The first person Fanny saw when she opened the lavatory door was Jeffrey Lassiter. She blinked and reared back. "What is wrong?" She knew shock and fear showed on her face. That should prove to Jeff that she was upset over Marcus.

"Nothing. You seemed so . . . upset, I decided to come over here to make sure you were all right. Are you?"

He has mean little eyes, Fanny thought. *Why didn't I ever notice that before?*

"I always get upset when I come here. I never know if the news is going to be good or bad." She tossed her purse onto the floor by the chair she usually sat in. "Excuse me a moment, Jeffrey. I want to check with the nurse."

"Take your time. I'll keep my eye on your purse."

Fanny nodded. She stayed at the nurses' station longer than usual as she made small talk and accepted a cup of coffee. How many seconds would it take him to go through her purse? Five, ten? A whole minute. He'd have to paw through the junk, open the zipper compartments. Two minutes?

"If you're sure you're all right, I'll get back to the casino," Jeff said when she sauntered over to her chair.

"I'm fine. I appreciate you taking the time to drive over here. I'll call you later in the week."

"You know I moved into the penthouse, right?"

"No, I didn't know that," Fanny lied. "It's quite comfortable. It looks different now than when your father lived there. He was partial to black and white, chrome and glass."

"You're sure there is nothing I can do?"

"Everything's fine. Thank you for coming."

Her heart hammering in her chest, Fanny watched as Jeffrey walked away. How did CIA spies do this day in and day out? She felt wiped out, frazzled, down for the count.

"You pulled it off, Fanny. That's my girl. He suspects, but that's okay. Get those pictures and the keys. NOW!"

"I have other things to do right now, Ash. The charge nurse told me the doctors want to talk to me. They're with Marcus now. I think there's been some kind of change in his condition."

"Those pictures could screw up Sage's life, Fanny. You have to destroy them. That's a goddamn order, Fanny!"

"I don't have to listen to you, Ash. This isn't the navy." So much for words, Fanny thought as she headed for the ladies' room. The ugly pictures and the keys safe in the zippered compartment of her purse, Fanny took her place in the waiting room to wait for her conference with Marcus's doctors.

The knitting needles clicked furiously as Fanny's thoughts ran rampant. How did Jeffrey Lassiter get the pictures of her son and daughter-in-law? Was Ash's illegitimate son blackmailing her son? How could Birch's wife do such a thing? Her instincts about the young woman had been right. That brought it all back to Sage. She believed with her heart, with her mind, with her gut, that Sage would never betray Iris and his family. If her instincts in regard to her son were right, what other explanation was there for the obscene, ugly pictures? When her meeting with the doctors ended she would take a trip up to Sunrise. She could do nothing for Billie until later in the day.

Fanny adjusted the granny glasses perched on the bridge of her nose. Maybe she should think about Billie instead of the ugly pictures in her purse. On the other hand maybe she should think about Marcus and what the doctor was going to tell her. Was John Noble here? If he was, the medical center was allowing him to participate because he was a friend of the family and for the long years of service he'd given to the center before his retirement.

She heard the steps, knew they were coming at her from behind. Fanny wadded up her knitting and shoved it into the large canvas bag. She took a deep breath and waited. Was the news going to be good or bad? Why wasn't she feeling something? Why wasn't her heart pounding in her chest? Why didn't she feel light-headed? She'd felt all those things with Ash. Why was Marcus's condition different than Ash's? Marcus was her husband. Ash *was* her husband, too . . .

Six doctors! Fanny's heart fluttered in her chest. Ash said Marcus was going to live. Damn, she had to stop pretending Ash talked and visited with her. If she wasn't careful, they'd come after her with a net. She let her breath out in a slow *swoosh* of sound.

She felt at a disadvantage. Ash had always told her never to sit at a meeting. Standing he said, put you on everyone else's level. Eyeball to eyeball was always best. Fanny was on her feet in the time it took her heart to beat twice. She inclined her head slightly to acknowledge the five white coats. John Noble was in a three-piece suit.

John stepped forward. Fanny thought she'd never seen him look so inscrutable. "There is bad news and good news, Fanny. Marcus woke around two this morning. That's the good news."

"Marcus woke and you didn't call me! Why, John? That's unforgivable."

"Yes, it is. That's part of the bad news, Fanny. We started to run some tests immediately. You couldn't have done anything except to sit here just the way you were doing. It was a judgment call. The trauma to Marcus's head is much more severe than we originally thought."

"Is Marcus going to live, John? I want you to tell me the truth."

"There is no reason to think otherwise at this time. His quality of life is . . . we think it will be very different, Fanny."

Fanny drew in her breath. "What does that mean exactly? Spell it out, John."

"The tests . . ."

"Just tell me, John."

"Indications point to Marcus suffering brain damage, Fanny. He doesn't know me. It's doubtful he'll know you."

Fanny shuddered. "Is . . . is he like . . . is he like Philip was in the beginning? I really need to know, John. Don't sugarcoat this. I want it straight."

"Philip recovered and led a productive life after his stroke. Marcus's condition is different. We're going to run some more tests, Fanny. We just don't know yet. He's awake. In my opinion and in the opinion of my distinguished colleagues, that's a good thing."

Fanny backed up to the chair she'd been sitting on. John reached out to help her, but she shrugged off his hand. "What . . . what should I do? Shouldn't I do something? Why are you just now finding this out? Couldn't you tell earlier? I don't believe this. Surely something can be done. Do these things reverse themselves?"

"Fanny, when Marcus fell, he hit his head on the concrete. It was a horrendous blow. It's a miracle he survived at all."

"Are you saying his brain is scrambled?"

John's voice was careful, edgy sounding when he said, "I don't think I'd put it quite like that."

"That means . . . that means . . . How can God do this to me, John?"

John Noble bit down on his lower lip. He took a minute to compose himself. "Fanny, I'm just a retired doctor. I don't have the answers you're looking for. Is there anything you want to ask my colleagues? They're the best in their fields. They've done everything humanly possible. Aside from running a second series of tests, it is what it is. We're going to give Marcus a bit of a rest now and start the tests after lunch. You can visit with him now."

Fanny stared at the man who had been a friend most of her life and at the stoic specialists in their crisp white coats. She nodded. She was halfway down the corridor when she remembered her purse. She went back for it.

Fanny looked through the plate-glass window of the ICU room, her mind totally blank as she stared at her husband. He looked the same as he had yesterday. She wiggled her fingers. Marcus smiled and did the same thing. *Please, God, let all those doctors be wrong.* She lowered her head, tears dripping onto the molding around the window. When she looked up again, Marcus was still wiggling his fingers. Fanny bit down on her lower lip, breaking the skin. When she tasted her own blood, she backed away from the window out of fear that her frenzy would allow her to put her clenched fist through the glass.

"Whoa. What can I do for you, Fanny? Let's sit down and talk. Please, Fanny."

Fanny wiped at her eyes. "I don't know what to do, John. I didn't go in because I don't know what to say. How can a person as strong and vital as Marcus suddenly turn into someone who might not recognize me? We're married. We lived and loved together. All of that can't be gone. It just can't. Why me? Why Marcus? I don't know what I'm supposed to feel, what I'm supposed to do. He's my husband. Now you're telling me he could be a borderline idiot. I hate the word, but it is what you said in a roundabout way. I almost put my fist through the glass a few minutes ago. I don't think I can handle this. No, no, that's a lie. I *know* I can't handle this. Look at me, John. I'm not Sallie Thornton. Marcus isn't Philip Thornton. I cannot do what Sallie did. I simply cannot do that. I don't care what that makes me in your eyes. I refuse to allow myself to turn into Sallie Thornton. Do you hear me, John? I absolutely positively will not allow that to happen to me." Fanny's voice rose to a high-pitched scream.

"It's a shock, Fanny. Right now you're overwrought. When you've had time to think, to come to terms with Marcus's condition, things will fall into place. Look, I'm not saying Marcus is, using your term, an idiot. I don't like that word any better than you do. We need time. We need more testing. The general consensus was that Marcus would not wake. He did. I personally am taking that as a positive sign. Marcus is in excellent physical condition for a man his age. That's another plus. I probably shouldn't tell you this, but over the years I've seen many things in many patients. Patients lived when they should have died. Patients died when they should have lived. I'm betting all my medical knowledge on the fact that right now, at this point in time, that Marcus is just confused. He's been in that gray place where there were no sights, sounds, or familiar faces. He's in the light now. Time, Fanny. You need to give it time and let your conscience be your guide."

Fanny's eyes popped wide. "Did you say the word 'conscience'? Oh, no. All my life I've had to deal with my conscience. Everyone depended on Fanny's conscience. Do not ever talk to me about my fucking conscience, John. Never, ever! I mean it. That's not going to work with me. I will not turn into another Sallie Thornton. You can take that one to the bank. I'm walking out of here, and I'm not coming back. Tell anyone who needs to know. Don't call me. Don't write to me. I'm out of here."

"Fanny, wait. You're walking out on your husband? You can't do that, Fanny."

"Who says I can't? You? I'm going to do it. Watch me." Over her shoulder she called out, "I'll pay the bills, but that's all I'm going to do."

John's voice was so low-pitched Fanny had to strain to hear the words. "Are you saying you're going to *abandon* your husband? You'll never be able to live with yourself if you do something that drastic."

Fanny stopped in her tracks. *"Abandon?"* she said in a choked voice. All her life she'd never understood that particular word. Her own mother had abandoned her and her brothers. If there was one word in the English language she hated, abandon was the word. "Don't do this to me, John. These things just keep slapping me in the face. When does it stop? When is it over? Why me?"

"Sallie always said God never gives you more than you can handle."

"Don't talk to me about Sallie, John. I'm not denying my responsibility in regard to Marcus. I will not be a slave to . . . to Marcus the way Sallie was to Philip. I raised four children. I will not . . . be a custodian for someone who . . . who . . . I have a life. I used to have a life, and I want it back."

"Fanny, I can't let you leave here feeling as you do. I wouldn't be much of a doctor or a human being if I didn't try to make things right for you."

"You can't. No one can. I'm leaving."

"You didn't go in that room, did you?"

"No, I didn't. I can't."

"I'll go with you, Fanny. Don't you owe something to Marcus? How hard is it to say hello? What will you do if he recovers completely? How will you explain what you did to him and to yourself? Your family will never understand, nor will they forgive you. Just five minutes, Fanny. Then if you still want to leave, I won't try to stop you."

"You couldn't stop me even if you wanted to. All right, John. I'll say hello." Fanny steeled herself to walk back down the corridor to the ICU ward. She didn't stop to peer through the window. She opened the door, her back ramrod stiff, and marched over to the pristine white bed.

Fanny's eyes filled with tears as she approached the bed. It took her several minutes before she could bring herself to speak. "Hello, Marcus?"

The man in the bed stared at her with no sign of recognition. His voice was coarse and ragged-sounding. "Hello."

He looks thin, Fanny thought, *and in need of a shave.* His eyes were dull and listless, so unlike the intense, sparkling scrutiny she was used to. *How pale and waxy his skin looks.* "Do you know me, Marcus?"

"Are you a nurse? This is a hospital."

Fanny reached for the bed rail to support her unsteady legs. She shook her head. "I'm not a nurse, but this is a hospital. How do you feel?"

"Not so good. Can I go home?"

"Where do you live, Marcus?" Fanny asked.

"I live ... I live ... in a house," he said triumphantly. "Should I go to sleep now?"

"That might be a good idea," John Noble said.

"Will you come back?" Marcus asked. The question was directed to Fanny, not to John.

Fanny didn't trust herself to speak. She nodded as she ran from the room.

Outside in the cool sunshine, Fanny looked upward. "I never really asked You for anything. When I did ask, it was for other people. I'm asking You now, fix it or give me the strength to handle this. I can't do it on my own. I know I can't."

In the car, Fanny lit a cigarette. Earlier she'd had a plan. She was going somewhere to do something. She couldn't remember. All she could think about was Marcus and what lay ahead of her.

The engine turned over. Sunrise! She was going to Sunrise to talk to Iris, but she couldn't remember why. Then she remembered the ugly pictures in her purse. She was going to do something else, too. She had to think about Marcus and what would be best for him. Not her. But then she'd known that. Why else would she have spit and snarled at John the way she had?

Somewhere, some place, it had been ordained that she was to end up like Sallie Thornton. What had John said? It is what it is. Ash said she couldn't swim against the tide.

Tears rolling down her cheeks, Fanny drove out of the parking lot.

No matter what she did or didn't do, life would go on.

Ash and Simon had always said life was made up of winners and losers.

Fanny howled her despair as she turned off the road that would take her up to the mountain.

Was she a winner or a loser? Even a carnival fortune-teller could give her the answer to that question.

"I can't do any more, Harry. My hands won't move. I can't feel my fingers."

"We're going to die out here, Sunny."

"Like hell we are," Sunny blustered. "What number are we on?"

"This is stupid, Sunny. How do you expect me to count dominos and dig out this snow?"

"The same way I am. If I can do it, so can you. All I said was I was tired, and that I couldn't feel my arms and fingers. We have one space dug out and the other one is almost complete. We just need to rest and resume counting. I was up to 1844, so that means give or take a few, you're with me. We can't go to sleep, Harry."

"What time is it?"

"Does it matter? We aren't going anywhere. I'm going by touch because I can't keep my eyes open. I know what we can do, Harry. We can plan Thanksgiving dinner. Then we'll plan Christmas dinner. We'll decorate the tree. I have a really good memory, so I'll describe all the different ornaments and you'll pretend to hang them on the tree. This is all going to happen at Sunrise. *After* we finish building the domino bridge. I promised Dad, and I hate to break a promise, Harry. Break's over, time to get back to work. Start counting."

"One thousand eight hundred and forty-five. One thousand eight hundred and forty-six . . .''

"I can't do this, Dad. I'm too tired. I need to sleep. I'm sorry if I'm disappointing you. I want to do it, but I can't. Don't be mad."

"I'm not mad, Sunny. I'm pissed. The one thing that was always a constant in your life was that you weren't a quitter. I was so proud of you. Maybe I should have told you more often how proud of you I was. I told you to keep your eyes open."

"My eyelids and my eyelashes are full of ice. I can't keep them open. What difference does it make as long as I don't go to sleep? I can't wait till I get this goddamn bridge built. I only have one thousand four hundred and eight more dominos to go. I am going to sleep for a week."

"Oh, no, you are not going to sleep. When you finish the bridge, you have to dismantle it, counting backwards. Then you can go to sleep."

"That's a pretty sleazy trick, Dad. That's not what you said in the beginning. You didn't say anything about taking the bridge down. What do you think the odds are of me doing all that?"

"Damn good. You have guts, Sunny. You're the only one who had the guts to stand up to me. I respected that even if I chewed you out. I damn well expect you to do this, Sunny. That's a direct order! I don't want to hear you whining either. Keep going. Help is on the way."

"Harry needs to rest, Dad."

"No, Sunny, Harry can't rest. Listen to me, prod him, poke him, he's dozing off as he scoops out the snow. Do it, Sunny. Yell at him. Curse him if you have to. Make him fighting mad. Tell him you're stronger, tougher than he is. Men hate hearing shit like that. He's nodding off, Sunny."

Sunny poked Harry with the snow shovel. "Wake up, Harry. If you die on me out here in the middle of nowhere, I'm going to leave you. I'll cover you up with snow and say you got lost. Don't give me any shit that you're tired. I'm a girl, and I'm more tired than you are. My condition is worse than yours to boot. What number are you on? Don't tell me you can't remember either. I don't want to hear anything but numbers coming out of your mouth. Do you want to get married over Christmas, Harry? I'm tired of living in sin."

"One thousand eight hundred and fifty-seven. I'll think about it. You're too damn bossy. Would you really leave me out here?"

"Damn straight I would. I told you not to go to sleep. You're nodding off. You're slacking off, too. Look, if we scrunch we might be able to squeeze into that opening. Just a little more, Harry. I think we can finish the bridge and then start to take it down."

Harry jerked upright. "What?" he squawked.

"After we build it, we have to dismantle it, counting backwards."

"Shit!"

"Yeah, that pretty much sums it up. So, are we getting married or not?"

"I won't be any good to you. My balls are frozen."

"I feel certain they will unthaw or defrost. Which sounds better, Harry?"

"Forget about my balls. Let's get back on the bridge."

"My father said we have to dismantle it. He said he respected the fact that I was not a quitter. What do you think of that, Harry? Because I'm not a quitter, means you can't be one either. How will that look if you cave in?"

"All right already. Crawl in there now. Is there room for me? There better be because my right hand just went out on me."

"It's okay. If either one of us weighed one pound more, we

wouldn't fit in here. It's tight, but it's okay. They're going to find us, Harry. I know they will. Why are you breathing like that?'' Sunny asked fearfully.

''I don't know,'' Harry gasped. ''I think I breathed in too much cold air. Just let me sit here quietly for a minute. You do the counting.''

''Okay. Pull the collar of your jacket up over your mouth. I think it's about nine o'clock. Birch and Libby are up, and I know they're out here looking for us. I just know it. I feel it in my bones. I can't feel anything else, but I feel that. We survived so far, Harry. When it stops snowing we can get back on the snowmobile and head back for the lodge if no one comes to find us. There is still a little gas left. I love this igloo. I mean it. If my dad was here, he'd be so proud of us. We might do dumb things but we aren't stupid. Two thousand four hundred and sixty-nine. I never saw so much snow in my life. It has to let up soon. The snow's melting on my eyelashes. I don't feel so cold anymore. Two thousand four hundred and seventy-two. I wish I had a fried-egg sandwich and a hot cup of cocoa with melted marshmallows. When we go back to the lodge, that's the first thing I'm going to ask for. What are you going to ask for, Harry? Two thousand four hundred and seventy-five. Are you feeling better? Just nod?''

Harry nodded.

''Good. Let's suspend the construction of the bridge and start our Thanksgiving dinner. I'm making the stuffing. You're peeling the potatoes. We made the pies yesterday. We're drinking wine as we work. Wine warms you up. It's mind over matter. If you think warm, you will be warm. Two thousand four hundred and seventy-nine. They're going to find us, Harry. Jiggle my arm if you think they will.''

Sunny almost fainted with relief when she felt the small jiggle to her arm. Of course they would be found. The big question was, would they still be alive?

* * *

Fanny was halfway up the mountain when she jammed her foot down on the brake pedal, tires screeching. She turned around in the middle of the road and roared back down the mountain.

Radio blaring, the windows wide-open, Fanny talked to herself as she tried to reassure herself that Marcus would improve. The doctors could be wrong. They'd been wrong where Philip was concerned. Doctors weren't gods. Back at the medical center she'd been in shock and had reacted to that shock. What did those stoic men in the white coats think? As if she cared. It was her life, hers and Marcus's future and what was going to be best for both of them, especially Marcus.

It was a beautiful day, she noticed. The air was crisp and clear, but then the air was always crisp and clear on the mountain. In just a few weeks it would be Thanksgiving and then Christmas. Would her family celebrate Thanksgiving together? They had much to be thankful for. Surely her children would want to be together. Birch and Sunny would be home for the holidays. Ruby would invite Metaxas Parish. Marcus could carve the turkey. If he wasn't up to it, then perhaps Metaxas would take over. Birch and Sage preferred to gouge the turkey opposed to carving it. If Metaxas begged off, then the job would be given to Chue. She needed to give some serious thought to her newest daughter-in-law and her extracurricular activities.

The sun was so bright today. More so of late, she thought. For some reason the mountain always seemed extra bright. Maybe that was the reason they called it Sunrise Mountain. She reached up to retrieve her sunglasses from the visor and slipped them on. The world around her took on an amber hue.

Fanny settled back, her thoughts jumbled. She wished she knew who she was. Right now she felt like a stranger to herself.

That wasn't Fanny Thornton Reed back at the medical center. And who was that person who committed a crime back at the casino? Who was this jittery person behind the wheel? Ash would say she was someone who didn't know her ass from her elbow. "Oh, yeah, then why do you always come to me when things go awry? If I'm so damn terrible, why am I the one who always gets the short end of the stick?"

"It's your lot in life, old girl. You're dependable. You never let anyone down. You work overtime at being solid, dependable Fanny. You set that precedent early on, and we all succumbed to it. Things aren't always what they seem on the surface, Fanny. I shouldn't have to tell you that. The Fanny I know, the Fanny world knows, will never turn her back on Marcus. He needs you. Even when I was at my worst and needed you the most, when you hated my guts, you came through for me. You can't do less for Marcus. He is a good, kind, gentle man. He really needs you, Fanny. You can't stick him in one of those halfway houses or some institution. Remember when you went to see Jake the gambler's old friends. He'd be in a place like that. You promised to love and honor him. It pains me to say this, but he deserves everything you have to give him. He deserves more than I did, and yet you came through for me. That's who you are, Fanny. So what if you entered the penthouse and took a few things. You did it for all the right reasons. You can and will make that come out right if you use your head. You have Billie on the right track. I have no doubt that she will falter once or twice. You need to be a step behind her so you can catch her. Put her on a skimpy allowance, take over her bills. Sage will do the rest."

"Why is it, Ash, that you have the answers to everything? I can't fathom any of this. When are you going to go away and . . . and, you know, rest in eternity? If anyone sees me talking to you, they'll lock me up. When, Ash?"

"When you don't need me anymore. You'll know when that time comes."

"Will you say that final good-bye? Sometimes I am stupid."

"I'm not big on good-byes. You know that, Fanny. By the way, thanks for getting those wings back."

"You know what, Ash, it was my pleasure. I'm really sorry about screwing up like that. I'm on my way to the jewelers now. Are you going to hang around and watch?"

"Nah, I got things to do. The kids need me."

"That makes me feel so good, Ash, knowing you're watching over them. I'm worried about that storm, but I know they're safe in your hands. I need to thank you for that. How come your voice sounds so froggy and hoarse? Are you crying, Ash? You are, aren't you? I didn't know you had emotions and stuff like that up there."

"It's not me, Fanny, it's you. See you around."

Fanny reached across the console for a tissue. She cleared her throat before she wiped at her eyes and blew her nose. *Damn, he was always right.*

Twenty minutes later, Fanny held out Ash's aviator wings to Herbert Rothstein. "I'd like you to take the clasp from the back of these wings and attach it to this one. I'd like to wait, Mr. Rothstein. It's very important to me to take them up the mountain today."

"I can do it right now. Go to the café and have breakfast. By the time you get back I'll have them ready."

Fanny withdrew Simon's wings from her pocket. Later she would bury them at Simon's grave. She should have done that in the beginning. However, if she'd done that she wouldn't be standing here now, having Ash's wings repaired. Everything in life, she was learning, had a reason.

When Fanny returned, Ash's wings had been cleaned, polished, and now rested in a small, velvet-lined jeweler's box. Simon's wings were in a tiny plastic bag. "I'd like the same kind of box for these, too, Mr. Rothstein. I'd appreciate it if you'd glue a clasp on the back of these, too."

"I did that, Mrs. Thornton."

"Reed. My name is Reed now."

"My apologies. A gold box for Mr. Ash and silver one for Mr. Simon."

"That's fine. Thank you," Fanny said as she extended her credit card.

Back on the road to the mountain, Fanny started to cry.

"Now what's wrong, Fanny? That was a nice thing you did back there. Simon distinguished himself in the war. That should never be negated. Burying his wings is a good thing. I'm sure he's aware of what you're doing. Is that why you're crying?"

"I guess so. It's sad. I cared for him very much at one time. These wings are all that's left."

"Some people don't leave that much behind, Fanny. It's the way it is."

"When I go, Ash, what will I be leaving behind? Tell me. I need to know."

"The family. Our children, their children. No one has a right to ask for more."

"It seems like there should be more. You know, something people can look at and say, Fanny Logan Thornton Reed did that."

"That's pretty selfish coming from you. There can't be anything more important in this world than family. Mom and Dad started it. You and I took over. Now it's our children's turn. I'm so goddamn proud of that, Fanny, I could just bust. I know in my gut Jake is going to . . . I don't know what he's going to do, but he's going to do something to distinguish himself at some point in his life. You wait and see."

"Okay, Ash."

"Okay, Ash. That's it?"

"Okay, Ash, you're right. I knew that, I was just testing you. You passed the test."

"I had a hell of a teacher, Fanny. Thanks."

"Take care of the kids, okay."

"You bet."

16

Sage wasn't sure how long he'd been alone. Minutes, hours? He wasn't even sure how he knew there was no one behind him. He'd lost track of time a long time ago. All he knew was that he was alive, he was numb with cold, and no one had answered his hoarse shouts for a long time. He needed to rest, to swallow a little snow. He allowed himself to crumple into the snow.

He knew he was on higher ground because the trees were denser. The scent of pine resin was sharp in his nostrils. The air was thinner, singeing his throat and lungs. He felt as though he'd used the last of his strength. Would he be able to get up and move again? He shouted Ruby's name again, as loud as he could. It was less windy now, the snow lighter, or else it was a hopeless wish on his part. He looked upward, blinking to clear his vision. Black clouds scudded across the sky. He stumbled and fell, picked himself up, and stumbled again, landing facedown in the snow. He cursed under his breath, every dirty word he'd ever heard. Where in the hell was he? He shouted Ruby's name again to no avail.

Sage's legs refused to hold him upright. He dropped to his knees and crawled upward, his movements automatic, robotic. He hunkered into his coat and crawled forward as swirl after swirl of snow slapped and stung his face. Now the snow was thicker, heavier, the wind strong and gusty. Then he tripped and fell, his face smashing into something cold and hard, something that wasn't snow. The breath knocked from his body, he fought his fear as he tried to calm himself. Was it a rock, a large boulder, a clump of granite? His numb hands brushed at the snow. He worked feverishly, his breathing ragged and shallow. He had to stop three times to fight off momentary bouts of dizziness. He wouldn't give up. He couldn't. Birch was out here and Birch needed him.

Minutes later he saw the shiny black machine that to his eye looked like a giant bumblebee with tail feathers. The key. Where was the key? Was this the snowmobile Metaxas's friend said he would leave? One machine? Were there more? He called Ruby's name again and again until his voice was little more than a croak. He could hear Ruby's name echo down the mountain. He waited to see if his own name could be heard. All he could hear was the sound of the storm all around him.

Sage dug farther, his hands everywhere as he searched for the other machines. There should be seven. Or was it six? He couldn't remember. Would the machine start? He said a small prayer as he turned the key. He almost fainted when the engine turned over. "Oh, baby, I'm in business now," he chortled as he climbed into the seat. He angled the machine to the left as he catapulted from the drift. Seconds later he was skimming off into blind whiteness. He slowed the machine as he tried desperately to get his bearings. Better to continue upward to the lodge and start from there. Up, up, the machine went, straining, the engine whining and struggling to do his bidding.

He veered sharply to the right as a copse of trees came into view.

What seemed like an eternity later he saw a dim light ahead. The lodge? He offered up another prayer. The barn! He slowed the snowmobile, then cut the engine. A minute later he was in the barn, staring at the oil lamps and the line of snowmobiles on their track. Four machines were missing. Four! Birch and Libby? Who were three and four? People from the lodge?

Sage ran from the barn to the snowmobile and climbed on. He pressed the gas pedal and roared to the entrance of the lodge. He left the engine running while he ran into the lodge, shouting to anyone who could hear him. He listened to the night clerk as his heart thundered in his chest. "What time is it?" he bellowed. "Ten o'clock! That means he has a two-hour head start on me. If they find their way back, tell them . . . hell, you know what to tell them."

Sage raced back to the barn and gassed his machine, topping it off. At the last second he filled two gallon plastic containers with extra gas and put them on the seat next to him. He was off, snow spewing behind him in a six-foot wake. His goggles in place, he could see faint signs of tracks from a previous machine. He switched on the light, hoping the glow would outline the tracks. It did nothing. Better to save the battery and blow the horn. He let loose with a loud blast. There was no return blast. He stopped, climbed out, and looked at the ground. He was definitely following a set of tracks. He pressed the horn again and again. He peeled off in a rain of snow. Every other minute he leaned on his horn.

The snow was coming down harder, almost in sheets, the wind furious and wicked, the visibility at zero minus. He blew the horn again. *I'm coming, Birch. I'm coming.* From somewhere off to his left he thought he heard a return blast. He blew the horn again and waited, his ears straining to hear any sound other than the howling wind. He heard it then, the faint sound of a matching horn. He swerved the snow machine and headed in what he thought was the direction of the sound he'd just heard. He tapped the horn again and again, then switched on the light. When he saw a flicker of light in the distance, he almost jumped out of his skin. He no longer felt the cold or the numbness. He pressed the horn for a full minute. The return blast of sound was closer, a tenth of a mile if that far. He flicked the light on and off as he tapped the horn again, two long blasts and one short one. He was closer now, the light ahead more visible, the sound of the horn sharper.

The sound of the double engines ahead roared in his eardrums as he brought his machine to a stop. "Birch!"

"Sage! Jesus, is it really you, Sage! How the hell did you get here? Christ, I can't believe this!"

"That about sums up my feeling, but it's me, frozen balls and all. I take it you haven't had any luck."

"Diddly."

"I got separated from Metaxas and Ruby and the guys he brought with him. I found the snowmobiles by accident. At one point they were behind me. I've never *heard* of a storm like this much less been in one. We can catch up on the bullshit stuff later. Should we fan out or stick together? This stuff ain't lettin' up at all. I don't think I have any skin left on my face."

"We have to stick together and hope Metaxas and the others find the snowmobiles like you did. I'm afraid to go too far. We brought extra gas, but under these conditions we don't know how long it will last."

"I brought two cans. Birch, can Sunny survive this? I've tried not to think about it since leaving the lodge. I thought it was you. All my instincts said it was you who was in trouble. I didn't have a clue that it was Sunny and Harry. I thought *you* were in trouble."

"Take a good look at me, Sage. I am in trouble. Libby and I've been looking for Sunny for almost three hours. We're down to the wire here, gas-wise, and I can't see two inches in front of my face. She's smart, but she isn't in good physical shape. Neither is Harry. I'm not really hopeful. If the goddamn snow would just let up, we might have a fighting chance. I won't give up if that's your next question.''

''I'm here. I was traveling blind. You saw my light and heard my horn. Maybe if we keep doing that, she'll hear us. The same goes for Metaxas and Ruby. If you have a better idea, I'd like to hear it.''

''Let's try to think like Sunny. She would have been cautious. Harry more so. That leads me to believe they headed in a straight line thinking they'd follow their tracks back when they had enough. I think they would have planned on about thirty minutes to ride like the wind and then another thirty to get back. Do you see anything wrong with what I just said?''

''One little thing. One of their snowmobiles ran out of gas and the other one didn't have a full tank. There is no place to hole up around here. The snow is drifting as fast as it falls. I don't think they took extra gas. They wouldn't think they needed it. They could huddle together for body warmth, but they're both so damn skinny I doubt they have an extra ounce of fat between them. I do think they took some stuff from the supply closet, but I don't know what. They're the ones who lit the first lantern in the barn. Libby and I lit the rest of them. We at least know they were thinking.''

''Now we have to worry about Ruby and Metaxas.''

''They'll be fine. Picture Metaxas in your mind's eye. Do you think for one minute he'd let anything, and I include this pissy-assed storm as he would call it, interfere with his plans? I don't think so. He'll protect Ruby with his life. How far do you think this is from the lodge? Do you see them getting this far?''

''Three, maybe four miles. No. That's why we stopped. That's how we heard you. We were trying to decide if we should head back. We did stop from time to time and veered off for about a quarter of a mile each way. We didn't want to lose sight of our original tracks. They're probably frozen to death somewhere, Sage.''

"I don't want to hear that, Birch. I didn't come all this way and almost get killed to hear you talk like that. We're just blowing smoke. Let's head back before the tracks fill in. Ten minutes and we'll stop. We'll flash our lights and blow all three horns. Every ten minutes, Birch. You okay with that?"

"Okay, I'll take the lead, Libby behind me. You bring up the rear."

Two long, endless hours passed. Birch tapped his horn and brought his machine to a stop. "I have a quarter of a tank of gas left. Let's blast the horns for thirty seconds. Lights on for ten seconds and then off for ten seconds. Libby and I will have to head back to the barn to refuel. You'll have to come with us. We can't afford to lose you, too. Metaxas should have found us by now. Or else he's out of gas the way we are. The other possibility is he didn't find the snowmobiles the way you did. Okay, horns and lights."

"I thought I heard something. Did you hear something, Birch?"

Libby and Birch both shook their heads. Sage felt his shoulders slump. "I'm not imagining it, I think I heard something. Let's try it again."

"There. What was that sound? It came from the left."

"It's a snowmobile," Birch shouted. "It's a whole line of them."

"It's Metaxas and Ruby," Sage cried. His shoulders straightened immediately.

The line of machines growled and snarled as they came to a grinding halt. Metaxas's voice was the roar of a lion. "Any luck?"

"None. We're almost out of gas. We're about four miles from the lodge. We were going to head back to gas up."

"We'll follow you. We're almost out, too. Lead the way, son."

"Wait a minute. If Birch is here, with Libby, who are we looking for?" Ruby shouted.

Sage shouted in return, "Sunny and Harry. They've been out here since around two this morning."

"Oh my God!"

"Don't you go bawling on me now, Ruby. We'll find her. I give you my word. You okay with my word, sweet baby?"

"Yes. Yes, I'm okay with it, Metaxas."

Sage jerked his hand forward, a signal for Birch to lead the way back to the barn.

It was nine hours to the minute since Sunny and Harry had careened out of the barn to play in the snow.

Nine hours of gale-force winds, heavy snow, and single-digit temperatures.

Fanny knocked on the kitchen door. It felt strange to be knocking on the door of her own house.

"Fanny! What's wrong? Has something happened to Sage? What are you doing here? Tell me the truth."

"Iris, nothing's wrong. I came to visit. Billie and Bess went home. I just wanted to be in familiar surroundings. Marcus woke up this morning."

"Fanny, how wonderful! I'm so happy for you. I prayed every single night. The kids did, too. I know Sage did, too. I knew he'd come out of it okay. I just made coffee. Would you like some?"

"Silly girl. I'd love some. Marcus is . . . they said . . . what they said was . . . I don't know if I believe them or not . . . but they said he has brain damage. They said his life as he knew it is over. It's like he's an eleven-year-old. He didn't know me or John. I want to cry, but the tears won't come. There is so much I don't understand. When I make a mistake the world grinds to a halt. How are you, honey? You look a little peaked to me."

"It's a lot of things, Fanny. It's not my pregnancy. I feel physically fine. Mentally I'm a basket case. I'm truly sorry I went off on you, Fanny. Things got out of hand. I guess I let them get to that point. I should have confronted Sage. Instead I decided to be a martyr. Suspicion is so deadly. Part of me, the good part, knows Sage would never betray me. The other part of me, the bad part, says men are men and some men get caught up in things they can't handle. Birch could handle something like that but not Sage. I don't know how I know this. It's a feeling, okay."

"Where did this come from, Iris? Sage was deliriously happy about your pregnancy. Does this have anything to do with Jeff?"

"Yes. Fanny, I sank so low I followed Sage and spied on him. Then I had Ruby follow him and spy on him. I hate myself for doing that. But, to answer your question, Sage had the card key to Room 719."

"How do you know that, Iris?"

"I saw it. He was in the garage one evening for a long time. He acted strange when he came in. That night he threw his suit on the chair and I went through it to check his pockets because I was going to town the next day and would drop off the cleaning. Then Sage brings it back at the end of the week. The card was in his pocket. I left it there. The next morning I pretended to be asleep and I watched him take it out and put it inside his jacket. He didn't go to work that day. I was so devastated. No offense, Fanny, but everyone in this family knows what Room 719 was used for. I thought of it as like father, like son. I'm so sorry I didn't have more faith in Sage. I'm sorry I didn't talk to him. All I've been doing is watching the weather channel. That storm is absolutely horrendous. I'm worried sick."

Fanny thought about the obscene pictures in her purse. Instinctively, she clasped it tighter in her lap. "Iris, look at me. Your husband, my son, did *not* have an affair with his brother's wife. I want you to believe that.''

"Sage said he didn't like Celia from the moment he set eyes on her. She spooked him that day at the airport, and then he said she was evil. He sounded so sincere. He even hired a private detective to look into her background. I don't know if he got a report back or not. Please don't tell anyone I told you that. Birch would never understand something like that.''

"I won't tell anyone. Tell me something, Iris. Now that the kids are here, does Sage still sleep soundly?''

"If you mean can I still bang a metal pan with a metal spoon in his ear, yes. He barely wakes up when the alarm goes off.''

"Birch is the same way. Nothing wakes those two. Do you ever push him out of bed or make him roll over, that kind of thing?''

"I pushed him out of bed one night and he slept the rest of the night on the floor. He was snoring so loud I couldn't stand it. I asked John Noble about it once, and he said lots of people are sound sleepers. He said it wasn't anything to worry about. Why do you ask?''

"It's one of those things mothers like to know,'' Fanny said lightly.

"Is there anything I can do for you, Fanny?''

"I wish there was. You did your share helping Billie out. I'm having a hard time with that. She's seeing a shrink today. That's the first step. We'll take it one day at a time. Recognizing and dealing with it up front is the second step. I feel confident my daughter will get a handle on it.''

"Oh, Fanny, I know she will. I'll help in any way I can. I think we should talk about Celia, Fanny.''

"What good will that do?''

"She's going to cause trouble. I can understand Birch getting carried away with her. She's so beautiful she takes my breath away. That stupendous figure of hers is to die for. I hope Ruby didn't make a mistake by hiring her.''

"I hope so, too. I just adore Ruby. She fits in like she was meant to be in this family."

"She belongs, Fanny. She's one of us. She tried so hard not to step on toes in the beginning. We all went to her with our problems because . . . because you were doing other things, and we didn't want to intrude. She made it clear from the beginning that she was a temporary stand-in for you. She bought a ten-million-dollar plane for Birch and Sage. Can you believe that?"

"Ruby's like that. She's a wonderful friend. Ash loved her in the end. There is nothing I wouldn't do for her. I think she feels the same way. You're right. She belongs to this family. She earned her place."

"Fanny, do you really think Sage is all right?"

"I *know* he's all right. Ash told me himself. Don't ask me to explain that statement."

Iris smiled. "I won't. All night and all morning I've had this strange feeling like someone is . . . *hovering* nearby. I went out to the cemetery twice and can't explain why. I had this overwhelming sense of peace while I was there. I wanted to stay, but I had to come in to get the kids off to school. After Chue picked them up, I went back out and had the same feeling all over again. I felt like there was a cocoon all around me. Listen, let's talk about something else. Let's talk about you and Marcus."

"Let's not. I have a lot of thinking to do. I won't abandon him. Do you mind if I take Daisy back with me? I miss her terribly."

"Can we keep Fosdick and Growl Tiger? The kids are very attached to them."

"Sure. By the way, where are they?"

"They're the first ones in the van when Chue blows the horn. They love going to school. Chue keeps cookies in the van for them."

"What would this family do without Chue and his family?"

"I don't ever want to find out, Fanny."

"You know what, I don't want to find out either."

"Iris, I don't know if you want to know this or not, but Room 719 is no longer closed and locked. It's just another room that's rented out on a daily basis. Sage made sure of that. I think it's important for you to know. Rushing to judgment can be and is a dangerous thing to do. You are and your family are blessed, Iris. Please, don't ever forget that. I guess it's time for me to go back to town. Thanks for the coffee. I hope I helped a little. Don't worry about Sage. I have it on good authority that he's fine. I hear the van!"

Iris opened the door. Daisy leaped into Fanny's arms as her pups circled her feet barking ferociously, their tails wagging miles to the minute.

"Oh, Daisy, I missed you." Fanny dropped to her knees to tussle with Daisy's pups. "Isn't it wonderful the way animals love unconditionally? I wish people could do that."

"I do, too. Thanks for coming up, Fanny. I've missed our talks. When Sage gets back, and I know he will make it home safely, I'll talk to him. I don't want to live with mistrust. I don't want you worrying about us. We'll make it work."

Fanny's voice was sad when she said, "Sometimes life just gets in the way of things. If you're honest and up front and things are in the open, it's easier to work things out. At least that's the way I perceive it. If you need me, call."

"That works two ways, Fanny. The kids miss you."

"We'll get together soon. I promise."

"I'll hold you to it."

"I'm going to stop at the cemetery for a few minutes. Do you have an old wooden spoon or a trowel handy?"

Iris reached under the sink and withdrew a small pail of gardening tools she used for her indoor plants. "Just leave it on the wall. I'll pick it up later."

Fanny withdrew the silver box from her oversize purse and set it on the ground. Fifteen minutes later, Simon Thornton's grave looked the same as it had when she first entered the cemetery. She left the pail on the wall and walked around the property to the edge of the mountain. Once again she fished in her purse. Jeffrey's key ring, minus Ash's aviator wings, sailed through the air. Fanny dusted her hands together in a gesture of defiance.

Now it was time to get on with the new life that had been foisted upon her.

Fanny's first stop when she returned to town was the bank. In an hour she'd reversed what remained of Billie's trust fund. She then asked to have Billie's signature removed from the corporate business accounts. "This bank will be held liable if you honor any checks bearing the signature of Billie Thornton. Is that understood?"

"Absolutely, Mrs. Reed. Is there anything else we can do for you today?"

"No. Thank you for your help."

Fanny's next stop was the corporate offices of Sunny's Togs and Rainbow Babies.

"Mom! Imagine meeting up twice in one day," Billie quipped.

After telling Billie about the change in Marcus's condition, Fanny said, "I reversed the trust fund, Billie. I also removed your name from the corporate accounts. You can no longer sign checks. I really hated to do it, Billie."

"I understand, Mom. I screwed up. I expected you to boot my butt out of here."

"That's the next step if you don't hold the line. I mean it, Billie. I was sick to my soul when I reviewed your trust account."

Billie nodded, her face miserable.

"What time is your first meeting?"

"In an hour. I'm actually looking forward to it. It didn't go so well with the shrink. I was belligerent and testy. He was cool and professional. Once he almost threw me out. Then he switched up and said I could leave anytime I wanted. To use a quote from Sunny, this dude won't put up with my shit. End of quote. I guess it's what I need. I'm to go three times a week. A hundred bucks a pop. That's going to seriously eat into my salary."

"Speaking of your salary, it's been cut in half. When you've proved yourself to my satisfaction, I'll reinstate it. I consider trust to be one of the most precious things life gives us. You violated that trust. Until you earn it back it has to be my way or no way. I hope you can live with that, Billie."

"Half! That's pretty steep, Mom."

"Yes, it is. You'll take home enough to pay the rent, the utilities, food, gas, and have a small allowance to fritter away. There won't be enough left to save. I want your word that you will not borrow from your sister or brothers. That goes for Ruby and Iris, too. I'm willing to take your word. Please don't make me regret my decisions."

"Mom!"

"It's the way it is, Billie. Do you realize thousands and thousands of homeless people could have been fed and housed with the money you gambled away? I want you to think about that every time you have the urge to hit those gaming tables. It's going to work out, honey. It may take a while, but you can do it." Fanny sat down and folded her hands. "It seems at times that our family's lot in life is to endure. I'm not sure why that is. Sunny has had more than her share. She's handling it even though she has more bad days than good days. You can't do less, Billie. You're tough. You're young and resilient. You, like Sunny, are my daughter. I'm here to offer support, but I expect you to cut the mustard as your father would say. Do you want me to go to the meeting with you?"

"It's not allowed. I can handle it, Mom. Do you think you'll ever be able to forgive me?"

"I think so."

"I was hoping for a qualified yes." Tears filled Billie's eyes as she stared at her mother.

Fanny held out a tissue. "You have to earn my forgiveness. That doesn't mean I love you any less."

"Mom?"

"Yes, Billie."

"I worked like a tired old dog for years. I helped build these companies. You said without me there wouldn't be a Sunny's Togs or Rainbow Babies."

"That's true. And then you took all that and threw it away. You cheated people. You lied and you stole from those people who loved you the most. You worked like a dog because it was your choice. You loved what you did. You made the choice to gamble. If Sage hadn't caught on to what you were doing, you would have destroyed the business. I want to leave you with one thought. Some people in this world never get a second chance, even when they deserve it. You're one of the lucky ones. If you hold on to that thought, things might be a little easier. Right now you're in a very scary place. It's dark and ugly. All you have to do is find the tunnel that leads to the light. If you falter, call me, any time of the day or night. I have to go now. I went to Sunrise to get Daisy. She's in the car. Lord, I missed that little dog. I'm going home to cuddle with her."

"Marcus?"

"I'm going to think about Marcus. I have to find a way to help him."

"You're like a mother bird, Mom, with all her wounded chicks. I don't know what any of us would do without you. Give Daisy a hug for me."

"Let me know how the first meeting goes."

"I will, Mom. I love you."

Fanny smiled. "And I love you. Bushels and bushels."

* * *

"Well that was some pretty sappy dialogue if you want my opinion. Do you think it worked?"

"Go away, Ash. It's how I felt. The rest is up to Billie. She has this quiet determination and dedication unlike Sunny, who has guts out the kazoo. She'll make it. I know she will. You want her to fail, don't you? That's unconscionable, Ash."

"Jesus H. Christ, Fanny, where did that come from? How can you say such a thing?"

"Because you could never remember her name, that's why. I'm getting pretty fed up with you and your sudden appearances. I have things to do and places to go, and they don't include you. When I get up there, it will be time enough to have all these discussions."

"I'll be old and gray by then."

"You were old and gray when you died, Ash. I'm getting older by the day, and under this Clairol stuff on my hair I'm as gray as you were."

"You dye your hair! That's sinful!"

"You sound so virtuous. I find that remarkable. Just leave."

"I thought you wanted to talk about Marcus and those pictures. That was pretty neat of you to throw Jeff's keys down the mountain. You have a regular junk pile down there."

"Putting the keys in Lost and Found minus the wings would have been a dead giveaway. I'm sure he has an extra set someplace."

"You're going to abandon Marcus, aren't you?"

"You have no right to say something like that to me. Especially you, Ash. I took you in, and I took care of you. We were divorced, and I didn't abandon you."

"I was there, Fanny. I saw you. I heard you. That's exactly what you were planning on doing."

"For ten seconds. I won't deny it. I panicked. I've accepted it. I know what my duty is, and I don't need you to remind me."

"*Those are words, Fanny. I'm looking for a special word here. Commitment. That's the biggie right now.*"

"I have a marriage license that says I'm committed. I'll handle my life the way I see fit. Why don't you go sit on a cloud or something."

"*Later. Business first. All I'm trying to do is point out the error of your ways. You do make errors, Fanny. I want to know that I wasn't wrong about you. I want to know that you'll step in and do what needs to be done. Not grudgingly but willingly.*"

"Go to hell, Ash."

"*You toed the line with Billie a while ago. You handled that just right.*"

Fanny's voice was sarcastic when she said, "Thanks."

"*So what are you going to do with those pictures?*"

"None of your business, Ash Thornton."

"*I think you need to go to Room 719 and check it out. The decor in that room was different from the other rooms. More fitting, if you know what I mean.*"

"You son of a bitch! That was the room where you used to take your women. I don't need to go there. I saw the bedspread and the drapes."

"*Did you see that sparkly dress on the floor? Maybe some of those little sparklers fell on the floor. They get mashed in the carpet, and you have to pick them out. It was a long time ago, Fanny, and it didn't mean anything. It was wrong. It wasn't a good time in my life. For whatever it's worth, I apologize.*"

"Go to hell."

"*You said that already. Are you going to check it out?*"

"Why? I'm certainly never going to show those pictures to anyone, so what is the point?"

"*You'll always wonder if you don't. It looks to me like Sage was dead to the world and Miss Hot Pants Celia was just*

*POSING him for the camera. He doesn't have his eyes open
in any of the pictures. I think Jeff took the pictures. What do
you think of that, Fanny?''*

"I think you're a little late. I already figured that out myself."

"Attagirl, Fanny. So, what are you going to do?''

"I think I'll show the pictures to Celia. It's possible she was
hoping to drive a wedge into this family. Maybe it was her
intention to pit Birch against Sage. Blackmail. I don't know,
Ash. Maybe I'll hide the pictures and wait to see what happens.
I like to think about things before I rush into something, unlike
you."

*"You're gettin' feisty again, Fanny. I'm liking what I'm
seeing and hearing. See you around, old girl. So those golden
hairs aren't yours after all. Tsk, tsk.''*

Daisy jumped into Fanny's lap as she burst out laughing.

"We'll deal with Celia when the time is right, Daisy. We
have other things to do right now." Fanny hugged the little
dog, a feeling of peace settling over her as she drove out to
the desert to the small house she called home.

Celia Thornton threw her canvas bag into the backseat of
her newly leased BMW. She uncapped a bottle of mineral water
and drank deeply. The hot lights she'd worked under all day
had taken their toll on her skin and her mouth. She drank
greedily from the bottle. She couldn't wait to take a shower
and moisturize her skin, especially her face. She'd done well,
and the end was in sight, as was a very generous paycheck.

The engine turned over. Foot on the gas pedal, lights switched
on, she was about to pull into traffic when she felt hands on
her throat. She slammed on the brakes as she tried vainly to
see who was behind her.

"Thought you'd pull a fast one, huh? That kind of behavior
doesn't work with me, Mrs. Thornton. What did you do with
my keys, and where are those pictures?"

Celia went limp so that Jeff's hands would relax their hold on her throat. "What are you talking about?" she managed to gasp. "You saw me when I left. I didn't take your damn keys, and I didn't take the pictures. What the hell are you saying, Jeff?"

"I'm saying someone entered the penthouse and took them. You were the only one there. I don't give a hoot in hell about the pictures, but I do care about my keys and my father's aviator wings."

Celia wiggled in her seat till she was turned and facing Jeff. "Look somewhere else, Jeff. I didn't have time to do what you're accusing me of. Go through my bag. Why would I want your stupid keys? I would like the pictures though. If they fall into the wrong hands, there could be a lot of trouble. When did you notice they were missing?"

"This morning. Fanny Logan called and wanted to meet with me downstairs, and when I got there she was in the ladies' room. She wanted to have breakfast and talk, but she got a call and had to run off to the medical center. I was kind of suspicious, so I went to the center, and, when she wasn't looking, I went through her bag. I also went through her car. She seems to be a very trusting person because the car wasn't locked. Needless to say, I didn't find either the keys or the pictures. So that brings me back to you. Besides, Fanny is the one who gave me my father's wings. What would she want with my keys?"

"Well, I didn't do it. Maybe she took them as an afterthought once she saw the pictures. She wouldn't want you to have the wings if you're the kind of person who has pictures like that. Think about it before you go off half-cocked. I thought there was only one key to the penthouse."

"I thought so too. Obviously I was wrong the way I was wrong about Room 719. I have to give the Thorntons credit, they know how to cover their asses. There is a pair and a spare to everything that has a lock. I want those keys. They're mine. Those wings belong to me. They're my good-luck charm."

Celia's trilling laughter sent chills up and down Jeff's arms.

"Don't tell me someone as educated as you are believes in good-luck charms. That's too funny for words. I don't give a damn about your stupid keys. I knew I never should have let you keep those pictures. I was right. You're sloppy. When you're sloppy things go wrong. I had you down as a tight-assed perfectionist. Man, was I wrong."

"Shut up, Celia. I need to think. Why would Fanny Thornton set me up?"

"It's Fanny Reed, Jeffrey," Celia said sweetly. "She's probably onto you. The whole damn family is probably onto you. You don't belong. It's that simple. Fanny's children overrode her decision. Everyone is laughing at you behind your back. I hear the talk. Get it through your head. You aren't good enough for them just the way I'm not good enough for them. At least I landed on my feet and have a job that pays some decent money. I'm earning it, too. All you do is collect a paycheck. It's charity they're handing out to you."

"I don't give a good rat's ass about that crap. Money is money. If they're laughing, they'll be laughing out of the other side of their faces in a few more weeks. You, on the other hand, Celia, have everything to lose and nothing to gain. That was an incredibly dumb thing you did with Sage. I'm embarrassed to have had a part in it."

"That's pretty funny coming from you. You were the one with the pictures in your possession. That makes you as guilty as me if we're placing guilt. If you're right and Birch's mother has the photos, she isn't going to let anyone see them. There are no negatives because they're Polaroids. She'll never show them to Birch because Birch will not believe Sage wasn't fooling around with me. He'll take the view that pictures don't lie. Fanny won't confront Sage. I think I'm in the clear here. At least for the time being. You, on the other hand, have a problem. If I were you, and this is just my opinion, I would hit those tables and get as much money as I could. I'd take that little operation of yours and head out to the desert, where no one knows you. I'm glad you stopped by, Jeff. I feel a lot better. Don't ever do it again. If you do, I'll shoot first and ask questions later. I bought a gun, and I have a permit to carry it. I'm Mrs. Birch Thornton, and I work for the family. You're from the other side of town, and all you're doing is taking up space and collecting a check. Who do you think the police will believe? Trust me when I tell you Fanny is not going to buck her kids again. You need to ask yourself something, Jeff. If Fanny did take the pictures and the keys, what did she do with them? Where would she put them to keep them safe? Work on that. Now get the hell out of my car. You're stinking it up.''

"Bitch!"

"Bastard!"

Sunny's head lolled to the side. "I can't keep this up, Harry. What number are we on?"

"Two thousand nine hundred and forty-one. I thought I heard something."

"You're hearing the wind in the trees. What did we cook for Christmas dinner? I forget."

"I forget, too. What did you give me for a present?"

Sunny laughed hysterically. "A wool scarf. Did we get married? How did I look in my gown in the wheelchair?"

"Like a bride. Your dress was all puffed out, and you couldn't see the chair at all. Jake had on a tuxedo, and Polly was wearing a red dress trimmed in white fur. She looked as pretty as you. Jake shook my hand and said he'd always take care of both of us."

Sunny started to cry. "Did he really say that, Harry?"

"He did. I love him, Sunny. I love Polly, too. I'd give everything I own, which is almost nothing, to be able to be a real father to them. Do you think they know that, Sunny?"

"Hell yes they know that. They're my kids, Harry. They

understand. God, what if we never get to see them again? What number are we on?''

"Three thousand nine hundred and thirty-six. We're going to see them again. I know we are. What did I give you for a present?''

Sunny sighed. "Earmuffs. Neither one of us was very original. If we get out of this, I'm going to get you a present that will blow your socks right off your feet. I have to go to sleep, Harry. I really do. Just for ten minutes. You wake me up, okay?''

"I need you to talk to me, Sunny. We have to talk to each other. That's how we stay awake.''

"Oh, Harry . . .''

"If you go to sleep now, you'll never wake up. Listen to me, Sunny, I'm talking to you. Salute me. Show me some respect. I gave you an order, and you're deliberately disobeying me. I'll have to punish you.''

"That's a joke. You can't do anything worse than this to me.''

"Let's have a little respect, Sunny.''

"Dad, I'm so cold I can't feel any part of my body. I can't count anymore because my tongue isn't working. I can't see, and I can't feel. I did everything you said, and nothing is working.''

"It is working. You're alive. I want you to stay that way. Just hang on a little longer. Try singing.''

"Come off it, Dad. If I can't count, how do you expect me to sing? I don't know any songs. I have to go to sleep.''

"If you go to sleep, Sunny, the next time you open your eyes you'll be standing next to me. Jake will be sending you notes in balloons like he sent me. Is that what you want?''

"No. Dad, help me. I wish Mom were here.''

"I wish she was too, kiddo. All you have to do is hang on a little while longer. I want your promise to try. You never

broke a promise. The Sunny I knew was always as good as her word.''

"Not like you, huh? You always made promises and forgot about them."

"I know, and I'm sorry. I don't want you to be like me."

"I don't want to be like you either. I want to be like Mom."

"I want you to be like your mother, too. Sing, Sunny. As loud as you can. Make Harry sing, too. Promise me."

"Okay, Dad."

"Harry, we're going to sing now. Really loud. My mother would want me to sing. Dad says it will help. I don't want Jake sending me balloons like he did for Dad. Can you sing, Harry?"

"First you want me to count, then you want me to cook and shop and buy presents and now you want me to *sing!* Make up your mind, which is it?"

"We're going to sing. Let's do 'Ninety-nine Bottles of Beer.' At the top of our lungs. Don't ask me why we have to be loud. Dad said loud. It was a direct order."

"Oh, okay. We have to follow orders or things don't work. You start!"

"Okay, here goes. Ninety-nine bottles of beer . . ."

The wind shrieked and howled in Sage's ears. Would he ever hear normally again? Now he was hearing other sounds, like someone singing off-key. It would be just like Mataxas to be serenading Ruby as they rode along on the snowmobiles. His guts churning, his eyes straining to see into the distance through the swirling snow was taking its toll. How much longer could he continue. He'd had no sleep the night before. All he could say for himself was that he was alive. He knew the others weren't faring any better. At least Birch, Libby, and he had youth on their side and were in reasonably good physical shape. He wondered who would be first to call a halt until the snow let up. He wouldn't, that was a given. Birch would search till he dropped. So would Libby. Metaxas didn't know the meaning of the word quit. Sage had to assume his men were of the same caliber. Ruby adored Sunny and considered her the daughter she'd never had. Ruby would go till she dropped, too.

"We're all here for the long haul," Sage muttered to himself. He flashed his lights and tapped his horn twice. The sudden silence was overwhelming. He shook his head to clear it. Beer! Who the hell was singing about beer! He could use one, though. In the time it took him to blink, Sage was off, the snowmobile skimming over the small mountains of snow in the direction he thought the sound was coming from. None of the rescue party would be singing because it took too much energy.

"Go get her, Sage!"

"I'm going, Dad, I'm going."

"See you around, kid."

"Dad, wait."

"You don't need me anymore. You did good, Sage. Really good. I'm damn proud of you."

Later he would think about these strange conversations. He pressed his hand on the horn and kept it there. For one brief second he took his hand off the horn to flick on the light. He shouted then, his voice carrying on the wind, fighting with the blaring horn.

"Sunnyyyyyyy!"

17

The moment Fanny pulled into her driveway she knew something was wrong. Daisy leaped from the car, her barks sharp and shrill as she ran first to the kitchen door, then to the front door and finally back to Fanny, pawing her legs, backing up and running to each door.

Her legs wobbly, Fanny opened the trunk of her car, where she rummaged for the tire iron. She hefted it a couple of times to get the feel of it before she advanced to the front door, her breathing ragged-sounding. Earlier she'd locked the door, but it was open now, the knob turning under her hand. The moment the door swung inward, Daisy raced through the house, her bark sharper and more shrill than before. To Fanny's ears it meant intruder, intruder in our midst.

Her house was a shambles. There was no other word to describe the interior. The cushions on the sofas and chairs had been slashed, furniture overturned, lamps leaning drunkenly against the walls. Only a few shards of jagged glass on the large-screen television remained. The VCR was halfway across the room. Carpeting was ripped loose at the corners and pulled back. The bookshelves were empty of books and plants, the contents scattered everywhere. The pictures that had once belonged to Sallie were ripped into shreds, the canvas strips hanging loosely from the ornate frames Sallie had treasured.

The kitchen was a total disaster, the canisters upended, flour, sugar, and coffee everywhere. A lone tea bag hung from one of the blades on the overhead fan. The refrigerator door stood open, ice cubes melting, the contents of the bottles and jars spilled on the floor. An empty milk carton clung precariously to the open door. Canned soups, packaged goods, cleaning supplies were piled high in a corner. All Fanny could do was shake her head in despair as she headed for the master bedroom.

The mattress of the king-size bed was half-on and half-off the bed, the sheets wadded into a ball. The down comforter was empty of the fleecy feathers. Daisy sneezed as a feather landed on the end of her nose.

Fanny stood still, her eyes raking the total chaos. Her closet doors were open, shoes strewn everywhere. Her clothing as well as Marcus's was slashed and gouged, some items still on the hangers, some on the floor. Her jewelry was scattered over the dresser, hanging lopsidedly from the open drawers.

Everything on top of the vanity in the bathroom was on the floor—her cosmetics, Marcus's shaving gear, her blow-dryer and curling iron. Bars of soap, washcloths, and perfume bottles filled the toilet bowl. The lid of the toilet tank was in two pieces, half in the shower stall, the other half in the bathtub.

Tears rolled down Fanny's cheeks. Whoever had done this was filled with rage. Uncontrollable rage. That someone was looking for something. And that something was probably what was in her purse.

She had to get out of here, and she had to get out of here now. She called to Daisy, who was chasing a trail of feathers across the floor. The little dog looked at her before she pounced on a feather, trapping it with her paws. The second time Fanny called her, the dog trotted over to her and waited to be picked up.

"This is not good, Daisy. Only someone who is full of hate could do this. We're going to stop at the bank and put this stuff in our safety deposit box. Then we're going back to the hospital. Today is Friends of Animals Day, so that means you can make the rounds with Nurse Fisher. I'll visit with Marcus. Hey, they might even let him see you through the glass." Fanny continued to jabber to the little dog as she picked her way through the debris. Her keys were still in her hand. There didn't seem to be any point to locking the door. She shoved the keys into her pocket and drove away without a backward glance. This was just someplace where she used to live. It was a house. Once she'd told Marcus she loved it because it had no memories and that they would build their own as they went along. She would come back to pack up what was left of her belongings and never return. Never, ever.

It was after two when Fanny turned Daisy over to Nurse Fisher, who immediately decked her out in a tiny straw hat and a small straw basket full of lollipops for the children in the pediatric ward. Daisy knew the drill and trotted off happily, knowing the children would end the visit with her favorite biscuits. "I'll be in ICU. Call me when you want me to pick her up," Fanny called out.

To the charge nurse on the ICU floor Fanny said, "Have they finished with my husband's tests?"

"Yes, Mrs. Reed. They brought Mr. Reed back fifteen minutes ago to a private room at the end of the hall. You can stay as long as you like. However, he is sleeping right now."

Fanny nodded. "Perhaps I'll just sit here for a little while and have some coffee until he wakes up."

"I'll fetch it, Mrs. Reed."

Fanny sat and smoked, her mind in turmoil. She should call the police and report the ransacking of her home. Thank God she'd stopped at the bank. Ash's wings and the hateful pictures were safe for now.

"*So what are you going to do, Fanny? This is about as serious as it gets. I wish to hell you had listened to me. Oh, no, you had to go and involve that kid in your life and the kids' lives. Do you see now what he's capable of? Take my advice and get him out of the casino. You need to do it today. Pay him off. Give him the money for his contract and boot his ass out of there. Call Clem if you don't have the guts to do it. Or else, have Neal get the bouncers to do it. If that doesn't work, call the police.*"

"Stop it, Ash, you're making me nervous. I refuse to live in fear. This is your fault. You should have told me he was a . . . troubled person."

"*He's not troubled, Fanny, he's crazy. He was the kind of kid that set cats on fire when he was little.*"

"I don't want to hear that. Stop it, go away. You should have told me what he was capable of instead of keeping everything a secret. This is your fault, Ash, not mine."

"*No. You need to listen to me. I paid a fortune in shrink bills for that kid. His mother refused to believe there was anything wrong. The only reason she agreed to take him at all was because I threatened to cut off their monthly checks. He's smart, you can't take that away from him, but that's all he is. He's cruel and sadistic. Don't you remember, Fanny, you found the shrink bills and wanted to know what they were for? I lied and said I was going. You believed me. Christ, I didn't want anyone to know I had a kid like that. You should have let well enough alone.*"

"Don't blame me, Ash. If you'd been honest with me, this wouldn't be going on now. I'm living it, so you don't need to tell me how serious this is. The person who destroyed my home is a person filled with sick rage. I didn't have a clue, Ash. I just assumed because he was your son he would be as normal as our children. I just didn't know."

"What is past is past, Fanny, and it can't be changed. For me to say I'm sorry isn't going to help matters. You know I'm sorry. If I could turn the clock back I would, but I can't. What I do regret is you never gave me credit for doing anything right. You homed in on all the negatives, and there were a lot of negatives, but there were some damn good positives, too. Our kids remembered those positives these past hours, and they're alive now because of it. I'll be so damn glad when you finally get your life straightened out, Fanny."

"Ha! No one will be happier than me when that happens. Marcus is alive. I guess I owe you one for that."

"Nah. You knew it all the time. Things just kind of piled up on you. He's gonna be okay, Fanny. Time is all he needs. And you. It pains me to tell you this, but you really should fix yourself up a little. You look a little ragged around the edges."

"Really."

"Thick in the middle, too."

"What else, Ash?"

"You look like Grandma Moses with those glasses on your nose. Spruce up a little. Give old Marcus some incentive to get well."

"Are you trying to tell me something, Ash Thornton."

"Hell yes. You need a do-over."

"Go to hell, Ash."

"When was the last time you SIZZLED, Fanny?"

"None of your business."

"I'm just trying to help."

"For your information, I'm one of those people who simmer and smolder."

"Smolder's good. I like smolder. It brings to mind banked embers that explode into raging fires."

"Take back that Grandma Moses bit."

"Look in the mirror, baby."

"Marcus likes me the way I am."

"Yeah, sure. He's flat on his back. What other choice does he have? Wait till he's up on his feet."

"If I could blow your socks off, I can do the same for Marcus. Hit the road, Ash."

"Ahhhh, what a memory that was."

"Daisy! How'd you do? Did the kids love you? Of course they did. How about the seniors? Did they love you too?"

"They wanted to keep her. Daisy let each one of them pick her up and hug her. She gave kisses to everyone. She did her job, Mrs. Reed. Tonight all the seniors will have something to talk about over dinner. See you next month, Daisy."

"Okay, big girl, let's see if Marcus is awake. He's in his own room, so maybe they won't kick us out. No barking."

Marcus still looked pale, but when he opened his eyes they appeared less glassy and more focused.

"Woof."

"Daisy!"

At the sound of her name the little dog leaped from Fanny's arms to jump on the crisp white spread. She bellied up to Marcus and started to lick his face.

"Marcus, you recognize Daisy?" Fanny said, her voice breathless with wonderment.

"It's pretty sad when the first kiss I get is from a dog and not my wife."

"Oh, Marcus, you know us. They said . . . I thought . . . Move over, Daisy."

"Mrs. Reed! You can't bring a dog in here!" a nurse in crisp white said angrily.

"Who said I can't?"

"Well . . . I . . . Dr. . . . ."

"Phooey. We're here and we aren't leaving."

"Germs . . ."

"We don't have any germs, and we brushed earlier. With baking soda."

"Well, I never . . ."

"I want them to stay," Marcus said in his new croaky-sounding voice.

"And we want to stay. If we leave, Marcus will get upset. He shouldn't get upset," Fanny said as she smothered her husband's face with kisses.

"Doctor will have something to say about this when he finds out."

"So go already and tell him," Fanny said.

"Marcus, do I look like Grandma Moses? You scared me out of my wits."

"Kinda. You look different."

"You mean haggard? Maybe sloppy? Tired?"

"Kinda. You look like I remember. I had so many bad dreams."

"I never remember my dreams. Do the doctors know you're . . . you know, with it? Did they talk to you? Did you answer them? They said you . . . were having some difficulty."

"Don't know. Can't remember. I remember the dreams. Ash was in all of them."

"Ash!"

"I'm tired, Fanny."

"Of course you are. We'll leave now and come back tomorrow. Sleep well, Marcus. I love you."

A smile touched the corners of Marcus's mouth as he drifted into sleep.

"C'mon, Daisy, time for us to find a new home." Fanny's step was lighter, her heart less heavy when she strode past the nurses' station, Daisy in her arms. Marcus was alive and well. He'd smiled at her, called Daisy by name. "Thank you, God."

"Mrs. Reed, Mrs. Reed, Doctor said . . ."

Fanny laughed aloud. "Ask me if I care what Doctor. Whatever-his-name-is said. My dog did more for my husband than all those tests you put him through. Guess what,'' she called over her shoulder, ''I'm bringing her back tomorrow and the day after tomorrow. If you don't like it or Doctor Whatever-his-name-is doesn't like it, look for another job.''

''*Attagirl, Fanny. Kick ass and take names later.*''

''Did I do good, Ash?''

''*Damn good. Hole up at the casino. Do what you did when you barred Simon from the premises. Pay Jeffrey off and get him the hell out of there.*''

''Okay, Ash. Marcus is going to be just fine. Just fine. I wish I could tell you how happy that makes me. My world is right side up again. I owe you another one for that.''

''*Nah. Take care of yourself, Fanny.*''

At the casino, Fanny asked for the keys to the suite of rooms kept for what Ash had always called visiting royalty. Translated it meant high-rollers or, as Sunny put it, a luxury comp for someone who was prepared to drop a half million bucks in a high-stakes poker game.

Fanny dropped the card key into her purse. She rummaged for a minute until she pulled out the crackly envelope she'd taken from her safety deposit box. Jeff Lassiter's contract. The amount of the cashier's check made her wince. She was cutting her losses. Big time. She sought out Neal and spent ten minutes huddling with him. ''It's not that I don't want to confront Jeff, Neal. I'm afraid of what I might do if I find myself face-to-face with him. Take some Security people with you and escort him from the premises. Under no circumstances is he permitted in this casino or hotel ever again.''

''My pleasure, Fanny. I bet Ash is smiling from ear to ear over this.''

''You're probably right, Neal. I'll be in the high-roller suite until I can find a place to live.''

''Do you want me to call you when he's gone?''

"No. I don't want to know anything about that young man. Thanks."

"Let's go get you some chicken, Daisy," Fanny said, picking up the little dog. "Then we're going upstairs, where I'm going to show you how happy I am. I am, you know. I feel like singing. I might even sing to you." Fanny squeezed the little dog until she squealed. "I'm just so happy, Daisy."

"No muss no fuss, guys," Neal Tortolow said to the beefy Security guards. "We take him down the private elevator to his car. I'll drive the car out to the street and the two of you will escort him to it. If he ever gets within a foot of this place, you're all on the unemployment line. Ring the bell."

Jeff Lassiter opened the door, an ugly look on his face. Neal slapped the contract and the certified check into his hand. He nodded to the Security guards as each of them took hold of Lassiter's arms. "We'll send your belongings to your mother's house."

"What the hell do you think you're doing? Take your goddamn hands off me. I'll sue your fucking asses off."

"It's a free country. As of this minute, you are trespassing. Once we escort you outside you can do whatever you want. Go to a lawyer, go to the police, it's your choice. Come near this casino, and you'll be carted off to jail. I filed a restraining order an hour ago," Neal said.

"I want my belongings, and I want them now!"

"Tough shit, mister," one of the guards said.

"It'll be tough shit if any of my money is missing," Lassiter snarled.

"You should have put your money in the bank the way normal people do," Neal snarled in return. "Tell me how much there is, and I'll go back and get it now."

"You don't need to know how much there is. Just get the

metal security box under the bathroom vanity. It has a combination lock, so it better not be tampered with.''

"Eat shit, Lassiter," Neal said as he spun around on his heel to head for the elevator. To the guards he said, "Hold him here till I get back."

Jeff Lassiter leaned against the front of his new car, his face full of rage. Obviously Fanny Thornton had put two and two together and come up with the number four. He was sorry now that he hadn't blown up the cozy little house in the desert. He did like a good fire. From all he'd been told, Fanny Thornton Reed was a creature of habit and comfort. By all rights, if she was the one who had taken the pictures and his father's wings, she would have secured them in the cozy little house in the desert. People like Fanny Thornton Reed couldn't comprehend that people like him would actually break and enter her sacred domicile. If he lived to be a hundred, he would never understand how she could give up the Thornton name. He himself would kill to carry that treasured name. Well, hell's bells, he could do just that. All he had to do was go to a lawyer's office, show all his voluminous paperwork, and ask for a name change. He could prove paternity. His mother would back him up. All he had to do was threaten to cut the television wires and she would do whatever he wanted. And he wanted to change his name. He started to laugh, an unholy sound that echoed around the underground garage.

Neal stepped out of the elevator, the metal box in his hands, just as Lassiter's laughter circled around him. He felt himself cringe. His eyes narrowed. He'd heard laughter like that once before. Simon Thornton had laughed like that the night Neal and the same Security guards dragged him from the penthouse after he'd beaten Ash. A cold chill ran along his arms. He shoved the metal box into Lassiter's hands. To the guards he said, "Take him outside, and I'll drive this pimpmobile out front. If he tries any funny stuff, deck him."

"You and what army?" Jeff sneered.

"Keep it up, and you'll be wearing these super-duper tire-tread marks all over that ugly face of yours. There are a million pairs of eyes on you, so I'd be careful if I were you. That advice is free. Get his stinking ass out of here," Neal said as he turned the key in the ignition. A devilish grin on his face, he gunned the engine, exhaust billowing up and around the fancy sports car. He peeled rubber and raced down the length of the garage and up the ramp and out to the street, where he screeched to a halt. The moment he stepped from the car, Lassiter was shoved inside.

Arms akimbo, the three men watched as Jeff settled the box on the passenger side of the car, fastened his seat belt, and fired up a cigarette. He took his time looking in the rearview mirror as well as the side view mirror before he turned on his signal lights and inched into traffic. The window down, he leaned out and raised his middle finger.

"The same to you, asshole," Neal muttered under his breath. "Okay, you guys, back to work."

Jeff drove aimlessly. Technically, as of this minute, he was homeless. What were his options? Return to his mother's and the sickening smell of liniment and the sound of raucous game shows? Take a hotel room or rent a furnished apartment? Buy a house? Hang out at Celia's fleabag apartment? He opted for the latter. First, though, he had to stop at the bank and stash his money in his safety deposit box. Then he would go to Celia's apartment to wait for her. An hour with Celia would tell him if it was Fanny Thornton Reed or Celia who had his belongings.

He had all the time in the world. And he was rich. After tonight he would be even richer.

It was ten minutes past seven when Celia fitted her key into the lock of the dingy apartment. She flicked on the light switch next to the door, gasping when she saw Jeff Lassiter sitting in the living room's only chair. "What's wrong?"

"It depends on your point of view. I'm only going to ask you this once, so I would advise you to tell me the truth. Did you or didn't you take the keys and the pictures?"

"No!" The single word exploded from Celia's mouth like a gunshot.

Jeff's voice took on a singsong quality when he said, "I hope you aren't lying. If you are, that means I ransacked Fanny Thornton Reed's house for nothing. I really did a number on it. She won't want to live there ever again. The keys and pictures weren't there. That brings me back to you. By the way, Fanny Thornton Reed had my ass booted out of the casino. I'm homeless and jobless. What do you think I should do, Celia?"

"Why are you asking me? What did you do to Fanny's house? Did it ever occur to you that maybe, just maybe, someone from the casino went into your apartment when you were sleeping? Why would Fanny Thornton want your keys? Furthermore, she didn't know about the pictures. You saw me leave. I had nothing in my hands. My carry bag was by the front door where I dropped it. I took the money out and handed it to you. I don't have a key to the penthouse, and you know it. There was no way for me to get back in, so don't go getting any funny ideas. Now that you're homeless and jobless, let's call this deal off. I'll be going on the road, so there is no point in discussing this any further. You have your deal about ready to fly, don't you? Let's part without hard feelings."

"No, my deal isn't ready to fly. We're going to keep going with our plan. I've been barred from the casino, so that means you work it tonight. They can't throw you out. You play all night and win as much as you can. I'll meet you when the sun comes up at Fanny Thornton Reed's house. That's the last place anyone will think to look for either of us. Make sure no one is following you. I've taken the liberty of writing down the directions. Don't screw this up, Celia."

"Or what?"

"You don't want to know."

For the first time since meeting Jeffrey Lassiter, Celia felt total fear. She tried to brazen it out. "And while I'm doing that, what are you going to be doing? If you say Fanny isn't going to return to her house, that means she's probably staying at Babylon. They'll call her if I start winning. Then what do I do?"

"Do I have to do all your thinking? You continue to play. All they can do is change the dealer, shut down the table for an hour or so. If things get out of hand, make an announcement. Tell everyone who you are and see the reaction you get. Crowds love that kind of crap. You're an ingenious person much like myself. Fight fire with fire. Just make sure you take the house for everything you can. Don't screw up."

"In the meantime those pictures are out there somewhere." Suddenly Celia felt like crying.

"That's something we both need to remember. I stopped by a lawyer's office today. I'm changing my name to Thornton. I turned over all the paperwork. Proving paternity was no problem. How do you like the name Jeffrey Thornton?"

"It has a definite ring to it," Celia said carefully.

"I think so. My uncle Simon was a nutcase, did you know that? My old man shot him dead. Then he bought the farm. They died within minutes of each other. Mrs. Fanny Thornton Thornton Reed gave my father a sendoff, and my uncle was simply planted. It's a crazy family."

"Then why do you want to belong to it?"

"Because it's my right. I have the same blood. It's my goddamn right. Why did you marry Birch Thornton?"

"For his money. Greed, pure and simple. It isn't going to work. It's over. Can't you see that? They're onto you. If changing your name makes you happy, then you should change it, but the Thorntons will never accept you any more than they'll accept me. Sooner or later you'll end up in an alley somewhere with your throat slit from ear to ear. Things like that happen in this town. You just never hear about them. Jeffrey Lassiter Thornton will become a statistic. Is that what you want? This town will never accept you.''

''And you have all the answers?''

''No. I have a few. I know I screwed up. My greed got in the way. You'll probably laugh your head off when I tell you this, but I'm going to tell you anyway. I'm pregnant. That's why I want out of this mess. I'm going to have to make it on my own. If Ruby keeps me on, and with the money I've stashed from our little venture, I'll be okay.''

''A kid! How'd that happen?''

Celia shot Jeff a disgusted look. ''It happened, okay. Now I have to deal with it. No more late nights, no more drinking and smoking. No more gambling in smoky rooms all night long.''

''How do I know you aren't lying?''

Celia reached into her bag and withdrew a lab report. ''Read it.''

''Okay, you aren't lying. You're off the hook. Tonight's your last night, so make it count. My mother told me how hard it was for her to be pregnant with no one to look out for her. She needed someone. A person, a body. She said she could have gotten by with less money from my father if he'd just been there for her. It wasn't her choice. It was his. A kid needs two parents when possible. Nobody gives a damn about the kids. All they do is think about themselves. Don't be so quick to give up the Thornton cushion.''

Celia stared at Jeff. She thought she saw tears in his eyes.

''You're missing the point, Jeff. I don't love Birch.''

''What the hell does love have to do with anything?''

''It has everything to do with it. You're a prime example. I don't want to get into this. I'll take the low road and hope for the best.''

''I can't dig you as a mother. You could give the kid out

for adoption to people who will love it. The kid's going to need a live-in set of parents. A kid needs a hands-on father and a mother who bakes cookies and goes on Scout trips.''

"Do you have any idea how strange that sounds coming from you? The kid will be my ace in the hole down the road. That's my thinking now. It might change as time goes on. I might turn out to be the world's best mother. The flip side of that is I might turn out to be the world's worst mother. Only time will tell. To go back to your suggestion, I could never give a child away. I might be a lot of things, but I would never abandon my own flesh and blood. I'm out of here now. Stay if you want.'' She picked up the directions to Fanny's house. "I'll see you in the morning.''

"Celia, wait. Put yourself in Fanny's place. If you took the pictures and the keys, where would you hide them? I went through her car and purse within an hour. She didn't stop anywhere except the medical center.''

"I'd put the keys down my bra and the pictures in my pocket. Then I'd hide both things in a safety deposit box. If that's what she did, you'll never get them. Cut your losses and go on from there.''

"This place is a dump.''

Celia looked around. "It's worse than a dump. For now it works.''

"I expect big bucks, Celia.''

"There is something I want you to remember, Jeff. I haven't forgotten the other night. Nor will I forget it anytime in the near future. Paybacks are a bitch. The second thing you need to remember is I'm going up against Fanny Thornton.''

Jeff snorted. "Just mention your ace in the hole. C'mon, all we had was a little fun. Sex is sex. It didn't mean a thing.'' His face turned ugly and hateful. "Get over it.''

Celia slammed the door on her way out. She was almost to the street when she remembered that she hadn't checked her answering machine. When she got to the casino she would call

Jeff to check it and to tell him not to answer the phone in case Birch called. Her stomach started to churn. She should never have allowed Jeff to stay in her apartment. Stupid. Stupid. Stupid.

Her stomach in a knot, Celia climbed behind the wheel of her car. How was she going to deal with her mother-in-law if something went awry this evening? If Fanny had the pictures, her attitude would be less than understanding if Celia were winning big at the tables. Maybe she should just flash the lab report under Fanny's nose, let her figure out which one of her sons was the father of her unborn child. There was no way Fanny would let homemaker Iris know about her husband's presumed infidelity. No way at all. There was no way Fanny would allow Birch to see the pictures either. *So, for the time being, the father of this child is up for grabs where Fanny Reed is concerned,* Celia thought smugly.

She sighed deeply, God she was tired. She'd been tired from the moment she stepped foot on American soil.

She stopped for a red light. *All I want right now is a nice place to live with some decent money in the bank, so I don't have to worry about bill collectors. A job that isn't a killer and a strength zapper would fit right into my wish list. Something part-time would be nice.*

Once all the hoopla was over with The Chicken Palaces, part-time might work. At least for a while. She closed her eyes for a moment but was jolted awake when a horn blared behind her. If she did have a wish list, it would be for a hot bowl of soup, a long, leisurely bath, and twelve hours' sleep. Instead, she was headed for a gambling casino where she would gamble the night away in a skintight dress, spike-heeled shoes, and enough makeup on her face for heads to turn. She'd sip free drinks and smoke free cigarettes until her throat became scratchy and her eyes started to water.

"I don't want to do this anymore. Die already, Jeffrey Lassiter Thornton or whatever your name is today," Celia muttered as she swerved into the underground garage, where she parked her car in her husband's parking slot.

"Seventy-nine bottles of beer . . ."

"Harry, stop. Did you hear something?"

"Just you. You can't sing worth a darn, Sunny."

"I know. Just listen for a minute. I thought I heard a horn."

"I guess a horn is better than hearing a dead person talk to you. I'm sorry, Sunny, but I can't buy into that. Wait, I think I did hear something. You're right. It does sound like a horn. Maybe someone out there is looking for us on a snowmobile. I'll crawl out and give ours a blast. Keep singing, Sunny."

"What number are we on? It's Birch. I know it's Birch. I can feel it."

"I don't care who it is as long as they can get us back to the lodge. I think we're on eighty-five."

"God! Is that all we did?"

"Time has no meaning, Sunny. I was just guessing. Okay, I'm going to give the horn a blast. I'll wait ten seconds and do it again."

"That's good. Ninety-three bottles of beer . . ."

"Seventy-four, Sunny. You need to get it right in case your father really is out there somewhere listening."

"Oh, boy, oh, boy. I heard that real clear. Did you hear that, Harry?"

"Yeah." Harry blasted his horn for ten long seconds and received an even closer blast in return.

"I told you Birch would find us. It's Birch. We're saved, Harry. We aren't going to die out here alone after all. Do the horn again, Harry, and keep doing it. Turn on the light too."

"Sunny! Harry!"

"Sage! Sage, is that you? I hear you, but I can't see you."

"Sunny, where are you? Blow the horn."

Harry leaned on the horn with his elbow until he heard the snarl of the snowmobile careening to a stop next to their own.

Sage climbed from his snowmobile to scoop his sister up into his arms. He squeezed her so hard she yelped, her voice hoarse and craggy-sounding. "I've never been so glad to see anyone in my life. You too, Harry. Does that machine work?"

"Yeah. There is only a little gas left. We decided it was better to hole up here, where there was a little protection."

"I like your igloo," Sage laughed. "You're alive, that's all that matters. Were you two singing 'Ninety-nine Bottles of Beer'?"

"Yeah. Dad made me do it. First he made us build this igloo. Then he made us build the domino bridge and take it down. We wanted to go to sleep so badly, and he wouldn't let us. He made us sing. Can I go to sleep now, Sage? Please."

"Not yet, Sunny. I have to find the others and let them know you're safe. We branched out to cover more distance."

"What others?"

"Ruby, Metaxas, and some of his men. Birch and Libby. They're both wild and blaming themselves for this. How the hell do you think I got here in a storm like this?"

"I just kind of figured Dad helped you the way he helped me. He did, didn't he?"

"Shhh. We'll talk about it later. It's a damn good thing you were singing, or I might not have found you."

"Yeah, that's what Dad said. I want a fried-egg sandwich and some hot cocoa."

"Ready, Harry?"

"Yeah."

"On the count of thirty, blast your horn. Stay as close as you can. Sunny will be watching you. I can find my tracks. I actually think this damn storm is finally starting to let up. A goddamn igloo, huh?"

"Yeah. You know Dad with his neat ideas. It worked. We were cramped, but we weren't that cold. On the other hand we're numb, so I don't know if we're frozen or not. How mad is Birch?''

"He's not mad mad, Sunny. He's worried sick. I had this feeling something was wrong, that's why I came.''

"Will he forgive us, Sage?''

"Of course. Birch loves you, Sunny. Don't ever do a dumb-ass thing like this again. Do you hear me?''

"Sage?''

"Yeah.''

"We survived. Harry and I survived, using our wits. That doesn't make what we did right. Both of us know now that we can't survive on our own. What would have happened to us without your gut intuition or whatever that thing is twins have?''

"Birch would have found you.''

"We don't know that,'' Sunny blubbered.

"I know that, Sunny. Birch would have searched for you until he dropped. That's a given. What in the damn hell got into you anyway?''

"If I tell you will you yell at me?''

"No.''

"We wanted to *play* in the snow. We can't do things like that anymore, Sage. My God, some days we can't go to the bathroom without help. Do you have any idea how that feels? We had a plan. We were prepared. I wanted Harry to have some fun. He's never been in the snow before. I'd damn well do it again, too. So there!''

"I hear you, Sunny. It's okay. If you want to do something crazy, the next time let us know so we can be on the fringes.''

"We left a note. My only regret was that we didn't have our dogs.''

"I see lights ahead. The snow really is letting up.'' Sage gave his horn a one-two blast. Harry did the same thing. "We're going to ditch Harry's machine and get it later. He can ride with Ruby.''

Birch was off his snowmobile in the blink of an eye. For a

moment he stood rooted in the snow before he galloped over to where Sunny was. "I should blister your ass for pulling a stunt like this. I might even *think* about doing it later. I was sick to my soul when I found out you were gone. All I could think of was what my life, what all our lives would be without you. Empty. Libby was as sick as I was . . . am. She wants to quit and is blaming herself."

Sunny swiped at her tears. "That's probably one of the nicest things you ever said to me. I'm sorry for causing you worry. I did it for Harry. We survived. It was and is important for us to do things, to stretch our limits. This was the wrong time and the wrong place. You know what, I'd damn well do it again. I just told Sage the same thing. Give me a hug, you big galoot. Ah, don't cry, Birch. I was okay. We had a few bad minutes, but Dad got me through it. He was right there every time I needed him. He was really worried about Harry. Thanks for caring, Birch. So," she hissed, "did you sleep with Libby? If she's leaving, it's because of what she feels for you, not because of me and Harry. I love you! I love all of you! This is what family is all about. Look at Metaxas and Ruby. They might not have gotten together if it wasn't for this crisis. Think about that, Birch." Her voice was so weary, so sad, Birch felt his eyes puddle up again. "Harry's okay, isn't he?"

"Yeah, he's okay." Birch's hold on his sister became fierce. "You hang on now. I'm taking you back to the lodge."

"Thanks, Birch. For everything."

"Thank Sage. He's the one who found you. He's the greatest. I need to tell him that more often."

"Yeah, you do. Everyone needs to hear nice things once in a while. I have to go to sleep, Birch."

"I thought you wanted a fried-egg sandwich."

"I want that, too. I just love everyone."

Sage plowed through the snow next to his brother. "Birch, did she tell you about Dad?"

"Yeah. We'll talk about it later, okay. I need to talk to you about a couple of other things, too."

"I have a little sharing I want to do myself. We'll hunker in and wait out the rest of this storm. I gotta tell you, Birch, I've never seen snow like this in my life. I feel compelled to tell you what we all did was incredibly stupid. All of us could have died out there. What we did defies all logic."

"We had to do it. Sunny is our sister. I kept thinking about you the whole time, asking myself what you would or wouldn't do. Thanks for coming, Sage."

Sunny started to cry.

"That's it with the bawling," Metaxas roared. "We're all alive and well. We should be laughing and celebrating. Pile in everyone, we're going home. Our passengers are alive and in the need of food and warm beds. Not another word!"

"I love it when you take charge," Ruby said, leaning against Metaxas's chest. She blew her nose loudly. "You said we'd find her, and we did. I don't even want to think about what might have happened if you hadn't taken matters into your own hands and got us here. I will always be grateful to you, Metaxas. They're going to be all right, aren't they?" Her voice was so anxious-sounding, so full of concern she couldn't help but start to cry all over again.

"Yes, sweet baby, those two are going to be just fine. They'll feel the aftereffects for a few days and maybe get a rip-roaring cold, but we can head that off at the pass with some antibiotics and some good old Texas down-home remedies. Sweet baby, I know every one of those remedies. Trust me."

"With my life. I have to pee, Metaxas."

"Then we best see about gettin' you womenfolk back to the lodge. I'd like it a lot, sweet baby, if we could share the same room," Metaxas drawled.

"I was kind of thinking of something a little more . . . *intimate*. I was thinking more in terms of the same *bed*."

"Sweet baby, I am your man. Climb aboard and follow me.

This old Texan is leading the way. You young'uns stay close, you hear!'' Metaxas bellowed.

"That's nice. That's really nice. I'm so glad Ruby is happy,'' Sunny murmured. "Isn't it great, Dad?''

"Tell her I'm proud of her, Sunny."

"Why can't you tell her? It would mean more coming from you. She loved you, Dad. She loves all of us. You most of all. She talks about you all the time. Did I do good, Dad? Is Harry really going to be okay? How come you don't talk to Birch?''

"You sure do ask a lot of questions."

"It would be nice if you'd answer them.''

"You did real good, Sunny. I'm so proud of you I could just bust. Harry is going to be right as rain in a few days. Birch isn't ready to talk to me. He hasn't forgiven me for a lot of things. If he ever needs me, I'll be there for him. Tell him that for me, Sunny."

"I'll tell him, Dad. Dad?''

"What, Sunny?"

"Can I go to sleep now? I did everything you said.''

"Sure, baby. You earned it."

"Will you watch over me, Dad?''

"Always and forever, Sunny."

Sunny snuggled into the cramped space in the snowmobile, next to her brother, wet snow stinging her face. Suddenly she felt deliciously warm as a soft, gentle hand brushed back the frozen tendrils of hair on her forehead.

"What did you say, Sunny?'' Birch shouted.

"I was talking to Dad. He said it was okay for me to go to sleep.''

"No, Sunny, it is not okay. Please, stay awake.''

"Dad said it was okay. He gave me a message for you. He said if you ever need him, he'll be there for you. You have to forgive him first. That means you have to open up your heart. Don't worry about me. Dad is watching over me and Harry.

'Night, Birch. I love you. Tell Sage I love him. Tell everyone I love them.''

Birch clenched his teeth so hard he thought his jaw would shatter. "You damn well better be watching over her. I'm not buying into this gobbledygook. I'm not into spirits and spooks. If Sunny believes she talks to you, that's okay, but it's not okay with me. You should have done all these good things when you were alive. Being dead isn't going to cut it with me. I can't conceive of me ever needing help from the netherworld. Stop that crap with Sunny before she goes off the deep end.''

"If you believe that, exactly who are you talking to?"

The snowmobile swerved and almost plowed into a two-foot-high drift next to a clump of pine trees. "What?"

"What, SIR? Show some respect. Do you talk to yourself? I've been called a lot of things in my day, but I don't think anyone ever called me a spook. I resent it."

"Get real."

"I can't. I can only deal with the cards in my hand. The message was simple. It stands. Tuck it away for future reference or discount it. The choice is yours."

"You're dead."

"That's a brilliant observation. Sunny's fine, she'll sleep round the clock. Harry will be fine, too. You'll all fly out of here, and your lives will go back to the way they were."

"Like I didn't know that."

"There's a lot of things you don't know, Birch. You play the same games I used to play. You hate me, but you're following in my footsteps."

"That'll never happen."

"It already happened. You were unfaithful to your wife. You not only raised your hand to her, but you struck her. With all my faults, I never raised a hand to your mother."

"What you did was worse."

"There is nothing worse than abuse. Nothing."

"I don't get it. Sunny said if I ever needed you, you'd be

there for me. I don't need you, so what the hell are you doing here?"

"*You were talking to me. I responded. Get it through your head—I don't want you to be like me. I want you to be your own person. The person I know you can be. I won't make any promises where Sunny and the others are concerned. See you around, Birch.*"

"Not likely."

Birch brought his snowmobile to a stop behind Metaxas's machine. The big Texan was out in the blink of an eye, Sunny in his arms. "Lead the way, sweet baby."

Birch watched, hands on hips, as two of Metaxas's men picked Harry up. He felt confused, disoriented.

"Birch. Thanks for coming to our rescue. Sorry is just a word, but it's the only one I know. I want you to know we couldn't have made it without your dad helping us. Sunny's sleeping, isn't she?"

"Yeah, she is."

"I saw the light first and then I started to feel warm all over. I guess your dad thinks I belong. At first I thought it was all bullshit, that we were delirious, you know, half out of it, for a while. Man, I became a believer real fast. Anyway, thanks."

Birch nodded. Harry was right the first time. It was all bullshit.

"Are you okay, Birch?" Libby asked.

"Yeah. How about you?"

"Cold, but that's okay. A cup of hot tea and some dry clothes will fix me right up. This is just a guess on my part, but I think tea and warm clothes aren't going to do it for you. Am I right?"

"We'll talk later, Libby. Go with Ruby and help Sunny get settled. We'll take care of Harry."

"Whatever it is, Birch, cut yourself some slack. You're too hard on yourself."

"Save some of that tea for me, but I want something in it besides sugar, okay?"

"Okay."

"Now, what am I supposed to do?" Birch muttered. "Do I listen my heart or do I listen to someone I lost all respect for, someone who is dead?" He was still muttering under his breath as he held the door open for Metaxas's employees. Harry offered up a high five that Birch returned, a silly grin plastered on his face. There were some things in life that were better left unanswered.

18

Birch Thornton sat alone, staring at the fire. For the past several hours he'd been guzzling scotch and smoking one cigarette after the other. He looked around, wondering why he was alone. He hated being alone, hated thinking the kinds of things that were buzzing inside his head. His nostrils told him they would serve dinner shortly. He wondered if he'd be dining alone since everyone else was still sleeping. His eye fell on the scotch bottle. He'd had enough, but then again, what was enough? Who decided how much was enough? He wished he could put a face to that particular person. He shoved the bottle farther away on the table.

The flames danced in front of him, toasting his legs. Warmth had never felt this good. Was his mother worried about them? And Celia, was she even aware of what had gone on here in Vermont? Yes to the first and no to the second. How much longer was Libby going to sleep? She probably wasn't sleeping at all. She was probably curled up in front of the fire in her room thinking horrible thoughts, just the way he was. Everyone was alive, safe, and well. That had to count for something.

Birch's feet thumped down hard on the floor. He had to get up, move around, clear his head. He smelled fresh coffee, roast beef, and cinnamon. Dinner would be plentiful and hearty. Would anyone eat? He walked to the front windows to stare out at the white world that surrounded the lodge. How much longer would they be lodgebound? A day, two, three? He wished he could open the door, walk out, and never come back. He'd done that once before when he left Nevada after his accident. He'd run away to find himself. The only problem was, he hadn't been successful. The same demons plagued him, and now he'd made matters worse. His father was right. He was following in his footsteps. Hell, he was *wearing* his father's shoes.

He didn't hear his brother or see him until he felt his comforting hand on his shoulder. "I thought you'd sleep the clock around, Sage."

"I thought I would too, but here I am. What's wrong, Birch? Two heads are better than one. It always worked before."

"That's because we were kids. We *thought* it worked."

"If that's the case, then why did we always come up with our answers?"

"I don't know," Birch said.

"Let's sit down and have a drink."

"I've already had more than my share. Something weird happened to me earlier. It's bothering me."

"I'm listening, Birch."

"I guess I was more or less daydreaming on the ride in. Maybe I was just so numb with cold I didn't . . . I had this conversation with Dad. I was a little bent out of shape over Sunny. She said . . . what she said was she'd been talking to him. She kept mumbling and muttering. At first I thought she was delirious. I'm not sure that she wasn't. She said she had a message from Dad which was, when and if I needed him, he'd be there for me. It pissed me off. Like he was ever there for us. Oh, yeah. I was muttering to myself. You know kind of railing him out, that kind of thing. He fucking answered me.''

''Stuff you didn't want to hear, huh?'' Sage said, propping his legs on the table in front of the fire. ''I swear, I didn't think I'd ever be warm again. This feels so good.''

''Yeah. He said he didn't want to see me turn out like him, and yet I'd set the wheels in motion. He *knew* . . . things. Maybe it was my own guilty conscience. You want to believe that crap, don't you?''

Sage's voice was barely a whisper. ''Yeah.''

''Sunny too.''

''Sunny too,'' Sage said.

''It's bullshit, Sage.''

''If it's bullshit, then why are we even talking about it?''

''Because I can't get a handle on it, that's why.''

Sage looked thoughtful as he too stared into the flames. ''I think it's one of those things that either you believe or you don't. I lived through it, so that makes me a believer. I rather think Sunny feels the same way. Harry could go either way. Then there's Ruby, who says she talked to him, too. Metaxas said he showed him the way down. He swears he carried on a conversation with a voice that said his name was Major. That big Texan is not one to buy into what you call this bullshit. Let's say it's an either or and let it go at that.''

''It's not that easy. I said some ugly things because it was how I felt at the moment. Guilt sucks. I slept with Libby this morning. I'm asking Celia for a divorce.''

''Oh.''

''That's it, oh. Is that the best you can come up with?''

''Are you planning on . . . what about Libby?''

''She says she's going to leave the center. Not because of Sunny but because of me. She . . . we went to bed because it . . . it was one of those one-for-the-road memories that would carry us to our rocking-chair days.''

"Dad was right, you are following in his footsteps. What the hell kind of thinking is that? That's how he used to rationalize things. The bottom line is you were unfaithful. On top of that, you knocked your wife around. No matter what, you can't justify that. Dad never laid a hand on Mom."

"I'm getting a divorce."

"That doesn't make it right. All marriages have ups and downs. You gotta work at it night and day. It's not easy, Birch. Do you love Libby? Or is it a sexual thing?"

"She's wonderful. She's down-to-earth. She's not money-grubbing. She has ethics and values. We have everything in common, unlike Celia and me. She's warm, caring, and I know she feels what I do."

"All of the above, and yet she went to bed with a married man. That old dog ain't gonna hunt, Birch."

"Don't be so goddamn virtuous, Sage. Don't sit there and tell me you've never been tempted."

"That's exactly what I'm telling you. I love Iris so much my heart aches sometimes. We like each other, Birch. We're friends as well as lovers and parents. Iris and the kids are my life. I can't conceive of ever wanting that to change."

"The good son. The good husband."

"I hope so. As I said, it's my life. This is just off the top of my head, but hear me out. Start with Dad dying and you not coming for the funeral. Maybe if you can lay that to rest, the other things will fall into place. Think of it as a jumping-off place."

"I couldn't make it. I tried. I wanted to come. It didn't work out. Don't you think I regret not going to my own father's funeral?"

"Of course you do, and it's all tied into guilt. Work through it, Birch. If you have to get professional help, then get it. There is no shame in asking for help. I believe one hundred percent in my heart that I wouldn't be here if it wasn't for Dad. Nothing and no one will ever be able to convince me otherwise. Even when I made it to ground he helped me. Sunny too. How can both of us be wrong? It's what it is.''

''The word you're looking for is bullshit.''

''That's your word, not mine,'' Sage said.

''Looks like it's just going to be me and you for dinner. The desk clerk said she'd try to patch a call through for us. Let's check it out. Mom must be worried sick.''

Fifteen minutes later Birch held out the earphone so Sage and he could both hear his mother's relieved voice. ''I was worried but not that worried,'' she said. ''Your father told me it would be okay. Lately he's been visiting. I know that sounds weird, but it happened. He's watching over all of us. Are you absolutely certain Sunny and Harry are okay?''

''We're certain, Mom,'' Sage said. ''Birch doesn't quite believe the stuff about Dad.''

''He will when he finds himself in trouble. I had a problem with it at first. I'm okay with it. Maybe we're all ready to be locked up. Take care of yourselves and give everyone a hug for me, even Metaxas.''

''Will do, Mom.''

''I want to call Iris. I know Mom will call her, but I want to hear her voice. Pour yourself a drink, Birch, you're whiter than that snow outside. Do you want me to call Celia for you when I'm finished?''

''Yeah.''

Thirty minutes later, Sage held out the speaker to his brother. ''It's ringing. Supper's coming and I'm so hungry I could eat a horse.''

Birch reached for the headphone and held it to his ear. He blinked at the sound of the voice on the other end of the line. ''Who is this?''

''Jeff. Jeff Lassiter. Celia isn't here, Birch. Can I take a message?''

Birch clenched his teeth and balled his hands into tight fists.

"What the hell are you doing in my wife's apartment, Lassiter?"

"I'm staying here. Your mother paid me off today, and Tortolow escorted me off the premises. He took out a restraining order on me. That's the news. Celia went club hopping. She said I could stay here until I found a place of my own. Are you having trouble with this, Birch?" Jeff asked in a voice he would have used to discuss the weather. "Hey, by the way, I hear congratulations are in order. I bet you're going to make a hell of a father. Celia now, she's kind of flighty and greedy, but she might adapt to motherhood. Anything else, Birch?"

Birch broke the connection. He swallowed hard, his tongue thick in his mouth as he stumbled his way to the dining room. He sat down with a hard thump, his eyes glassy and unfocused.

Alarmed, Sage jumped up, half a butter roll stuck in his mouth. He tossed it on the floor. "What's wrong?"

"My world just ended is what's wrong. I called Celia, and Jeff Lassiter answered the phone. He said Mom paid him off and filed a restraining order. He sounded like he was discussing a summer rainstorm. He said Celia said he could stay with her until he found a place. Then the son of a bitch congratulated me on my new upcoming role in life—fatherhood."

"Huh?"

"You heard me."

"Since when does anyone believe what that jerk says?" Sage blustered. "Was Celia there? Did you talk to her?"

"Old Jeff said she went club hopping. I need a drink."

"I'll get it. You look like you're going to fall flat on your face. Stay put."

"I got news for you, Sage. I couldn't move if my life depended on it. Scotch isn't the answer either."

"I know that. I just want to put some color back in your face. This has not been a good day."

"Sure it was. We found Sunny and Harry. Celia . . . Jesus, now what the hell am I going to do?"

"I don't know, Birch. I don't think anyone can help you with this one. On the other hand . . ."

"I know that look, Sage. On the other hand, what?"

"Nah. You'd never go for it."

"Go for what? Don't talk in riddles. Look, right now I don't know what I'm supposed to be feeling. What?"

"Well, I was kind of thinking about . . . you know . . . Dad."

"Get off it, Sage."

"Okay. Congratulations! There is no feeling in the world that makes you feel better than looking down at your firstborn."

"For someone like you and Iris. Celia and I . . ."

"Sometimes things go sour. It's just too damn easy to get a divorce. Now, if what Lassiter said is true, there is a child involved. It's not just Celia, you, and Libby anymore. There is an innocent child in the mix. You need a clear head, Birch."

"What I need is to talk to Celia."

"That too. Can I do anything?"

"I've never been shy about asking for your help. I guess this is one of those things I have to deal with myself."

"Libby?"

"I think I'm falling in love with her. She's so real. Of course I thought Celia was real, too. Actually she was real when we were in Costa Rica. At least I thought she was. Maybe it isn't Celia at all. Maybe it's me. I guess I really am The Emperor's son. Now that's a pisser, isn't it?"

"I'd say so."

"I'm going to my room. All that liquor has made me woozy and it's stifling in here. I need to think."

"Thinking's good. I do that a lot. What should I say to Libby if she comes in for dinner?"

"Say whatever feels right to you. Check on Sunny and Harry, okay. I might fall asleep in the middle of my soul-searching. I understand it's pretty heady stuff."

"Go!" Sage said. He sighed deeply as he loaded his plate. Another Thornton was coming into the fold.

* * *

It was a welcoming committee that had no equal. Balloons and streamers were hanging from the rafters, dogs barked, and children laughed as everyone hugged everyone else. Mountains of food and a cake in the shape of an airplane filled the tables at Sunrise.

"I never want to see snow again as long as I live," Ruby said.

"Then, sweet baby, we'll go to some lush island paradise where the sun shines seven days a week. After the wedding, of course. Listen up, everyone, we may never come back. The door will always be open to all of you," Metaxas boomed.

"Ten days is more than enough," Sunny said in a raspy voice. "Harry and I are really sorry we caused you all such worry. We also want to thank you for coming to our aid. I think we should make a toast now to the person who got us here safe and sound. My dad!"

Fanny's eyes filled with tears. *I wish you were here, Ash, to hear this.*

"I know what you're thinking, Fanny, and I know Ash is up there somewhere listening. You know it too."

"Yes. Yes, I do know that. Are you sure this isn't too much excitement for you, Marcus?"

"Are you kidding? I love this. How many times do I have to tell you I love this family of yours? Now that everyone is home safe, we need to think about relocating. Where would you like to live, Fanny?"

"Let's move into the penthouse for the time being. I can redecorate, and you can play the slot machines while I'm doing it. When you're fully recovered, we'll go on a trip somewhere. Just you, me, and Daisy. The way I look at it, this is the first day of the rest of a very long and happy life. The kids and I really haven't had much of a chance to talk. Do you mind

Marcus, if we talk about their father a little? I'd like to hear their stories. I think Birch needs to hear them, too. He looks so lost. Celia is so quiet. I have such bad feelings about their marriage.''

"Stay out of it, Fanny."

"I will. Are you sure about Ash?"

"I'm sure."

"Listen, everyone, I want us all to share, if you don't mind, your experiences in Vermont. I have my own to share also. Believe it or not, Marcus has his own story, too. Who wants to go first?"

"I will," Sunny said, her face solemn as she reached for her son Jake's hand. "I guess I started it. This is how it was . . .''

It was almost dusk when Marcus, the last to contribute, wound down his story. The food was half-eaten on the plates, the ice cream melted, the coffee cold. No one seemed to mind. "To Ash, may his wings broaden and encircle us all."

"And to top it off, I have something in my purse for someone at this table. It's so special there are no words to describe it." Fanny reached into her purse, all eyes on her hands. She withdrew a small tissue-wrapped package and held it out to Jake. "Your grandfather wanted you to have this. There is a message engraved on the back. You need a magnifying glass to read it. It's special, Jake."

Tears streaming down the little boy's face, he ran from the room, the tissue-wrapped package clutched tightly in his hands. "No, no. Let him go. He needs time alone with his gift."

"What did it say? What was the message?" everyone asked at once.

"I don't know. Ash didn't tell me. As I said, you need a magnifying glass to read it. I'm sure Jake will decipher it. I have the feeling it's a private, personal message that was meant for Jake alone." The family nodded, understanding perfectly.

*   *   *

"Warm pumpkin pie with real whipped cream," Iris said, her voice breathless.

Fanny reached for Marcus's hand. He squeezed it. It was like old times. All her chicks were in the nest. "I have to go to the ladies' room, Marcus. I want you to think about something while I'm gone. What kinds of wonderful things are we going to do with the rest of our lives. Traveling is wonderful, but we're too young to retire. We need to *do* something, you know, contribute. It has to be something we can do *together*."

Fanny excused herself from the table. The upstairs bathroom was closed. She leaned against the wall to wait. Who was missing from the table downstairs? Jake, of course. Chue's wife had gone outside for something but had come back and was standing by the stove. Celia. Celia had left the table earlier. Who was in the bathroom?

The hallway was long and well lighted. How many times she'd walked the space to the room at the end, the room that once held the old iron safe. It was Jake's room now. She noticed that the door was closed. Jake was probably sitting on his bed with his grandfather's wings in his hands. She knew in her heart that the little boy's eyes were full of tears. Her own felt misty at the thought.

The room across the hall had been Sallie's schoolroom. Polly and Lexie shared it these days. Simon's old room was a guest room, and Ash's room was being painted and redone for the twins.

Fanny walked down the hall to the room that smelled faintly of fresh paint and wallpaper paste. She looked around. One wall was decorated with colorful Disney characters. Two walls were painted white. She wondered what was going to go on the fourth wall. The old rocker, the one she'd rocked all her children in, was under a sheet, the petit-point cushions worn but still beautiful. How like Iris to keep them. Iris was as sentimental as she was. Two cribs were under a flowered sheet. She raised the sheet at the corner. Birch's and Sage's old cribs. They'd been sanded and varnished. New plastic strips attached to the rails. The word tradition skittered around inside her head. She walked over to the huge walk-in closet. Sunny's crib had been in the corner. It was still there, the slats mangled, the headboard gouged and nicked. Irreparable, but Iris had kept it. Maybe she could work a miracle and have it fixed.

Feeling a presence in the room, Fanny turned. "Celia."

Celia nodded. "It's a pretty room. It will probably be even prettier when it's finished."

Fanny's voice was cool, aloof. "It used to be Ash's room when he was young. Birch and Sage took it over when they were ten or so. It has a wonderful view." *Don't think about those ugly pictures, Fanny.*

"I never had a room of my own. I never had much of anything growing up."

"Really," was all Fanny could think of to say. She wouldn't ask questions because she didn't want to know anything about this young woman who had married her son.

"Were you waiting to use the bathroom?"

"Yes."

"Do you think Iris will mind if I look around?"

"I don't know, Celia. Why don't you ask her?"

Celia nodded as Fanny left the room.

Fanny stood in the hallway for a few seconds and wasn't sure why. She listened a moment, a small smile tugging at the corners of her mouth. The rocking chair still creaked. She'd tried everything to erase the creaking sound but had been unsuccessful. Obviously Iris hadn't been successful either. In the end, she'd adapted to the sound and the slight creaking noise had become comforting. She heard that sound now and knew Celia was rocking in the chair. How strange.

Fanny was washing her hands when she heard heavy foot-steps go past the bathroom door. Birch's footsteps. Birch had always come down hard on his heels, Sage on the other hand was a sole walker. Fanny shook her head. How strange that she should think of that now. She sat down on the edge of the bathtub to wait.

"There's a big powwow going on in there. Don't you want to know what's going on?"

"It's none of my business, Ash. What are you doing here anyway? I thought you just showed up in emergencies. I'm not ungrateful so don't misunderstand."

"What makes you think this visit isn't an emergency?"

"Everything's quiet. All my chicks are in the nest. Oh, Ash, I gave Jake the wings. That's why you're here, isn't it? Celia saw . . . heard . . . is that . . . ? He had tears in his eyes, Ash. He ran to his room. I did what you wanted, Ash. I made it right."

"Yeah, yeah. Thanks, Fanny."

"You sound funny. You're crying, aren't you?"

"Nah. It's kind of cloudy here. Damp. You know humidity, that kind of thing. It creeps into your voice."

Fanny's voice was soft, compassionate. "I understand, Ash."

"I know you do. So, are you going out there to listen?"

"You want me to eavesdrop? I've never done anything like that in my life."

"There is a first time for everything. Remember those pictures."

"That's one of the reasons why I can't go out there. I can't look at her. She was rocking in *my* rocking chair. I *heard* her."

"Maybe she's getting practice."

"For what? Oh, Lord! Ash, are you telling me . . ."

"Figure it out for yourself, Fanny."

"I can't spy on my own son, Ash. No, I won't do that."

"How about lingering in the hallway for a moment or two? Your seams could be crooked, your shoelace untied, that kind of thing."

"Ash, where have you been? We wear panty hose these

days. That means no seams and the only shoelaces I have are on my sneakers, and I'm wearing heels. I'm going to stay here a few more minutes and then I'll leave.''

"Damn it, Fanny. That's just like you. Tomorrow you'll be trying to conjure me up to find out what happened. I'm not doing your dirty work."

"I'm not doing yours either. So there."

"Don't call me. I'll call you."

"Fine," Fanny snapped.

Five minutes later Fanny quietly opened the door. Satisfied no one was in the hall, she tiptoed her way to the stairs. She could hear voices, her son's raised in anger. She almost tripped over her own feet in her hurry to get down the stairs. The sounds from above stayed with her until she reached the landing, and then the children's laughter took over. She sighed mightily. Sometimes it was better not to know everything.

Birch's voice was cool, controlled and angry. "What are you doing up here, Celia?"

"I went to the bathroom. Was I supposed to ask for your permission? Your mother was in here, so I stopped in to see the room. I surmised from the fresh paint smell that this is going to be the new babies' room. From the look on your face I guess I did something wrong again. Excuse me. I'll leave."

"Wait, Celia, we need to talk. This is as good a place as any."

"I don't agree. I don't even know why you insisted I come here with you today. You certainly don't want to be with me, and I don't want to be here. I also don't intend to fight with you. I'm glad everyone came out of the storm safe. I congratulated and complimented everyone. What else do you want from me?"

"I told you. I want to talk."

"There really isn't anything to say, Birch. This has all been one big mistake. I'm leaving when we go back to town. You can file for a divorce, or I can. The choice is yours. We never should have gotten married.''

''Why did you marry me, Celia?''

''Because you were rich, and I was greedy and stupid. It's all my fault. The only way to make it right is to walk away. Your family doesn't like me, and I really don't like them. I'm not like your sisters and your mother, and I won't remake myself to fit into a mold that fits the Thornton women. Now, if you'll excuse me, I'll leave by the front door and walk down the hill. I need the exercise. I'll leave the explanations up to you.''

''It's not a hill. It's a mountain. Tell me something. Did you ever sleep with Jeff Lassiter?''

''Sleep with him! Do you mean as in going to bed with him and *making love?* No, I did not. I should ask you the same question. I saw the way you and Libby looked at each other. I'm a woman, so I can sense these things. Don't go getting self-righteous on me. I'm out of your life. Keep your damn money, your mountain, and your trust fund. No one ever gave me anything in my life. My mistake was thinking you would.''

Birch raked his hair with his fingers. ''Celia, it wasn't . . .''

''Don't make it worse by trying to justify it, Birch. You screwed around with Libby. I know it, and you know it. Hell, everyone downstairs knows it. It shows on both your faces. So, who's going to file, me or you?''

''Let's not rush into anything here. We need to sit and talk like responsible adults. We aren't kids.''

''I am sitting. You're perched on the second step of a ladder. There is nothing else to say. I'm taking all the blame here. You're off the hook. I guess I'll see you around. Then maybe I won't. In the scheme of things I don't suppose it matters. By the way, I don't want anything.''

''Celia, wait!''

''There is nothing to wait for, Birch. I'm going to Los

Angeles. Ruby has an office there. I'll work out of it until . . .
for now. Ruby was the only one who . . . you know what. It
doesn't matter. What does matter is, I can't let her down. If
you need me to sign papers or anything, send them on.''

Birch stared after his wife's retreating back. It was a trick.
It had to be a trick. He loped over to the window. By stretching
his neck he was able to see his wife walking down the driveway,
her shoulder bag slapping against her thighs. She didn't look
back.

Birch didn't know if he should run after his wife or not. He
felt sick to his stomach. His head started to pound a moment
later. She hadn't said a word about the baby. Did Lassiter lie?
What was Celia doing here in this room rocking in a chair?
Trying it out for size? Imagining what it would be like to
rock a baby? How matter of fact she'd been. She'd correctly
interpreted his feelings for Libby. Libby with the wraparound
smile. Libby, Libby, Libby.

After today there wasn't going to be a Libby or a Celia in
his life. Tomorrow, Libby was leaving for New York to take
a job in White Plains. She said she'd send a Christmas card.
He knew she wouldn't. He wanted to cry. He'd screwed everything up just the way his father screwed up things. He truly
was following in his footsteps. Son of a fucking bitch!

*"It's pretty cold out there, and it's a long way down the
mountain!"*

"Who asked you? You did enough damage to this family.
Don't go sticking your nose into my business."

*"What business is that? I can't screw up your life because
you already did that. A person could make something like this
come out right, but that person would really have to be unselfish.
You aren't. We both know that. The kid is going to grow up
without a father."*

"Butt out. She didn't say anything about a kid. If you think
I'm going to believe that *other* son of yours, you're crazy. He's
just as fucked up as you were. She's a grown woman. If she

wants to freeze her ass off walking down the mountain, that's her business. Christ, she doesn't know the difference between a hill and a mountain. Get out of my life. I don't need you, and I don't want to talk to you either. Go rattle someone else's cage.''

"She told you the truth."

"Like you really know a thing or two about truth. All you ever did was lie to Mom and us kids. If my life depended on it, I wouldn't believe anything you said."

"Your loss, Birch. Every day of your life you're going to wonder about your child. The kid won't even know you. She probably won't tell him about you. She might even give him her maiden name. Jake, Polly, and Lexie will never get to know him. A kid needs a father."

"If I'm so damn much like you, why would a kid want me for a father? If I do turn out like you, I'd be doing the kid . . . get the hell out of here."

"No problem."

"Birch? Are you up here? What the hell are you doing in here? Where's Celia? Iris sent me up here to tell you the pie's ready. We've been waiting for you."

"Celia left."

"Where'd she go?"

"Down the mountain. She said one or the other of us should file for divorce. She's going to L.A. She didn't say anything about being pregnant. Maybe Lassiter lied. For some reason I think he was telling the truth."

Sage sat down on the rocking chair. His thoughts took him to the brown manila envelope that had arrived at Sunrise while he was in Vermont. The private detective's report on Celia. He hadn't opened it and would probably never open it because he'd stepped over the line into his brother's private life. At four o'clock in the morning he'd crept downstairs and locked the envelope in the safe. One of these days he'd destroy it.

"What are you going to do?"

"I guess I'll take a page out of the old man's book and put it behind me. Life goes on. I'll go back to Atlantic City and when the casino is done, I'll run it."

"Libby?"

"Libby will get on with her life. She's going to New York tomorrow."

"Wait a minute. I don't understand. If Celia is going to divorce you, that means you're free to be with Libby."

"She won't see it that way."

Sage's eyes narrowed. "You're going to let both of them walk out of your life. Just like that."

"Isn't that what the old man would do?"

"Yeah, but you aren't Dad. You have choices, options here. It's up to you, Birch."

"I feel like my world caved in. Look. I don't want to talk about this. Let's go get that pie."

"You're just going to let Celia walk down the mountain."

"That's what our old man would have done. It's over, forget it."

"Sure, Birch, whatever you say. I'll meet you downstairs."

The moment Sage heard his brother's footsteps on the stairs, he went into his room, closed the door and dialed Chue's number. Charlie, Chue's seventeen-year-old grandson answered the phone. "Do me a favor, Charlie, take your grandfather's pickup and give Mrs. Thornton a ride to town." He listened a moment and then laughed. "I happen to know Iris made two extra pies for you guys. Your grandfather will bring them down later. Thanks, Charlie."

Fanny slipped into her coat. "We had such a good time. Invite us again, Iris."

Iris laughed. "The door's always open." She hugged her mother-in-law.

"Did you and Sage iron everything out?" Fanny whispered.

"Yes. I was so stupid. He couldn't believe I would think such awful things. Making up was wonderful. Being separated for eight days was pure hell."

"I'm glad it worked out. I knew it would. What happened to Celia?"

"Sage said she and Birch had a tiff, and she walked down the mountain."

"And Birch let her!"

"Sage called Charlie to give her a ride. Don't say anything to Birch."

"Of course not. Guess we'll see you on Thanksgiving."

Iris stepped aside as Libby approached and reached for Fanny's hand.

"Mrs. Thornton, I'd like to say good-bye and thank you for giving me the opportunity of working at the center. I'll miss all of you. I feel like you're my family."

"Are you sure you won't change your mind?" Fanny asked as she took the young woman into her arms.

"No, I can't. My replacement is someone I handpicked for Sunny and Harry. They're both good with this. I'm going to miss them, all of you. Perhaps I'll come back for a visit one of these days."

Fanny pressed a folded envelope into Libby's hands. "It's just a little something to make the transition easier. Promise to call and write."

"I will. Tell Birch I said . . . tell him . . ." Her eyes filling with tears, Libby ran to the van.

"Don't even *think* about touching that one, Fanny," Marcus hissed into her ear.

"How did I miss that, Marcus?"

"You were too busy enjoying your grandchildren and eating all that food. We both need to go on a diet. Let's get a move on. I want us to curl up on those red chairs and hold hands."

"You are my man, Marcus Reed. Lead the way."

"Fanny, wait up," Ruby called.

"Is something wrong, Ruby?"

"No, no, nothing's wrong. Metaxas and I wondered if we could have about thirty minutes of your time when we get back to town. If Marcus is too tired, it can wait till tomorrow."

"Marcus?"

"Sure. How about the Harem Lounge? Drinks are on me," Marcus said.

"Spoken like a true Texan," Metaxas boomed. "We'll follow you down the mountain. I never knew anyone who actually lived on a mountain. Or owned a mountain. I learn something every day."

Fanny smiled as her eyes raked the room for a sign of Birch. She knew instinctively where he was. She looked at Sage who nodded. She wondered who it was in the small cemetery who would be giving him comfort.

"Don't worry, Mom. I'm going to make him stay the night. Jake and I already have it all worked out. Birch loves that kid and enjoys every minute he spends with him. Plus, Jake can give him some insight on Dad."

Fanny shook her head. "It's amazing. A child giving one of us insight. Good night, honey. Thanks for having us. Help Iris in the kitchen. She refused everyone's help."

"That's because cleaning the kitchen after company is what Iris calls our quality time. It's a good thing, Mom. Drive carefully."

"Where's Billie? I didn't see her leave?"

"She left about fifteen minutes ago. She said she had a bad headache and wanted to get to bed early."

Alarm showed on Fanny's face. "Do you . . . ?"

"I don't know, Mom. Call her when you get to town. If you need me, whistle."

" 'Night everyone," Fanny called.

*   *   *

Billie Thornton garaged her car, unloaded the trunk of all the goodies Iris had pressed on her. She wouldn't have to cook for a week. Her arms full, she headed for the underground elevator that would take her to her high-rise apartment. It took her ten minutes to sort through the packages and stack them in the freezer. She used up another five minutes mixing a drink and kicking off her shoes. Her watch told her it was only eight o'clock. She switched on the television, flipping through the channels for something that would hold her interest. A minute later she turned off the television, reached for her coat, and left the apartment.

A walk in the cool evening air would be good. Who was she fooling? Certainly not herself. She knew exactly where she was going and what she was going to do. *Count to ten, once, twice, three times. Call your counselor. Count again until the urge passes. Do it, Billie.* She tried and failed. How much money did she have in her purse? Not much. Possibly $30. She retraced her steps, running this time, counting as she raced along. She danced from one foot to the other, her stomach churning, her eyes glassy until the elevator stopped on her floor. She ran then, faster than she'd used to run on the mountain when she was a child. Her hands trembled as she tried to fit the key into the lock. When she finally succeeded in getting the door open she bolted inside and ran to the dining room, to the corner where a large blue water bottle stood. Her breath exploded from her mouth in hard little gasps as she dropped to her knees and upended the bottle, silver dollars rolling all over the floor. She scrambled to retrieve them.

Count to ten, call your counselor. One, two . . . Did she need to roll the silver? How much was here? Once she'd calculated she had close to $800. She stopped for a second trying to remember if she had coin wrappers or not. No, she didn't have any. What she did have was a canvas bank sack for coins, but where was it? She couldn't think. She was dizzy now, hyperventilating. *Count to ten, call your counselor.*

The coins went into her denim carry bag she was never without. Damn, it was heavy and dragging down her left shoulder. She didn't care. All the weight did was slow her down. That was okay, too. *Stop! Call your counselor, take deep breaths. This will pass.* In the lobby, Billie fished in her pocket for a quarter. Her hands were shaking so badly she dropped the coin four times before she was able to fit it into the slot. She dialed the number she'd memorized. "Shit!" What was the woman's name? She couldn't remember. Sara, Sybil . . . Sylvia. Yes, Sylvia. She waited doing her dancing two step, the denim bag on the floor at her feet. "Come on, come on, answer the damn phone already!" She broke the connection just as a voice on the other end of the phone said, "Sorry, I was in the shower. Hello . . . hello."

Billie trudged along, people staring at her. She glared at them as she shifted the denim bag from one shoulder to the other. The moment she saw Babylon's high-rise sign, she crossed the street and entered the first casino she came to. Had she known what she looked like, she might have detoured to the ladies' room for a quick repair job. Instead she headed for the nearest money changer. "I'd like bills for these," she said in a jittery-sounding voice. She brushed at her hair. *Count to ten. Call the counselor again before you do this.* Maybe she had stepped outside, maybe she was in the bathroom. *Try again. Don't blow this. Count to ten.*

"This is good. Thanks," Billie said, stuffing the bills into her pocket. She walked the floor to the next money changer and did the same thing. *This is good,* she thought. *The bag is getting lighter. Count to ten. Call your counselor.*

On the other side of the casino floor, in the casino's main office, two men sat staring at a monitor. They looked at one another and nodded. One of the men pressed the Security button. The door was opened almost immediately. The men pointed to the monitor and the Security guard nodded briefly. "Be discreet. Don't call attention to the young lady. Bring her here. Don't frighten her."

"I'll make some calls," the second man said.

"Neal, this is John Dallas. Do you by any chance know how I can locate Mrs. Thornton? Excuse me, Mrs. Reed. She's there. I need to speak to her. We have your pigeon. Thanks aren't necessary. We put the word out the minute you spoke to us. There isn't a casino in town that will take her money. You know we take care of our own. Four tickets to the Lakers game? You send those suckers right over, Neal. Sure, I'll hold on."

Billie knew she was being hustled. Her shoulders slumped as the two Security guards, who resembled Wall Street bankers, escorted her to the office across the floor. She didn't cry until she was inside, her shoulders shaking. "You aren't going to believe me but I'm glad you dragged me in here. I tried not to do it. I really did. Do me a favor, though, please don't call my mother."

"She's on the floor now heading this way. We don't do business that way." The older of the two men walked over and dropped to one knee. He cupped her face in one hand. "Look at me, Miss Thornton, and listen carefully. There isn't a casino in this town that will take your money. Every establishment on the Big White Way is off-limits to you. Do you understand what I just said?"

"Yes, but how ... why ... I don't understand," Billie gulped.

"This town owes its business to the Thornton family. We can't allow you to destroy what your grandmother and your father built here. Your addiction would destroy it in insidious little ways. At the moment you might not believe we're helping you, but we are."

Fanny was a whirlwind as she rushed to her daughter. "Oh, Billie, why didn't you call me? Did you follow the steps? What happened?"

"Mom, this is how I get. I can't control it. These men helped me. Right now I don't see it that way. Tomorrow I will. I'm sorry, Mom. I'm okay now. It's passed. I did try to call my counselor, but there was no answer."

"You have to keep trying until you reach a counselor. Take your daughter home, Mrs. Reed."

"Thank you. Thank you for . . . everything. It doesn't seem adequate, but it's all I can come up with right now."

"Mrs. Reed, your daughter is not welcome in any casino in town. Perhaps one day that will change. None of us wants her money. Perhaps she'll understand that tomorrow."

Fanny turned and smiled at the man's slow wink. She nodded slightly. "I think, Mr. Dallas, Ash Thornton would be very proud of you tonight. I know I am. Tomorrow is a bright new day. I'm looking forward to it. Good night, gentlemen."

Fanny's voice was stern, yet gentle, when she said, "This was probably the best thing that could have happened to you. Now you know you aren't welcome anywhere."

"Are you saying I'm a pariah?"

"Yes. If your next question is, did I alert the other casino owners, the answer is no. Word gets out. There are no secrets in this town just as there are no clocks in the casinos. Your father always said, as did Sallie, this town takes care of its own. Be grateful, Billie, that they do. Now there is a little matter of some outstanding money. Hand it over."

"Even the silver dollars?"

"Every single one. And the money in your pockets."

"Okay, okay."

"Way to go Fanny!"

"Is she going to make it, Ash? This was pretty scary."

"She's your daughter, Fanny. My money's on Billie."

"Oh, Ash, you finally remembered her name. Did you have anything to do with this?"

"Me?"

"Yes, you."

"*Nah.*"

"Liar."

"Did you say something, Mom?"

"I talk to myself sometimes."

"That's not good, Mom."

"In this case it is. Trust me."

"If you say so. Did I ever thank you for being my mother?"

"Hundreds of times."

"Wanna hear it again?"

"You bet."

19

Fanny led Ruby to a small table in the far corner of the Harem Lounge. "I really don't like sitting on a stool at the bar. That's for men. There are days when I actually miss this place. They're few and far between, but they do come. I met Marcus here for the first time. Let's have a cup of coffee and relax. Is anything wrong, Ruby?"

"Wrong means different things to different people. From my perspective there is nothing wrong. Are you sure Marcus doesn't mind sitting at the bar with Metaxas?"

"Not at all. He enjoys his company, and his name intrigues him. By the end of the evening I bet he knows the whys of it all."

"I don't even know. It is a strange name. I never heard it until I met Metaxas. He said it's because he's one of a kind. That could be true for all I know. It is a mouthful, though."

"Ruby, I want to thank you again for going with Sage to Vermont. Without you and your plane we could have faced a tragedy. I will be forever grateful to you."

"You said we were family, Fanny. I took you at your word and only did what you would have done. I don't mind telling you I was petrified." Ruby leaned across the table and dropped her voice to a hushed whisper. "Listen to me, Fanny. Ash . . . Ash . . . what he does is . . . he . . . talks to me. He says things that make sense, things that . . . they don't scare me, they . . . they seem so real. He seems so real. Am I crazy, Fanny? I know we talked about this at Sunrise and everyone had a different spin on it. What do *you* think, Fanny? I really need to know."

Fanny smiled wearily. "On the surface, Ruby, there is a logical explanation for everything. It could be our subconscious working overtime or our own common sense. In the case of Sage and Metaxas, weather balloons. Sunny was always athletic and she camped, skied, and did all sorts of outdoor things. Little things you learn along the way stick with you. You don't realize it until you face some monumental event in your life. When it's down to the wire, Ruby, it's whatever works for you. Speaking for myself, I choose to believe. However, I'm not going to take a full page ad out in the *Nevada Sun* and announce it to the world. I don't mind if the rest of the family knows because it brings us all closer. I think we all have a higher comfort level now believing Ash is looking after us. At least I do. Did I help, Ruby?"

"It's pretty much how I feel, too. It was so real, Fanny. Metaxas believes. Here is this bigger-than-life Texan, someone you know just by looking at him is in total, complete control, telling me he had this . . . ethereal experience. It was like he was talking about his grocery list. If it were anyone but you and Metaxas, I think I'd run for cover."

"Is that what you wanted to talk about, Ruby?"

"That was part of it. I was wondering, Fanny, if you would allow me to get married at Sunrise. I'll do all the planning. Iris is busy, and with her being pregnant, I don't want to burden her."

Fanny grinned widely. "Will you let me handle the details, Ruby? Sunny and Harry are getting married over Christmas. Sunny was pretty adamant about it. They didn't pick a date yet. Is that too soon or too late or were you thinking about spring or summer? Can I make your dress? Or do you want a gown? I have the time, Ruby. A double wedding would be nice."

Ruby beamed. "I think so. Metaxas will agree to anything I want. He's wonderful, isn't he, Fanny?"

"I always thought so. I'm so glad it worked out for you."

"Me too. That's what I want to talk to you about. I'll be moving to Texas. I want to *give* you Thornton Chickens. It really belongs to all of you. I have no children. The lawyers can handle the legal end of it. I'm sure it isn't going to be one of those cut-and-dried things. I thought . . . that you and Marcus could run the business. It's going to be important for him to have something to do. Retirement is wonderful when you're old. Both of you are so vital, so energetic. The company could use you. Everything's set with The Chicken Palaces. I hate to admit this, but Celia did a bang-up job."

"I never understood that, Ruby."

"I wanted to get her away from Iris and Sage. Iris thought . . all kinds of things. It seemed like the thing to do at the time. It worked, too. She's going to be working out of our Los Angeles office starting tomorrow. I want you to keep her on. I gave my word, and I don't like going back on it. I didn't have a problem with her. I don't think you will either. If you and Marcus agree to take over, you can terminate her employment if she doesn't live up to her contract. I don't think that will happen, though. She's going to get some very nice residual checks. This is all off the top of my head, Fanny. I want to go with Metaxas without any worries. I never made a secret of how I hate the chicken business. I never wanted it, but how do you give something like that back? Sallie made it possible for Dad and Mom to have it. It was Sallie's money that funded it from the git-go. Mom said that a hundred times. There is . . . ah, one other little thing, Fanny. The . . . ranch goes with the deal. I know, I know,'' Ruby said, throwing her hands in the air.

"The ranch too! Oh, Ruby, I don't . . . oh Lord, that means Marcus and I would . . . oh, Ruby, I don't . . .''

"What she means is okay, we'll do it!'' Marcus said from the bar.

"Marcus, the ranch goes with the deal. It's a package,'' Fanny said.

"I'll throw in my yellow Wellington boots,'' Ruby said. "You need them to wade through the chicken poop. Dad's are green. They'll fit Marcus. They never wear out!''

"Fanny, how can we refuse an offer like that?'' The laughter in her husband's eyes brought a smile to Fanny's face.

"I don't know the first thing about being a . . . madam. Ruby, I don't think I could do *that*.''

"It goes with the deal. You don't actually have to do anything. The ranch is run like a business. It has its own business manager, its own accountant, its own bank account. You review the account four times a year and that's it.''

"Sallie must be up there spinning in circles at this turn of events. Lord, what will the kids think? Marcus, do you really . . .''

"I think it's a great idea. We'll be together in our Wellingtons. You can make curtains for the chicken coops. It will give us something to do. You said you wanted to contribute. Let's face it, Fanny, the world eats chicken. We can do that free-range thing Birch was talking about. The possibilities are endless. We'll talk about the ranch end of things later. What is the asking price?''

"There is no price, Marcus. Ruby wants to give the company back to the family.''

"*Give?*''

"Yes, give. As in *free*.''

"I might have some trouble with that. That's not good business sense, Ruby."

"Makes perfect sense to me," Metaxas drawled. "They'd laugh me right out of the state of Texas if I brought home a wife who owned a chicken ranch. It's my sweet baby's decision. Whatever she wants is what I want. It's yours."

"Ruby, I don't know what to say," Fanny said.

"Just say yes. Please."

"Well, I . . ."

"Please, Fanny," Ruby implored.

"Can . . . can you wait a few minutes? I have to go to the ladies' room." Fanny was off her chair and headed for the women's lounge around the corner from the bar. She ran to the stall at the end of the room and locked the door. "Ash! I need you. Right now. C'mon, c'mon, I don't have all night."

"This is the ladies' room, Fanny."

"No one else is in here. Whisper. What should I do? I'm dithering here, Ash."

"Those yellow Wellingtons will look good on you, Fanny."

"Is that a yes, Ash?"

"Thornton Chickens belongs to the family. Ruby's doing the right thing. Be gracious in your acceptance."

"What about the . . . you know . . . ?"

"What about it? It's the oldest profession on the books."

"Damn it, Ash, listen to me. I've tried these last years to be my own person. I made up my mind I wasn't going to end up like Sallie. It's a goddamn package deal is what it is. What about the kids?"

"The ranch is a separate entity, Fanny. If you really want my opinion, I say go for it. Just think about it, Fanny. Picture this, two or three Chicken Palaces in every big city in the United States. You could become bigger than those hamburger joints. You don't have anything else to do. Give it a shot."

"What if Marcus and I hate it?"

"You won't. It's going to be good for Marcus. A man needs

to feel he's doing something worthwhile. Taking up space, traveling, gardening isn't his answer. This is something he can sink his teeth into."

"And the . . . ranch?"

"Just part of the deal, Fanny. Fanny?"

"What?"

"Mom wasn't a madam. She did things other people wouldn't do to survive. I didn't understand that for a long time. It was Red Ruby's choice to do what she did. Mom just cleaned up the business and helped her, the way she helped half the people in Las Vegas. Remember that, okay?"

"Okay, Ash."

"Can I go now? I really don't like hanging out in women's bathrooms. Tell Ruby I'll be at the wedding. She deserves to be happy."

"I'll tell her, Ash. Thanks."

Back in the Harem Lounge, Fanny took her place at the table.

"What did he say?" Marcus hissed.

"He said . . . he said . . . go for it!"

"Then it's a done deal?" Mataxas queried.

Fanny's voice was jittery, her face white. "It's a done deal."

"Fanny, thank you. Thank you from the bottom of my heart," Ruby said.

"We are one weird family, Ruby." Fanny leaned across the table. "Ash said to tell you he'll be at the wedding. He said you deserve to be happy."

Ruby burst into tears. In the blink of an eye, Metaxas had her in his arms and was carrying her across the casino floor singing, "Deep in the Heart of Texas" at the top of his lungs. Onlookers clapped and whistled their approval.

Fanny's voice was still jittery when she said, "I guess we're in the chicken business, Marcus."

"I can't wait to see you in those yellow Wellingtons."

"Sadist."

"Fanny, look at me. I love you so much my heart aches. I know in my heart that feeling is never going to leave me. I just wanted you to know."

"I think that's the nicest thing anyone ever said to me. Let's go home, Mr. Reed."

"We don't have a home, Mrs. Reed."

"Sure we do. Home is wherever we are. Together. Home is where your stuff is. We have some stuff upstairs. For now, until we move out to the ranch, it's home."

"Home is the sweetest word in the English language. Actually, it's the fifth best word after, Mom, Dad, kids, and love," Marcus said.

"Oh, yeah," Fanny said, snuggling against her husband's chest. "I love you, Marcus."

Be happy, Fanny.

Fanny stumbled and righted herself, her hold on Marcus's arm secure. If it had been daylight, her smile would have rivaled the sun.

"What did he say, Fanny?"

Fanny didn't bother pretending she didn't understand. "He told me to be happy."

"Are you happy, Fanny?"

"Marcus Reed, I am the happiest woman alive, and that is never going to change. So there."

"So there yourself, Fanny Reed."

Celia Thornton sat in her car staring up at the lighted window of her apartment. Was Jeff still there? Not that it mattered. Was it worth going up to the ugly, mean little apartment to disconnect the phone, to get the answering machine, and the few things she'd left in the bathroom? Her money was in her purse. Her clothes and incidentals were in the trunk of the leased car. She could leave right now and not look back. She rolled down the window to take deep, gulping breaths.

Fanny Thornton was the one who had the Polaroid pictures. There for one brief instant, in the upstairs bedroom at Sunrise, they had stared into each other's eyes. Fanny wasn't going to do anything. Of that she was certain. To do anything would be to destroy her family. Without words they'd come to an understanding: She would live her life and the Thorntons would live theirs. As long as those lives remained problem free, the pictures would remain safely hidden. She supposed it was a fair trade-off.

Celia leaned back against the plush leather seat. Earlier, Ruby had called her to tell her of her plan to turn Thornton Chickens over to Fanny and Marcus Reed. She'd almost fainted until Ruby said her contract would be honored by Fanny, and the sooner she could get to Los Angeles the better it would be for everyone.

The 260,000 dollars, her percentage from the blackjack tables, was safe under the seat. She knew in her gut, in her heart, in her mind, that Fanny would let sleeping dogs lie as long as she made herself scarce where the Thornton family was concerned. Instinct told her one claim against the family would end Fanny's silence. Until and unless Fanny was prepared to confront her, the stupid, ugly pictures would remain a silent threat. Celia was no fool. She'd played the game too long not to know how it worked. If she factored in her salary, she could live comfortably until the birth of her child. The residuals from the commercials would be icing on the cake and pay for day care if she decided to keep working after she gave birth.

Everything in her life had changed with the results of her lab test. Even her thinking had changed. One minute she was Celia Connors Thornton, married to one of the richest men in Nevada. One second later she was Celia Connors Thornton, mother-to-be. The greedy, conniving, manipulative Celia Thornton ceased to exist the moment she read the lab report. She felt vulnerable, scared, and lost.

She thought about her future. Maybe she'd learn to cook. Maybe a lot of things. Ruby had said something about a new series of commercials with a family for The Chicken Palaces. She'd play the mother and actors would play the children and husband. According to Ruby it was Audrey Bernstein who came up with the idea of using two little girls named Corinne and Jessica, who would become household names once the commercials aired. It would probably work, too. Everyone loved a family.

What was she waiting for? Why was she sitting here staring at this seedy building? If she drove all night, she could make L.A. by morning. "I'll never have to see Jeff Lassiter again," she muttered. She thought about the formula Jeff had given her that was safely hidden in the bottom of her makeup case. Anytime she wanted, she could head for Atlantic City and do what she'd done in Vegas for Lassiter. If she wanted to. "I hope you croak, you bastard!"

Celia switched on the headlights and turned the key in the ignition. The engine snarled to life in the quiet night. She was about to pull away from the curb when a Jeep Cherokee pulled in front of her, the headlights blinding her.

"Celia, wait!"

Birch! Celia slammed the car in reverse, the headlights trapping her in their bright glare. She was about to shift into first gear when Birch reached the door.

"Celia, wait!"

"For what?"

"I want to talk to you. What's a few minutes out of your life?"

"I'm in a hurry, Birch. I thought we said everything that needed to be said on the mountain."

"Where are you going?"

"I told you. Los Angeles. I plan to drive all night. What can you possibly want from me? I have nothing to give you."

"Just tell me the truth: Are you pregnant?"

"I don't have to tell you anything. Please get out of my way."

"If you are pregnant . . ."

"Yes," Celia drawled.

"You hate kids. You said that yourself. What I'm trying to say here is, if you are pregnant, don't do anything foolish. I'll take the child."

The sound Celia made deep in her throat was somewhere between a sob and a howl of misery. "I'm not good enough for you, but my child is? If I'm pregnant, that is. If we're talking hypothetically here, how do you know I won't turn out to be the world's best mother? I could turn out to be a better mother than your own. I will never, ever forgive you for what you just said. Was it your intention to offer me money for the child, assuming I'm pregnant? Don't bother to answer that question. I can see it in your eyes. Get the hell away from me."

"Let's not end it like this, Celia."

"You're the one who slapped me around, Birch. You're the one who was unfaithful, and you don't want to end it like this. Go to hell."

"You aren't blameless here."

"That's true. I'm not. That's why I'm leaving. I'm sorry for my part in all of this. I got by before I met you, and I can get by again."

"Yeah, thanks to my family. Ruby is paying you five times what the job is worth. You took the casino for some heavy money. Thornton money."

"That's the way the old cookie crumbles. A girl's gotta do what a girl's gotta do. I'm beginning to hate the Thornton name. I'm giving it up. Your half brother petitioned the courts to have his name changed from Lassiter to Thornton. Too bad I couldn't just give him my name. He could have saved some legal fees. I'll give you thirty days to file for the divorce. If you don't, I will. I don't want anything from you or your family, so that should make it quick and easy.''

"Are you pregnant, Celia?"

"None of your damn business. You gave up the right to know anything about me when you went to bed with Libby Maxwell. Look, Birch, this was all wrong. I'm willing to take the blame for everything. The only way I can make it right is to walk away, which is what I'm trying to do right now. When something's over it's over. We can't get it back because we didn't have anything to begin with. You're going to get on with your life, and I'm going to get on with mine. I doubt if we'll ever see each other again. I wish you the best. I mean that. Now, if you'll excuse me, I have a long drive ahead of me.''

"You are, aren't you?"

"If you don't move, Birch, I'll smash that Jeep. We're just two people who used to know each other."

Birch stepped aside, a stunned look on his face. He watched Celia's car until its taillights were barely pinpoints of red light in the dark night.

"It's not the end of the world, Birch."

"Sage! Where the hell did you come from?"

"I followed you down the mountain. It is what it is. You have to accept it."

"Did you hear the whole thing?"

"Half the neighborhood heard it. She didn't admit to being pregnant. You have to accept what she said and get on with it, and you have to take responsibility for your actions, Birch. Come on, let's go to Babylon, and I'll buy you a beer."

"Am I like Dad, Sage?"

"Yeah, in some respects, but then so am I. At this point in time, Birch, that's not a bad thing. It was all a long time ago. I believe I learned from Dad's mistakes. I hope you did, too. We're not perfect people, and we don't live in a perfect world.

That means mistakes are okay as long as you learn from them and don't repeat them.''

''What the hell am I supposed to do now?''

''What do you want to do, Birch?''

''The truth?''

''Yeah, that's a good place to start.''

''I want to put on my running shoes and run till I can't run anymore. I want to pretend my name is Joe Smith and that I live in Perth Amboy, New Jersey.''

''Nah, that's the easy way out. Guess what, Birch. Joe Smith of Perth Amboy, New Jersey, would trade places with you in a heartbeat.''

''What if she is pregnant, Sage?''

''That's why they have lawyers. Celia could turn out to be the best mother in the world. If she's pregnant, and we aren't sure that's the case. I told you, don't believe anything that jerk Lassiter says.''

''Celia told me he's petitioned the court to take the Thornton name. She, on the other hand, is giving it up.''

''So? Do you want to fight that, too?''

''I was making conversation.''

''Then let's make conversation someplace else. This isn't the best part of town, you know. How could you let your wife live here?''

''That and a hundred other things are the reason I want to be Joe Smith from Perth Amboy, New Jersey.''

''It isn't gonna happen. Let's go get that beer.''

''Celia's a survivor.''

''That's good to know, Birch. If that's true, you can stop worrying about her.''

''She was pretty decent there at the end, all things considered.''

''Everyone has good and bad in them. Even Dad,'' Sage said pointedly. ''I'll follow you, and we'll park at Babylon. By the way, when are you leaving for Atlantic City?''

"Tomorrow on an early flight. Sunny's staying on another week. Life's going to be kind of dull with us gone, huh?"

"I can take dull for a little while. Mom's got Billie under control. It's going to be a struggle for a while, but it will work out in the end. Billie doesn't want to live with an addiction. Ruby and Sunny are getting married over Christmas, on the mountain. Iris is having twins, Chue and his wife are finally going to China for a visit. Mom's happy. Marcus is well. Our world is good, Birch. In fact, I don't think it gets much better than this."

"I'm happy for everyone. Don't start worrying about me, Sage. Sometimes you're like a mother hen. Just why the hell did you follow me down the mountain?"

"I followed you because I was worried. Plus, Iris pushed me out the door. I just want to help. I want you to know you can count on me no matter what happens."

"I do know that, Sage. I'm damn glad you're my brother. As long as I know you're in my corner it's okay."

"Can we go get that beer now? All this jawing is making my mouth dry."

Birch wrapped his arms around his brother. "Thanks for . . . you know, everything."

On the fourth floor of the ugly, decayed building, Jeff Lassiter stared through the grimy curtains. "Now isn't that just too cozy for words?" Too bad he couldn't hear all the cutesy words that went with the hugs and kisses.

Ten minutes later Jeff was adjusting his Ralph Lauren tie in the dingy bathroom mirror. His suit was custom-tailored, his shirt pristine white. He gave his hair a quick touch with the brush, knowing he could have posed as a Madison Avenue executive.

At the door he debated whether he should lock it or not. Why bother, Celia wasn't coming back. He walked out, leaving the door ajar. Tomorrow he'd think about where he was going to live. His attaché case full of cash secure in his hand, Jeff climbed behind the wheel of his car. His first and only stop for the evening would be the secret, private location where his Holy Grail warriors toiled night and day.

The team, because that's how Jeff thought of them, looked up at his entrance. They looked weary, red-eyed, and out of sorts. "Payday and dinnertime," Jeff said cheerfully as he plopped down Styrofoam dinner cartons. "T-Bones, loaded baked potatoes, garden salad, carrots, and peas. Rolls, apple pie, and coffee. Your pay," he said, placing sealed envelopes, each with a name on the front of the envelope, on the long folding table that doubled as a desk and catchall. "Dig in, guys."

Jeff distanced himself from his employees to sit on a wooden crate across the room. From time to time he looked up to see how the crew was progressing. The moment he saw the men and women toss the throw away dinnerware into a barrel that served as a trash container, he walked over. In his hand was a thick envelope full of cash. There was no name on the front. "So, who gets the prize?" When there was no response to his question, Jeff repeated his question, a definite edge in his voice.

A frizzy-haired young woman with owlish glasses spoke, the same edge in her voice. "No one in particular. We took a vote and will split the . . . prize."

"What that says to me is none of you are smart enough to do this project on your own. You've been depending on one another since we started. Teamwork is commendable. Split it. It makes me no never mind. Are we ready to wrap this up?"

The same frizzy-haired woman spoke. "We want more money."

"I bet you do. So do I. Guess what, you aren't getting it. We had a deal. Now, let's see the prototype." When no one moved to do his bidding, Jeff said, "How much more?"

"Fifty thousand each."

Jeff shrugged. "Okay. Where's the prototype?"

"Where's the money?"

Jeff opened his attaché case. He'd known it would come down to this and was prepared. The envelopes were sealed, his workers' names scrawled on the front. He pushed them across the table and watched through narrowed eyes as they were opened, the currency counted.

A loose-jointed individual with two Ph.Ds., one in engineering and one in mathematics, bent over to lift a heavy carton onto the folding table. Thick binders and loose-leaf notebooks were placed next to the carton. "The specifications," he said. Lassiter nodded.

"We're leaving. You got what you paid for."

"You were well compensated," Lassiter said.

"Yes."

"You're dismissed. Let's have a test run here."

"You read the instructions on page one and you pull the lever," someone called over their shoulder.

"This thing weighs a ton. How about carrying it out to my car."

"That's not our job," the Ph.D. said.

"Asshole," Jeff said under his breath.

Jeff thought he heard the frizzy-haired woman say, "It takes one to know one."

Oh, well, one way or another, he'd get the prototype to his car. His next stop, Atlantic City, where he would peddle his Holy Grail to the highest bidder. On the other hand, Monte Carlo had a nice ring to it. He swayed dizzily when he thought of the millions of dollars that were within his grasp. He sat down on one of the stools to leaf through the specifications. The basic allure was the intermittent reward system that would allow a person to win enough to stay hooked—but not on a predictable schedule. That was good, he'd asked for this. Jeff flipped the page, mumbling as he did so. This prototype had the ability to become harder as the player's skill increased, making it even more addictive. Designed to keep people fascinated—to keep them playing.

Jeff continued to peruse the specs, grinning as he did so. What he had in front of him was worth every cent he'd paid out. Time to pack up his future and head on out. He wouldn't be sorry to shake the dust from this town off his shoes.

Jeff whistled. He had it all now, the ultimate gambling machine, the Thornton name, a fortune in cold hard cash—and one small niggling worry. It had been too easy to walk away with all that cold hard cash. Somewhere along the way, one or two of the owners should have kicked up a fuss. It was all just a little too easy. He started to sweat.

Maybe it would be better to wait till morning, when the sun was out. Strange things happened to people in the dark. Besides, he needed a safe place to secure the prototype. In addition, he needed to make copies of the specifications and secure at least one copy in his safety deposit box. People in this town would kill to have what he was looking at. People killed and robbed just for a stake at the blackjack table.

The long night stretched ahead of him. He passed the time memorizing the specifications and nibbling on the T-bones he picked out of the Styrofoam boxes in the barrel. Maybe he should revise his game plan. The French Riviera was on his list of places to visit someday. Why not now? He could survive there with his passable French. His arm snaked out for the phone. He hoped he would remember to have it turned off first thing in the morning.

Thirty minutes later, Jeff stared down at his scribbled notes. He now had a confirmed reservation for Paris. He'd take in the sights for a few days, rent a car, and set up a new life for himself.

Let the Thorntons self-destruct. He wouldn't be around to witness the havoc. He'd be leading the good life, the easy life of the megarich. And he would be rich. There was no doubt about it. With what he had in his hand he could name his price and live happily ever after. He'd probably become fluent in French, marry an equally rich woman who would bear him beautiful children whom he would treasure more than his wealth. And when his beautiful, wealthy wife got fat and sloppy he'd take a mistress the way his own father had done. Oh, yes, life was looking wonderful.

It didn't occur to Jeffrey Lassiter that with his impending name change, he could self-destruct as well.

20

~

"A penny for your thoughts, Fanny."

"Marcus, I didn't hear you come up behind me. I'm feeling sad, and I should be feeling happy. In a few hours it will be a new year. I'm so glad Sunny went back to her original plan to be married at sunrise on New Year's Day. Christmas was so hectic with everyone here. Ruby and Metaxas are just as happy. Did you see that sparkler he gave her? I think it's bigger than the one Elizabeth Taylor has. I felt like I should put my sunglasses on. They're so happy. Do you feel like things are coming to closure for everyone, Marcus?"

"In a way. Bear in mind, Fanny, when things come to an end there are always new beginnings. We're the perfect example. On January 2 we start our new jobs. I cannot tell you how I'm looking forward to working again. We'll be side by side in our Wellingtons."

Fanny laughed. "Everything is falling into place for everyone. That's what really makes me happy. I love this mountain. If there was one constant in my life beside the kids, it was this mountain. There was a time when I knew every inch of it. The kids did, too. I think Iris plays with the kids going up and down the way I did. Sage built a fort once, and the kids ate and slept there for weeks on end.''

"It looks very dry to me. I can't get over what a strange year it's been weather-wise. Floods and all those tornadoes in Texas and Oklahoma, the extra dry weather in the plains states, rain in the East. Not to mention that horrendous snowstorm in Vermont."

Fanny's eyes were thoughtful as she stared across the mountain. "I'm surprised Chue didn't find a way to water it. The mountain I mean. He's so nervous about leaving tomorrow. As nervous as he is, that's how excited his wife is. He's never flown before. When he came here with his family, they traveled by boat. I tried to reassure him by saying he'd be flying in a Coleman-Thornton plane. I don't know if it helped or not. Bess said John was going to slip him some tranquilizers so he'd sleep the whole trip. They're leaving for town right after the weddings and will stay at Babylon, then take an early-morning flight on the second."

"Once he's on his way he'll be fine."

"He really doesn't want to go, Marcus. I feel bad that we all talked him into it. He's going along with this trip because he knows we want him to do it. It was an all-expense-paid trip from Mr. Hasegawa, so he couldn't refuse and save face. It's so still. Nothing seems to be moving. Do you think it's an omen of some kind?"

"No, I do not. What I do think is we should go indoors and join the family."

"You go in, Marcus. I want to stay out here a little longer. I have some visiting to do."

"Okay, but don't be too long."

Fanny walked out to the cemetery and sat down on the low brick wall. As always, a feeling of calm and peace settled over her.

"Now, aren't you glad I stopped you from swallowing those pills?"

"Ash! Guess you're here for the wedding, huh? Yes, I am very glad you stopped me from taking the pills. I heard something in town yesterday, Ash."

"About Jeff?"

"Yes. They're saying he left for France. He built some kind of slot that's going to net him a fortune. I feel relieved that he's gone. I'm sorry if that bothers you. My question is, how do *they* know? Have they been following him? Sometimes it's all so mysterious. I'm grateful that they stepped in where Billie is concerned, though. Sometimes I think I have a whole posse of unknown faces watching over us. Is it true, Ash?"

"He's gone, Fanny. Accept things for what they are. It's easier that way. As much as I hate to say this, I must. Jeff was and is a bad seed. Say a prayer that he stays where he is for a long time. You don't want or need him in your life. I don't like the look of the mountain. It doesn't feel right."

"You had to say that, didn't you, Ash? It's always like this. One problem is taken care of and laid to rest and another one crops up. You're spooking me."

"You were spooked before I got here. I heard you talking to Marcus."

"You need to stop eavesdropping. We were making conversation, nothing more. Listen, Ash, are you going to do something . . . you know, spectacular for the double wedding? Or, are you going to stand in the background? How are you going to handle that? Are you *ever* going to tell me what was engraved on the back of your aviator wings?"

"Nope."

"Okay. I should go in. Is everything okay up there? Now that things are almost back to normal what are you going to do with yourself?"

"I thought I'd take in Atlantic City. Birch is hurting really bad. He might need me."

"That's nice, Ash. Don't let him follow in your footsteps."

"I'll do my best."

"Wear him down, Ash. You're good at that. It always worked with me. I worry about him."

"I know you do, Fanny. He's looking for something, searching."

"He's looking for you, Ash. He just doesn't know it. If he does, he won't admit it. It's a burden. Are you up to it?"

"He's my son, Fanny. Of course I'm up to it. How's Jake?"

"Jake is . . . Jake. He's such a robust little boy. He's bright, mischievous, and so honest and caring he makes me want to cry sometimes. He talks about you all the time. He adores Harry and, of course, you know he loves Sunny with all his little heart. You redeemed yourself with Jake in my eyes, Ash. That's the main reason I put up with you. It's okay to cry. Sometimes crying makes things better. Big guys cry all the time. That's what all the slick magazines say. I should go in now. I'll see you in the morning. It would be nice if Sallie and the others could attend. Do you think you could work on that, Ash? Now, about that signal—"

"I'll see what I can do."

"Okay, Ash. Good night."

" 'Night, Fanny."

Just as the sun rose over the mountain, the minister's words rose to a crescendo. "Sunny and Harry, I now pronounce you husband and wife. You may kiss the bride!" The cleric repeated his words a second time, his words ringing over the mountain for Ruby and Metaxas.

"Look!" Jake said.

Fanny's hand flew to her mouth as the others gasped. Up above, the clouds swirled and parted, then came together to form a pattern of figures. All the figures seemed to be holding hands. "Sallie, Philip, Devin, and Ash and Simon," Fanny whispered.

"Clouds, Fanny," Marcus whispered.

"Try telling that to them," Fanny said, jerking her head in the direction of her family.

Tears streamed down Sunny's face. Sage offered up a snappy salute, while Ruby wailed her pleasure. Billie grinned from ear to ear, her fist shooting high in the air. Out of the corner of her eye, Fanny watched as Jake's thumb rubbed the wings on his collar as Birch stared out across the mountain, his eyes glazed.

"How'd you like that, Fanny?"

"I was kind of expecting something a little more, you know, *boisterous*. This is a double wedding."

"You should have said you wanted boisterous. I thought subtle would do it."

"You did good, Ash."

"Fanny. Keep your eye on the mountain. Are you listening to me? It doesn't look or feel right. Promise me. Birch senses something. Look at him."

"I noticed, Ash. Right now his head is full of memories. I promise. We're going to drink a toast to you when we go indoors. Sunny and Ruby just wanted a champagne breakfast. Sunny said it was classy. Thanks, Ash."

"Remember your promise."

"Did I ever break a promise where you were concerned?"

"No, and that's why I'm counting on you."

"Champagne, everyone," Sunny called happily. "We need to make toasts this morning. Happy New Year!"

The sound carried over the mountain, ringing in everyone's ears as toast after toast was made.

"Ruby and I saved the best one till last," Sunny said, holding her glass high, her hand trembling. "To my dad, the man who's responsible for me being here today!"

"To my grandfather!" Jake bellowed, tears streaming down his chubby cheeks.

"To my brother, Ash," Ruby said, tears puddling in her eyes.

"Boisterous would be good right now, Ash."

"You got it!"

The chandelier over the dining room table swayed, the crystal teardrops tinkling as they touched each other. The sound was light, melodious, and happy.

"Someone must have opened the kitchen door," Birch said. "The wind is really whipping up out there."

The two new brides, the two new grooms, and the assembled guests smiled.

And smiled.

"That was hardly boisterous, Ash," Fanny said, a giggle in her voice.

"Cut me a little slack, Fanny. I didn't have a lot to work with. Those fried-egg sandwiches look good. I bet this wedding breakfast is a first. Julia Child probably wouldn't approve. Remember when she did that cook off thing? I saw those ninety-nine bottles of beer on the kitchen counter."

"Sunny needed to do that. I think she did it for you. They aren't for consumption."

"Pay attention to the wind, Fanny."

Fanny looked out the dining-room window. "Do you think it will snow, Marcus? There's usually some snow by Christmas and New Year's. I wonder why it's so different this year."

"It's too warm for snow. It is getting windy."

Fanny's voice dropped to a whisper. "Ash said to watch the mountain and just now he said to pay attention to the wind."

"Then that's what we'll do."

"You aren't humoring me, are you, Marcus?"

"I would never do that, Fanny."

"Miss Fanny, may I speak with you in the kitchen?"

"Of course, Chue. Are you getting excited about your trip?" Fanny asked as she excused herself from the table.

"Miss Fanny, I do not wish to make the trip. I do not want to go. I spoke with my wife about this, and she understands. Please do not be angry with me."

"Oh, Chue, it's all right. We all thought . . . of course you don't have to go. Is there a particular reason?"

"It doesn't feel right. I feel a coward, but I cannot do it. I don't wish to leave the mountain."

"You know what, Chue, that's good enough for me. I understand completely. To all of us you are the mountain's protector. I know what you mean about it not feeling right. I sensed it earlier myself."

"You are not angry with me?"

"Never in a million years. I'm angry with myself that we cajoled you into thinking you wanted to take this trip. At our age, Chue, we are too old to do things we don't want to do. Life is too short to be miserable. I'll tell the others. We were going to give you a royal send-off."

"I know this. I am very sorry."

"Guess what, Chue. I'm glad you aren't going for purely selfish reasons. It bothered me that my mountain would be unprotected while you were gone. It would be the first time in more years than I want to count. What about Akia?"

"She is going to Chak-ago."

"Chicago? Why?"

"To buy stuff, she said. There is a cousin there also. I will leave now and unpack my satchels. I wish to watch the wind. The wind bothers me."

Fanny hugged the old Chinese. "I know. Ash told me to pay attention to it. He said he doesn't like the way our mountain looks or feels."

"Yes, he has said this to me also."

"Truly, Chue?"

"I will go now. It was a fine wedding. Thank you for inviting my family."

"Our family, Chue."

The old Chinese smiled. "Yes, our family."

"Happy New Year," Fanny said as she went to each of her children to kiss and hug them. "It's a whole new year for you, Billie. I know you will persevere and prevail as well. Call me anytime things start to overwhelm you."

"I couldn't do it without you. Thanks for being my mother."

"Sunny, I hope this New Year will bring you all the happiness you and Harry can handle. If you need me, call."

"I love you, Mom."

"And I love you."

"Happy New Year, Mom," Sage said, wrapping her in his arms. "I love you, too, but you already know that. If you and Marcus need help with the chickens, we're available on the weekends. I think Jake might like going out there with you guys. He knows Dad worked there for years. You'd be surprised at what that kid knows about chickens and all because Dad used to tell him about trooping through the chicken poop with those damn boots."

"Thanks for telling me that, Sage. Of course I'll have him come out. He'll love the baby chicks."

"I've got to get going, Mom. Happy New Year. The first weekend you have free, think about coming to Atlantic City. I know Uncle Daniel and Uncle Brad are dying to show off their work. Thanks for being my mother, too. I'm going to try to keep an open mind about . . . Dad. Who knows, I might get comfortable with it one of these days. I'll call on the weekend. I promise."

"Guess it's our turn," Ruby said, her eyes moist.

"Promise to write and call," Fanny said, her own eyes moist.

"Are you going on a honeymoon or isn't that something I should be asking?"

"In a week or so. Metaxas has some business he wants to clear up. And he has to make a thousand or so phone calls to get him and Sage off the hook with that unauthorized airport landing in Vermont. Every agency and organization that has anything to do with flying or airplanes is after his hide. Sage's, too. It's a given that they'll lose their licenses. Metaxas said he's a horse trader from way back. Translated that means he'll make it come out right. He said not to worry, so we aren't going to worry. It's behind us. I wish you and Marcus the very best for this New Year and all the years to come. I love you, Fanny Reed, and I couldn't wish for a more wonderful sister-in-law. The next time you talk to Ash, tell him I love him so much I can't see straight. I don't care if people think we're crazy or not. I know we're not, and that's all that matters."

"I'll do that, Ruby. You take care of her, Metaxas, or you'll have me to deal with. You hear?"

"I hear you. I love this mountain. What say we buy us a mountain, sweet baby?"

"It wouldn't be the same. This is a family mountain, and as such you now have a share in it, right, Fanny?"

"What is ours is yours, Metaxas. We'll carve your name on one of the trees. That means you'll live forever on the mountain. Old Chinese proverb. That means you belong. Chue started the custom years ago. The moment this family takes you under their wing, Chue is on the mountain with his hammer and chisel."

Metaxas beamed. "I swear, that's one of the nicest, kindest things anyone ever said to me. Thanks, Fanny."

"Will you promise to call before you leave? I always like to know where my family is."

"Of course we'll call. As I said, it's going to be at least a week. I'm so happy, Fanny. I wish I was a writer, so I could put into words the happiness I feel."

"Ruby, you don't have to do that. It shows on your face, in your voice. Your happiness is oozing out of your pores. Guess that doesn't sound so poetic, huh?"

"Oh, hell, who cares. I want you to remember something, Fanny. Under no circumstances can you give back that chicken business. We're clear on that, aren't we?"

"Absolutely."

"We're going to say good-bye and head down the mountain."

"Ruby, what is going to happen to your plane and the one Metaxas flew into Vermont?"

"Do you want my best guess?"

"Uh-huh."

"I think that's part of the horse-trading business. The state will get to keep them. Tell Sage and Birch I'll buy them another one."

"Please don't, Ruby."

"You're the boss. Be happy, Fanny."

"You too, Ruby."

Fanny's voice was groggy when she said, "Marcus, what time is it? It's still dark outside. Why are you getting up now?"

"We're in business now, Fanny. That means we have to get up with the chickens." He slapped at her rump, laughing so hard he dropped to his knees.

Fanny rolled out of bed, laughter bubbling in her throat. "You want to hear the roosters crow. Admit it, Marcus. Okay, I'm up. I think this is going to be the ultimate challenge in our lives."

"The best part is we're up to it. I'll put the coffee on and get our boots ready. I bought you a present when I was in town yesterday. It's one of those His and Her gifts. Actually, I got three of them. One for Jake, too. What do you think?" Marcus said, tossing her a tissue-wrapped package.

"A baseball cap that says Thornton Chickens. This is great, Marcus."

"That's not all it says. Look under the brim."

"How sweet. It says 'Fanny.' Jake is going to love his."

"Gift-wise it hardly compares to the island paradise Metaxas is buying Ruby. Are you going to wear it?"

"Of course I'm going to wear it. Proudly. Jake is coming down this weekend to help. We're paying him a dollar an hour. Sage said he spent the money seven different times already. God, I love that little boy. It's hard to believe it's a week since the wedding."

"Uh-huh. Time is money, Fanny. The chickens are waiting for us."

"Go!"

When the bedroom door closed, Fanny dropped to her knees at the side of the bed. "Thank You, God." She bowed her head and offered up a short prayer.

As the day wore on Fanny did her best to hide her smiles when Marcus kept saying things like, I really like this. This is great. I'm having the time of my life. I do love chickens. At four o'clock, he called time out, and said, "This sucks, Fanny. I stink and so do you. How could we have been so stupid that neither one of us cared that the help here consists of day workers who come by when the mood strikes them? Did Ruby tell you the workforce was nonexistent?"

"No. I knew that, though. We're committed, Marcus. Ruby said under no circumstances are we allowed to give back the business. This is just our first day."

"Oh, God!"

"Don't ever offer me chicken for dinner, Marcus. I hate these creatures. There has to be a better way."

"Yeah, you hire people to do this and we sit in the office."

"Isn't that cheating?"

"Who cares? I say we call every agricultural school in the country and ask for résumés from their graduating class. If we throw in these goddamn boots, they'll probably knock our doors down applying for jobs. We could offer throwaway clothes for the day workers. Bonuses. Something!"

"Marcus, there isn't enough money in the world to pay someone to do this. That's why this business has stayed in the family. We can do this. I know we can."

"I don't want to do this, Fanny. You don't either. I'm sorry I bought these hats."

"I love mine," Fanny said, pushing hers farther back on her head. "God, it stinks!"

"We'll have to throw away our clothes because we'll never get the smell out of them," Marcus said.

"What time are you getting up tomorrow, honey?" Fanny asked, tongue in cheek.

"I'm not."

"I hate to keep using the word committed, Marcus."

"Stop saying that, Fanny, I don't want to hear it."

"Something's wrong, Marcus."

"You're telling me."

"No. Watch the chickens. They're clustering. *Hovering.*"

"You said they get restless when there is a full moon. They do look kind of skittish now that you mention it."

"We're not due for another full moon for a few weeks. We have to check for snakes or some wild animal. Even with all the protectors in place it's possible for something to slip through. Philip always played music when something like this happened. He even installed a stereo system for just this reason. I know how to work it, so you check for stray animals. Don't take too long, Marcus. The more restless the chickens get, the more prone they are to fighting."

"Now I've heard everything. No damn wonder you can't *give* this business away," Marcus muttered as he stomped his way through the pens.

Fanny slipped out of the yellow boots to enter the office. She crossed her fingers that she would remember how everything worked. She pressed buttons, turned knobs, and within minutes soft, restful, music invaded her ears. She ran to the window to see what effect it was having on the chickens. To her eye it looked like they were still clustering, still hovering near the edges of the pens. "Damn." She turned up the volume just as the phone rang. She stretched her arms to snag the receiver, her eyes never leaving the chickens. "Yes, hello. Fanny Reed speaking. Slowly, Chue, I can't make out what you're saying. Stop, take a deep breath. Now, tell me what is wrong."

Fanny listened, her face draining. "We'll be right there, Chue.

"Marcus!"

"Fanny, what is wrong? Why are you looking like that? Talk to me, Fanny. What is wrong?"

"That was Chue on the phone. The mountain's on fire!"

"Jesus! Let's go!"

"What about the chickens? Call the kids, the fire department, everyone you can think of. The mountain can't burn, Marcus. It just can't."

"Move, Fanny. Don't just stand there babbling. You know what to do. Do it!"

Fanny raced from the building, out the door and up the winding, flower-bordered walkway to the main part of the ranch. She didn't take time to appreciate the lush shrubbery, the softly whirring sprinklers, the velvet lawns and the pristine white veranda complete with padded rocking chairs and pitchers of frosty lemonade. Instead she bellowed at the top of her lungs. "Arletta! Arletta!"

Arletta Vandercomb was a vision of beauty with her perfectly made up face, her elaborate hairdo, and her costly afternoon dress that fussed and flirted about her ankles as she rose from one of the rockers.

"Mercy, Miz Reed, what is all the fuss?"

"I'll tell you what all the fuss is, Miss Vandercomb. My mountain is on fire, and I need you and your . . . ah . . . ladies to help with the chickens. It's a messy job. You probably know that. Now, Miss Vandercomb! Hustle, hustle. Time is of the essence.''

"I don't think we're equipped . . . my girls don't know the first thing . . ."

Something snapped in Fanny. "Cut the crap, Arletta. It's time those girls learn how to shake their asses doing *real* work. That means you, too. The schedule is posted on the door of the office. I'm counting on you and I'm depending on you. If you let me down, or if those chickens suffer, you'll be peddling your asses out on the highway for two bits a night. There is only one game in town, and it has my name on it. Now move it!''

"Yes, ma'am.''

Fanny glanced toward the porch to see Arletta's girls lined up against the banister, their faces full of shock. Her own face burning with shame, she snarled, "I want to see your asses wiggling down this path right now. Now means this instant, and if you don't understand what I just said, your new home is the highway.''

The mad scurry left a trail of wind that swirled around Fanny.

"Man, I love it when you kick ass, Fanny. Head for the mountain. The chickens can smell the smoke. That's why they're so restless.''

"Oh, Ash, am I going to lose the mountain?''

"I don't know, Fanny. Get going.''

"I'm going, I'm going. This is crazy, Ash. What can I do except be there? Fires are dangerous. Oh, God, how did this happen?''

"I told you years ago to post NO TRESPASSING signs. Did you listen to me? No, you did not. Somebody trespassing left a fire burning or a cigarette wasn't completely crushed out. A camper who thought his fire was out and it wasn't, which would make it an accident. The why of it doesn't matter, Fanny. It

is. You have to deal with it. Make a call. You know the number. You're going to need all the water in town."

"I'll call from the truck."

Marcus's Jeep Cherokee was running when Fanny hopped into the passenger side of the truck. She took a moment to notice the shock on her husband's face as she reached for the phone. "What do you call those things the ladies are decked out in?"

Fanny looked over her shoulder. "Teddies, and those fancy things on their feet are feathered mules. Their perfume alone will knock the chickens out. It is what it is, Marcus. C'mon, c'mon, burn rubber," she said, hysteria ringing in her voice.

"There is no answer, Marcus," Fanny said, her face full of dismay. "They always answer. Sallie swore to me that there would always be a voice at the other end of the line. She swore to me, Marcus."

"Always can't be forever, Fanny. I made all the calls. Things are under way."

"Do you know if the houses are safe?"

"For now."

Word spread faster on the Big White Way than the fire on the mountain. Loudspeakers blasted from one end of town to the other announcing the closing of all casinos and hotels in the next ninety minutes due to an impending water shortage. Accommodations to transport all guests to Reno would be complimentary.

Skeleton crews remained on duty inside the casinos as workers and management rushed to do what they could to save Sallie Thornton's mountain.

They came from everywhere once the television and radio stations carried the news. Old, young, fit, and feeble came to help.

Food, coffee, cold drinks appeared suddenly, with children rushing to hand it out to anyone who needed it.

"I have people on the way, Fanny," Metaxas said quietly. "If we can't save your mountain, we'll replant it. Trust me, Fanny."

Fanny started to cry, Ruby's arms around her shoulder. "It'll take a hundred years to restore the mountain. I won't be here to see it. So many people. Where did they come from? I didn't know they cared. I can't just stand here. I have to do something."

Fanny leaned on Ruby's arm as she was about to get up from the rock she'd been sitting on. Once before she'd seen these same feet or at least she thought she had. Then they'd been encased in shiny black shoes. Now she was staring at Timberline boots and denim clad legs. She raised her eyes, her face soot streaked. "We're bringing water from everywhere, Mrs. Reed. As you can see, the fire is in the middle and spreading in every direction. Get your family off the mountain as soon as possible."

"They're on the way down as we speak. I didn't expect . . . you shut down the whole town! To save Sallie's mountain! I don't know how to thank you."

"Is that another way of saying you accept us?"

"I've always accepted you. It was Sallie's legacy to me. I'll find a way to make up your losses. It might take me a while, but I will do it."

"NO!" The single word was a thunderbolt of sound. "We take our losses just the way Babylon takes theirs. Sallie looked out for us. Ash did, too, in his own way. As your husband said, sometimes you just have to give back."

Fanny swiped at her dirty face. "Just out of curiosity, how are those riverboats doing?"

The man closest to her smiled. "You see, I knew you'd get it. Revenues couldn't be higher, thanks to you. We'll talk again when this is over."

"I have to do something, Ruby. I can't just stand here and watch the mountain go."

"What can you do, Fanny?"

"I can dig ditches and drag hoses. Keep your eye on my kids."

"The hell with that idea," Ruby snorted. "Your kids are on the mountain doing whatever they can. Besides, they are old enough to take care of themselves. Iris sent the kids along with Chue's grandchildren to town. She's working at the floor tent. I'm with you for whatever good I can do."

"If this mountain goes, my life will never be the same. I don't suppose that makes any sense to you."

"It makes all the sense in the world. Come on, I want to get some use out of these ugly mountain boots. If I can sling chicken crap, I can drag a hose. I know how to work, Fanny. Like you, I'm not one of those delicate prairie flowers. Let's show these men a thing or two."

It was close to the dawn of a new day when Fanny and Ruby climbed the mountain to the ridge to gratefully accept a cup of coffee from Iris. "I can swallow, but I'm too tired to chew," Fanny said, stretching out on the ground. "All I can see are the whites of your eyes, Ruby."

Ruby gulped at the coffee. "My blisters have blisters. I didn't think you got blisters when you wore gloves. The wind is shifting, Fanny. It's going to take the houses if it gets any stronger."

Fanny bolted upright. "Iris, is there anything in the house you want to save? Tell me now, and Ruby and I will get it out. The wind's shifting."

"Sallie's rocking chair. The kids took their treasures with them. I gave Jake the photo albums to take with him. We can live without the rest of the stuff."

"You should leave, Iris. All this smoke can't be good for you. Do you think you can talk Chue into going with you? He's too old to be fighting a fire."

"Try telling that to him. He'll never leave, Fanny. His life is this mountain, and he has the right to try to save it. He's working like a Trojan."

"We'll get the chair and put it in the trunk. Promise me you'll leave right away."

"I promise."

"Fanny?"

"Yes."

"Stay safe. I don't want anything to happen to you."

Fanny nodded. "The wind is picking up. Where's your car, Iris?"

"In the courtyard. Fanny, save that picture of Jake and Ash that's on the mantel. I forgot to give it to Jake."

"Will do."

Thick gray-and-black smoke swirled across the road as Fanny and Ruby raced to the house. Minutes later they had the rocking chair in the trunk. Ruby clutched the gold-framed picture to her chest as Fanny peeled away from the courtyard, gravel spewing backwards. Both of them leaped out of the car the minute Fanny came to a complete stop, the tires squealing.

"Go, Iris, and drive carefully. Go, honey. We'll tell Sage where you are. We'll take care of him. The kids need you."

"I'm going, I'm going. Take care of yourselves."

"Go, Iris, the smoke is getting worse."

"God, Ruby, what are we going to do? There is no way to save the mountain."

"Stop it right this minute. You don't know that. The whole damn town is on this mountain trying to save it. That means something."

Fanny reared back, her head stretching on her neck. "Ash, where the hell are you?" she screamed at the top of her lungs. "You always have the answers to everything. Tell us what to do. If there is nothing we can do, tell us that too. I need to know, Ash."

"I am a little busy, Fanny. There is a lot going on here. What do you want from me?"

"Tell us what to do?"

"You can't win this one, Fanny. The wind shifted. Sparks are hitting the roof of Sunrise. Chue's back porch is on fire."

"Don't tell me something like that. Blow it out, Ash! You have more hot air in you than one of those balloons. God, what a stupid thing for me to say. If it's all going to go, why are we out here killing ourselves trying to stop it?"

"That fire is going to cross the road. If you trench it, there won't be anyplace for it to go. The asphalt is melting big time. Start digging, Fanny, and put some muscle into it."

"Will that save the houses, Ash?"

"Sage is hosing off the roof. Chue's doing the same thing. Move on it, Fanny."

"I'm going, Ash. Ruby, we have to dig a trench along the crest. I'll start. See if you can find someone to help us. Be careful on the asphalt. It's hot and sticky."

It was midafternoon when Fanny leaned on her shovel to stare at Ruby. "You look awful, Ruby. Are you as tired as I am?" Fanny asked.

"I could fall asleep leaning on this shovel. Your eyebrows are gone, Fanny."

"So are yours. The fire hasn't crossed the road. We should be thankful for that. Look at it this way, Ruby, we gave up our eyebrows to save Chue's house."

"I'd do it again, too," Ruby said smartly.

"Me too. I love that old man. We stopped it for the moment, Ruby, but to me the flames are higher and the heat more intense. The fire marshal wants us."

"He wants us to leave is what he wants," Ruby fretted.

"I'm not going anywhere. I have a deed that says this mountain is mine, and I'm staying! So there."

"They're going to start with the chemicals. They do that

from airplanes. I read that somewhere. Metaxas and Sage had their licenses lifted, so they won't be doing the flying.''

"Sweet baby, you and Fanny have to go down to the base of the mountain. That's an order now. I don't want to hear one word out of you, Fanny."

Fanny's voice was meek when she said, "All right, Metaxas, but only to the base. I can't see through the smoke and flames very well. It's gone, isn't it?"

"Almost. I'll rebuild your mountain, Fanny. That's a promise."

On the way down to the base of the mountain, Fanny said, "You can't rebuild a mountain. I appreciate Metaxas trying to make me feel better."

"Fanny, look at me. If Metaxas said he'll rebuild your mountain, he will do exactly that. He never says anything he doesn't mean. I've been meaning to tell you something these past few days but keep forgetting. The day Chue carved his name on my tree was an awesome thing to see. He just stood here, looking around like he was memorizing the trees, and he probably was. He said," Ruby's voice choked up. "He said he now belonged to the mountain. This is kind of corny, but he said his spirit will live on forever as long as those trees live."

"Oh, God, Ruby, did they go? Did they burn?"

"Are you kidding? Chue doused them good. Sage said he used some kind of stuff mixed with other junk. He hooked the bottle onto his garden hose and prayed for hours. They were still there earlier. They didn't burn, Fanny. I mean the trunks. Some of the branches will have to be trimmed. Trust me. Metaxas will not let them burn."

"How is that possible, Ruby, with a fire like this?"

"God? Ash? Sallie? I don't know, Fanny. Maybe Chue's Chinese gods. It doesn't really matter, does it? The important thing is the trees are still standing. I think they'll still be standing when this fire burns itself out."

"I can live with that little grove of trees, Ruby. The day

Chue carved Sallie's name on the tree she was so happy. He couldn't read or write English, so Sallie printed everyone's names for him. The letters were so neat, so precise. It's our place on the mountain. I feel like Metaxas does. Our spirits will live on here forever and ever. Devin has his own tree. Chue was so anxious over that. Philip is the one who told him Devin belonged, too. What that means is Sallie has two trees. Did you see the tree with the yellow ribbon on it?''

"It's for Iris and Sage's twins, right?''

Fanny nodded. "It's a young tree, and it will grow with them. See, Ruby, everything happens for a reason. If Chue had gone on his trip, we wouldn't have known how to save the trees. He knew though. Another crisis in my life. Have you seen Marcus?''

"Not for a while.''

"God, Ruby, I forgot to tell you about the chickens.''

"You're not giving them back. Don't even bring them up. They're yours. Forever and ever.''

"Right now they belong to 'the girls.' ''

"You mean . . . No!''

"I did. I told them their asses would be on the highway if they didn't go down to the pens and you know . . . take care of the chickens. They were quite resplendent in their teddies and feathered mules. Miz Arletta was sitting on the veranda sipping lemonade when I broke the news. I have to tell you, Ruby; I can't handle that. I'm going to ship the lot of them to Reno and Beaunell's establishment. Excuse me, Beaunell's sister's establishment. I'm not cut out to be a madam or a madam's keeper. I'm going to find a way to make that chicken thing work. It's my mission in life. I'm going to take a catnap right here on the side of the road. Wake me up in fifteen minutes.''

"I will if someone wakes me up. Do I still have eyelashes, Fanny?''

"Itsy bitsy little ones. Do I?''

"Nope."

"I don't care, Ruby."

"I don't either, Fanny."

"Sleep tight, Fanny. Your mountain is in good hands."

"Truly, Ash. Are our trees and the houses going to make it?"

"You bet. You don't think for a minute I'd let anything happen to those trees, do you? That's our family, Fanny."

"Say something nice to Ruby," Fanny said. A second later she was sound asleep.

"Ruby, thanks for coming and helping Fanny. I really like that guy you married. I was watching when Chue carved his name in the tree. The second richest man in the country had tears in his eyes and no dollar signs in sight. I like that. Listen, kiddo, be happy."

"I know this is a dream because I'm so exhausted. But, just in case it isn't, Ash, will you sing to me. When I was a kid, I always wanted a brother or a sister to sing me to sleep."

"Hush little baby don't you cry, your big brother is going to . . ."

"Mom, it's Sage. Iris and I want you to come up the mountain this morning if you can. I know it's April 1, and no, this is not an April Fool's joke. Can you and Marcus make it? Iris is making lunch. Good, we'll see you in an hour or so."

"Did she say yes?" Ruby dithered.

"She said yes," Sage grinned.

"Everything is in place. We are going to blow your mother right off this mountain this morning," Metaxas said.

"I still don't believe you can, as you put it, rebuild a mountain."

"It's my wedding present," Ruby cooed to the new baby in her arms. She looked over at her husband, who was holding the second baby, a look of pure fright on his face. "Actually, it's our wedding present to all of you. Metaxas said he would rebuild this mountain, and he's going to do it. What do you think is going on out there with all those men and women?''

"I never saw so many strange-looking vehicles in my life. Or so many hard hats. If it really is possible, how long is it going to take?'' Iris asked.

"It will be done by the end of summer. We couldn't start till now because the ground was too hot. It's under control. This mountain will be as beautiful as it was before the fire. You have my word.''

"Miss Ruby Fanny Thornton has the hiccups.''

"Mister Metaxas Ash Thornton has something alien in his trousers,'' Metaxas said, handing the baby over to Iris.

"It's great of you two to agree to being godparents. Mom was thrilled when you said yes.''

"Are you kidding? Just remember that you and Iris agreed all the kids could spend the summer with us on our new island. That means these two precious bundles. We'll have a nurse on call and a real nanny on the premises. You and Iris are long overdue for a vacation. When it's up, you can stop by our island and pick up the kids. Or, you can stay and visit.''

"Only a fool would turn down an offer like that,'' Iris said.

"Is everything okay at Chue's house?''

"Yep, uncles, aunts, cousins, and more cousins arrived a week after the fire. Everything is good as new with the exception of the view. Every day he sprays our trees with that magical stuff that saved them. Boy, no one, not even the fire marshal, can figure that one out. He's got this wicked-looking hypodermic syringe a foot long that he fills with something that looks like glue. He shoots it into the ground at the base of the trunk twice a day. Then he sits down like this little fat Buddha and watches the trees. I think he's defying them not to grow. Three days ago he spotted new growth. He rattled something off in Chinese that could be heard all the way down the mountain. End of story.''

"Has anyone heard from Birch or Sunny? And how is Billie?" Ruby asked, finally relinquishing her hold on her godchild.

"The building is moving along at breakneck speed. Sunny and Harry are happy. Birch is a little testy. He was served with his divorce papers, and that put him into a funk, but he's okay with it. Their target date for completion on the casino is still the same, January 15 of next year. You will be on hand for the ceremonies, won't you?" Sage asked.

"Absolutely. Billie?"

"Billie is acing it all the way. She has a handle on it now. She's back to her old work habits. She's still seeing Adam. Have you heard from Celia?"

"Not directly. I think she's doing well. The public likes the image she presents. She bought herself a condo. The last note I had from her said she subs in a private school two days a week. She didn't ask about anyone, if that's your next question. It's best to let sleeping dogs lie. She'll get on with her life, and Birch will get on with his. By the way, how are the Kingsleys?"

"They're busy in Washington doing the political and social thing. Mom said they were going to come out this summer for a visit," Sage said.

"Then all is well that ends well," Ruby said happily.

"I hear a car," Iris said. "It must be Fanny and Marcus."

"You go out first, Metaxas. Fanny's going to be in shock. I don't think she ever quite believed that this could be done."

Metaxas lumbered over to the door, a smile as radiant as the sun plastered all over his face. "What do you think, Fanny?"

"I don't know what to think. Are you taking out the dead trees?"

"We're taking them out along with all the burned and charred soil. We're going to grind out each and every stump, grade the ground, nourish it, and plant new trees. Big trees, Fanny. I bought a forest in Oregon. We're taking out the trees and bringing them here. We'll replant in Oregon when we finish with this."

Fanny's voice was full of awe. "You can do that! I don't know what to say. My Lord, how much is this costing?"

"Fanny, look at me. We both know I'm rich, so let's not belabor the point. I worked all my life to get where I am. A man can have all the money in the world, but what good is it if you don't have someone to do for and to share with? Nothing in the world could ever give me more joy, more peace of mind, than to know I planted a mountain for those I hold near and dear. Ruby said we're a family. I take the word family really seriously. If you know what I mean. It gives me great pleasure, Mrs. Reed, to give you back your mountain. Tell me you accept."

Tears rolled down Fanny's cheeks. "On behalf of Sallie Coleman Thornton, I accept. Thank you, Metaxas, thank you from the bottom of my heart. I feel like I should say more, but I don't know what the words are, where to get them from. I owe you so much. You save my daughter's life and now this. Thank you seems inadequate."

"Thank you is more than enough. Hey, I have a tree with my name on it that has withstood the hands of time, two god-children, one of whom bears my name, and a whole new family to love. A man would be a fool to expect or want more, and I'm no fool. I say we go inside and drink a toast to this wonder-ful, one-of-a-kind family."

"I need to talk to you, Fanny."

Fanny whirled around. "I think that's a wonderful idea. Would you mind giving me a minute?"

"All the minutes you want, Fanny."

Fanny walked over to the edge of the mountain, to the same spot where she'd slid down on her rump the day she ran away from Simon. "Ash, what's wrong? Is it Sunny or Birch?"

"No. You always think the worst, Fanny."

"From long habit. I'll try and correct that. Metaxas is going to replant the mountain, Ash. Our trees are alive and well. It's almost too much if you know what I mean. Everything is so wonderful. Life is good again. I wish you were here. I feel kind of selfish soaking it all up. I'm babbling here and don't know why."

"I came to say good-bye, Fanny."

"Good-bye? Oh, no, Ash, not good-bye. Please don't say that. What does that mean? Will you ever, you know, talk to me again? I don't want you to go. You got me to this point in time. I depend on you."

"That's just it, Fanny. You can't do that anymore. You have the kids, Marcus, Ruby, and Metaxas. You don't need me anymore."

"I do. Don't say that! I don't want to hear that. Damn you, Ash Thornton, that's just like you. You set me up, then you knock me down. What will I do without you?"

"Cut me loose, Fanny. There is a pretty wonderful guy in our old kitchen who loves you the way you deserve to be loved. Hell, he even puts up with me. That's got to be a plus in anyone's book. Come on now, it's just two little words. How hard is it to say good-bye?"

"For me it's the hardest thing in the world. I can't do it. I damn well won't do it. So there. Are you going to wait for me, Ash?"

"Three's a crowd, Fanny. I think I overstayed my welcome. Come on, chin up and no more tears. You know you look ugly when you cry."

"I do not. You're trying to make me mad. It won't work. Can't you sort of, you know, kind of hang around on the fringes."

"I can't, Fanny. You go first."

"Ash, I can't do it. I want you in my life."

"It can't be, Fanny. You don't know how much I wish it were otherwise. Take care of Jake, okay?"

Fanny sobbed.

"Say it, Fanny."

"No!"

"Yes. Now, Fanny."

Blinded with her tears, Fanny teetered on the edge of the mountain. Her voice was the barest of whispers. "Good-bye, Ash."

"Good-bye, Fanny."

Fanny's scream ripped across the mountain, "Ashhhhh!"

Inside the kitchen, Ruby heard the sound. "Oh my God!" She ran then and caught Fanny just as she crumpled to the ground, her brother's name ringing in her ears. She crooned to her like a mother would to a child. "Good-byes are so very hard. When you say good-bye you know that one day you'll say hello again. When you need him the most he'll be there, Fanny. You need to believe that because I believe it. Come on now, time to get up and make that toast for Metaxas. You owe me, Fanny, and I'm calling in my marker. I want a smile on your face and in your voice. Tears are okay as long as they're tears of happiness."

"How'd you get so smart?" Fanny blubbered.

"The two best teachers in the world. You and Ash."

"I'm ready, but I need to blow my nose."

"The hell you do. Wipe your nose on your sleeve the way the kids do. Your husband is waiting for you, and my husband is waiting for me. Shake it, Mrs. Reed."

The toast was short and simple, their voices ricocheting down and then back up the mountain.

"To the family!"

Epilogue

~

California: 1991

He would have known her anywhere. Her little half-skipping step and the slight jiggle of her buttocks was one of his more pleasant memories. The shorts, cutoff frayed jeans, a white shirt tied in a knot at her midriff, and the scuffed tennis sneakers, long ponytail tied with a red ribbon were exactly as he remembered.

Birch Thornton sucked in his breath, his eyes going to his nieces and nephews to make sure they were all right. They were all sitting on a bench eating ice-cream cones. "Jake, keep your eye on the others for just a few minutes, okay?"

"Sure, Uncle Birch."

It was true that he would have known her anywhere, even from the back, but it was the sturdy little boy in the madras shorts, white tee shirt, and blue sneakers that made his heart pound in his chest. He tried to take a deep breath and failed.

"Celia, wait!"

The look of blind panic on his ex-wife's face made his heart pound harder. "Whoa," he said raising his hands in the air, his open palms facing her. He watched the panic replace itself with naked fear.

"Birch. I . . . imagine seeing you here."

Birch stared at his ex-wife, her tan fading in front of his eyes. "I bring my nieces and nephews here once a year. They're sitting right over there on the bench. I've been doing it for years now. Living in Atlantic City doesn't allow me to see them too often. I take them for a week every summer. It gives Sage and Iris a break."

Birch dropped to his knees. "And who are you? Do you have a name?" As if he didn't know.

"My name is Thorn Connors, sir. What's your name?"

"Birch Thornton." *My God, he's the spitting image of Sage at his age.*

"I know my telephone number and where I live. I'm going to school soon."

"That's good. Is this your mom?"

"Yes, sir. She's pretty."

"Yes, she is. Do you have a daddy?"

"Yes, sir. He lives far away. Someday he's going to come and see us."

"Enough, Birch. No more questions."

"My God, Celia, why didn't you tell me? I asked you, and you lied to me."

"No, I didn't lie. I told you it was none of your business. Go back to your family, Birch."

Birch's voice was tortured when he said, "Tell me why. I need to know. Six years, Celia, and you didn't tell me. You robbed me of his first five years."

"I didn't ask you for anything, Birch. It's not my intention to ever ask you for anything. If you don't mind, we're here on a holiday, too, and I'd like to get on with it."

"That's it! You expect me to walk away and forget this

happened. He looks like Sage. His cousins are sitting there on the bench. Don't you think it would . . . ?''

''No, I don't. I'm sorry this happened.''

''It did happen, and now we have to deal with it.''

''No, we don't. If you make an issue of this then I'll . . . I'll disappear. If I do that, though, you'll sic all those hot-shot Thornton shark lawyers on me, right?''

''At least one of them. This is all wrong, Celia. I have rights, too.''

''No, you gave those up when you and Libby did things you shouldn't have done. Look. I wasn't perfect. The truth is I was pretty lousy. I recognize that, and I take full responsibility. It's over, it's done, and we can't turn time backward. I've moved on. My son and I lead a very calm, peaceful life in a quiet little neighborhood. He has friends. I have friends. I teach a few days a week. We even go to church on Sunday. I learned how to cook and mend. This boy is my life, and you aren't going to change it. I've told him just enough. I didn't tell him any lies. In fact I named him Thorn. I wanted him to have some small part of his heritage.''

''When he gets older and starts asking questions, will you lie then?''

''I don't know. When that time comes I'll deal with it. Until then the situation stays as is.''

Birch dropped to his haunches again. ''Tell me, Thorn, where you live.''

''I live at 22 Sunrise Terrace in Santa Monica. Mommy said Sunrise is a special mountain. Someday she's going to take me there. That's where my daddy lived when he was little like me. It's a big mountain. Do you know where it is, sir?''

''Yes, I know where it is. It's beautiful. There was a terrible fire five years ago and it burned, but some very kind, wonderful people made it grow again. I hope your mommy takes you there someday.''

"She promised. You should never break a promise. Isn't that right, Mommy?"

"That's right, Thorn."

Before Celia could reach for her son's hands, Birch had him in his arms and was striding toward the bench. "I want you to meet some wonderful young people, Thorn."

"Birch, no. This isn't good. Don't make me call Security."

"Go ahead. Make a fuss, Celia. This is the right thing to do. Thorn, this is Jake, Polly, Lexie, and these two little people are Ruby and Metaxas. We call him Tax. Guys, this is Thorn Connors."

"Hi ya," Thorn said.

Jake stared around at his sister and cousins, his face puckered into a puzzled frown. "How come he looks like us, Uncle Birch?"

Birch shrugged. "I kind of think he looks like his mother."

"My mom's pretty," Thorn chirped. "She's the prettiest lady here. She makes raisin cookies."

"My mom makes raisin cookies, too," Ruby sniffed.

"We live on a mountain," Tax mumbled.

"I live at 22 Sunrise Terrace."

"That's not a mountain," Lexie said.

"There is going to be a war of words in another minute. Let's bury the hatchet for the afternoon, Celia, and give these kids a day they'll always remember. When it's time for you to leave, I won't stop you. Deal?"

"Deal."

"It feels right, Celia. For whatever it's worth, I'm sorry."

"I am too. How are things in Atlantic City?"

"Lonely. How are things at Sunrise Terrace?"

"Lonely."

"How come you never remarried?"

"Did you?"

"No. Not even close," Birch grinned. "No matter what you say, we did have something once."

"That was another time, another place," Celia said.

"We could go back there and take . . . your son with us. It's something to think about. Kids get school vacations. We could view it as a test of sorts. Will you think about it?"

"I'm not that ugly person I was years ago. It was a bad time in my life. I made a new start. I have a new life. Old habits, old memories belong in the past. We can't go backward."

"I know. The future could be really bright and sunny. There is this chicken ranch in Nevada my mother and Marcus have been trying to unload for years. I'd almost be willing to give up the gambling business and raise a family on that ranch. Do you think that might be worth thinking about?"

"It might."

"We're going to be here for three more days. Do you think you might have an answer at the end of that time?"

"It's entirely possible, Birch."

"You're on a roll, son. When things are meant to happen they happen. I have a feeling those boots are your size. The kid reminds me of you and Sage. The mountain can always handle another child. I'm going to leave you with a thought, son: Anything worth having is worth working for. Do you think you can handle it? Are you up to it?"

"Dad?"

"Yeah."

"Can we talk again? You know, later, when things are calmed down."

"I'd like that, son."

"Yeah, yeah, me too. I really would."

Celia linked her arm in Birch's. "Did you say something?"

"I was thinking it would be nice to see Thorn on the mountain with the others."

"I was thinking the same thing. Look how well they get along. Did you notice that, Birch?"

"Actually I was thinking about how well you and I are getting along. Do you think it's short-term or long-term?"

"Definitely long-term. What's your opinion?"

"Definitely long-term."

A long time later, when the sun was starting to set, Birch looked from one tired child to the other, and then at his ex-wife. "Is this a family or what?"

"I'd say it is definitely a family."

"Can you see Thorn and you becoming a part of it? You know, at some point?" Birch said, an anxious tone to his voice.

"Possibly at some point."

"Can I hold on to that?"

"Just don't let go, okay?"

"Okay."

For a sneak preview of
the first book in Fern Michaels's
brand new Kentucky trilogy,
KENTUCKY RICH,
coming soon,
just turn the page. . . .

Prologue

❧

The two brothers watched from the window as a black limousine crunched to a stop in the middle of the gravel driveway. In silence, they watched a uniformed driver step out and open the rear passenger door. Their jaws dropped when they saw a slender, long-legged woman dressed in brown-leather boots, well-cut jeans, and white shirt emerge and look around. A sun-darkened hand reached up to adjust tinted glasses before she tipped the brim of her pearly white Stetson to reveal a mane of thick sable brown hair.

"Who the hell is *that?*" Rhy Coleman demanded of his brother.

"How the hell should I know?" Pyne said. "Whoever she is, she's coming up to the porch. I think you should open the door."

When his older brother made no move to greet their guest, Pyne started toward the door, but it opened before he could reach it. The strange woman blew in like a gust of wind. Without a glance in the brothers' direction, she headed straight for the stairway leading to the second floor.

"Hey! Just a damn minute!" Rhy shouted. "Who the hell are you to walk in here like you own the place?"

She turned to face them and smiled as she lowered her dark glasses. "I do own it, Rhy, at least a third of it. Don't you recognize me, big brother?"

Rhy's eyes widened with shock.

Pyne walked toward her. "Nealy! Is it really you?"

"In the flesh," she said, thinking it funny that neither one of them had recognized her. She'd known them the moment she'd seen them, not by the family resemblance but by the slump of their shoulders. Her smile vanished as she glanced back at the stairs. "Where is he?"

Pyne's head jerked upward.

Nealy nodded. "You two stay here," she ordered. "This is between me and him. I have something I want to say to him, and I don't want either of you interfering. Do you understand? This is my business, not yours." When there was no response, she repeated her question. The brothers nodded reluctantly.

Nealy stared at the two men. They were strangers to her; she felt absolutely no emotion for them—not love, not hate, not even curiosity. They were just two men standing side by side in the hallway.

It had been over thirty years since she'd seen her brothers. Over thirty years since she'd left this house with Emmie in her arms. Over thirty years since she'd set foot on Coleman land. And now, after all this time, here she was, back in Virginia.

Home.

The word made her shudder. She turned her back on her brothers and gazed at the staircase that led to the second floor. As a child, she'd climbed those stairs hundreds of times, maybe thousands. Usually to run and hide so she could whimper in safety.

Shoulders stiff, back straight, she mounted each step with the same mix of confidence and caution she used when mounting her horses. At the top, she stopped and looked down at her brothers, who appeared to be debating whether or not to follow her. "Go about your business while I take care of mine." She hurled the words at them in a cold, tight voice to ward them off. Nealy remembered another day, long ago, when they'd stood in the same spot watching her. She glared at them now as she had then and waited until they walked away before making her way down the hall.

Nealy hesitated only a moment outside of her father's bedroom, then opened the door and walked in. The room was just as she remembered it, gray and dim with ineffective lighting, a few pieces of battered pine furniture and worn-out, roll-down shades covering the two windows.

Her nose wrinkled at the smell of dust, mold, and medication. Hearing a groan, she turned her gaze toward the bed and saw a mound of quilts . . . her father, the man who had sent her fleeing from this very house over thirty years ago. How old was he? She knew he was over a hundred, had read about his getting a card from Bill Clinton when he turned one hundred, but gave up because she simply didn't care.

As she walked toward the bed, she sensed rather than heard someone follow her inside the room. One of her brothers, no doubt. Damn, didn't they know an order they heard one? Of course they knew, she reminded herself. If there was one thing Pa was good at, it was giving orders.

A frail voice demanded to know who was there. Nealy stepped up closer to the bed and heard a footfall behind her. Rhy or Pyne? she wondered. More than likely Pyne. In his youth, Pyne had been the one to show concern about things and people. Rhy, on the other hand, had taken after their father, not giving a tinker's damn about anything or anybody.

"It's Nealy, Pa."

The voice was stronger when he spoke a second time. "There ain't nothin' here for you, girl. Go back where you came from. You don't belong here."

"I don't want anything, Pa," Nealy said, looking down at the load of quilts on the bed. They looked dirty, or maybe it was just the lighting. Clean, dirty . . . what did she care? She pushed the Stetson farther back on her head so she could get a better look at the dying man without any shadows over her eyes.

"Then what are you here for?"

Nealy felt a hand on her shoulder and glanced back to see Pyne. The hand was to tell her to take it easy.

Like hell she would. Her father had never taken it easy on her. Not even when she was so sick she couldn't stand on her own two feet. She removed Pyne's hand with her own and gave him a warning look. More than thirty years she'd waited for this moment, and neither Pyne nor Rhy was going to take it away from her.

"I came here to watch you die, old man," she said, looking her father straight in the eyes. "And I'm not leaving until I hear you draw your last breath. I want to see them dump you in the ground and cover you up. I want to make sure you're gone forever. Only after I've danced on your grave will I leave. Do you hear me, old man?" She glared at him, her eyes burning with hate.

The old man's face became a glowering mask of rage. "Get out of my house!"

"Still ordering people around, are you? Well guess what? I don't have to take your orders anymore. I repeat; I came here to see you die, and I'm not leaving until you go to hell. That's where you're going, Pa. Hell!" There, she'd said what she'd come to say. Why didn't she feel a bigger sense of satisfaction? Why did she feel this strange emptiness?

"Pyne! Take this devil child away from me. Do you hear me?" the old man gasped as he struggled to raise himself up on his elbow.

"I'd like to see him try," Nealy said bitterly. Then she felt her brother's hand on her shoulder again. "I'd like to see anyone even try to make me do something I don't want to do. Those days are gone forever."

The old man gurgled and gasped as he thrashed about in the

big bed. Nealy watched him with a clinical interest. Her eyes narrowed when she saw drool leak from his mouth. God did work in mysterious ways, she thought as she remembered the day her father decided to take her drooling dim-witted child to the county orphanage. Spawn of the devil was what he'd called Emmie. She stood staring at him until he calmed down, then stretched out her leg and, with a booted foot, pulled over a straight-backed chair and sat down facing the bed. For long minutes she stared at her father with unblinking intensity until, finally, he closed his eyes.

"Okay, he's asleep now," Pyne said. "What the hell are you doing here, Nealy? We haven't heard a word from you in more than thirty years, and all of a sudden you show up just as Pa is getting ready to die. How did you know? Can't you let him die in peace?"

Nealy removed her Stetson and rubbed her forehead. She didn't really care all that much for hats, but she'd always longed to wear a pearly white Stetson, just like the Texans wore. These days she was into indulging herself and doing all the things she'd always longed to do but for one reason or another had never done.

"No, I can't let him die in peace," she said, her voice even now, calm. "He has to pay for what he did to me and Emmie." Her eyes narrowed as she watched her brother closely, wondering what he was thinking before she realized she didn't care. She really didn't give two hoots what her brothers or anyone else thought. "As to how I knew he was dying, I make it my business to know what goes on here. And you know why I'm here, Pyne. I want my share of this place for Emmie."

Pyne chuckled softly. "Your share? You just said you'd made it your business to know what goes on around here. So how come you don't know that Pa refused to make a will? There hasn't been any estate planning, Nealy. And neither Rhy nor I have power of attorney. The IRS is going to take it all. Whatever's left will be a piss in the bucket."

Nealy bridled with anger. Leave it to her gutless brothers to let their father go to his deathbed without so much as a power of attorney. "We'll just see about that," she said. "Call the lawyers right now and get them here on the double. Offer to pay them whatever they want. Just get them here. If we work fast, we can still get it all into place. As long as Pa's still breathing, there's a chance. Now, get on it and don't screw up, or you'll be out on the highway along with your brother."

Pyne stammered in bewilderment. "But . . . I can't. Pa wouldn't . . ."

Nealy stood up, took her brother by the shoulders, and shook him. "Don't tell me what Pa would or wouldn't do. It doesn't matter anymore. He's dying. There's nothing he can do to you, to any of us. Don't you understand that?"

Pyne Coleman stared down at his fit and *expensive*-looking younger sister. After all these years she was still pretty, with her dark hair and big brown eyes. Once when they were little he'd told her she looked like an angel. She'd laughed and laughed. Back then they had been close out of necessity. It was all so long ago. And now here she was, over thirty years later, just as defiant as ever and issuing orders like a general.

Nealy suffered through her brother's scrutiny, wondering what he was thinking. She was about to ask when Rhy stuck his head in the door. "You better come downstairs, Pyne, there's a whole gaggle of people outside. They said they were relatives, *family*. I didn't know we had a family. Do you know anything about this?"

Pyne didn't seem the least bit surprised. "I know a lot about it," he said, smiling. "Pa told me about them a month ago, right before he had his stroke, but he didn't say anything about them coming here. I wonder what they want." He took Nealy's elbow and steered her toward the door. "I'll make you a deal. You make *our family* welcome while I make that phone call to the lawyers."

Nealy jerked her arm free, walked back to her father's bed-side, and leaned close to him. Only after she was satisfied that he was still breathing did she follow her brothers downstairs.

In the foyer, Nealy set her hat down on the telephone table and checked her hair and makeup. With all the skill of a seasoned actress, she worked a smile onto her face as she headed toward the door. Rhy wasn't kidding when he said there was a gaggle of people outside. But *family?* Whose family?

"Hello," she said. "I'm Nealy Coleman."

1

Thirty years earlier . . .

Nealy eyed her brother warily. After what he'd said last night, she didn't trust him anymore. But what could she do? She was too weak to move. "Am I dying, Pyne?"

"Don't be ridiculous. Doc gave you a shot and said you'll be fine in a little while. Listen, Nealy. You have to get better real fast. Pa's planning on sending Emmie to the orphanage in the morning. Once he does that, I don't know if you can get her back."

Nealy pushed the covers away and swung her legs over the side of the bed. Her face felt hot, her skin stretched to the breaking point. And yet her body was cold.

"What do you think you're doing?" Pyne asked.

"Taking your advice. I'm going to leave."

"But . . . You're too sick, and Emmie's coming down with the same thing.

Nealy ignored him. Chills racked her body as she gathered her warmest clothes and took them into the closet. Minutes later she emerged completely dressed. She sat down on the edge of the bed and was pulling on her boots when the door opened and Emmie ran in. Tears streamed down Nealy's face as she hugged her. "I'll never let Pa take you away from me. Never." The toddler burrowed her head against her mother's chest. Nealy rocked her feverish daughter in her arms. She looked up when her brother came to stand in front of her.

"I knew you would react this way, so I came prepared." He reached his hand into his pocket, then handed her a neat roll of bills. "Tessie, Rhy and me . . . We scraped together all we could. It's almost $200. I wish it was more but . . . Wait a minute! I know where there's some more. Don't move till I get back," he said, excitement ringing in his voice. He was back within minutes holding a fat envelope. "There's four hundred dollars here. Tax money. I saw Pa counting it the other day. Don't say anything, Nealy. I'll deal with it later. Here's the keys to the truck. Tessie is packing up Emmie's things right now. There's not much time. Pa went to the barn with the vet, so if you're leaving, you best do it now. He made the call to the county orphanage last night, and they said they'd come for Emmie in the morning. I don't expect they'll go after you, but I covered the license plates with mud just in case." He reached into his other pocket and took out a napkin. "Doc Cooper left you some pills and gave me instructions to give them to you every four hours."

Nealy took the napkin from her brother's hands and opened it up. Staring up at her were five huge pills. "These are horse pills," she said, looking up at Pyne.

"Doc says what's good for horses is good for folks, too. He told me to cut them up in quarters. Just bite off a chunk."

Nealy stood up and tucked the napkin into her jeans pocket. "Thanks for the money and the pills." She used up another five minutes stuffing essentials into an old carpetbag that Tessie said had once belonged to her mother.

"You're welcome. It's cold out, but the heater in the truck

is working, and it's gassed up. I'm sorry about all this, Nealy. I wish there was some other way to . . ."

"Forget it Pyne," she said, cutting him short as she struggled to even out her breathing. "Pa is Pa, and that's it. Wherever I go and whatever I do . . . it's gotta be better than this." She gave the room a last look. "I love this place, Pyne. Maybe because I don't know any better or maybe because our Mama is buried here. Then again . . ." She shook her head, unwilling to voice her thoughts. "Am I going to get a chance to say good-bye to Rhy and Tessie?"

"No. Rhy's in the barn with Pa and Doc, and Tessie is standing guard at the back door. She made up a food basket for you and Emmie." He took the carpetbag from her hand and opened the bedroom door. "When you drive out, coast down the hill and don't put your lights on till you get to the main road. Don't stop till you're far away from here. When you get to where you're going, call Bill Yates and let him know how you are. He'll get a message to me. Can you remember to do that, Nealy? Jesus, I wish it didn't have to be like this. Make sure you remember to call now."

"I'll remember, Pyne. But I don't know where I'm going. Where should I go, Pyne?"

"Head for Lexington, Kentucky. Stop at the first breeding farm you come to. They'll take you in. You're good with horses, better than Rhy or I will ever be. Hell, you're better with them than Pa is. That's why he worked you so hard. He knew how good you were. You have grit, Nealy. Use it now."

"Good-bye, Pyne. And thanks . . . for everything," Nealy said, her voice ringing with tears.

"Go on, git now before Pa comes back from the barn," Pyne said gruffly. Then he did something that she would remember forever. He bent over and kissed Emmie on the cheek. "You take care of your mama, little one." He pressed a bright, shiny penny into her hand. Emmie looked at it and smiled.

Nealy held Emmie close as she negotiated the front stairs. "Pyne?"

"Yeah?"

"Emmie is not a half-wit."

"I know that, Nealy. Hurry up now."

Perspiration dotted Nealy's face and neck as she quietly opened the front door and headed for the truck parked in the gravel drive. After settling Emmie into a nest of blankets on the passenger side, Nealy climbed in and adjusted the seat. She saw Pyne toss her carpetbag into the back with some buckets and a shovel. Then she put the key in the ignition, but didn't turn it. The fact that she didn't have a driver's license suddenly occurred to her. She'd driven on the ranch and a few country roads, but she'd never driven on a major highway. If the state police caught her, would they send her back? Would her father tell them she stole the truck? Tessie would say she was borrowing trouble with such thoughts, and since she had all the trouble she could handle at the moment, she concentrated on the problem at hand, steering the coasting truck.

Nealy was almost to the main road when she stopped the truck to take one last look at the only home she'd ever known. SunStar Farms. Her shoulders slumped. Would she ever see SunStar's lush grassy pastures again? Or its miles of white board fence? Or April Fantasy, the stallion she'd raised and trained herself? Something told her she'd miss pasture grass, fencing, and a horse more than her own father and brothers.

Hot tears burned her eyes as she climbed out of the truck. She reached in the back for one of the empty oat buckets and the shovel. Moving off to the side of the road, she sank the shovel deep into the rain-softened ground, then filled the bucket with rich, dark soil. SunStar soil. That much she could take with her. She lugged the bucket back to the truck and hefted it into the truck bed. Her chest screamed with pain as she clamped a bigger bucket over the top to secure the dirt.

Gasping for breath, she leaned against the back fender and stared into the darkness. "They may think they're rid of me, but they aren't. I'll come back someday, and when I do, things will be different."

Nealy drove for hours, her body alternating between burning up and freezing. She stopped once to fill a cup with milk for Emmie and once to get gas. She took Emmie into the bathroom with her, careful to keep the wool cap pulled low over her face just in case anyone was looking for them. Satisfied that they had not attracted any attention, she climbed back into the truck. She gave Emmie some baby aspirin that she'd found packed among her things and broke off a quarter of one of the horse pills Pyne had given her.

Two hours later Nealy crossed the state line into Kentucky. She drove for another two hours before she left the main highway and headed down a secondary road with a sign pointing to Blue Diamond Farms. Maybe she could find work there, though why anyone would hire a sick teenager with a sick toddler was beyond her. On second thought, maybe she would be better off to find a cheap motel and stay there until they were both better.

Emmie tugged at her arm just as the truck bucked, sputtered, and died. Nealy steered it to the side of the road. She lifted the little girl into her arms and hugged her. The aspirin hadn't helped at all. Emmie was so hot she was listless. Fear, unlike anything she'd experienced in her short life, overcame Nealy. Emmie needed help—a doctor—a people doctor, not a horse doctor. She stared out the window and debated whether to take Emmie and walk down the road or cut across the field. If she cut across the field and couldn't make it, it might be days before anyone found them. With Emmie in her arms, she started down the road, only to turn around to get her bucket of dirt out of the truck bed. She could always come back for the rest of her belongings.

Twice she stumbled and almost fell but managed to right herself both times. She trudged on, the whimpering child clinging to her neck. "I can do this," she told herself. "I know I can do this." Like a litany, she said the words over and over.

The third time she fell she couldn't get up. Holding Emmie close to her she curled into the fetal position and cried. Then she prayed. And when she opened her eyes, she saw denim-clad legs and muddy boots. Through fevered eyes she looked up and saw the biggest, ugliest man she'd ever seen in her life. "Please, can you help me and my little girl?"

Nealy felt herself and Emmie being lifted, and somehow knew they were in good hands. "My bucket. Please, I can't go without my bucket," she said, when the giant took his first step. "I can't leave it. It's all I've got left." She felt him bend down, heard the click-clack of the handle, and closed her eyes.

Nealy went in and out of consciousness. She knew people were helping her, knew the hands were gentle. She could hear them talking about her and her daughter. Someone named Maud and someone else named Jess. She felt them take Emmie from her arms and didn't protest because the hands were good hands, gentle hands. "Please God," she prayed aloud, her voice scratchy. "Let this be a good place."

"This is a good place, child," the woman, Maud, said. Her voice had a lilting Southern drawl. "Jess and I are gonna take care of you and your li'l girl. Is there anyone you want us to call? Do you have a family, child?"

Until now Nealy hadn't considered what she would tell people who questioned where she'd come from. She couldn't think about it now because she was in too much misery to concentrate. "No, ma'am. It's just me and my little girl," she said for lack of a better explanation. Later she would give them their names and tell them something about herself, something that was close to the truth. Later, when she could think more clearly.

"All right then. Don't you worry about a thing. Jess and me will take care of everything. You just close your eyes and go to sleep. The doctor is on his way."

"I need my . . ." Nealy's voice gave out.

"Jess is on his way now to tow your truck into the barn. As soon as he's through, he'll bring your things inside."

Nealy had to make the woman understand that it wasn't her belongings that were important to her. It was the bucket of

SunStar soil. "No!" She struggled to raise up but Maud held her down."

"What is it, child?"

"I need . . ."

"Shhhh," Maud hushed her. "It's right here." She lifted the bucket for Nealy to see.

"Thank you, ma'am." And then she was asleep.

Fern Michaels likes to hear from her readers. You can e-mail her at *fernmic@aol.com*

Complete Your Collection of
Fern Michaels

___**Dear Emily**   0-8217-5676-1 $6.99US/$8.50CAN

___**Vegas Heat**   0-8217-5758-X $6.99US/$8.50CAN

___**Vegas Rich**   0-8217-5594-3 $6.99US/$8.50CAN

___**Vegas Sunrise**   0-8217-5893-3 $6.99US/$8.50CAN

___**Wish List**   0-8217-5228-6 $6.99US/$8.50CAN

Call toll free **1-888-345-BOOK** to order by phone or use this coupon to order by mail.

Name _____

Address _____

City_____ State _____ Zip _____

Please send me the books I have checked above.

I am enclosing $_____

Plus postage and handling* $_____

Sales tax (in New York and Tennessee)

                                            $_____

Total amount enclosed $_____

*Add $2.50 for the first book and $.50 for each additional book.

Send check or money order (no cash or CODs) to:

Kensington Publishing Corp., 850 Third Avenue, New York, NY 10022

Prices and numbers subject to change without notice. All orders subject to availability.

Visit our web site at **www.kensingtonbooks.com**